Holidays on a Mountain

Love is a Cabin Series
Book Six

Jacque Jacobs

Drawings by
Ken Czarnomski

Cover Photo by
Bill Johnston

An imprint
Drellag Press, LLC

Holidays on a Mountain
Love is a Cabin Series – Book Six
Copyright ©2022 Jacqueline E. Jacobs, PhD, Drellag Press, LLC
All rights reserved

This is a work of fiction. Names, characters, places, and incidents are products of the author's imagination or are used fictitiously and should not be construed as real. Any resemblance to actual events, locales, organizations, or persons, living or dead, is entirely coincidental.

An imprint of Drellag Press, LLC
Address: 2160 58th Ave. PMB 58 Vero Beach FL 32966
Website: LoveisaCabin.com

Printed in the United States of America
Paperback book: ISBN 13: 979-8-9873453-0-6
eBook: ISBN 13: 979-8-9873453-1-3

Other Works of Fiction by
JACQUE JACOBS

Love is a Cabin Series

High on a Mountain – Book 1*
Life on a Mountain – Book 2
Settled on a Mountain – Book 3
New Beginnings on a Mountain – Book 4
Community Unites on a Mountain – Book 5

Coming late Fall 2022
Holidays on a Mountain – Book 6 (Late Fall 2022)

Drawings by
Ken Czarnomski

Cover Photo by
Bill Johnston

An Imprint of
Drellag Press, LLC
Vero Beach FL

Acknowledgements

To my readers, thank you for making the journey with Bella.

In December 2020 when I started what is now the *Love is a Cabin* series, I could not have imagined I would actually write my first novel—let alone six novels in the ensuing ten months. With this publication, the sixth book in this series, I have so many people to thank. Many have encouraged me in this endeavor, and I hope I've captured my thanks to you personally and in at least one book.

I am deeply grateful for my immediate family members: Amy Garrett Kline, Bonnie Jacobs Coats, Kristopher Coats, Michael Coats, Cheri Jacobs Cheesman, Jack Cheesman, David Jacobs, Thomas Hall, Nancy Jacobs Hitt, Chuck Hitt, Becky Clark, Diane Willis, and Deb Latch for your love and encouragement. You are my family.

Close friends are family-by-choice in my life. It isn't easy to know how to recognize people, so this is in chronological order of how long I've known each of these dear friends: Marilyn Burton, D.W. Presley, Ruth Jackson Johnston, William F. Johnston, EdD, Peggy Jones, EdD, Paula VanHooser, Sandra Council, PhD, Dondra T. Maney, PhD, Hal Burton, Georgia Hambrecht, PhD, Donna Duffy, Ken Czarnomski, Ann Alexander, PhD, The Wlosok family: Andrea, Pavel, Victoria, Natalia, and Karolina, Susan Lovelace, Bonnie MacDougall, PhD. I love you each and all. Thank you for enriching my life.

A special thank you to Dondra Maney, PhD, Susan Lovelace, and Ruth Jackson Johnston who have read every word in every manuscript and given me great suggestions. Thanks to the *Tuesday Writers* of the Laura (Riding) Jackson Foundation for sharing your talent and helping me develop my own.

Specific to *Holidays on a Mountain*, I owe special recognition and thanks to D.W. Presley, son of my dear departed friends Donald and Priscilla Presley, who I have loved from the day he was born. He has grown into an awesome husband, father, firefighter, and community leader. D.W. is Fire Captain in the Carbondale, Illinois, Fire Department. He gave me hours of explanation on how fires can be set and how they are fought. We owe a debt of gratitude to all firefighters who save lives and structures all over the country. Thank you, D.W., I hope you know how special you are to me.

One of the fun things about creative writing is I get to create the characters and name them whatever I choose. Many of you will see your name appear in my books—always used with love and affection, even if you end up the villain. In this book, there are some new names of people who I have known for decades: Karen Franklin and her husband, Mark. Mark really does own an executive apartment short-term rental business in Raleigh NC. Check them out if you need accommodations there https://www.peaksuites.com. There are some newly named characters in this book who are folks I'm getting to know in my life; Jackie Grady, Jen Renfrey, Jeanne Selander Miller, and Mary Ann Klein.

As I have acknowledged before, the creative talents of Ken Czarnomski, illustrator, and Bill Johnston, photographer, have made my books come to life. Thank you both from the bottom of my heart. Readers will be enchanted by the updated plat of Bella's land at the end of this book.

Special thanks to Chris Erdman for permission to use his poem, found at the back of this book, from the words of John Muir. (back poem)

Last, but certainly not least, this book would not be in print without excellent editing by Elaine Massung, PhD, https://academic-smartcuts.com; Cover design by Pixelstudio at https://www.fiverr.com/pixelstudio; Book formatting by Arkonna at https://www.fiverr.com/arkonna. Thank you for your own creative talents and for the quality work you produce.

Dedication

With abiding love and affection for my granddaughter,
Hannah Ashley Kimball, who loved the magic of Christmas
— she sings loudly with the angels.
(6/9/1997-6/6/2014)

Drawing by Ken Czarnomski

CHAPTER 1

Fall Into Winter

In the week before Christmas, festivities in the mountains moved into full swing. Tiny crystals glittered as the sun hit the snow blanketing the valley below, offering the illusion of protection from the outside world. Bella Anderson sat in her living room, her feet warmed by the new stove installed in the former firebox of her one-hundred-and-twenty-year-old ancestral home: Drellag Caban. She marveled at how the snow accentuated the peaks of the Smoky Mountains, likely helped by the inches of accumulation on the tall evergreens that made these hills unique. After almost three months back on the mountain, the vagaries of human nature had shown her crime in an upfront and personal way—ways she had never experienced when visiting these hills as a child, or even when living in the city. She had always felt safe and secure here. *What's changed: me or the world? Maybe both?*

The ringing of the kitchen wall phone early on Monday morning beckoned her. She remained grateful there was no cellular service on her mountaintop at 4,560 feet above sea level; she didn't mind getting up to answer the landline—her answering machine wouldn't kick in for seven or eight rings; mountain folks know to let a phone ring if they want to reach whoever they're calling.

"Drellag Caban, may I help you?" The wall calendar by the phone had a picture of Pigeon Forge before it became a wildly popular tourist destination thanks to singer and actor Dolly Parton. Bella understood the positive impact for the people of these mountains, but smiled at her memories of experiencing the town's tranquility with her Grandmother Hazel—a peacefulness perfectly captured by the black-and-white photo.

"I'm trying to reach Dr. Bella Anderson."

"Who's calling, please?"

"Detective Burton from Statesboro, North Carolina."

"This is Bella Anderson."

"Dr. Anderson, your number was provided by Dr. Carlsen at the university. Would you verify your address in North Carolina?"

"Is Victoria okay?" Bella pulled the long cord on the phone towards the kitchen table and sat. She couldn't imagine what was wrong. "Oh, my address..." She gave it to him.

"Thank you, for verifying the address, ma'am. Dr. Carlsen and your neighbor indicated your house sitter is away at a conference which we have verified." He paused. "I regret to inform you there was a fire at your home."

"What?" Bella's stomach lurched and her heart began to race. She took a deep breath to calm herself. "When did it happen, how much damage is there?" Bella's mind whirled. She had to get home.

"I'm sorry to tell you this . . ." He paused. "The house is a total loss. The fire started around two this morning and it took almost five hours to get it completely out. I'm sorry, ma'am."

"Thank you." Her voice was barely a whisper. "May I have your number? I would like to call you back."

Bella wrote the number on the calendar as the detective recited it, stood up and dropped the handset of the phone in the horseshoe-shaped cradle. Later she would wonder if she even thanked him for calling or said goodbye. She looked at the number and couldn't remember the detective's name.

Numb and in shock, she turned on the burner under the tea kettle. She walked into the living room to get her mug. *Gone? Everything is gone? Do they know Victoria was not there?* She scratched Wizard behind the ears as she passed her sheprador pup lying on his bed. *How do I know he was a detective in North Carolina?* She picked up the phone and dialed the number the man had given her.

"Detective Burton speaking."

Without a word, she hung up the phone and wrote his name by the phone number.

The whistling of the tea kettle and the ringing of the phone created a cacophony that brought Wizard to Bella's side; he leaned against her leg. She absently reached down and scratched his ears while she poured hot water in her mug.

The phone continued to ring. She let it.

The answering machine kicked in and she braced herself for the detective's voice.

"Morning, love of my life. I guess you must be out for a hike on this lovely morning. Give me a—"

She grabbed the handset. "Chad . . . Chad!" She burst into tears.

"Bella, hey, what's wrong? Catch your breath. Are you hurt?"

"Hold . . . on . . . please," Bella managed to say each word—one on the inhale, the other on the exhale. She wasn't accustomed to falling apart. She sat down again, took a deep breath, and let it out slowly as she heard Chad's steady breathing.

"Bella, I can be up there in twenty minutes." He prayed that was an accurate assessment with the newly fallen snow.

"No. No. Give me a minute." She slowly sipped her hot tea. "I just got a call from a detective in Statesboro."

Chad knew where her North Carolina home was. "Is Victoria okay?"

"I think so. I don't know." She sipped more tea as she tried to calm herself.

Chad propped his phone between his shoulder and his ear and searched for information about the police station in Statesboro. He sent an electronic pink note to Detective Billy Williams to call and find out if there was a problem at Bella's property there.

"Bella, please tell me you're not physically hurt."

"I am not."

"Take your time. I can wait until you're ready to talk." He could hear her shallow breathing.

"My home is gone." Her voice was barely a whisper.

He wasn't sure if he had heard her correctly; he was reluctant to speak.

She spoke again, more resolutely this time—trying to convince herself in the saying of the words. "My North Carolina home is gone, Chad. It burned to the ground."

"Oh, my Bella, I'm on my way. Nora will call you soon after I hang up. I love you and I'll be there soon. Now hang up the phone so Nora can call you."

"Okay." Bella hung up while Chad was still talking.

"Remember, I love you. I'm on my..." Chad heard the click of the disconnect. He dialed Nora's number, grabbed his jacket, and headed to the door. Chad opened the door to Billy Williams' fist; he was about knock.

"Come in. No, don't. Walk with me."

Billy took long strides to keep up with the sheriff. Chad headed to the back lot of the station while talking to Nora. Billy listened carefully to Chad's side of the conversation.

Marking Time

Nora had four-year-old Mac and two-year-old Lilly bundled up and ready to play in the first snow of the season when her mobile phone rang.

"Hey, Daddy. Awfully early for you to be calling."

"Good morning to you too. I need you to call Bella and talk to her until I can get up there."

Nora fully understood the official tone in her father's voice and did not question it. She heard the engine of his SUV start.

"Sure, Daddy. Something I need to know?" She looked down at her two children waiting for her to help put on their boots. She smiled and put her finger to her lips, a sign Mac knew meant to wait quietly.

"Apparently her home burned down during the night."

"Here, Daddy? Weren't you there?"

"Her North Carolina home. Talk about the kids, the snow, I don't care what, but talk to her until I get there. I need to focus on the switchbacks on that road, so please—call her now." He clicked off his phone without telling Nora he loved her; he never did that.

He lowered the window and told Billy he'd call him in a few minutes. "I want, no I need, to be on the road."

"Yes, sir." Billy waved him off.

Up on the mountaintop, Bella sat drinking her tea. She ignored the thoughts pushing into her head. *Gone? Everything is gone? Please let the detective be right that Victoria is out of town.* She sat up straight in her chair. *Why didn't Eric Carlsen call me?* She had always been friendly towards her former colleague at the university, but they weren't personal friends. The ringing of the phone broke into her thoughts. She let it go to the answering machine...five rings, six, seven...the answering machine kicked in.

"Hey, Bella, Nora here, just calling to—" Bella reached for the handset.

"Hey, Nora. Thanks for calling. How are you today?"

Nora wasn't quite sure what she should say ... what she *could* say. "I'm okay, Bella. Daddy's on his way up there. Hold on a minute." She bent down to Mac and Lilly to unzip their jackets then realized Mac was whispering to her.

"Is it Miss Bella? Is it, Mommy?"

"Bella, there's a little boy here who would like to speak to you. May I put him on?"

"Oh, yes, please." Bella smiled at the thought of Nora and Fred's son wanting to talk to her.

"Miss Bella?"

"Hey, Mac. Do you have a lot of snow at your house?"

"Yes. Do you?"

"I do. It looks like there is a big white blanket over all the trees up here."

Bella chatted with Mac like he was a long-lost friend. She reminded him of the fun they had at Thanksgiving several weeks back; eating at the big table in his dining room and the games they played afterwards. She bounced from one memory to another until she realized Mac had not said a word for several minutes.

"Mac, I'm so sorry. I have such nice memories of our Thanksgiving I didn't think about what you might want to say."

Bella had been pacing back and forth in the kitchen. Wizard followed her movements—swinging his head from left to right and back again. She stopped. "Mac, you're a very special friend to let me talk so much."

"It's okay, Miss Bella. Mommy said to just let you talk."

"You're sweet. Tell me what you're going to do today."

Mac looked up at Nora. She smiled and whispered, "Tell her."

"Mommy, Lilly, and I are going to go make snow angels. Do you know how to make snow angels, Miss Bella?"

"I do. Please ask your Mommy to take a picture for me."

"Okay, hold on." She heard his sweet voice repeat her request to Nora. "Miss Bella? Mommy said she would. Here, you want to talk to her?"

"Bella, hang on just a minute." Nora told her son to go play quietly with Lilly. He took his sister's hand and went off to their playroom. Nora smiled.

"Thanks, Bella. Are you okay?"

"It's gone, Nora. My home is gone." She took a deep gulp of air. "Except for the few things I have here in Drellag Caban. Everything is gone." She held her breath so as not to sob. She completely forgot about the clothes she had stored at Chad's when they came back from North Carolina last month.

"Bella, Daddy's on his way and should be there soon. Me, Fred, the kids . . . we're all here for you. I don't know what to say, or even what I can do right now, but we're here for you. We're your family. I hope you know that."

Bella could not hold back the flood gates. "Everything, Nora. Matt. . . everything that was Matt—it's all gone. My parents, my grand-mother, everything I had that was theirs. . . gone."

Nora would later wonder where her words came from. "Bella, I can't imagine losing all the material connections to my family. I can't. But I know this. You have wonderful memories of Matt, your parents, and your Grandmother Hazel. You tell stories about them all the time. Do you know you do that? It's a wonderful model for me to store away good memories of the people I love. I'm doing a better job of writing things on my calendar that are quick reminders of time with Daddy, you, Fred, the kids. I want to remember, but some days my life is so hectic I'm afraid I'll forget. Thank you for helping me to realize how important even the little things are."

Bella heard the engine of Chad's Ford Interceptor SUV coming up the road. She knew it could still be several minutes away since sounds had a way of traveling in the hills, even when muted by the snow. "Nora, I have to go. Your dad's almost here. Thank you for calling. We'll talk soon." Unaware she was on autopilot, Bella hung up the phone and ran to the bathroom to wash her face.

Winding Road

Route 54, the main county road through the valley, had been cleared during the night and Chad was grateful for the snow tires his mechanic had put on in anticipation of the early winter weather. He called Billy and learned a fire had indeed destroyed Bella's home. At first, he was annoyed that it took a return call before the detective in North Carolina would talk to Billy, but he soon settled—he knew he would expect his own officers to do the same: "Trust but verify."

Chad was finally on the smaller county road up to Bella's cabin where the switchbacks caused him to slow—he was well aware he could go over the edge. He let out a long breath as he crossed over the cattle grate on Bella's Creek and headed up towards Drellag Caban. He had tried to get Bella to come to the valley ahead of the impending snow, but she insisted she would stay put: she had never seen the first snow up on her mountain. The thought of how determined she could be assured him her grit would get her through this.

Bella was standing in the open door of the kitchen as he pulled up. Chad jumped out and ran through the light layer of snow to her. She all but fell in his arms almost knocking him backwards. Wizard's tail thumped against the kitchen door—a metronome setting a rhythm of urgency.

"Hey, hey. Come on. You're not dressed to be out here in the cold." Chad guided her into the kitchen and shut the door before fully embracing her.

She moved to hug him more tightly. Her hand hit his service weapon and she froze.

Chad took her hands and led her to a chair. He knelt in front of her. As a law enforcement officer for over thirty years, he knew the tragedies that could happen without warning and turn someone's life upside down. He also knew, like most people, Bella was mostly aware of such things by hearing or reading about them in the news—at least until she came up here full time in September. *I pray this is not the proverbial straw.*

"Bella, look at me, please." He put his hand under her chin and turned her face towards his. "I love you. I am here for you. I will do whatever you want to do. Let me get you some tea, then we'll go sit on the sofa."

Bella looked into the gray eyes of the man she had grown to love in the span of only three months. If anyone had told her five years ago when Matt died that she would someday fall in love with a sheriff, she probably would have laughed them out of town. Yet here he was. She lifted her hand and traced the outline of his face with her finger. She leaned in and kissed him deeply, with a longing that came from the very marrow of her being. He had come to her in her time of need on a day that started out as a quiet gathering of thoughts while sitting comfortably in her living room. A day that was shattered with one phone call.

Chad was overwhelmed with the need he knew was in her kiss and could feel in her arms as she clung to his neck. He picked her up off the chair with a strength that surprised them both. He took her into the living room and sat her on the sofa. He wanted to take her to bed, to shower her with love, but he knew now was not the time. Instead, he kissed her on the forehead as she leaned back against the long L-shaped sofa.

Bella took one of the loose cushions and hugged it to her chest. No more tears came.

After a few minutes, Chad reappeared with a mug of tea. She cupped her hands around it, allowing the warmth to spread to her chilled fingers and hands, and she felt her resilience in the face of a crisis start to return as well. Chad sat and put her feet on his lap and gently rubbed her legs.

Chad knew it would take time for the officials in Statesboro to determine the fire's origin. Billy had verified with Detective Burton that there was apparently nothing left but the block and brick foundation and some partial lower walls. He wondered if Bella would want to see for herself. He would do whatever she wanted—but he knew he would not let her go to North Carolina alone.

Bella spoke quietly as she looked up at the ceiling. "Thank you for coming, and thank you for having Nora call. I'd forgotten what it meant to have someone care about what happened to me." She looked at him and smiled. "I have to call the detective back. I think I hung up on him."

"No problem. Billy spoke with him. They'll keep us informed."

"Informed? Informed of what? He said everything was gone."

Chad wasn't sure she was ready to hear there would be an investigation to determine if the fire started from something inside the house—or if it was arson. He decided now was not the time.

He swallowed hard. "Yes, everything is gone but the foundation and part of the walls. The detective said the land around the house, and its distance from your neighbors, saved the fire from spreading to other houses."

"Oh no!" Her dark brown eyes were the size of saucers. *I never thought about my neighbors being at risk.* She took a deep breath. "Chad, Victoria's mobile number is on the list by the phone. Please call and make sure she really is at a conference and safe. I would prefer she hear from you that whatever she had in my home is gone."

He relaxed. Her comments showed the rational woman he knew her to be. He went to the kitchen and dialed Victoria's number; after a moment, Bella could hear his voice but not his exact words. There was a soft click as he hung the phone up.

Bella lifted her feet when he returned and put them in his lap again.

Chad rubbed the tops of her feet and smiled. "She's safe. She's in Phoenix at a conference. I made sure someone was with her before I told her. She's very concerned for you, and I told her you would call her soon. She has a presentation this afternoon, but Courtney will have her phone if you call."

"Thank you, Chad." She sat up and turned so that she was leaning against him. He put his arm around her and pulled her closer. They sat quietly with Wizard at their feet. She rubbed her foot against the dog's chest, and Wizard rested his head on her ankle.

The knock on the kitchen door startled both of them. Chad kissed her forehead and stood to see who was there.

CHAPTER 2

Of all the paths you take in life,
make sure a few lead to the mountains.

John Muir

Decisions to be Made

Agent Quinn Isaacs of the Immigration Enforcement Agency looked out the window of the home that had belonged to the late Joe Johnson. Joshua had offered his father's house to Quinn anytime she was in the valley, and she had been here so often recently she thought she should talk to Joshua again about renting the house or at least compensating him for the utilities. So far, he had refused.

"Good for someone to be in the house. If things change, I'll let you know. Nothing to worry about." His words played in her head. She couldn't help but think things might change given that Joshua had recently married Carla Long. The marriage united the Valley Store and The Corral, the two major businesses in the valley. It wouldn't surprise her if the union affected how things were run at both venues; after all, Carla had left The Corral to help out at the grocery store. *Stop it, Quinn. Joshua has put a lot of trust in you, and you have to return the favor.*

She took a deep breath to clear her head then returned to studying the snow out the front window. County Road 54 was cleared, at least here in the valley. She needed to get to her own home in Round City and check in with the special agent in charge. She hoped they were wrapping up the most recent case involving the illegal immigrants found in the valley.

She packed up her things and was headed to the front door when her secure work phone rang.

"Isaacs here."

"Boss said to tell you he needs you in the office in less than thirty minutes."

She shook her head at the officious tone the junior agent took with her. *I may have to jerk his chain one of these days—I have ten years in the IEA and a graduate degree on him.* She decided now was not the time. *Why did he call on my secure phone?*

"Thank you, Agent. Message received." She pressed the key to hang up. *All the gender equity training in the world isn't going to change the behavior of insecure men.* Her way of dealing with him was to shut him down with the click of a button.

She turned the house thermostat down to sixty, made sure all the lights were out, and sent a text to Joshua to thank him. "See you next time." She added a smiley face.

Her SUV started up easily, and she was glad to be headed down to the lower part of these hills, not climbing them. *Wonder what the director needs? Why didn't he text me himself?* She drove as fast as she dared, knowing that cleared roads were not always any safer ... and sometimes worse if the slush had turned to ice.

Difficult to Decide

"Morning. Come in." Chad opened Bella's door to builder Arthur Gillett, who was working on Bella's new guest cabin. Her garage was almost completed and the dog run to the shed was getting a few finishing touches. Chad knew Bella had agreed to let the inside work in the smaller cabin wait until the outside work was done.

"Morning, Sheriff. Just wanted to check with Miss Bella this morning and see if this sign suits for the new cabin."

"Morning, Arthur." Bella walked into the kitchen as if nothing out of the ordinary had happened in her life this morning.

"Morning, Miss Bella. Won't take but a minute if you can spare it."

"Of course."

"We'll finish up the final wiring on the heating coils under the walk out/dog run to the shed, and then I can show you how to run the control." He reached down and patted Wizard. "Should make this boy pretty happy to have warmth under his feet when he needs to go outside on a day like today."

"That's great, Arthur. Thanks."

"Well, just wanted to see if this sign works for you for the new cabin." He removed the piece of cloth from the sign: *Solasta Caban – Elevation 4,532'*. Rays of sun radiated on the trees. The basic shape matched the sign on Drellag Caban.

"Oh, Arthur, it's perfect! The rays of sun convey the meaning of Solasta: shining."

"Yes, ma'am. That's what I was trying to do. Glad you like it."

"How did you get the elevation? It didn't occur to me it would be twenty-eight feet lower than Drellag Caban."

He pulled back his jacket sleeve and showed her his wrist. "This watch has an altimeter built in. Just a gadget my son gave me for Christmas last year."

Bella nodded her head. "Clever."

Chad had seen the similar watch Sergeant Sylvia Whitehorse had given her husband, the local fire chief. "I'm putting one on my list for Santa."

Bella looked at Chad. "Then you better be nice. Santa doesn't bring gifts to naughty girls and boys . . ." Her voice trailed off.

Chad watched her and tried to be unobtrusive when he stepped in a little closer—she was unsteady on her feet.

After a moment, Bella said, "I may have to go to North Carolina in the next day or two. Is there anything you need from me to keep working?"

"No, ma'am. Appreciate the trust you give me to have a key to Drellag Caban. Helps to have a bathroom and access to a phone up here."

"Absolutely. Well, no definite plans yet, but I'll let you know one way or the other."

"Sure, Miss Bella." He looked at Chad and Bella. He was pretty good at reading faces, and he was pretty sure something was wrong ... but he doubted it was in their relationship. "Let me know if you need me to do anything."

"Thanks, Arthur. I appreciate it."

Chad opened the door and shook Arthur's hand on his way out. "Thanks, Arthur."

"You bet, Sheriff."

Chad closed the door.

Bella filled the tea kettle at the sink. "Have you eaten breakfast?" She didn't turn around.

"I'm good. May I fix something for you?"

"I've eaten. Have time to talk?"

"Anytime." He pulled out a chair at the kitchen table and sat.

"Is it likely they'll figure out what started the fire?" Her question showed no emotion.

"I think it may take some time, but they'll be thorough and I've got Billy following up with them. The detective in Statesboro seemed very cooperative." He was not about to tell her at the moment that Billy informed the detective about the Zimmerman case and the fact someone involved had ferreted out Bella's addresses and phone numbers.

"Okay. I understand that. I'm torn with whether I should go or not. If it's all gone, what's the point?"

"It's up to you. No decision has to be made right now. You'll need to contact your insurance company, and you might want to reach out to your attorney there. You could also call Gray Olson and ask him to handle it for you."

"Yes. Let's do that. Gray knows you, and I won't have to talk to anyone." She paused, and he could see the deep sadness in her eyes. "That's not fair to ask of you. I'll call him."

He reached across the table and took her hand as the tea kettle whistled and the phone rang.

"You get the kettle. I'll get the phone." He knew she didn't want to answer the phone, and he didn't want someone saying something on the answering machine that would add to her grief.

Morning in the Valley

Joshua had been at the Valley Store since six. He was always appreciative that the county trucks cleared the roads through the night. The hospital and schools had their own plows. One of the local house painters had a winter business plowing driveways and the few parking lots in the valley. Joshua knew The Corral was cleared first and then his store. Snow wouldn't keep the locals away, but a plowed parking lot would minimize the risk of fender benders.

It was after eight when the first customer ventured in.

"Morning, Miss Andrea. You're out early today." He wondered what she'd think of the music now playing in the store.

"Dropped Natalia and Karolina off at school, so I decided to get my shopping done in case they end up with early dismissal." She stopped. "Joshua, I love the music." Then she looked around. "You've changed things around." She smiled and nodded her head in approval.

Joshua smiled in return. "Let me know if you need help finding anything. Moved some things around over the weekend. Help yourself to the coffee or tea over yonder." He nodded his head towards the new counter.

"Why, Joshua, what a wonderful idea!" Andrea walked over to the counter. She noticed the wooden box with a slit in the top. The sign said, "Free coffee and tea. Help yourself. Donations will go to the scholarship fund for local students." She turned and looked back at Joshua. "The donation box is perfect." She smiled, took a bill out of her pocket, and put it in the box. She poured hot water from the carafe and put in a tea bag. "Thanks for having tea."

"Thanks for being the first to donate to the scholarship fund. Not sure if you've heard, but Melody is the first recipient. She's got a full ride to university. Sure hope it's UT."

"Oh, I think that's what she wants if the way she and Natalia talk is any indication. I don't think she has to worry about being admitted."

"No. I don't think so either. Let's just pray it works out for her."

"You bet. Well, I'll let you get on with your day." Andrea looked down and saw that a cupholder had been attached to the shopping cart. She put the tea in to cool as she walked up and down the aisles.

The silver bell over the front door jingled, and Joshua looked up to see the county manager—and one of his best friends—walk in. "Morning, Joshua."

"Morning, Harold. Thanks for making sure our roads got plowed."

"We have a pretty good crew. They monitor the weather so they can spring into action as soon as they're needed. I'll pass on the thanks. Just stopped to get some coffee—" He stopped and looked around. "I don't remember smelling coffee in here before . . . or hearing music."

Joshua pointed towards the new coffee counter.

"Well, bless my soul! That new wife of yours sure doesn't let any grass grow under her feet, does she?"

Joshua laughed. "Have to admit all this was her doing. The coffee idea came from the sheriff; the music was Carla's idea."

"Did you ever know a law officer who didn't drink coffee?" Harold chuckled.

"Nope, don't think I ever did. What brings you in . . . oh, yeah, coffee. Guessing you mean the grounds, not the cup you can get over there."

"I'll get one next time. Just need to grab the coffee for the office for now. Have to run." Harold moved closer to Joshua. "An FBI agent is going to be here to talk to me this morning."

Joshua knew no one was in the store but Miss Andrea. "On Zimmerman?"

"I assume. I'll let you know unless they tell me it's confidential."

"Well, you'll tell the truth, and I'm here to corroborate if they want to talk to me."

"They might. Told them everything when their agent was here before. Oh well."

"Reckon they're just being thorough."

"Reckon so. Let me get on the move." He headed to the coffee aisle then paid and was out the door.

Joshua noticed Harold was whistling along with the Christmas music.

News Travels

Chad decided not to speak. He lifted the phone to his ear. *Don't need to give away that I'm here if there's more to this fire than a terrible accident.*

"Dr. Anderson, you there?" It was Billy.

"How may I help you?"

"Oh, hey, boss. Just had a call from the detective in Statesboro. Seems the newspapers there are sniffing for a story. He wanted to give us a heads-up that they may try to find her number here."

"Got it. Thanks. Anything else?"

Billy tried to figure out why the sheriff was being so coy. "No, sir. That's all unless you have something for me."

"Nothing at the moment. Thanks for the call." Chad hung up and saw Bella staring at him.

"For you? Do you need to leave?"

"No, not at all." He sat back down at the table and saw she had made him a cup of coffee. He reached across the table and put his hand on top of hers.

"Bella, that was Billy. I don't have a lot of experience with reporters given our local paper is a weekly."

"Yes, I know. *The Tuesday Tattler.* What's your point?"

"Billy said the detective from Statesboro called to let us know reporters are trying to find out about the fire."

For a moment, her eyelids fluttered and her chin sagged towards her chest, but just as quickly she looked up at him, alert and attentive. "And?"

"He just wanted you to know reporters might try to find your number here. Suppose it depends on whether they find someone who knows where you are."

"My neighbor does, but he won't tell them. No one at the university *should* tell them under privacy laws but that doesn't stop some folks. The number here at Drellag Caban is still listed under my Grandmother Hazel's name; I just never wanted to change it."

He heard some of Bella's stubbornness returning. *Good. You need to draw on that strength.*

"I suppose a thorough investigative reporter could find the number eventually—if she traced my genealogy." Then her head snapped up. "But why on earth would a reporter care about my house burning down?"

"Slow news day?" He tried to make light of it.

"Ha ha!" She turned her hand over and held his by the palm. "I needed the laugh."

He looked into her eyes. "Then I'm glad you *could* laugh."

"Chad..."

He heard the serious tone he'd come to expect when she was thinking through an idea.

"I think I want to ..." she looked up at the kitchen clock; it was 10:15 a.m. "... ask you to call Gray and get his advice. Then I want to call Doc Jim and ask him if he can take care of Wizard for a few days."

Wizard looked up, cocked his head towards her, then settled back on his bed.

"Done," Chad said.

She looked into Chad's eyes. "Then I want to know what you're not telling me."

His eyes did not waver.

She stood. "I'm going to walk Wizard while you call my attorney. Given he was your father's partner, I assume he'll know you wouldn't call unless I asked. If he needs me to tell him, holler." She put on her coat and boots and looked at the dog lying on his mat. "Come on, boy. Let's go see the workers."

The Sheriff's Station

Sergeant Sylvia Whitehorse was headed down the hall towards the front of the station when a familiar voice called her name.

Sylvia turned around. "Morning, Detective. Busy morning?"

"Not here." Billy Williams looked around. They were just outside the conference room and Billy nodded towards it.

"What's up that's so secretive?" Sylvia looked skeptical but stepped in.

Billy shut the door. "Dr. Anderson's house burned down."

"Oh no! I need to call Mike and see what we can do to help."

"Whoa, sorry. Her house in North Carolina burned to the ground last night."

"Is the sheriff up at the Anderson place?" Sylvia pulled out a chair at the conference table and looked at Billy. He pulled out a chair across from her.

"Yep. For quite a while now."

"Any word on the cause of the fire?"

"Nothing the detective in Statesboro is sharing. I suspect it will take some pretty thorough investigative work to sort it out."

"Think it's linked to anything that's gone on here?"

"You mean Zimmerman?"

She shrugged.

"Your guess is as good as mine. I've informed the detective and told him the person in question is in the hands of the FBI, IEA, and the Drug Enforcement Agency. I think it caught the North Carolina detective up short."

"Why?"

"Given that the house was vacant—"

"It isn't! What about her student living there?" Although her voice was calm, Sylvia's concern was evident.

"According to the detective, she's away at a conference. I *knew* there was something I needed to tell the boss." He took his phone out of his pocket.

Sylvia held up her hand.

Billy recognized the focused look she got when ideas were running through her head.

"When did you last talk to him?"

"Twenty minutes or so ago. He was pretty brief in his answers."

"Then let's leave the information about her house sitter for now. Pretty good bet the boss has already verified it, and if they want us to follow up, he'll call." She refocused on Billy. "It burned to the ground?"

"Apparently, just the foundation walls and some of the brick walls are left."

"That's a hot fire," she said absently.

"Anyway, I just wanted to give you a heads-up. The boss is likely to need us to cover if he takes her to see the house."

Sylvia nodded and continued to stare straight ahead. Suddenly she stood. "Thanks, Billy. Let's keep this between us and the sheriff for right now."

"Yes, ma'am. I agree."

She walked out without another word and headed straight to her office and closed the door.

Billy wandered back to the lab where Elizabeth, their star forensic tech, was working on a few pieces of the food truck that had exploded a few weeks earlier. "Not satisfied yet, Alexander?"

"Nope. There's just something that isn't quite clicking for me. I know Chief Smallwood approved the final report on the cause of the fire. It was a cheaply built little explosive device."

"Then what's got a burr in your saddle?"

Elizabeth looked at him and rolled her eyes. "When I find it, *if* I find it, I'll let you know. If you need me to do this off the clock, just say so."

"Whoa, no need for that. You're good at your job, and we need you to go beyond the obvious. No problem. No problem at all." Billy walked to his desk and saw the light flashing on his desk phone.

Elizabeth sighed. "Billy, got a minute?"

He turned back to her. "Always."

"What happened to the boy who was driving that food truck?"

"Phil Harper?" Then he realized she likely didn't know his name. *They all have a name.* "He was a pawn in a very dangerous game."

"I heard he was young. Sometimes I do all this forensic work and never know anything about the case, victims, or criminals."

Billy stared at her. "Sorry, Elizabeth. That never occurred to me. The crime originated in Round City and since the DA covers both them and us, he was transported there." He watched her face. "If you find something, let me know. We'll want to share it with Chief Smallwood. Thanks for your diligence."

"You bet. Back to work." Elizabeth returned to her analysis.

Meltdown

Wizard walked beside Bella. "Good boy, Wizard. In a few days you'll be able to go outdoors in your new run. Excited?" Bella looked down at him and rubbed behind his ears. "Hope you're going to like it." She walked past the shed, which was now linked to Drellag Caban by the joint walkway and dog run. At the far side of the shed, she leaned against the wall and looked out over the wide expanse of the valley to the northwest of her cabin. *When I arrived three months ago, I didn't plan on having a decision made for me about where home would be. Of course, I didn't plan on drugs being run through my property and my shed having an ATV rammed into it.*

She heard her name being called.

She stepped around the edge of the shed and almost ran into Chad. He kissed her, took her hand, and headed back towards the cabin. She had long legs but she was almost at a trot to keep up with his quick pace. She stopped completely.

"Chad, stop. This minute."

"I'll explain once we're in the cabin." He looked at her with pleading in his eyes. "Please, Bella."

She didn't argue and picked up pace to stay with him. They stamped the snow off their boots at the door and headed into the kitchen. Wizard walked to his bed and snuggled down.

"What's so important?" Bella knew she sounded more demanding than Chad deserved. She was unnerved by the urgency of his actions.

"Bella," he took her hands. "No one is hurt, and you will process all of this going forward. Gray Olson needs to talk to you . . . us, if you want me there, as soon as we can get there." The phone rang. Chad shook his head, upset that he had not turned off the volume on the answering machine.

They both stood frozen in place as the answering machine clicked on.

"This message is for Bella Anderson. This is Detective Burton in Statesboro. It is imperative that I speak with you as soon as possible. Please call me back at . . ." He recited the number and the call clicked off. There was no goodbye.

Bella stared at the answering machine and then at Chad. He knew something, and she wanted to know what.

"I've talked to Doc Jim, and he'll take Wizard. We need to get to the valley. Do you need anything from here to be away for a few days, or do you have things at my place that you can use if you want to go to Statesboro?"

"I want to know what's wrong. This is not like you."

He let out a long breath. "You know the old saying that there's a reason physicians shouldn't treat their family members?"

"Of course, lack of objectivity."

"Right. Same is true for sheriffs. I missed a really important element in the loss of your home because I was hyper focused on you."

"What? Tell me what you missed!"

Chad actually liked her demanding tone. It was the Bella he knew would come through this tragedy. "An obviously expensive home burned down while the owner is in the mountains and her house sitter is on the other side of the country."

"Yes. So?"

"I forgot there would be questions about whether you had motives for burning it down." His voice was low, barely above a whisper.

"Do *you* think *I* had it burned down?" Her voice was firm and un-equivocal.

"Never. But I can't protect you from being investigated, except to make sure you have the best legal advice you can get. Gray is waiting."

Chad had seen Bella when she was annoyed, but he had not seen her when she was determined.

"Please get Wizard's crate and make sure the cabin doors and windows are locked. I need a few things and my computer. I'll be ready in less than ten minutes. Please tell Arthur I'll call him when I know my plans for the rest of the week." She turned and headed for the bedroom. She saw the shocked look on Chad's face and knew her tone was harsh. She threw her arms around his neck and sobbed, "I'm sorry."

He hugged her as they stood rocking back and forth, gently swaying as he whispered his love, hoping to assure her everything would be all right.

CHAPTER 3

In God's wildness lies the hope of the world—the great fresh unblighted, unredeemed wilderness. The galling harness of civilization drops off, and wounds heal ere we are aware.

John Muir

Round City

Quinn arrived in Round City in twenty-six minutes. She liked living in a small town without the cacophony of the bigger cities like Knoxville and Nashville. But, like most places now, the modern world still encroached. The proximity to two major interstates and the cover provided by the mountains meant they were on a prime route for human trafficking and smuggled illegal immigrants. *The last two years the state of Tennessee has led the nation in combatting human trafficking. We were a significant part of the state's success.* She wondered why the random thought popped into her head.

She parked and headed into the local IEA office. The administrative assistant buzzed her in. "He's expecting you." She nodded towards the director's door.

Quinn knocked and entered. "Morning, sir."

"Morning, Isaacs. Have a seat."

She did.

"I thought we'd wrapped up our part in the case with the commissioner from the valley, but I just had a call from the FBI. They need someone who can move among the folks in the valley and get some information. By the way, sorry I didn't text you myself. I was on the phone with the FBI, so I asked Agent Lawton to call you." He caught the look on her face. "Problem?"

"No, sir. None at all. Just trying to figure out why the FBI needs us to follow up on what is primarily their case."

"Apparently, a house in North Carolina burned down during the night, and it belonged to a resident in the hills over that way."

"Okay . . ." She watched the director.

"Seems the woman might be a friend of the sheriff's, and someone has raised questions about the sheriff's ability to be objective."

Quinn stopped herself from laughing. "Sir, if there's one thing I know about any of the folks in the valley, it's that Sheriff Oliver is by the book—no matter who you are. He recused himself *and* welcomed us, the DEA, and FBI on the recent case." She shook her head trying to imagine who would think someone could sway Chad Oliver's objectivity.

"Fair enough. Just head over there and see how you can help." He looked down at the piece of paper on his desk. "Name's Anderson. Dr. Bella Anderson."

Quinn tried to keep her face devoid of any reaction by writing the name on her notepad. "Anything specific they want to know?"

"Something about threats that were made on the sheriff through her. Know anything about it?"

Quinn chose her next words carefully. She knew threatening phone calls had gone to the house's landline, and still needed to be investigated, all of the threats were specifically about the sheriff. "It was part of catching Zimmerman. Didn't know that her *home* in North Carolina had been threatened. I'm on it. Report back to you or someone in the FBI?"

"The SAC who called me said you should connect with Agent Bill Michaels. Seems he's already in the valley. Better get on it. Keep me in the loop."

Quinn hated how unwilling the director was to learn new strategies for leadership. His dismissive ways went out a decade ago. She stood and said, "On it, sir. I'll keep you informed."

As she walked out to her SUV, she decided to focus on the fact that he *did* apologize for not texting her himself. What she couldn't figure out was why this couldn't have been done on a secure line. *Maybe a throwback to 'step and fetch, girlie?'* Then she realized he had no way of knowing she had spent the night in the valley. *None of his business who I spent my evening with anyway.*

She dialed the cell number Bill Michaels had given.

"Michaels here."

"Isaacs, sir. Are you in the valley yet?"

"Yes, ma'am. Headed into a meeting. You headed this way?"

"I am. Want to meet?"

"Sure. The Corral at eleven?"

"Works for me. See you there."

FBI and Harold

Harold pulled into the county offices just as he saw Agent Bill Michaels of the FBI getting out of his vehicle talking on the phone.

"Morning, Agent Michaels."

"Morning, Mr. Cooper." Michaels slipped the phone in his pocket.

They walked together towards the front door. Harold opened the door and Bill Michaels entered.

"Excuse me just one minute." Harold stopped to his receptionist's desk. "Abigail, here's the coffee. I'll be in a meeting, not sure how long."

"Sure, Mr. Cooper. No problem." She knew the man with him was an FBI agent.

"This way." Harold walked to his office. They entered and shut the door.

"I won't take much of your time, but I just need to review a couple of things related to the former commissioner, Mr. Zimmerman."

Harold tried to hold back the disgust he felt from reaching his face. "Anything I can do to be of assistance."

"Thanks. We have the minutes and videos of all the meetings in which Mr. Zimmerman participated. Thank you for providing those."

"Public record, as you know." Harold tried to sound professional, but not officious.

"Indeed. I appreciate the promptness with which you provided them."

"Happy to be of service."

"My specific question has to do with the meeting when Mr. Zimmerman told the other county commissioner there was a new business coming to town which the men would like."

Harold couldn't keep the look of disgust off his face. "Yes. What about it?"

"The video doesn't cover the entire room in which you meet, so I am wondering if there was anyone else there who doesn't normally attend your meetings. Someone not from this community?"

Harold sat without moving. *Was there? I don't think so. Think, Harold, think.*

"You may not remember..."

"Agent Michaels, our community is small and we like it that way. I don't remember who was at the meeting specifically—so few folks ever come. However..." His voice reflected the confidence he felt, "I promise you if there had been someone *not* from this valley, I would remember." He shook his head. "Nope, no one extraordinary. *That* I would remember."

"Good. That's all I needed to know."

"Don't suppose you can tell me why?"

Michaels smiled.

They both knew the answer.

Michaels stood.

So did Harold.

"Thank you for your time, Mr. Cooper. Nice little community you have here."

"Thank you, Agent Michaels. Come back and visit when you can enjoy it."

"That would be a pleasure. Have a good rest of the day."

Harold walked him to the front door. *What was that all about?*

Michaels walked to his car and headed to The Corral to meet Quinn Isaacs. *Good man, Harold. Guess you'll find out some day... if the former commissioner, now bona fide criminal, ever goes to trial. Sorry I can't tell you he's claiming the video is doctored—and his friend from Detroit was in the meeting who can corroborate his side of the story.*

Headed to the Valley

Chad put Wizard and his crate in the back of his SUV. "Sorry, boy, not enough room for the crate and you. We'll be down the mountain soon." He scratched the pup behind the ears and closed the crate door. Wizard curled into a tight ball and rested with his nose poking through the slats. Chad chuckled. As he turned to go back inside, he saw Bella standing in the doorway of Drellag Caban.

"Windows and doors are all locked, thermostat is set on that fancy new stove, and the pup is ready to ride." He smiled as walked towards her.

"Thanks."

"Anything else?"

She carried a small canvas bag but no suitcase. "No, I'm good. I'll follow you down in my Jeep."

He stepped in front of her. "Bella, I took *my* Jeep home. You can use it anytime you need. Yours is fine here. If you find you absolutely have to have it, I can send someone up to get it. I'm asking you to ride down with me."

She looked at him for several seconds. "You're right. I'm in no condition to drive. Thanks for thinking of it. I'm ready when you are."

Chad recognized the robotic response of grief. He took her hand and walked her to the passenger side of his SUV and opened the door. He half thought, no wished, she might give him some pushback, but she didn't. He put her bag on the back seat behind him and got in.

Bella reached over and put her hand on his arm. "I need a minute, please."

He started the car so it would be warm, then he put his hands in his lap. He looked at her.

"Chad Oliver, I love you. I don't think I've told you today—shame on me."

He could hear a quiver in her voice. "I love you too."

"I know. Right now, I wonder if I am worthy of your . . ."

Chad put his hand up to stop her. "Don't say it."

"Worthy of your time and energy when you have so many people to serve." She gave a wan smile. "I'm pretty much in shock at the moment, but I'm confident enough to know that I believe I *am* worthy of your love. However, even love doesn't change how I feel." She looked into his gray eyes. "I feel like I've been nothing but trouble since I met you. Maybe I'm the character in the cartoons with the cloud over his head all the time."

Chad laughed. "I'm so glad you're older than I am. If I mentioned that comic strip, more than half my staff would look at me wondering what I was saying. Now I can say I learned it from an older woman."

"Don't push it, fella." She poked his ribs and just missed his service revolver. She knew it. "Guess I'd better be careful. I may be nine days older than you, but you're the one with the gun. Let's go see what Gray has to tell me."

He leaned across the console and kissed her. "It's going to fine—it likely won't be fun."

"Then let's stay here and make out."

He rolled his eyes. "Now you're aging both of us!" He put the SUV in gear and started down her road. As they reached the place where their mobile phones picked up a signal, the ping sounds created a tune as their phones joined the network. Chad knew one of them was his secure phone; he took it out but waited until he passed the last switchback before listening to the messages. All of them were from Bill Michaels of the FBI. The last one asked Chad to meet him and Quinn Isaacs at The Corral.

Bella did not look at her phone to see if her notifications were texts or phone calls. She would wait until she talked to her attorney. Then she could honestly say she hadn't seen any messages on her phone. *I did, however, hear the message on my house phone.* She turned her head and stared out the window at the trees laden under a blanket of fresh snow and leaned her forehead against the cold of the window.

Their first stop was Doc Jim's. Chad convinced Bella to stay in the SUV while he took Wizard out of the crate.

Doc Jim called out to him. "Don't need the crate, but if you want to unload it, feel free."

Chad shook his head, closed the back door of his SUV, and walked Wizard up to the porch. "Thanks, Jim. We'll let you know how long no later than tomorrow. That work for you?"

"As long as she needs. I love having this boy visit, and I'm tickled pink to help Bella."

"Thanks, Jim. Be in touch soon." Chad shook Jim's hand and returned to the car. Bella was waving; Jim waved back as Wizard's tail thumped against the front porch.

A few minutes later, Chad pulled up in front of the small building that had been the law offices of his father and grandfather for almost fifty years of the seventy-five years the practice had been in business. He missed his dad—especially in moments when he needed legal advice. *As much as I hate that my divorce was handled by my dad, he gave me good advice: keep the peace with Mary, keep your nose clean, take care of your daughter, and get her out of the house before you file for divorce. I did.*

Gray Olson and his sister were now the partners of the firm, which retained the name of Chad's father. Chad appreciated the sentiment and loyalty it represented. He stopped the SUV and hopped out. Bella was out her door by the time he got around to it. *That's my love. Back in charge.*

"Do you want me to go with you?"

"Should you?"

"Good question. Since Gray is my attorney too, maybe we could ask him. I have some information from those phone calls that might be pertinent. Shall we?" Chad opened the front door, and they were greeted by Gray Olson.

"Morning, folks. Sorry you had to come out on a morning when you should be enjoying the first snow. Come on in. Coffee? Tea?"

"Water for me, please," Bella said.

"Coffee would be great. I can get it and the water. Something for you, Gray?"

"No thanks. I'm good." Gray didn't bat an eye at Chad's familiarity with moving around his offices. "Come on in, Bella." They walked into the office that Bella knew used to belong to Chad's dad.

Chad handed Bella a glass of water and sat his coffee down on the table where the two were already seated. It was 10:50 a.m.

"I'm very sorry to hear of your loss, Bella. I can't even imagine how to process something so monumental under any conditions but being up here has to make it more challenging." Gray stopped talking. He knew his southern manners could make him say more than he should.

"Thanks, Gray. It will take some time for it to sink in and feel real, although I have no reason to doubt the detective. Chad said we need to talk about what I can expect going forward. I would like him to stay as long as he can, if you think it's all right."

Chad looked at Gray.

"Bella, the process may be complicated because of our personal relationship. I would normally be the one working with the law officers in Statesboro, but I assigned it to Billy Williams from the beginning." He saw she was alert and attentive.

She nodded.

"At the very least, the insurance company is going to want to be sure you had no involvement in the destruction before they pay out the kind of money your home is going to merit."

Chad saw Gray nod as well.

"The added complication is it may be related to the case with Zimmerman."

Bella looked from Chad to Gray then back to Chad. "Oh my. That never occurred to me."

Chad smiled at Bella. "Either way, our personal relationship will cause me to recuse myself from any part of the investigation that might be conducted locally."

"Oh, Chad, is that a problem?"

"None." Chad's tone conveyed the love he felt for her.

Gray saw they were holding hands. He smiled.

"Now, the information I need to share before Gray advises you on what to do is this: the calls I received while on the way down the mountain were from an FBI agent who was the lead on the investigation here which resulted in the arrest of Zimmerman and others. The agent is here in the valley along with Quinn Isaacs from the Immigration Enforcement Agency. They've asked me to meet them at eleven at The Corral. I'd like to call and ask them to meet me at the station so that Sergeant Whitehorse is present and I can officially pass the baton to her on this."

Gray nodded and glanced at his watch. "Good plan. How about you have them meet you at eleven thirty? That'll give us time to talk through what I want to tell Bella, and then if you need to go, we'll be fine."

"I'll make it noon. Excuse me for just a minute."

Some Days Start Later Than Others

Carla walked through the door of the Valley Store at ten thirty. Joshua was at the register finishing up with a customer.

"Hey, Carla. Seems strange to see you over here. Miss being at The Corral?"

Carla looked at the woman, someone she'd grown up with. "Not for a minute. My last boss was a tyrant. This one is sweet as corn smothered in butter in the summertime, *and* I get the added benefit of him being my husband." She grinned.

"True as a preacher's sermon on Sunday. Always good to have a job with benefits." She winked at Carla. "Catch you two later."

Carla walked behind the counter and hugged Joshua.

"Morning, sleepyhead." He smiled at her when he said it. "I'm glad you were able to sleep in. I do wish you hadn't driven on these roads though." He patted her belly. "Precious cargo, to say nothing of the person carrying it." They were ecstatic about the pregnancy.

"Sweet of you, Joshua. I wouldn't have driven if I thought it was dangerous. As predicted, the snow is already melting. You know how the first snow is. Been busy?"

"Steady. Tell you the truth, though, I'm glad you're here. Skip is going to be a little late with our delivery today; not surprising, given the weather. Once I get the order in, I need to make a couple of propane deliveries. Feel good enough to hang around 'til Melody gets here?"

"I'm fine. Doc Fred said just to sit when I can and not to lift. I've been pretty good about following those directions over the last month, haven't I?"

He kissed the top of her head. "You have." He turned as the silver bell above the door jingled. "Catch you in a bit." He headed back to the storeroom as Carla greeted the customer.

She pulled the stool up, sat down, and smiled. *A few more weeks, Baby Johnson, and we can tell the world.*

"Here you go, Miss Carla. That's all I need today."

She rang up the sale, thanked the customer, and leaned against the post holding up the loft office above the registers. She rested her hands on her abdomen and smiled.

The Corral

Quinn parked on the side of The Corral and entered through what folks called the locals' door. She liked the idea of being a local. *I'm here so often now that it's practically true.* Before she could get too distracted thinking about her reasons for being a regular visitor to the valley, she saw Agent Michaels coming in the front door.

"Morning, Cheri, we'll sit in the corner if that's okay."

"Sure, Miss Quinn. Nice to see you today. Coffee?"

"I'll have iced tea, unsweet. Not sure about Agent Michaels." She was glad the server had quit addressing her as agent. She was younger than the server but, coming from these hills herself, she understood the propriety locals showed to people who they viewed as having important positions or a level of education above their own. *No sense fighting it. At least we've moved to Miss Quinn.* She extended her hand to Bill Michaels.

"Coffee, please. Black." He nodded to Cheri. He shook Quinn's hand and motioned to her to have a seat. He sat opposite her. "Just had a text from the sheriff. He's asked us to meet him at his office at noon. Does that create a problem for you?"

"None. My director has me over here as long as you need me." She didn't tell him she wished she had stopped at home to repack her bag so she could just stay.

"Guess you've heard Ms. Anderson's North Carolina home burned to the ground."

"*Dr.* Anderson," Quinn stopped herself. She knew she put a little more emphasis on the title than was necessary, but she was tired of it. *If the person had been a male, I have little doubt you wouldn't have said, 'Mr. Anderson.'* She took a sip of her tea. "Please, fill me in."

"No details to give on the fire. Apparently Detective Williams contacted the Statesboro police and informed them the phone threats last month extended to Dr. Anderson's home phone."

"Yes, her landline received the calls threatening the sheriff. In fact, your agency had her home and her house sitter under surveillance for several days, right?"

"We did." He held up a finger for Cheri to wait a moment as she set the coffee down. "Hungry, Agent Isaacs?"

"No thanks, help yourself." Quinn smiled. *My reaction was because of my boss. Michaels didn't deserve my snippy response to Ms. Anderson.*

"Thanks, I will. I'll have two eggs over easy, ham, a biscuit and grits, butter only."

"Yes, sir." Cheri headed to the kitchen.

Quinn hesitated. "I apologize for my curt comment earlier."

"No problem. Tough time."

Cheri was back with his breakfast in short order. "Here you are, sir."

Quinn surveyed the platter. "Now, there's a southern breakfast."

"Best there is. Didn't even need to ask for blackberry preserves." Michaels grinned.

"You can count on it here. Enjoy. Now, tell me how I can help."

The Sheriff's Station

"Williams here."

"Billy, it's Sylvia. Just had a text from the boss. He'll be here at eleven forty-five and wants to meet with the two of us. No details. Also, he wants the conference room ready for a meeting at noon."

"Are we in that one too?"

"No idea. He said there'd be at least two guests. Do you have time to put on a fresh pot of coffee in the conference room?"

"Yes, ma'am. Your wish is my command. I'll check that there's water too." Billy hoped she knew he didn't make the best coffee in the world, but he wasn't going to be the one to tell her.

"Thanks. See you in the sheriff's office shortly."

"On it."

Billy hung up the phone. *Who are the guests? Guess this means the boss has come off the mountain. Hope Bella's okay.*

Sylvia looked down at the pad of notes she had taken while talking to her husband, Mike Smallwood, the local fire chief. He was an expert on fires, and in the twenty-plus years he'd been a firefighter, he had called the cause of every fire accurately, every time. She knew that Elizabeth Alexander was checking out something related to the food truck that had blown up, but she was confident it wouldn't change the cause identified by the fire inspectors. *Based on what Mike told me, I think my hunch about Bella's home burning to the ground is right. That had to be a very hot fire.* She reread her notes.

Sylvia looked up when Billy knocked on her open door. "Coffee's on. Anything else?"

"No. Thanks for that. I'll see you in . . ." she looked at the wall clock, ". . . less than ten in the sheriff's office."

Billy shrugged and walked away.

Sylvia wondered who the two guests were.

Legal Advice

Bella listened attentively as Gray explained that she would, at the very least, be interviewed by an insurance adjuster. "Given the report you received that the home is a total loss, they will do everything possible to make sure you were in no way involved. Is there anyone else who stands to benefit from the insurance on your home?"

Bella shook her head. "No." She hesitated. "Sorry, I was trying to recall if I ever took Matt's name off the policy. But I remember taking it off, so I'm the only person insured."

"Okay. I'd like to talk about my recommendations on your participation in the interviews, but first, Chad, is there anything we need to know?"

"I'll recuse myself from the investigation, and we will give the FBI agent permission to conduct it. Agent Michaels is fair and impartial.

I think having me out of the picture should go a long way in helping the insurance adjuster, too."

Gray nodded.

"Gray," Bella's voice was soft but confident. "On the one hand, I can see no purpose in going to see what remains from the fire." She waited a beat. "It was my home for over two decades and everything I had of my late husband, my parents, and grandmother . . ." Her voice caught. A tear ran down her face.

The two men sat quietly. Chad squeezed her hand.

"The original drawing of the Anderson property was in my home there. It was a special treasure of my grandmother's." She looked at both men. "I suppose these are the things you don't realize you run the risk of losing if you keep them anywhere but a safety deposit box."

Gray spoke quietly and with a warmth Bella felt envelop her.

"This may not be the time to say this, but Chad's dad always told me, 'If you live your life well each day and celebrate all the good that comes to you, you will never have regrets.'"

Chad nodded. "I haven't thought of that in more years than I care to claim. He did say that. He was right."

"I'm assuming you derived a great deal of pleasure from seeing that drawing in your home. Right?"

"We did. Thanks, Gray. I have always tried to live each day—just may not have done the celebrating as well as I should have. I'll work on it."

Gray smiled. "Unless Chad has anything else, I see it's getting on time for him to meet the folks who can help get this resolved. Do you have time to stay, Bella?"

"I do." She leaned over and kissed Chad. "Thanks for everything. I'll see you later today." She leaned her head back. "Oh, I forgot we rode down together."

"Not to worry. Just call. I'll answer my phone. If I can't get away at that moment, someone will come get you. You'll be fine." He kissed her and headed for the door.

As the door closed behind Chad, Gray said, "Bella, I'm not one given to sentimentality, but I want to tell you I'm happy as a clam that you're in Chad's life. He's a very fine man, like his father, and he deserves to know the love of a good woman."

"Well, aren't you the gentleman! Thank you. I'm the one who's lucky to have him in my life."

"Fair enough. Now, let's talk about what may be ahead of you."

CHAPTER 4

*Abuse no one and no thing, for abuse turns the wise ones to fools
and robs the spirit of its vision.*

Tecumseh

Victim's View

Bella listened to Gray's advice and agreed she should talk with the insurance adjuster by herself. If the adjuster was rude or pushy, Bella could ask to stop the interview and call Gray.

"I have nothing to hide. There was nothing for me to gain by burning down my home, and far more to lose in the memorabilia of my family life." She glanced at Gray. "I have no family now. Like me, Matt was an only child, and we had no children. I'd have to go back several generations to connect with family. There is no way I would have been part of losing those connections."

"Bella, most of the time, the truth emerges in all things. Sometimes the road is bumpy getting there. Do you know the value of your home?"

"I assume the land has its own value, so the replacement of the home itself is probably five or six hundred thousand dollars. I truly have no idea."

"Have you increased the coverage of your insurance as property values have risen?"

Bella looked at him. *Is he telling me what's going to be asked by an adjuster?*

"Our agent advised us a number of years ago to do replacement value on our home. I don't know when that was, or if it's even something that's done anymore. Should I call my agent?"

"Yes, we'll do that in a few minutes. Did you know your house sitter would be out of town?"

"No, I didn't. I never asked her to keep me informed. I felt whatever time she was there was time the house wasn't empty. Should I have expected her to tell me?"

"Not at all. You understand they will interview her, too?"

Bella nodded. "Thankfully, she's finished her thesis. I would hate to have this . . . oh no!" Her eyes were wide. Then she relaxed.

"What's your concern?"

She gave a short laugh. "I finished my dissertation many years ago, and we didn't have computers and backup drives and the cloud. I always kept a copy of my dissertation wrapped in foil, in a plastic bag, inside the freezer in case of . . ."

Gray nodded. "I get it. Glad you thought of that now. Not important when you talk to anyone else."

Bella nodded. She blinked several times in rapid succession.

"Bella, are you all right? Want to get up and stretch?" She didn't answer. He reached over and touched her hand. "Bella, everything okay?"

"Oh, Gray. Sorry. Yes. Everything's fine. Sometimes my mind wanders."

"Sure, no problem. A few more questions. Then we'll wrap this up and call your insurance agent."

"I'd like to call Victoria while I'm here in case she has any legal questions about her personal effects. She can talk to my attorney in North Carolina if she needs to."

"Let's do that now."

Bella dialed Victoria's number.

"Dr. Anderson, This is Courtney."

Bella remembered Courtney, another graduate student and friend of Victoria.

"Hey, Courtney. Guess Victoria isn't available."

"No, ma'am. She told me to tell you not to worry about her and just take care of yourself. She'll be free any time after 5:00 p.m. Arizona time."

"Thanks, Courtney. Tell her I'm glad she's at the conference. I'll call another time."

"Sure will. Take care, Dr. Anderson."

"You, too, Courtney." Bella ended the call.

"Not available?" Gray said.

"No, I'll call her later. Now, to the things we need to talk about."

"Take a minute. We've got time."

"Fine, Gray. That's just fine." Bella's eyes looked ahead but did not focus on anything in particular.

Preparing for Visitors

Chad turned on his computer to check for messages, but he saw nothing out of the ordinary after a scan of his emails and pink notes. He was about to close his inbox when there was a knock on the door.

Chad opened the door to Sylvia and Billy. "Come in." The three walked to the round table in his office.

"You okay, boss?" Billy studied Chad's face.

"Fine. I'm just fine." Chad cocked his head towards Billy. "Bella's fine too." He decided to save the inquiry. "Need to focus here as we don't have much time."

"Yes, sir."

Sylvia remained silent.

"FBI Agent Michaels and IEA Agent Isaacs will be here at noon. I'm not sure if this involves DEA Agent Nations or the State Bureau of Investigation. I assume it's related to our previous case on Zimmerman, or maybe even the burning of Dr. Anderson's home in North Carolina. In either case, you'll be in charge, Sergeant. I'll recuse myself."

Both nodded but did not speak.

"If Dr. Anderson decides she wants to go to North Carolina, I expect to go with her. I will take leave for a few days as soon as we know the nature of the FBI visit."

They nodded again.

"With any luck, this is a tragic event related to something in her home, and it will be behind us quickly. However, we know better than most folks that there are few coincidences in life."

"Boss," Billy said. Chad turned to look at him. "I don't think she had anything to do with the fire, but don't you think folks will be asking that?"

"Of course. I do not wish to discuss it with you so that you are each at arm's length for anything that may come of this."

"Sure, boss."

"Yessir," Sylvia said.

"Last thing. Sylvia, has the county finished the formalities on offering the administrative position to Cecelia?"

"Yessir, she started today."

Chad blinked and looked at her. "Of course she did." He paused. *Oh, yeah, I was out of here this morning before she came in. I completely forgot.*

"Not like you didn't leave here in a hurry to see Bella, Boss." Billy bit his tongue as soon as it came out.

Sylvia tried to defuse the blunder on Billy's part. "She's in the office next door, shall I get her?"

"Thanks for helping her settle into the office. I'll get her. Back in a minute." As he walked to the door adjoining his office with the office now occupied by Cecelia, he heard Sylvia speak even though it was almost a whisper.

"Really, Billy?"

Billy didn't need to reply; he was already admonishing himself and he knew that Sylvia rarely made comment.

Making a Plan

Bill Michaels and Quinn Isaacs were walking up to the front door of the sheriff's station when Sam Nations, an agent with the Drug Enforcement Agency, hopped out of his SUV.

Quinn raised her eyebrows at Sam. "Well, well, well, look what the cat dragged in!"

"Well, good morning to you too, Agent Isaacs." He turned the FBI agent. "Just ignore her, Agent Michaels. It's an old rivalry from our college days at UT."

The FBI agent looked from one to the other. "Good thing our past experience tells me it doesn't interfere on the job." He smiled and shook Sam's hand.

"Much," Quinn said under her breath.

"Allow me," Sam stepped ahead of them and opened the door. He hoped the FBI agent didn't know about the times the former personal relationship between him and Quinn *had* interfered. *Those days are behind us.*

Cecelia was chatting with the desk deputy while waiting for their guests. She walked towards the locked door between the inner workings of the station and the reception area when they entered. The deputy buzzed the door open.

"Welcome, I'm Cecelia Kennedy, Sheriff Oliver's administrative assistant. Please follow me."

"Well, well, the sheriff's added some class to this place," Sam said.

Quinn elbowed him.

Bill Michaels followed Cecelia and ignored Sam's comment.

"Please have a seat. May I get you coffee? Water?"

"Congratulations on the new appointment, Cecelia." Sam extended his hand and smiled. "Glad to see your boss finally recognized he needed an admin. He couldn't have made a better choice."

"Thank you, Agent Nations." Cecelia smiled. She and Sam had gone to school together, but she was not here as his classmate; she was the sheriff's administrative assistant. She took seriously the responsibility of representing Chad in the most professional way possible.

Bill Michaels was standing by the coffee pot. "Thanks, Ms. Kennedy. We're pretty accustomed to serving ourselves. Anyone?"

Quinn held up her Yeti and shook her head.

Sam said, "Sure. Black for me. Thanks."

"If you don't need anything from me, the sheriff, Sergeant White-horse, and Detective Williams will be with you in a moment." She went to open the door and almost fell backwards as Chad opened it from the other side.

"Sorry. Did I startle you?" He looked at Cecelia.

"I'm fine, sir." She slipped out behind him and headed back to her new office. She smiled as she recalled the desk deputy telling her that they'd miss her in dispatch, but everyone was happy for her promotion.

Chad walked in and shut the door after Sylvia. "Don't need intro-ductions, do we?"

The three visitors stood as Chad walked in and everyone shook hands.

"All good."

"Nope, we're fine."

"Good to see you, Sheriff," Bill Michaels said. "We'll try not to take up too much of your time."

"Whatever you need, Agent. We're glad to see you back in our neck of the woods." Chad set both his personal phone and secure phone on the table in front of him.

Sylvia, Billy, and Sam knew Chad well, and they looked from the sheriff to each other and down at the table. It wasn't like the sheriff to have phones so visible in a meeting.

Billy sat opposite Quinn. He caught himself before he made a re to her about the sheriff having his phones out. He reminded himself this was not the time for bantering—no matter how much he enjoyed the time he spent outside of work with Quinn. He also knew everyone at the table had been part of saving his life when his car was forced off the highway in the Zimmerman case. He owed them respect.

"Just for clarification, I was in the area for an interview related to former county commissioner Zimmerman when I was contacted about the fire at Dr. Anderson's home. At this time, we have no specific evidence to link the fire in North Carolina to the Zimmerman case, but we can't rule it out either." Agent Michaels glanced at Quinn when he used Bella's title.

Quinn's face was expressionless.

"As a formality, I need to ask some questions specific to Dr. Anderson. Is it accurate, Sheriff Oliver, that you are in a personal relationship with Dr. Bella Anderson?"

"Yes, I am dating Dr. Anderson. Are you available to lead this investigation, Agent Michaels?"

"I am. Agent Isaacs and Agent Nations have also been sent by their respective agencies to assist. If the destruction of the Anderson home in North Carolina is related to any ongoing investigation or case, we may have to tug on a number of threads to find where it leads. I haven't brought in anyone from the SBI, but I spoke with Assistant Director Elliott Nelson, who has assured me if this leads back here, they are available."

Chad nodded. "We are fortunate to have you here, and I am grateful for all of you. So, I am recusing myself and will leave our agency's part in this investigation, linked or not to Zimmerman, in the very capable hands of Sergeant Whitehorse. She will work alongside you and provide whatever local resources or access you need. For the record, I am taking voluntary leave for a few days." Chad saw his personal phone light up. "Please excuse me."

Sylvia had never seen the sheriff answer his personal phone in a meeting—ever.

He lifted the phone to his ear. "Hey." He listened. "I'll be there in ten minutes or less. Okay? See you soon." He put the phone in his pocket.

Even the federal agents who knew the sheriff were surprised he took the call. It wasn't like him.

"That was Bella. I'm going to pick her up, and we'll either be at The Corral for lunch or at my home. Sergeant Whitehorse knows how to reach me."

"Before you go, Sheriff … Chad. Do you happen to know if Dr. Anderson will be available if we need to talk to her?" The FBI agent watched Chad.

"I have no doubt she'll make herself available. My personal assessment at the moment is that she is struggling with the need to go see for herself that her home is gone. Feel free to call her and ask. She is quite capable of making her own decisions and availability known." He looked around the table and stood. "If there's nothing else, I'll leave you to your work and thank you for trying to wrap this up as soon as possible, for all concerned. This kind of loss is not the best way to start the holiday season."

Bill Michaels stood and shook Chad's hand. "We're on it. Thanks for your cooperation."

As soon as Chad was out the door, Michaels spoke to the other three. "This may have nothing, or everything, to do with the Zimmerman case. We need to be thorough and swift to minimize the impact on the victim. On the other hand, the insurance adjustor and the detective in Statesboro will be conducting their own investigations. Of course, we'll cooperate, but I'd just as soon not have them in the middle of the Zimmerman case unless it's warranted."

Quinn's eyes lit up. *Not only a quick learner but a focused agent. Let's do this!*

Sam was watching Quinn's face and knew her brain was running in high gear. He missed the sparring they did as students at UT, but he also knew he was responsible for the end of their personal relationship. *Focus, Sam. Let's do this!*

"Sergeant, is it possible," Sam and Quinn immediately looked at the FBI agent, "to see the visuals from the work we did earlier?"

"Yes, sir." She opened the laptop in front of her and projected the illustration of the elements from the Zimmerman case on the screen.

"Thanks. Detective Williams, apologies if this causes any stress for you." He looked at Billy.

"I'm good, sir. Let's figure this out so Dr. Anderson can get on with her life. She's had more than enough unpleasant things happen to her in the last three months."

"Oh? Maybe we need to start there. Let's make sure we all know the same pieces."

Billy started when Bella first came up to the mountains in September and the all-terrain vehicles used her land as a path to run drugs.

Tell Me Why

Chad walked into Gray Olson's office. Gray and Bella were chatting in the reception area. Chad took a quiet deep breath—Bella looked and sounded like herself. "Sorry to keep you waiting."

"Although I've kept Gray from his work, I've enjoyed our conversation. Thank you, Gray. I appreciate your advice and particularly your suggestion that I meet somewhere neutral with the adjuster." She turned to Chad. "Gray suggested I talk to James and see if we can meet in the back room at The Corral."

"Great idea. I'm sure there'll be no problem. There's also a small room at the library which I'm sure Dona will let you use. Good thinking, Gray. Neutral territory generally goes a long way to soothing any ruffled feathers. I also like the idea someone will be close by if Bella needs them."

"Why would I need someone, Chad?"

"I don't think you do, but I like to plan for all contingencies when I can." He winked at her.

"I'm not sure what contingencies would necessitate me having someone available, but maybe you could advise me on that later." The message she was in control was loud and clear, to both Chad and Gray. "We've taken enough of Gray's time." She moved towards the door.

Chad slapped Gray on the back and chuckled. "You'll get a bill. Don't worry about it." He reached out to shake Gray's hand. "Thanks, Gray. You're a good man."

"Remember, Bella. Call anytime. If you think the adjuster or these feds are getting too pushy, we can move the meetings here."

"I think I'll be fine. The shock is ebbing. I've held my own with a bunch of college professors for decades and, believe me, they can try to put you through the ringer over a single *idea*. They'd make an insurance adjuster look like a middle school student in his first debate." She shook his hand. "Thanks, Gray. My chariot awaits."

"You two take care."

Chad opened the outer door to Gray's offices and Bella stepped outside.

"Look, the snow is starting to melt. Doesn't look like this will be the foundation for the winter snow."

"At least not in the valley I'd venture. Hungry? It's well past lunch time."

She looked at her watch. "Do you have time?"

"I'm on leave: signed, sealed, and free to do whatever you want or need." He kissed her as he opened the door to his SUV for her.

"I could eat." She looked at him. "Although I might end up changing my mind, right now I think I want to be around people, good people. Let's go to The Corral."

"Your wish is my command." He backed out of the lot and turned the corner to drive the block and half to the restaurant. His hand rested on her arm. He backed into a parking space in the side lot and turned off the engine, then he leaned over and kissed her. "I love you, Bella Anderson. You know that, right?"

"I do know that. I love you too. Now, last one into the restaurant pays." She hopped out and headed for the side door. He let her go.

"Miss Bella, hey!" Cheri was just inside the door when Bella pulled it open.

"Hey, Cheri. Okay if we take that back booth?"

"Anywhere you like. Light crowd today."

"Ha! First snow of the season and you'd think everyone who lived here was from Florida," Chad said.

"Well, Sheriff, more and more of them are!"

"Fair enough, Cheri. Fair enough."

"Hot tea, Miss Bella?"

"That would be great. Thanks. I would like whatever the soup of the day is and a grilled cheddar cheese sandwich on whole wheat." She took off her coat.

"Double that. Any chance the soup is tomato?"

"It is!" Cheri beamed.

"Perfect." Bella and Chad laughed in unison.

They hung their coats on the rack near the back booth and sat down. Chad leaned across the booth and stroked Bella's cheek. "You doing okay?"

"I think so. Something happened earlier, and I want to tell you about it . . ."

Cheri returned with their drinks.

Bella smiled at Cheri. As she walked away, Bella continued. "Remember when I said I had visions about Billy's wreck?"

Chad nodded.

"While I was listening to Gray, I had a vision of something spilling at my home but I couldn't see where." She looked at Chad to see if he was going to make fun of her.

"Black and white or color?"

"The liquid?" She looked at him with squinted eyes.

"No, your image. Sorry, vision." His voice was steady and calm. There was no hint of derision or dismissal.

"More sepia tones, like a silent movie from the 1920s. I wasn't focused on how the vision appeared but the detail of it." She looked straight into Chad's eyes, then she looked away. "Do you think I just wanted to see that? To think that someone deliberately burned down my house rather than accept that there was faulty wiring or something like that?"

"I think you had a vision. How it's related to what happened, I have no idea. Your visions around Billy's wreck went a long way to saving his life. Our organized, systematic search was the right way to try and find him, but you provided information we didn't have, and it was plausible in the circumstances. So, don't discount what you shared."

"Thanks, Chad."

Cheri set their plates in front of them. Bella looked up at her. "Bless you, Cheri, for putting dill pickles on the plate. I forgot to ask for them."

"No need here, ma'am. The cook pouts when someone asks to leave off the pickles." Cheri leaned in closer. "Mostly it's folks not from here."

Chad laughed. "We are stuck in our ways, aren't we?"

Cheri turned to leave. "I reckon that's the truth. Enjoy your lunch."

"Smells real." Bella lifted her spoon in a mock salute.

"Think people not from here know what that means?"

"Smells real? Seriously? Does it matter? We do." She smiled and lifted a spoonful of soup to her mouth.

"Listen to this woman, she's smart as all git out."

"Exam time." She took a bite of her sandwich and looked at Chad.

He was so happy to see a little of her spark back. "How much of my grade depends on the answer?"

"Forty percent."

"Okay, at least I'll still pass if I miss it. What's the question?"

"What is the meaning of 'as all git out?'"

"Anything I say is going to be a guess, and once I do, I would love to know what the English scholar can teach me about it."

"Might ruin the ease of saying it." They both laughed.

"Afternoon, Sheriff. Ma'am."

Neither had seen Walter walk up to the table.

"Afternoon, Walter." Chad said nothing more.

"Good afternoon." Bella glanced up.

"Sorry, didn't see you had your lunch. I'll talk to you some other time, Sheriff. Enjoy your meal." He turned and walked off.

Chad shook his head slightly and leaned closer to Bella across the table. "I hope I am never in such need of attention that I behave like Walter."

"Never hurts to say hello. I suspect every community has a gossip. At least we know who ours is." She smiled. "Now, that doesn't get you out of the exam."

"Oh, yes, ma'am." He took a bite of sandwich and wondered why more exams didn't include food to serve as a distraction. "My considered opinion," he said after swallowing, "is the meaning has to do with a full measure of something. Like this soup is as good as all git out. It means compared to all the tomato soups in the world—it's at the top."

Bella sat up straight and clapped her hands slowly. "The pupil gets an A. For an A-plus, what is the etymology?"

Chad studied her eyes. Then he grinned and said, *Huck Finn!*"

Bella laughed and slapped her hands together, almost spilling her soup. "Give the man a star. Oh, wait. He has one. He's the sheriff."

He pulled back his sweater and showed her his badge. "The professor wins!" His six-pointed star gleamed.

"I don't think I've ever noticed your badge."

"Whoa, you don't get off that easily. I want to know if I'm right about the etymology."

"If memory serves, it's not the earliest reference to the phrase, but it is one of the earliest in this country."

"See, I'm edumacated."

"You are indeed, fine sir." She pointed to his bowl. "However, your soup's getting cold."

"To see you smile, I'd eat it with ice cubes."

"Ugh. Not tomato soup!" She ate the last spoonful of hers.

"Tell me what you'd like to do with the rest of this day."

She looked at him, grateful for his love and for rescuing her today. "I think a little time with two cute kids would do a lot for me. Possible?"

Chad took his phone out. "Hey. What time is nap time?" He listened. "Perfect. Finishing lunch at The Corral and I have a lovely lady who needs a kid fix. Okay if we come over?"

Chad lowered the volume of his phone but put it on speaker since no one was near them.

"Daddy, you don't ever have to ask. After all, it's not like I haven't walked in on you in your altogether." Chad quickly turned the speaker button off as he turned beet red.

Bella laughed.

"See you shortly. Love you." He hung up.

"Oh, what I would give for a picture of your face a moment ago," Bella said and reached across to take his hand. "It was priceless."

"Always glad when a moment of humor at my expense gives the lady a laugh." He squeezed her hand. "Let's go. If Nora told Mac you're coming, there'll be no containing him."

CHAPTER 5

And into the forest I go, to lose my mind and find my soul.
John Muir

Pulling at Threads

"Sounds like Bella Anderson has had a rough start to retirement. Was there any link between Zimmerman and the drugs run on her property?" Bill Michaels looked at Sam Nations.

"None we could find. Even though Zimmerman's stepson, Steve Phillips, was involved and is in prison, the only link we could find was that he and Nick Brown connected over their mutual dislike for their stepfathers, nothing more."

"Bill, it seems to me that the four local boys connected by being in juvenile detention together. Prior to Hansen's incarceration, he went to the same private high school as Phillips, and Brown and Culverson were both from the local high school. The question I have for Sam is how any of them are connected to Calhoun, the boy who died in the meth lab explosion. Do we know that?" Quinn turned to look at Sam.

"Calhoun was from this area and his college roommate was the one who taught him how to cook methamphetamine. The roommate is in jail now. Three of the five boys involved are deceased, and the two in jail aren't talking—if they know anything. Our interrogators are pretty sure the boys were just mules and didn't know Calhoun. It's hard to go beyond what's been presented here. Our agents will continue to look for a link from these boys to any other suspects dealing street drugs, particularly meth."

Quinn nodded. "Okay. Sounds like there's nothing related to the prior crimes on Dr. Anderson's land that provide a link at this time."

Bill Michaels looked at Billy. "Detective, what do you think?"

Billy took a sip of his water before speaking. "If, and for now it is an *if,* the fire in North Carolina ties back to something here, the only logical thing is Zimmerman's lackeys. Zimmerman's still in custody, right?"

Michaels nodded.

"Then someone he set in place before his arrest, or someone he's reaching from custody, is the most likely connection." He took another sip.

"Seems you might have something else on your mind, Detective," Bill Michaels had a measured tone.

Billy went to the whiteboard. He drew a box and wrote "Anderson NC Residence" inside it. He then drew two lines leading from it, one to the left and one to the right. At the end of each line, he drew another box. He turned to look at the group.

"There are only two possibilities for how the fire started, right?" They all waited. He wrote "accident" in the right-hand box, then moved to left and wrote "ignited." He turned back to the group. "Let's do the easy one: accident. From my point of view, the firefighters in North Carolina will track that one down. Except for Bella Anderson being an upstanding member of our community and a friend, it isn't our concern. Right?"

Bill Michaels sat back and wondered why someone so analytical was content working in such a small community. "Go on."

"If we consider 'ignited,' there are at least three possibilities I can see, and this is where I think we need to brainstorm." He drew a single line down from the left box and connected three boxes to it. He wrote "owner," "our case," and "revenge on owner."

Sylvia had been quiet until that point. "Under owner, draw two boxes, 'self' and 'hired,' and then mark an X through self."

"Why?" Michaels asked.

"Because she was here last night."

"Do you know that for a fact?"

"I wasn't with her . . . " Sylvia looked around the group, "but, according to the sheriff, he was with her until almost midnight. She couldn't have made it to Statesboro and back in that amount of time, particularly given the snowstorm that started shortly after midnight." They all knew people's personal lives often had to be dissected as they tried to solve a crime. Sylvia didn't have to like it, but she would never back away from trying to find the truth.

"Let's make it a question mark for right now then." Michaels was matter-of-fact in his response: no judgment.

Sylvia continued. "As for hired, that only becomes a concern for this group if the person was hired by her across state lines and we are asked to become involved by the North Carolina police." She looked around the table. Everyone was nodding.

They spent the next hour and a half dissecting the other two possibilities related to ignited.

Billy looked around the table. "Alexander, our ace forensic tech, has done additional work on the recent explosion of the food truck."

All eyes turned to him. He thought he saw Sylvia bristle slightly.

"She has corroborated Chief Smallwood's investigation of an improvised explosive device, but she did find traces of an accelerant that appears to have also been planted. I share that just because it may turn out the same accelerant was used at Dr. Anderson's."

Sylvia knew Alexander was exploring other possibilities to the explosion of the food truck prior to the Powwow last month, but she was also very protective of her husband and his reputation.

Finally, Michaels said, "Okay. Lots of good discussion. Time for a break. We'll reconvene in fifteen minutes and then I'd like us to divide up how we're going to pull on the threads that are in our bailiwick."

Everyone stood and walked out of the conference room without comment. It was 3:40 p.m.

Providing Comfort

Bella sat with her legs tucked under her on Nora's sofa and leaned against Chad. He had his arm around her. The flames of the gas logs behind the glass in Nora's fireplace danced rhythmically, and the floor-to-ceiling glass wall on either side of it framed the mountains beyond. Nora sat in a large, overstuffed armchair with her feet on the ottoman. Chad propped his up next to hers.

"Daddy, I can't remember the last time we were able to sit and enjoy a fireside chat about normal, everyday things—I like it."

"Me too, my special daughter." He ran his big toe up the bottom of her stockinged foot.

"Stop it!" Nora giggled as she jerked her foot away. "Bella, he used to do that to me all the time as a kid. He knew I was ticklish on the bottom of my feet, and I think he liked pestering me."

"As a baby, I used my thumbnail, and you cooed and smiled and stole my heart." He smiled at Nora. "No way I'm going to pass up a chance to remember that."

Nora moved her feet out of his reach. "I'm glad you cherish the memory, but I don't coo and smile anymore when you do it. So, truce. Please."

"Fair enough. No more … for today." He smiled. "Kids should be getting up soon, right?"

"I'm surprised Mac hasn't been in here already. Making angels in the snow must have worn him out."

"Thanks for letting them go out and do it again with us. Your dad and I appreciate it. I can see it takes a lot of energy to get them bundled up enough to go out in the cold."

"I'm glad we could make memories together." Nora stopped. She hoped she hadn't broken the relaxed mood they were sharing. "How about staying for supper? I have chili made and the corn bread won't take too long. We could eat about five. Fred called and said he should be home early tonight. I know he'd love to see you."

Bella looked at Chad. Mac came into the room and walked directly to Bella, climbed up on the sofa, and put his head on her lap. "I'm happy you're still here."

Nora and Chad looked at each other and smiled. They were delighted with anything that made Bella feel she was part of their family.

Bella tousled his hair. "Should your grandpa and I stay for supper?"

Mac hopped off the sofa and started to jump up and down. He stopped. "Sorry, Mommy. That's outside behavior."

"It's okay this time, Mac. I know you're excited to have Grandpa and Miss Bella here. I bet Miss Bella might like to see your Lincoln Log fort. Why don't you show her?"

Mac took Bella's hand and she followed him into the playroom.

After they left the room, Nora leaned towards her father. "Daddy, how I can help Bella? I'm devastated about her loss; I can't imagine how she feels."

"You're doing it, sweet girl. Distractions help in these situations and ones that involve children are almost always the best. She has enough reality coming soon. Thanks."

"Daddy, I'm happy for you, and I really love Bella. I know you tried to make marriage work with my mother, but you two were never going to know what love was together."

"Whoa, young lady. The best thing in my life came from your mother—you. Don't you ever forget that."

Nora kissed Chad on the cheek. "You're the best, Daddy. I love you forever."

"And I love you more than you can ever know. Thanks for being your amazing self *and* a friend to Bella."

Nora wagged her finger in front of Chad's face. "I'm waiting on you to make her my bonus mom. Get on with it!" She tapped him on the head and headed over to the kitchen area of the great room. "Come on, make yourself useful."

Out of the Mouths of Babes

Bella marveled at the range of materials available to build and create in Mac and Lilly's playroom. She looked at the easel. "Whose picture is this?"

"Lilly's. I think she's an artist. What do you think?"

"I think she uses color in beautiful ways, and her drawing shows lots of creativity."

Mac looked at her. "Miss Bella, she's not a *famous* artist. Lilly's only two."

Bella reached over and hugged him. "That she is. Now, show me the inner workings of this fort."

Mac gave her detailed explanations of each part of his fort and how he built it to protect the people inside. He moved the small plastic figures in and out of spaces and talked about them.

"Did you know we don't need a moat to protect our houses now?" He sounded like he was fourteen, not four.

"That's true, Mac. I've learned something about our houses."

"What?" He said it with all the sincerity of a four-year-old.

"They provide shelter, a place to be together, and a place to make memories. That's why we call them home."

"I like my home. Do you?"

"I do, Mac."

"I like your home too."

Her voice caught when she tried to speak. "I like my home too. I can't wait for you to see Solasta Caban. It will be finished soon. I hope you can come up and spend the night."

He threw his arms around her neck. "Me too."

Bella saw Chad watching them from the doorway. She had no idea how long he had been there.

"Hey, you two, time to wash up for supper."

Bella looked up at him. "What time is it?"

"Five fifteen."

"Already? Time flies when a four-year-old has your attention!"

"That it does." He walked in and offered his hand as she stood.

"Come on, Miss Bella. I'll show you where you can wash your hands." He looked up at Chad. "You too, Grandpa."

They heard Fred's voice call out in a loud boom. "I'm a hungry monster. I'm looking for a little boy to have for a snack before supper."

Mac ran over behind the chair in the playroom. He peeked around the corner of it at Bella and Chad. "Shhhh . . . don't say I'm here."

"Not a word," Bella put her finger to her lips. She and Chad stepped out of the room, almost running into Fred in the hallway

"Hey, folks." Fred kissed Bella on the cheek, and she returned the kiss. He gave his father-in-law a bear hug.

He raised his voice again and called out, "I'm looking for a snack before supper." He stomped his feet in place. "I'm a hungry monster. Seen any delicate morsels around?"

"Not that I can see." Bella shook her head.

"Nor I, Mr. Monster." Chad tried to sound like he was scared.

"I'm going to find that little boy. I'll bet he's hiding under his bed." Fred stood in place and stamped his feet like he was moving down the hall.

Mac started giggling and Fred moved to the chair, leaned down, and scooped him up. He pulled up Mac's shirt and blew on his belly. He made chomping noises.

"Daddy, Daddy, stop," Mac laughed. Chad stood with his arm around Bella as they watched from the doorway. He knew he had missed too much of this by working all the time: one more reason to be grateful for Bella in his life.

Chad spoke, sounding like the sheriff, "Okay, folks, to the table. I'll have to arrest you for loitering otherwise."

"Grandpa, you can't 'rest me. I haven't done anything wrong." He looked into his father's face. "Have I, Daddy?"

"No, my son, you have not. Let's keep it that way. Come on, hand-washing time."

Once seated at the table, they all joined hands and Fred said, "Let us pray. Heavenly Father, thank you for this time with our family and for the blessings you bestow. You give us strength in difficult times and courage to face the unexpected. Bless this food to our use and us to Thy service. Amen."

They all echoed "Amen."

Bella was about to take her first bite of cornbread when her mobile phone rang. She apologized as she took her phone out of her jeans pocket. She did not look at the screen but turned off the ringer then put it away. She started to eat.

Who Goes First?

Quinn caught up with Billy as he headed to his lab.

"Hey!" He smiled at her. "Want to take a walk?"

"Sure, let me stop in the ladies' room, and I'll be right with you. Inside or out?"

"Too cold outside without your coat, so let's not go out. Come with me. You can stop off down this way."

Quinn knew this was a different hallway from the other ladies room she had used. She saw a sign on a door reading "Detective Bureau" as they walked. Billy stopped and pointed to the ladies' room on this hall.

After Quinn stepped inside, Billy leaned back against the wall to wait. He was glad this hallway took them out of direct sight of the conference room. Quinn emerged and he nodded further down the hall.

"Does this lead to a dungeon?"

"Close enough." He had his key out and opened a small room, ushered her in, and closed the door. He pulled her into his arms and kissed her.

She kissed him back and said, "Detective, we are on duty." Then she pulled him into a more passionate kiss.

"I'll take this duty any day." He flipped on the light.

Quinn saw they were in a small room lined with bookshelves and all manner of supplies. "So, they trust you with the keys?"

"I come in here and covet the old file folders we used for reports before we had computers."

She laughed. "We have a case to solve, you know."

"I do know, and we will. You don't think I'm going to leave Bella Anderson to the big city yokels, do you?"

"That's the detective thinking I love to hear."

They talked for several minutes and agreed that they would be a united front on the strategy Quinn had presented to tug on the strings that might help solve what had happened to Bella's home.

"Depending on our timeline, I'll likely head back to Round City as soon as we finish. Gets dark early now. With the snow melting, the roads can ice over quickly. Otherwise, I'd offer to buy supper at The Corral."

"As much as I'd love that, I want you safe. And we need to focus on solving this case." He kissed her lightly. "You go first. No sense giving folks something else to talk about."

"What? Listen to Mr. Gossip himself; who told me about the sheriff and Bella?"

"Okay, okay. I'm as guilty as the next person. I just don't like gossip about a woman I'm becoming very fond of."

She kissed him lightly and said, "The feeling is totally mutual. Now, get to work." She flipped out the light switch, chuckled, and slipped out the door.

A few moments later, Billy followed her. She was chatting with Bill Michaels when he returned to the conference room.

"Okay, folks. Listen up." All eyes turned to the FBI agent.

"Sergeant Whitehorse and I had a chance to talk during the break and we are agreed that the best strategy going forward is based on Quinn's proposal just before the break. Let's run through it."

All eyes turned back to the whiteboard, and they went through the role of each agency and what was expected of the representatives from that agency.

"Sounds like we have a solid plan. I'm going to head out before dark catches me on Route 54 and get on the highway to Statesboro. I've spoken with Detective Burton in North Carolina. We'll meet at eight tomorrow morning. For this team, I'd like a conference call at three tomorrow unless I let you know differently. Questions?"

There were no questions. Sam Nations said he was headed back to Knoxville.

Quinn said she'd be in Round City tomorrow.

Billy, unable to have a whole day go by and not make some kind of quip, said, "Well, Sarge, I guess that leaves thee and me in paradise. Who can argue?"

Sylvia rolled her eyes. "Indeed, Detective. Indeed."

Sylvia walked down to the new administrative assistant's office to speak to Cecelia. Billy caught up and walked beside her.

"Sarge, have a minute?"

"Sure, what's up?"

"Something tells me you have some thoughts on this which might not have come up in the meeting. Care to share?"

"Let me check on Cecelia, and I'll meet you in my office in ten minutes."

"10-4." Billy turned and walked away.

Sylvia stepped through the open door to Cecelia's new office. "How was your first day?"

"Great, thanks."

"I'm glad you already know that no day is particularly typical or routine here, but this one for sure has not been."

"I know. In some ways, it was helpful for me not to have the sheriff here."

"Really?"

"There were so many reports here to read, I'm not sure I could have gotten through them and done whatever he might have needed."

"Did you get bogged down in any?"

"Not really. Being a dispatcher for so long, I'm familiar with most of the language, so it didn't slow me down." She picked up a printed document and showed it to Sylvia. "Without the sheriff here, I don't know how he's going to want me to report this to him, but maybe you could tell me if you think this can serve as a starting place?"

Sylvia looked at the paper and then at Cecelia. "Cecelia, you have been underutilized for way too long. This is amazing." Across the top of the paper were headings reading "Issue," "Local concern(s)," and "Regional/State concern(s)."

"I have no doubt you and the sheriff will fine-tune this quickly, just like I have no doubt it will shorten his twelve-hour days considerably. I'm very happy you're in this role."

"Thanks, Sylvia. I'm excited. I just hope I can make things easier so the sheriff can focus on being more proactive like he wants to be."

"No doubt you will, Cecelia. Now, go home. It's the end of your workday."

"Night, Sergeant."

Sylvia walked out of Cecelia's office and wondered if having a job that didn't involve a rotating schedule would get boring. She thought it would for her. She walked to her office to find Billy waiting outside her door.

"May I?" He indicated opening the door.

"Please. Go in and have a seat." She followed him and shut the door. "Now, what's your question?"

"I don't have a specific one, but you were even quieter than normal today. Why?"

"Processing the ideas, mostly."

"Yes, you're top-notch at that. I also know you're married to a fire-fighting genius. Even if you haven't discussed this with him, I have a feeling you know more about fires than all the rest of us put together. Why didn't you speak to that in the meeting?"

"Nothing to say—we haven't seen the property. We have a vague explanation of a standing foundation and parts of brick walls, and were told it took almost five hours to put it out."

He studied her face. "And that doesn't paint a picture for you?"

"I don't know what time they received the call, how long it took the trucks to get there, where the water source was, if they had to use foam, and how many firefighters it took. And those are just the immediate questions. The only thing I think I know is it had to be a very hot fire to burn a house to the ground. The questions in my mind are how hot was it and why?"

"May I ask why you didn't raise that in the meeting?"

Sylvia looked at him. Like everyone, she knew Billy loved to tease and joke around. He was also one of the brightest minds she knew, and he never joked his way through solving a case. "I've learned a lot from Mike over the years, but this is not my area of expertise. I would not knowingly contaminate a case by having folks try to make some piece of evidence fit an observation I have."

Billy nodded his head. "Makes sense. If you had used the term 'hot fire,' everyone there knows what your husband does. Even for little ole me, it would immediately make me assume the fire was started by someone. Thanks for sharing with me. Just like you've learned from Mike, I learn many things from watching and listening to you. Sorry I'm not better about telling you."

"Thanks, Billy. I appreciate it. We have a great team here. Better than most law enforcement groups, I suspect. Makes it easier to do a tough job."

"That it does. Now, get out of here. I saw Sergeant Eddie on my way down. All is calm in the valley—the first snow has that effect. Night, Sarge."

"Night, Billy."

The Valley Store

"Melody, let's close this place." Joshua walked down the steps from the loft office over the cash registers.

"Mr. Joshua, it's only six o'clock. You sure you want to close?"

"I am. We've hit dark already, so I'll run you home." He saw a flicker of concern in her eyes. He knew how much she depended on her salary from her part-time job in the store. Her mother had multiple sclerosis and couldn't work anymore. "You can take those ledgers you were working on home if you have time to work on them."

"Oh, sure. I didn't mean anything about leaving early. I have a big test tomorrow, but I can do the ledgers too."

"No rush on them. I've closed up the back. Hand me that cash drawer, and we'll be out of here." He took the cash drawer upstairs and put it in the safe. *I'm going home and check on my wife. I can balance that drawer in the morning.*

"Sure thing, Mr. Joshua."

Joshua pulled in front of Melody's home. "Tell your mama I said 'Hey!'"

"She'll be tickled pink. Night, Mr. Joshua. See you tomorrow."

"Good luck on that test. I'm sure you don't need it."

"Need all the luck I can get! Thanks. Night."

"Night, Melody."

He watched until she was inside. *I know Dad always thought of her as the granddaughter he never had. I wish he were alive to meet the child we're going to have. I wonder if I'll live to see my child be a senior in high school. I never thought I'd be a dad, and certainly not at sixty-three. I'm sure glad Dad lived to eighty-five. Makes me think I have a chance of seeing him or her grow up. Wonder which it will be?*

He drove home. Carla was smiling as she waited for him in the doorway of the kitchen.

"Welcome home, husband."

"Glad to be home, Mrs. Johnson." He kissed her and pulled her into a hug. As much as he had loved his first wife, he couldn't remember the last time she was able to meet him at the kitchen door.

Day's End

Chad went to light the fireplace as soon as they entered his cabin. He normally would have taken off his service weapon and put it in the gun safe, but he didn't want to take the chance of disturbing Bella, who had settled into the peaceful afternoon they had at Nora and Fred's.

"I'll just put my things away," Bella said. "Be back in a minute."

"No rush. Want a glass of wine?"

"Sure, if you're having a beer. If not, I'll make tea."

Once the fire was lit, Chad took off his gun and put it in the safe, then he poured her a glass of Kim Crawford Sauvignon Blanc and popped the top on his Fat Tire Ale. He was already sitting on the sofa when she entered the living room.

Bella took out her phone and saw she had multiple texts and three voice messages. She looked at Chad. "I didn't get a chance to tell you I called the detective in Statesboro while I was with Gray. He wasn't available. I said I would be available after nine in the morning unless it was urgent... then he call anytime. His assistant said he would call if he needed me."

"Good. Glad to hear it. I suspect one of your other calls is the insurance adjuster. They tend to move fast. Many of them are retired detectives, and they know the importance of not letting time alter responses or expectations. Want me to listen to your voice messages with you?"

"That would be helpful. Here goes." She pushed play on the first message.

Chad slipped his arm around her shoulders and pulled her towards him while they listened to each message. She pulled her feet up on the sofa and leaned into him.

When the recordings finished, she had heard from the assistant for the insurance adjuster, her insurance agent, and her neighbor. She returned text messages to Victoria, her former department chair, and Eric Carlsen, her former colleague.

"Well, news travels fast, doesn't it?"

"That it does. But it doesn't sound like it's anyone you might not have expected. Right?"

"I suppose. I'm kind of surprised that Carlsen told our department chair. He doesn't like her." She chuckled. "Ha! He doesn't like anyone but himself unless he needs something from you."

"Sounds like a nice guy." Chad let the sarcasm slip out.

"I got along with him for the most part. We share a common interest in southern dialects, so I suppose I was helpful to him at times. With me gone, he was the only choice for Victoria's thesis, so I have tried to remain cordial."

"Can't imagine you doing anything else." He kissed her on the cheek. "Do you want to call the insurance adjuster?"

"Since he asked to meet at ten tomorrow, I guess I better. Thanks for asking James if I could use the back room at The Corral. Would I be lying if I tell the adjuster I want to meet him there because the road to my cabin is treacherous right now?"

"No, ma'am. Even I, the lowly sheriff, would accept that explanation. In fact, I'd believe it." He smiled at her.

She hit the number on the voicemail and waited. She smiled when the adjuster's phone went to an automated voicemail. "This is Bella Anderson, and I will be happy to meet with you at ten tomorrow, Tuesday, at The Corral Restaurant on Route 54 in the Valley community. You can call me any time after nine thirty tomorrow if you need directions. I'll see you there." She touched the "end" button on her phone then leaned forward and put it on the coffee table where Chad rested his feet. She reached over and tickled the bottom of his foot; he jerked it back.

"Whoa, no fair." He faked a hard glare. He couldn't hold the expression and burst out laughing.

"No fair? Fair? *You* are going to talk about fair." She tickled the other foot and he put both of them flat on the floor. "We women have to stick together, you know."

Chad rolled his eyes. "Great, I was already outnumbered one on one with my daughter. With two of you, I don't stand a chance."

"Good. Remember that." She turned and scooted onto his lap and put her arm around his neck and kissed him. Then she leaned on his shoulder and said, "I want to do my lists for today. Okay?"

"By all means."

She slid off his lap but left her legs draped across him. She took her glass of wine and took a sip. She looked into the fire as she spoke.

"My Not-So-Good List. It would be easy to take every element of the destruction of my house and drag out this list, but it's enough to say the burning of my home. Although related, it's a not-so-good task that others will have to investigate to determine the cause of the fire, and perhaps end up having to find who did it, if that turns out to be the case. Makes for a pretty hefty Not-So-Good List. The Good List far outweighs it though. First, today started with a beautiful, pristine snow across these mountains, and it was the first time I've seen the first snow in all the years I've been coming up here. Then the man I love came to rescue me."

She sat up and kissed him on the cheek then continued. "Nora called, and she reminded me earlier today that I carry the memories of Matt, Mother, Daddy, and Grandmother Hazel with me and share them with others. I'll miss the tangible mementos I had of them, but the memories are forever. Then I had a good meeting with Gray and was reminded there are good people in the world trying to help us all have a civilized and fair society. He's a good man. The rest of the day with you, Nora, Mac, Lilly, and Fred was a precious gift. Thank you. It gave me perspective on what matters in the final analysis. I love you." She looked at him and smiled.

"Finished?"

She nodded.

"My turn. I'm learning from your lists and may end up being able to label mine like yours, but, for now, I am sad that you lost your home and your family memorabilia. I am here to do whatever I can to help find the cause and be by your side through the process of resolving it. I also enjoyed our time with Nora and her family, and I am even more aware, thanks to you, of how easily I could have let these years slip away, buried in my work. I don't have to... and I won't. I'm confident the team who is aiding in the investigation will do everything they can to protect you and your interests. Let's let them handle it. And, lastly, I'm going to brag. I am proud of myself that I trusted my team to run the show without me. Now, let's enjoy our drinks and the fire and then call it a day."

She lifted her wineglass to his beer bottle. "To us."

"To us."

CHAPTER 6

Fortunately wrong cannot last. Soon or late it must fall back home to Hades, while some compensating good must surely follow.

John Muir

First Call of the Day

"Isaacs here." Quinn answered the phone on Tuesday morning without looking at the screen; she hated the glare. Instead, she glanced at the muted light on the clock next to her bed. She sat up and shook her head, trying to figure out who was calling her at 6:30 in the morning.

"Hope I didn't wake you, Agent."

Oh, yeah, I bet. She automatically rolled her eyes as she recognized the voice of the young agent.

"How may I help you?"

"Not me. The director wanted me to tell you it's imperative to check your secure messages immediately."

"Message received. Thank you." She hung up on him. *I don't know how much more I can take of young agents who think the way to advance is to kiss up to the director. Try doing your job.* She knew the director well enough to know that if *he* wanted to be sure she received the secure message at a certain time, he would have called. *This young man probably waits in his car, and when the director arrives, he just happens to walk in with him. I can hear him now, 'Morning, sir. Some way I can help you this fine morning?' The director absently said, 'I'm good, Agent Lawton, thanks. Just sent the one message to Isaacs that needed to go out.'" Then the idiot thinks that gives him license to call me.* She splashed water on her face and headed to her computer. *Come to think of it, why would the director say that much? Maybe he did tell him to call.* She moved to her home office, turned on her computer, and started the process of accessing the secure portal.

The Day Begins

Bella rolled over and ran her hand across the sheets. Chad's side of the bed was cold. She sat up and saw it was just a few minutes before seven. She showered and went into the guest room to get dressed. She was glad Chad had suggested storing most of her dress winter clothes here when she brought them from North Carolina last month. She put on the slacks for her blue wool pantsuit, slipped a pale blue cashmere turtle-neck over her silk camisole, and hung the suit jacket on the doorknob. The gold necklace Matt had given her on their twenty-fifth anniversary sat in a small velvet box. She put it on. *This, Mr. Insurance Adjuster, is the only thing I have left of my late husband.* She knew she wouldn't say that to the adjuster, but even with Chad's love, she needed Matt with her for this interview. Her long brown hair was almost dry, and she ran her fingers through it one more time before leaving the bedroom. She stopped in the doorway. *Why didn't I bring more things with me? I'd still have them.* A sob caught in her throat. She straightened her shoulders and started down the hall.

Chad was sitting in his recliner reading *The Tuesday Tattler*, the local weekly paper. "Any good news?"

Chad lowered the paper, looked at her, and whistled. "Yes, ma'am."

"Great, what is it?"

"A beautiful woman just stepped into my line of sight and every-thing else in the world disappeared."

She resisted running her thumbnail up the bottom of his foot. "Why, thank you, kind sir. Let me get a cup of tea, and I'll join you."

Chad closed his recliner and stood up. "You sit, I'll get your tea. Toast? Eggs?"

"Just tea for the moment." She kissed him and sat down on the sofa, disappearing into her thoughts.

Chad returned after a few minutes and set the tea on the coffee table. "Something prompt that lovely smile?"

"Just thinking about Mac yesterday. He was so intense as he explained his fort to me. It's so easy to forget the innocence of children."

"As I watched the two of you, I realized how you brought one more treasure to my life."

"Oh?"

"Yesterday Cecelia started as the administrative assistant for our leadership team. It's part of my promise to stop working so much. As happy as I am that you put that need front and center for me, I saw what I would have missed with my family if you had not become part of my life. Thank you for both."

"The pleasure is mine, I assure you." She smiled at him and turned to look at the fire. "What does your day hold?"

"Hanging out waiting for the love of my life while she meets up with another man … is the adjuster a man?"

"I honestly don't know. It was one of those names that makes it hard to tell. The voicemail message was his assistant as you heard and the message on the answering machine is automated. You know, 'Please leave your message for Alex Armstrong.' So, your guess is as good as mine."

"Want me to find out?"

"No, I'll find out soon enough. For now, I'm content for us to sit here and enjoy the morning together."

"Works for me."

A few seconds later she said, "Chad."

"Yes."

"Should I ask the adjuster if it's okay for us to go see my property?"

"Don't see any reason why not. Do you want to ask Gray? We can call him."

"No need to bother him. I'll just ask."

"Do you *want* to go?"

"Yes. And no."

Chad nodded his head in understanding.

"Part of me thinks we should go, and I'll close out my safety deposit box, talk to a realtor, and put the property on the market as soon as it's okay to do so."

Chad thought for several seconds before he spoke. "Want some advice from a sheriff?"

"Not from my love?"

"Happens to be one in the same, but this is from a sheriff's perspective."

"Sure." She sat up a little straighter, and Chad noticed she reached down absently, expecting Wizard to be at her feet. She pulled her hand back and put it on her lap.

"I think it's too soon to do anything other than go see the property. Assuming I didn't know you, if you did the things you just outlined, I would think you could have had a part in the fire to get yourself and your financial interests out of North Carolina."

Bella nodded. "You're right. I didn't think of that."

"I know. You've done nothing wrong, so even with all that's happened around you and to you in the past three months, you don't think like a criminal." He leaned over and squeezed her hand. "I'm glad." He winked at her.

"How will I ever write a detective novel if I can't think like a criminal?" She rolled her eyes.

"You read. Learn from books and the internet or interview folks who do deal with criminals. You know, like law enforcement folks." He smiled and winked again.

"Touché! Research! Right up my alley. Thanks, Chad. You already know how random thoughts pop in my head. That was just one I needed to process."

"Happy to help." He didn't tell her he was glad he heard her say "us" if she decided to go to North Carolina. There was no way he'd let her go alone. He knew she would likely be followed, and he wasn't totally sure if it would be by the good guys or the bad—or both.

The Corral

Carla was glad the snow was mostly gone and the roads in the valley were cleared. She headed to The Corral to talk to James. She wanted to ask once and for all if he was willing to accept part of her share of The Corral, giving him 75% ownership of the business. She wasn't sure why, but she felt she wanted to have that discussion inside the restaurant.

"Carla!" Two servers were near the door when she entered, and she stopped to give them each a hug.

"Hey! Looks busy. Need help?"

They shook their heads and one said, "Nah, we're on the downhill slide. We've got it."

The other said, "What can I get for you?"

"I'm good, I'll just grab a glass of milk. James here?"

They laughed.

"Seriously? James is always here."

"Just checking. See you later." Carla was already headed towards the station where the servers filled drinks. She loved that the machine for dispensing milk kept it so cold. It was the only way she could drink it, and she knew she needed to drink far more than she had ever been willing to drink in her life.

She knocked on James's door and entered. "Morning, second man I love."

"Morning, Sis." He looked up and smiled. "Nice to see you." He did a doubletake when he saw the glass of milk. He grinned from ear to ear. "Well, I never . . ."

"Never what? Never thought you'd see me drinking milk? Well, the time has arrived!" She raised the glass in mock salute.

He stood and walked around the table to hug his sister. He didn't let go as he rocked her gently and said, "I couldn't be happier for us."

Carla pulled back. "Us?"

"Us! I think it's fair to say that neither of us expected to have a legacy for the Long family."

She sat down. "That's as true as oil rising to the surface when the rain hits the pavement."

"That's a new one on me."

"Amazing what you can learn when you read. Seems I have time to do that now."

"Then good for you, Sis. Good for you. What brings you here this fine day?"

"I need you to tell me whether you're going to fight me on shifting my share of the business. I don't want a public scene—although I'm willing to take you on."

James sat down behind his desk and looked at his sister. Tears filled his eyes. "Oh, Carla, Carla, Carla. Don't you see?"

"See what?" Her voice was no-nonsense and demanding.

"Things are changing. Not only are you and Joshua going to have an heir, so am I."

She stared at him. "What did you just say?"

"You, Joshua, and I will have an heir. Who knows, this new person may just become the tycoon of the valley, head of the Johnson and Long enterprises."

Carla began to cry. "Oh, brother of mine, I would never expect you to leave your estate to my . . . our child."

James's calm disposition shifted. "I'll grant you may not have thought about it, but you damn . . . sorry, darn well better expect it."

Carla laughed. She had never heard her brother use profanity. "Why, James Long, I do declare! You do interact with the real world from time to time."

"Regrettably," he said and laughed along with her.

"So, you're telling me I should rethink things?"

He nodded. "Actually, I think you and Joshua should sort out your things, and then I'd like the three of us to sit down with Gray Olson and think about how all of us can contribute to the newest member of the Johnson and Long clans."

Carla's tears turned to weeping. James didn't know what to do. He hadn't seen her like this since their parents were killed in a car wreck.

"You okay?" He asked, pushing a box of tissues towards her.

"Hormones. Lousy hormones. *This* is why men should be able to get pregnant. Screwed up hormones!"

He began to laugh. "Okay, baby sister. We'll get through this."

"We will." She picked up the glass of milk, took a sip, and frowned. "Ugh, it's warm!"

"I'll get you a cold glass. Back in a flash."

Bella's Meeting

Bella was surprised she enjoyed driving Chad's Jeep Cherokee. The seats were much plusher than her Wrangler. *It may be time for a new vehicle.* She pulled into the side lot and backed into the parking space. *Hmmm … I like the backup camera too.* She knew she was trying to think of anything besides the fact her home burned to the ground. As she entered the side door, she almost ran into Carla.

"Hey!" Bella smiled from ear to ear. "You look amazing." She lowered her voice. "Feeling okay?"

"Great! Doc Fred says I'm doing fine."

Bella hugged Carla. "That's great. I'm so happy for all of you."

"Joshua will be happiest when he can get a sky writer to announce it to the world." She laughed.

"I can only imagine."

"But, hey, what brings you here at this hour?"

"I'm meeting with an insurance …" Bella looked around… "adjuster. James said we could use the back room."

"Well, come on, let's go make sure he remembered to turn the heat on in there." Carla took Bella's hand, and they walked across the restaurant, past the bar, and to the door into the large community room. "Look at that, he does have a brain." Carla laughed.

"Carla, don't be so harsh on your brother. He's a really nice man in case you haven't noticed."

"Bella, truth is, maybe I haven't been as observant of that fact as I should have been. Now, you have a seat and I'll tell Cheri to get you some tea. The hostess will bring back anyone looking for you. That work?"

"That's great. Thanks, Carla. Take good care of yourself."

"I will. Joshua will have it no other way."

Bella nodded. "I'm sure of that."

Carla left, and Bella pulled out her notepad and pen. She wanted to write anything she needed to remember from the interview while also having something to focus on if she got nervous.

"Hey, Miss Bella. Miss Carla said you could use a cup of tea." Cheri set it in front of her. "I'll get you a couple of glasses of water too. Be right back."

"Thanks, Cheri."

What more could I ask of a place I consider my hometown? At least as close as I'll really come to having one.

"Here you go. Need anything else?"

"No, I'm fine. Thanks."

"We'll see your visitor gets back here."

A moment later, the hostess walked through the door accompanied by a tall, thin man in a suit and top coat. He carried a felt hat in his hand.

Bella thought the only thing missing was a magnifying glass to make him look like Inspector Clouseau. She stood. "Mr. Armstrong? I'm Bella Anderson."

"Morning, Dr. Anderson. Nice to meet you. Sorry for the circumstances."

"Me too. Please have a seat." She saw Cheri waiting. "Oh, sorry, would you like coffee? Tea?"

He turned to Cheri. "Coffee, please. Separate check."

Bella smiled to herself and sat down. *Careful, don't decide he's predictable. Just answer his questions.*

"I'll try not to take up too much of your time."

No small talk. Must not be from the south.

"I'm at your disposal. Thank you for agreeing to meet here. The road up to my cabin is not easy on a good day, and there will be icy spots after the snow yesterday."

"This is fine." He handed her a business card and said, "May I see your driver's license, please?"

"Certainly." She reached into her purse and pulled out the small case with her license and credit cards. She showed him the documents.

He wrote down the information and handed it back.

"I hope you won't take offense, but may I see your license and verification of your North Carolina certification? I'm aware that Tennessee does not require licensure for adjusters."

He handed her his driver's license and a laminated card. She took her phone and took a picture of both.

"Smart," he said.

"It was my insurance agent who advised me to ask for those." She smiled. "I don't have any experience with this."

"I'm sure. I see that you've never even had a car accident."

"And let's hope I don't." Her tone was casual and friendly.

"Where were you the last three days...from Friday through Monday?"

"Here. Well, not here in the restaurant, but in Drellag Caban."

"Drellag Caban?"

"Yes, that's the name of my home here."

"You consider this your home?"

"I do."

"How long has it been your home?"

"Since I was born. My great-grandfather built the cabin in the late 1800s. My parents lived in North Carolina for many years, as did my late husband and I, but this has always been my home."

"Do you consider your residence in North Carolina your home as well?"

"North Carolina has been my legal residence for all of my life."

"Then how is it you distinguish one home from another?"

"Mr. Armstrong, I have been fortunate to live in a lovely city in North Carolina from the time my parents returned there after my birth here in the mountains of east Tennessee. My parents always considered Tennessee their home, as do I. It is the home of our ancestors and for me, of my soul."

"So, there's an advantage to not having a home to worry about in North Carolina anymore?" He said it quickly and with an edge, just as Gray had warned her.

"The loss of my home in North Carolina has devastated me. I'm not sure about other clients with whom you interact, so you might find this unusual." She took a breath. "I've moved back and forth between my two homes with ease for decades and I expected to do that for many years to come."

"It's a huge expense to have two homes." He said it flatly. No question.

Bella waited.

"Isn't it? Don't you think most people would find it a huge expense to have two homes?"

"Perhaps. It is not my personal experience or situation."

"How's that possible? Aren't you retired?"

Bella sipped her tea. "I am retired, as I'm sure you have already verified. I suspect you can access my credit score. I pay my bills, I buy what I want when I want, and I am a frugal woman of Scottish ancestry." She knew Gray would not be happy with her response.

"Isn't it true you just had a claim on your home here?"

She was ready for that question.

"I have been loyal to my insurance agent all of my adult life and expect the same from the agency he represents. The damage to my property here was done by boys riding ATVs, one of whom is now deceased, and the other is in jail. What the insurance company chooses to do with the courts to negotiate the repayment of the payout on my claim is not my concern. I did not ask to have my property trespassed upon nor damaged." She looked him in the eye. "No more than I asked to have my home in North Carolina burned to the ground."

He looked away, unable to hold her gaze.

She waited a beat. "I understand you have a job to do, and I am willing to fully participate in your investigation. I *want* to know what happened to my home. I have a PhD in the English language and understand nuances many would find boring to learn. Please, do us both a favor and do not play games with me. Ask what you need to ask, and then go help find out how my home burned down."

"Uh, hum … I just have a couple more questions." He sat up straighter in the chair.

After identifying who could verify her whereabouts and with whom she had spoken in the past three days, Alex Armstrong knew he was finished—whether he wanted to be or not.

"Thank you for your time, Dr. Anderson. I am sorry for your loss. You will hear from your agent in due course." He stood and extended his hand; she shook it.

"Thank you for your efforts to determine what happened. I wish you safe travels, Mr. Armstrong."

He turned and left.

Bella sat and sipped her tea as tears welled in her eyes. She let them fall. She did not hear the door leading from the kitchen into the community room open.

Chad pulled out the chair next to her, sat down, and put his arm around her. He kissed her cheek, but did not speak.

"Did you hear?"

"Every word. Good job. Glad I'm not your interrogator."

She looked at him and saw the sparkle in his beautiful eyes—the gray eyes that disarmed her the first time she met him—then kissed him.

"Let's go. I need to hike a mountain. Know any?"

"I have a lunch packed by our good friends here at The Corral, and as soon as you change out of that lovely outfit, we'll head to the hills."

They walked out holding hands. She hoped the adjuster was sitting in the parking lot. "Oh, wait. I didn't pay for my tea."

"Me either. James said it was on the house." He walked her to his Jeep Cherokee and opened the passenger door.

"How did you get here?" She looked around for his work SUV.

"I'm on leave, remember? I walked down the hill. Felt good."

"I love you, you clever man."

"I love you more."

"Not a contest, remember?"

CHAPTER 7

There is a love of wild Nature in everybody, an ancient mother-love ever showing itself whether recognized or no, and however covered by cares and duties.

John Muir

Updates

"Hey, love, what's up?" Joshua smiled as Carla entered the Valley Store.

"Just stopped in to organize the final interviews for a full-time cashier. Decided I'd rather sit here and do it than at home. Okay?"

"Absolutely. You okay to climb those stairs, or do you want to sit in the back?"

"Anyone here?"

"Just us at the moment."

"Okay," she took a breath. "Joshua, I am pregnant, not crippled. I'm being careful; I promise." She winked at him. "I'll ask for help when I need it. It's hard for an independent woman to accept help when she needs it, much less when she doesn't."

Joshua studied her face and looked into her eyes. "You're right. I'm learning. Let's try again. Honey, cash drawers are set up, we're ready for customers. Where do you want to work?"

She realized she owed it to him, and the baby, to be a bit more careful than she might otherwise. *Wonder if that happens to all women; the first time they're pregnant? My age might make me too cautious—or too cavalier.* "Thought I'd sit at the table in the storeroom." She kissed him and started towards the back of the store. A moment later, she turned around and said, "Guess what? I saw Bella at The Corral."

"You did? How is she? I'm surprised she hasn't stopped in here."

"She said she was meeting with an insurance adjuster. James let her use the community room."

Joshua's brow furrowed. "Insurance adjuster? You sure?" They heard the silver bell above the door jingle and turned to see Bella and Chad.

"Just talking about you," Joshua said.

"I knew my ears were burning for some reason." Bella stood on her tiptoes to kiss six-foot-four Joshua on the cheek.

"Look at you. Pretty dressed up for these parts, aren't you?" Joshua stepped back and looked Bella up and down.

"How's your brother's wife supposed to compete with that look?" Carla said.

"Competition seems to be the word of the day."

Carla and Joshua looked from her to Chad.

"Come again?" Carla said.

Bella looked from Carla to Chad. "Sorry, just a comment I made to Chad a few minutes ago that everything in life is not a contest."

"Well, if you entered, you'd win first prize." Carla said with no hint of jealousy.

The tension in the room was broken.

"Well said, Carla." Joshua kissed her on the cheek. "My sentiment exactly." He reached over and shook hands with Chad.

Bella raised her hand. "If you have a minute, I wanted to update you on some news I got yesterday."

"We're as slow as molasses running up hill in the wintertime." Joshua pointed to a stool beside the register.

"I'm good. Thanks. I think Carla should sit."

Carla shrugged and looked at the other three. "A bunch of mother hens..." She sat and Joshua put his hand on her shoulder.

Bella looked at Chad and he nodded. "My home in North Carolina burned to the ground."

"What? No, it can't be." Carla's hands flew to her face.

"Bella, how'd it … sorry, it's none of my business. I hate hearing this. What can we do to help you?" Joshua slipped his arm around Carla.

"Nothing, I just needed to get through the meeting with the adjuster before I shared the news with my family." She smiled at them. *They are family!*

"Well, I doubt there are words that will help right now, but you know we'll do anything we can." Carla stood up and hugged Bella.

"I know. Thanks. I'd like to keep it among us for now, if that's okay."

"Okay? Are you kidding. We have the biggest secret in these hills. We know we don't have to worry about you sharing it. Yours is safe with us." Joshua looked at Carla for corroboration.

"Absolutely," Carla said.

"Well, we're off for a hike. I need some time in these hills." She looked at Carla. "And you, my sister-by-choice, stay off your feet!"

They exchanged hugs then the bell jingled again as Chad and Bella left.

Once the door closed, Carla gave a shudder. "Burned to the ground? Joshua, that's terrible."

Joshua hugged Carla close. "A tragedy. Glad she's okay, though. That's most important."

Carla nodded.

Unwinding a Thread

It was 7:00 a.m. when Quinn arrived at the office; she saw the director drinking coffee with the boy agent. They had not seen her enter the small building. She was fine with that. It was now almost 11:00. She was surprised Agent Lawton hadn't come looking for her by now. She had been through all the pieces of information the director had sent her. There was nothing in the director's secure email that warranted a phone call. *So, what's the deal?*

She picked up her secure phone and dialed Sam Nations.

"Nations here."

"Isaacs here."

"So it is. Good morning, I was about to call you."

"Were you? Must have been my psychic abilities that beat you to it."

"Likely so. Listen, I've pulled on a thread around the drugs and the prostitution ring, and I think we might have something we should both look at—may be related to Zimmerman. Do you have any time today?"

"Figuring out if there's a connection to Bella's house burning is my top priority. Where are you?"

"Headed east on I-40. Where do you want to meet?"

"Come to my office. Good for my boss to see that I have connections in places other than his kingdom."

"Ouch. I bet there's a story behind that."

"That's for a beer on a Friday night, away from prying eyes and ears."

"Gotcha. Be there at eleven thirty. Take you to lunch if you want."

She almost dropped the phone.

"Quinn, are you there?"

"Sorry, just recovering from a lunch offer I wasn't expecting. See you when you get here."

"Hasta luego." He missed talking to her in Spanish.

Quinn turned back to the computer screen. *Where was the person who made the threatening phone calls to Bella Anderson and Nora Oliver-Smith? Did we all assume he was arrested after tracking the vehicle that hit Billy?* She pulled up all the phone records that had been collected with a federal warrant. *Sam and I used to be pretty good at puzzles. Let's see what we can find in this one.* She printed out the records and put them in a zippered portfolio marked "confidential" to take to lunch.

Then she sat back and puzzled over the boy agent and the director. Agent Lawton knew she was next in command after the director. Maybe he didn't know she had no desire to be the director; it was purely an administrative job. She liked being in the field and solving crimes. *Might be time to take the boy agent to lunch. Ugh.* She stood and was headed to the ladies' room when the boy agent and director turned the corner. They were laughing.

"Morning, Isaacs. Didn't see you come in this morning."

"Locked up in my office the past four hours, sir. Research to do. Thank you for the information you sent. It will be helpful."

"Didn't think it was urgent. Just wanted you to have it."

Quinn stared at the boy agent, who she could have sworn turned a light shade of pink . . . no, red.

She kept walking. "You gentlemen have a nice day."

Five minutes later she almost ran to her office. She grabbed the portfolio, her purse, and logged out of her computer. She called Sam as soon as she got in her SUV.

"Meet me at my place. We can eat later."

Driving home, she started piecing together the early morning call from the agent.

Another Thread

"See you then." Billy replied to an electronic pink slip from Sylvia about a meeting at noon. He'd been at the station since 6:30 a.m. and decided to go home and grab a sandwich. *I don't think the Anderson house just burned down. There has to be a link here, somewhere.* He put the two documents he'd been reviewing about the links to Zimmerman's ownership of the two Round City motels in a folder to read over a quick lunch.

Sylvia stared at the documents her husband had given her on weather conditions, square footage, height of floors, building materials, and the five types of construction recognized by FEMA. She also studied the effects of combustibles in the environment and the accelerants it would take to burn a house down in a given period of time based on the location of the ignition point and response times. She had been an excellent student of mathematics in high school and college, and she had even toyed with the idea of doing a doctorate in math. Love won out, and she had returned to the valley when she and Mike Smallwood married. She had never regretted her decision, but she loved the opportunity to try and solve problems.

The county appraiser's office in Statesboro had the square footage of Bella's home and a photo was easily found online. *I wonder how many people even consider how much personal information is available about them from the simplest online search?* The online site had estimated Bella's home at $750,000 for tax purposes…which included the land value. Sylvia had a list of vacant land close to the property, but there wasn't much available to determine the value of the land by itself. She was deep in calculations when there was a knock at her door.

"Ready for me?" Billy asked, opening the door a crack.

"Hey! Come in. Give me just a minute."

Billy walked over and sat down opposite Sylvia at her desk. He looked around and started to say something then stopped. *This office is big enough for a table. Wonder why she doesn't have one?*

"Thanks." Sylvia gathered up her papers and laptop. "Let's go to the conference room so we can spread out and doodle on the whiteboard."

Billy nodded and followed her down the hall. After making sure the door to the conference room was closed, he asked, "Heard from the boss?"

Sylvia didn't take her eyes off the laptop screen as she set it up to communicate with the projector. "No, Detective, he's on leave. I don't expect to hear from him."

Billy got the message. No chit-chat. He sat and waited for her to start.

"Let's agree on a plan of attack. I want to discuss the fire itself, at least as much as we know at the moment, what we know from the threatening phone calls Zimmerman had made to Nora and Bella, and review the interviews with all the boys who rode ATVs across her land. What do you have?"

"Documents from our detective's work on ownership of the motels in Round City. I've found an interesting link to North Carolina."

"Then let's start there."

Billy pulled out the two documents and showed her the ownership records and how they wound through Michigan, Tennessee, the Cayman Islands, and even North Carolina. They both drew the same conclusion—Zimmerman had connections in North Carolina.

Sylvia stood and made a note on the whiteboard under "our case."

"Good work, Billy. I want us to talk through what I've found and then take a break before our three o'clock conference call. Okay with you?"

"Let's do it."

They focused on the notes she had written about the elements of a fire. She showed him her calculations, and he whistled.

"Whoa. Are you sure about that?"

She nodded.

Lovely Day for a Hike

Chad drove up behind the building on the tribal lands and kept going. "I called Chief Whitehorse and asked him if we could drive up here. He sent us with his blessing."

"I like the chief."

"So do I."

"I thought he was just making small talk at the powwow when he asked me about writing his stories down, but we've already met three times. We've discussed his timeline, his expectations, and what I think I could contribute."

"Is it something you want to do?"

"I've always wanted to learn more about our native tribe, and this is an amazing opportunity to do it. I told him I was concerned how others might view him telling his stories to a non-native."

"What did he say?" Chad hesitated. "If it's okay to tell me."

"I don't think this is confidential. He made a valid point; I am not writing about him. In a way, I am his scribe. He will retain total control of the content. I assured him I would not use anything I wrote with him in any way. I asked him if he wanted a lawyer to draw up a contract."

Chad stopped the Jeep and put it in park.

"And?"

"And I made clear that I would not take compensation for the work, but if he would feel better knowing we had a written agreement, I would understand." She smiled. "He said, 'I'm not so sure the history of written agreements between our peoples has served either side well. You either trust someone, or you don't.' He said he wouldn't have asked me to help him if he didn't trust me."

"Smart man."

"I'm working on the stories he's told me already." She looked out from the window. "Somewhere in particular we're headed?"

"Yes, I have permission to take you up to Mantle Rock. I apologize if I overstepped, but I explained to the Chief . . ."

"Oh, Chad! I didn't answer the text from him yesterday. How can he trust me to be reliable?"

"Whoa, as I was saying, I explained to Tom what happened. He asked me to extend his sadness at the loss of your home. He asked if there was anything he could do, and I told him I thought it would be healing for you to go to Mantle Rock. He agreed and wished us a good walk."

"I'm honored. Does the tribe own all this land?"

"It was actually deeded to the tribe in the early 1900s. No one knows if money or other land was exchanged, nor with whom. So, yes, technically they own it. More than that, most European descendants have respected their rights and not trespassed on the land."

"Then should we?"

"We should. I would never come without permission unless there was a crime here. We not only have permission but the chief's blessing. Let's go."

They both exited the Jeep and started up the path hand in hand.

Round City

Quinn was barely in her house when Sam pulled up in front. She left the front door unlocked and threw her papers on her dining room table. It had belonged to her mother's parents, who she suspected would be horrified to know she used it as a desk rather than serving the elegant meals it knew in their lifetimes. She went to the kitchen and put on a pot of coffee for Sam but grabbed a Diet Coke for herself.

Sam knocked as he entered and shut the door.

"I'm in the kitchen making you coffee. Come on back."

Sam walked in and saw her drinking the Diet Coke from the can. "Must be a rough day. Don't know the last time I saw you drinking on the job."

"Ha! You know more of my quirks than may be in my best interest."

"I may not have always done by right by you, but I do not kiss and tell."

"Sorry. I know that. Didn't mean to sound snarky."

"What is going on with you? Snarky? When did you start using that word?"

"Since the boy agent—" she stopped. She pulled a glass out of the cabinet, put ice in it, and filled the glass with what was left of the Diet Coke. "Never mind."

"Looks like we're going to be at your worktable. Need me to do anything?"

"No. Be there in a second." She handed him her glass and opened another cabinet door and took out a mug. She already knew he drank his coffee black.

She set the mug on a coaster in front of Sam and jumped in. "We need to do a quick and dirty search through these phone records."

"What?"

"The phone records from the threatening calls to Nora and Bella. Remember, we had the warrant for them, but I don't think anyone ever did anything with them. If the FBI did, we never heard about it. I wonder if everyone just assumed once the FBI arrested the guys who ran Billy Williams off the highway, that they were one and the same: drivers and callers. I'm not so sure about that."

"And this matters, why?"

"Because if the caller, or callers, were not caught because they were careless and used their own phones, they may be on a mission to punish someone for cutting off their cash flow from Zimmerman. Or, heck, who knows, maybe Zimmerman got word to them from prison. And that's another thing, did his wife just fall off the planet? No word on her and we even have evidence he tried to have her killed in that wreck on Route 54."

"Quinn." He looked at her. "I want an end to the Zimmerman case as much as you do. I would also love to help solve the mystery of Bella's house burning down. But, well, isn't all this a bit farfetched?"

"Sam Nations, you *know* I do not go off half-cocked. This is a thread that runs through your agency and mine, and I'm going to either eliminate those threads related to the fire at Bella's or pull it in and catch whoever did this."

"If anyone did ..." He muttered under his breath. "Do you have a plan of attack on the phone records? We have three hours until the conference call."

Mantle Rock

"Here, step up on this side." Chad pointed to a part of Mantle Rock that provided crude stairs to the flat part of the outcropping; a large tree served as a handhold. Chad did not tell Bella this is where Sam had been hurt a few months before. He couldn't remember if she even knew he had been. "Let's sit over here."

"Oh, Chad. I've only ever seen that ravine from the air flying into Knoxville." She sat down and pulled her legs up to her chest, rested her hands on her knees, and placed her chin on her hands.

Chad watched her. He remembered the first time he saw her sitting in that position when they were on a hike on her property. *There's something about that pose that shows absolute absorption in the surrounding environment ... to say nothing of how beautiful she looks doing it.* He spoke quietly. "I've only been up here once. It seems to me the hike to get here through the forest and the absolute magnificence of the view has made this a healing place for generations."

She turned her head to the side and rested her cheek on her hands as she looked at Chad. "I think I always knew how fortunate I was to have found Matt early in my life." She watched his face; his eyes held hers. "I'm sorry you haven't known that kind of love throughout your life." She reached over and stroked his cheek. "I did not, however, imagine I would know the love of two good men. Last night it occurred to me *your* love for me knows I've loved before and carries no jealousy. For me, it makes your love even more special. Thank you for loving me."

Chad had been stroking her back since they sat down. He pulled her close to him and kissed her cheek. "You, Bella, have not only saved my life, you have given me life. You are kind and gentle and feel life in a way and at a depth I don't know if I ever can." He pulled his head back and smiled at her. "But I want to learn. I want to live life, not just wander through it as I've done for far too many years. I love my work, and I truly want to be more proactive in improving the quality of life for our community. Thanks to you, I am beginning to see I have let the work of dealing with crime guide my days instead of waking up and ..." He went quiet. "What's the old saying? Something about 'Seize the day?' I haven't, but I'm learning." He kissed her gently on the lips. "Thank *you* for loving me."

They sat quietly, each in their own thoughts as they took in the wind, the sun, the smells and sounds of trees—and the forest hunkered down for winter. Bella laid back on the rock, warmed by the sun, and looked up at the sky. She pointed to two red tail hawks soaring above them in quiet patterns on the thermals. Chad looked up at them, and they watched the wonder of life in this isolated place which had been home to many life forms for eons.

Tears ran down her cheek as she watched the majestic flight. *I can learn from those birds. They have no ties to a specific place on this earth except when they build a nest to have their young. They fly above the earth with no destination and land wherever their path takes them. The loss of my home in North Carolina may be the message—I have taken a path back to my roots:* this *is my home.*

She stood and took Chad's hand as he stood up beside her. She put her arms around him and kissed him. "I love you. Thanks for bringing me here. You have opened my eyes. Let's go eat the lunch you forgot to bring up here."

"So I did!"

She turned and started down the stairs etched in the rock. They both heard the crack of a rifle. Chad pushed her behind the large tree.

CHAPTER 8

I am learning nothing in this trivial world of men. I must break away and get out into the mountains to learn the news.

John Muir

Unknown

"Quinn, what date does your dataset start?" Sam looked at the printout she had given him.

"Two months before the first threatening calls."

"I assume you have it on your computer."

"Of course, Sherlock." She pulled up the file.

He ignored the quip. *Something is definitely stuck in her craw.* "Do a quick data sort and let's see the patterns of frequently used phone numbers to Nora and Bella during that period. Then we can see if we can eliminate the numbers prior to the calls in question."

"Doing it now." She clicked some keys on her computer. "How do we know there weren't some trial calls before the first threatening message?"

"First, we know Nora's phone number is not public because her husband is a physician. So, it's safe to assume if there are any calls to and from her number to a given number, it's a legitimate call to her."

"Okay, that works for Nora. How about Bella?"

"Let's just see where the data lead us."

"You're right. I know better. Here, look." She turned the laptop so they could both see.

They looked for numbers that only called Bella once. There was one leading up to the first threatening call.

"Give me a second, I'll see who has that phone number." She clicked some keys and said, "Edwards Well and Pump. Know him?"

"Yes. He digs and services all the wells in the area."

"Okay, eliminate that number. We know there were nine calls including the ones that went straight to the FBI. Should be easy enough … hold on. Sam, look at this number." She pointed to the screen and then typed the area code into a search window. "Detroit. And look, here it is again *after* Zimmerman went to prison. Make a note to check with Bella and see if she answered or had a message on her answering machine—no, wait. It could have been a hang-up since the call is recorded as one minute." She leaned back in her chair and closed her eyes.

Sam watched her and knew not to interrupt. *Now we need to find out if that is a mobile or landline. If it's mobile, what tower did it ping off?*

Quinn turned to look at Sam. "Thoughts?"

"You first."

"Let's check for repeats now and then we'll come back to this." She looked at him. "Let's be systematic. We both know what we'll do next."

"Yes, ma'am. We do." He smiled. He had missed working out puzzles with her.

Unsettled

Chad had his sidearm out of his holster instantly. Based on the direction he believed the shot originated, he pushed Bella back as far as the large tree would shield her. *I can't believe I didn't think to have us wear hunting jackets. The orange would help if it was a hunter, even one gone astray.* He knew they were in deer season until January. He also knew no one should be hunting on the tribal grounds, which was clearly marked with purple stripes painted on the boundary trees. The stripes meant no hunting or trespassing. *Hunters know the law.*

"Do you think it was a hunter?" Bella whispered.

Chad nodded his head, hoping to reassure her, but he held up a finger for her to wait. *Someone after one of us would be much more likely to have tried another shot right away. A hunter would quietly stalk his quarry. We can't head down; the area is wide open for the first eighth of a mile.*

Bella held up her mobile phone.

He shook his head. He knew there was no signal up here.

Bella looked and saw there was no signal. *I should have known that.*

Filling in the Blanks

Sylvia and Billy were making notes on the whiteboard after a thorough review of the motel ownership information and the data she had on fire destruction specific to Bella Anderson's North Carolina home.

"Whitehorse here." Sylvia answered her secure phone.

"Sergeant, Ken Bennett needs to know if he has permission to go up on the tribal grounds."

"Put him through."

"What's up, Deputy?"

"Sarge, I'm on patrol by the tribal grounds and heard a rifle shot that sounded a little too close for comfort."

"Then head up the road behind the tribal building, no lights or sirens. Don't go in on foot until you call me. I'm sending backup and will clear it with Chief Whitehorse."

Billy already had his phone out. He told dispatch to send backup to Bennett—no lights or sirens.

"Come on, Daddy, pick up."

"Good afternoon, my daughter."

"Good afternoon. Not a social call. Shot heard on tribal grounds, do we have permission—"

"Get up there. Chad and Bella are at Mantle Rock. Go!" The chief hung up.

Sylvia dialed dispatch. "Send another … yes, I know you've sent one. I said send another. No lights or sirens. The sheriff is up there. I'm headed up. Detective Williams is in charge here." She headed for her office. Billy was with her stride for stride.

"Sheriff and Bella are at Mantle Rock."

"Would you rather I go?"

"No, I need to go. It's better to have a tribal member there just to be sure we don't create other problems." Sylvia knew her father would have already sent tribal members to help.

"Good point. I've got things here. Remember, there's no signal up there, so keep a relay going."

"Thanks for the reminder." She didn't take offense. She knew he was trying to cover all the bases. "Get two more teams ready in case we have to cover the area. Call Bill Michaels and tell him we have to delay the conference call."

"Tell him why?"

"No. Not 'til we know why."

"That's why you're in charge, Sarge. I'm learning."

"You do what you do very well." She was almost at the back door, stopped, and looked at him. "Billy, this is the sheriff. Chad and Bella. Coincidence?"

"Don't believe in them myself. Go."

Routine

It was 2:30 p.m., and Melody had arrived early. "Hey, Mr. Joshua. How's Miss Carla?"

"She's fine, thanks. Out on good behavior?"

"Early dismissal today." Melody was happy that Mr. Joshua was joking with her. She had enjoyed that about working with his father, Mr. Joe, and now it seemed Joshua had picked up where Joe had left off. "Good deal, means you can start on the bookwork." Carla was still in the back of the store, so Joshua went to check on her. *Sure glad I can ask if she has the interviews set up, that way she's less likely to think I'm making sure she's okay—even though I am.* He looked through the swinging door and saw she was not on her mobile phone, so he stepped into the storeroom.

"Hey, how's it going?"

"I've reached the four people for full-time work, and we'll interview them tomorrow. I've left a message for Natalia to call me."

"I don't remember talking about Natalia."

"Sorry, we didn't." She looked up at him sheepishly. "I figure if we have a full-time person Monday through Friday, and Natalia works Friday evenings and Saturdays with Melody, it will also free up Melody to take on more of the bookwork."

"I'm used to doing all that."

She thought he sounded hurt. "I should have talked to you about it. It just occurred to me when I was talking to the last interviewee." She kissed him lightly on the lips.

"Okay. I trust you; I just need time to process it. The kiss goes a long way." He smiled at her, not wanting to upset her or add to her stress levels.

"Honey, you've worked fifty- and sixty-hour weeks all your adult life."

"So have you."

"I know, but I want us to be able to do other things: day trips, dinner in Round City, afternoon at the zoo in Knoxville. We have to scope out places other than amusement parks to take our child."

Joshua moved in and hugged her close to him. "You're right. Absolutely right."

"Besides, we'll be busy enough once we work through the details that Gray recommended so we can rent out my house and Joe's. Look how much it takes for you to do the store and run the propane business by yourself." She bit her bottom lip and looked up at him.

"Okay, okay. I admit it; you're smarter than I am."

"No, I'm excited. I love you." She dropped her voice to a whisper. "We're going to have a baby, and we can do whatever we want. We can even choose the fun parts to keep for ourselves."

He hugged her again. "That's my wife—figuring out how to have fun." He winked at her. "Now, are you drinking plenty of fluids?"

"Yes, nurse husband." She held up her thirty-ounce Yeti cup. "Fourth one today. I'm about to float away."

"Well, don't." He turned to head up front.

Carla stood. "I was just getting ready to leave when you came back. I'm truly sorry I didn't talk to you about Natalia."

"No problem. You did and that's what matters. Love you. Get some rest, please."

"On it."

They walked to the front holding hands. He kissed her. "See you soon. I love you."

"I love you too."

The bell above the door jingled as Carla walked out.

"I bet Miss Carla doesn't know how to act without working all the time at The Corral," Melody said.

"She's adjusting, Melody. She's adjusting." He climbed the stairs to his loft office.

More Information

"Issacs here."

"Billy here. Have a minute?"

"For you, anytime."

Sam watched as a smile grew on Quinn's face and her voice carried a warmth that was at odds with data analysis. Just as quickly it faded.

"What?"

"There was a—"

"I heard *that*. Chad and Bella?"

"Yes."

"Sam's here with me. We're on our way." She hung up and shut down her computer then moved it to the small safe near her desk. "Hand me those papers, please."

"All of it?" Sam was impressed that she would lock up phone records. *Well, they were obtained with a warrant, weren't they?*

"All of it. Let's go."

"One vehicle or two?"

"Two. I'll call you on the way and tell you." She checked her back door. Sam had her coat off the coat tree, ready for her to slip on.

She grabbed it and said, "Thanks. Have to put on my vest first. Have yours?"

Sam slapped his chest. "Never leave home without it."

"Smart plan."

As soon as she got to her SUV, she put on her Kevlar vest, pulled her jacket on over it, and started the engine. She dialed Sam on speaker as she pulled out of the driveway. He picked up on the first ring.

"Apparently Chad and Bella are up at Mantle Rock. According to Billy, Ken Bennett was on patrol and heard a shot from that direction."

"Let's go. Lights and sirens. I'll lead."

"Billy said no lights and sirens near the tribal grounds."

"10-4."

Backup

The first of the two backup vehicles arrived, and the deputies were told via radio from Bennett to cover the park area to the left of the building. Sylvia arrived at the same time as the second backup vehicle. She told the deputies to stay below and watch for anyone on the road.

Ken was standing outside his vehicle. "Sarge, no more shots and no evidence of anyone coming down."

"If I know my dad, as the chief he'll have tribal members in these woods already. I promise you will never see them unless they want to be seen. I think you and I are going to head up the trail acting like we're a couple who managed to slip away from work. We can't hide our uniforms, so our conversation will have to be our cover."

"10-4."

"Feeling romantic, Deputy?"

"Just don't tell my wife."

"That's a good line to start with. Let's go."

Grabbing his hand, she said, "Oh, honey, I'm so glad you could slip away. Come on, I want to show you my favorite place on this side of the mountain."

"I shouldn't be up here, should I? Isn't this part sacred?" He tried to sound concerned.

Sylvia was scanning left and ahead and Ken was scanning right and behind. He was less worried about what was behind them on the lower level as he knew there were other deputies below. The tall evergreens still held some snow, and the air was definitely cooler as they ascended.

"Shhhh . . . We'll be in trouble no matter what; I'm your supervisor at work." Sylvia panted like she was winded and couldn't control the volume of her voice.

"Forbidden fruit." He pulled her arm towards him and ran like he was anxious to get to the top.

Sylvia knew the top of the next rise would put them close to Mantle Rock. Ken had no way of knowing it. "I'm going to show you something more beautiful than you've ever seen when we get to the top of this next crest." She turned and signaled they would slow.

"*You* are the most beautiful thing on this earth. Where are we going? Can't we just stop here?" He purposely slowed his gait and she followed suit.

Sylvia leaned in like she was going to kiss him and whispered in his ear. "The next rise will put us in shouting distance to Mantle Rock. If the sheriff and Bella are still there, he will have heard the shot too."

Ken whispered back, "Let's hope he didn't receive the shot."

"Come on, you crazy guy. We're almost there." Sylvia giggled and nodded to him to move.

Each of them knew they were potential targets if someone was on the other side of the crest trying to get to Chad or Bella. Ken was at a disadvantage as he had never been up here, so he followed Sylvia's lead. Sylvia was also aware she had to let Chad know they were headed towards them.

Tribal Help

Sam and Quinn arrived in the valley and turned off their lights and sirens after they passed the sheriff's station. Quinn called to tell Billy they were heading up.

"I know, Billy. Sam told me on the way over we'll go up the gully above the road where the food trucks were. It gets to Mantle Rock more quickly than the road up the back of the building. Later."

"10-4." Billy hung up the phone. He was frustrated because he wasn't on the ground to know what was going on. *And I thought being a detective would be more interesting than when I was a deputy! What was wrong with me? I'll be listening to the tales of this hunt for months to come.*

Sam told Quinn to pull behind him on the bottom of the road. He didn't know there was a deputy watching the gully. As soon as they pulled up, the deputy drove up and blocked Sam's SUV. Sam put his badge out the window and stepped out with his hands high. *I pray to God this is not some trigger-happy rookie.*

Amy Murphy saw him and indicated OK with her fingers. She slowly backed down the road. Quinn got out and Sam pointed her towards an opening in the cluster of trees just beside a small stream covered with a thin crust of ice. "Be careful. That water will be more than ice cold. Watch me as we climb. Once we get above the flat area, it will be really steep."

Quinn nodded and pushed him ahead. As soon as they entered into the narrow gully, she was in awe of Sam as he stepped on rocks in the stream and used tree branches as handholds. *If I had entered up here, I would never have seen the ease with which this could be done.* She followed right behind him. She stopped when she saw him raise his hand.

Sam moved the hand he had raised to his ear, indicating she should listen. They both stood still. Sam slowly moved his head from side to side. He was listening for the source of the crunch he heard in the woods. Was it an animal, or was it human?

Quinn could not hear any sounds other than her own breathing and her beating heart. *Why did I never think I had time to come on a walk out here with Sam when we were dating in college? He would have taught me how to distinguish sounds. I always blamed him for not bringing me, but it was really my fault.*

Sam saw two people going up the gully ahead of them. He realized it had to be two tribal members by the way they were navigating. He gave the low whistle one tribe member used to identify himself to another tribe member. Sam received a coded whistle back. He knew the code and understood it meant to hold back. Someone who did not know the signals would think it was birdsong.

Quinn heard the whistles but didn't realize one of them was Sam. She waited on him to indicate their next move.

What Next?

Chad heard the sound of voices coming towards the crest. He couldn't make out the words, but he was concerned when he heard there was one male and one female. With no idea whether the rifle noise was just an errant shot and the hunter had moved on, Chad remained at the ready. It had been almost thirty minutes. He knew sound bounced against rock and it could be difficult to locate it, but he was confident it came from above them, not below. *Now I'm going to have two more people to worry about. Probably some young couple from the tribe getting away from the folks.*

Bella sat with her back against the tree, her legs poised to jump up if Chad said to move. *We've been here for half an hour. How long will we wait to see if there's another shot?* She knew if Chad wanted to have a conversation with her, he would. She watched as he continually scanned the area without moving anything but his eyes and slight movements of his head. When she was the victim of trespassers, she watched him, Deputy Bennett, and Detective Williams scan her property in September as they moved up towards Drellag Caban. She had no doubt he was highly trained, and they would have moved if he thought it was safe to do so. She turned her head towards the trail they had come up. She heard voices. What were they saying?

A Serious Game

Sylvia nodded her head sideways towards the crest in the trail and signaled to Bennett that they would drop down and scan over it. They went down at the same time. Bennett didn't land high enough to look right over, but Sylvia did. She had done this many times as a child when playing with her sister, Jackie, and she had happy memories of throwing rocks to try and trick her sister and friends into thinking she was on the other side of Mantle Rock. She prayed the rock she was about to throw would hit the ground straight in front of the sheriff. If he took a shot, it wouldn't be coming their way.

Ken Bennett slithered up to the crest and looked over. He could see Chad and Bella. As he scanned beyond them, he found the shadows cast by the evergreens made it hard to see if there was anyone on the other side. He looked over at Sylvia.

Sylvia put her fingers to her lips. She showed him the rock she had picked up and indicated she was going to throw it. She prayed that there was only one shot towards the rock—and that it was Chad's.

She threw the rock with the precision of a major league pitcher, and it hit twelve feet in front of Chad, exactly where she had aimed it. She heard one shot. Then another. Someone screamed.

CHAPTER 9

Coming Off the Mountain

"Doc Fred said you can talk to him in about ten minutes, but it will have to be brief," said Angela, the head nurse in the ER.

Sergeant Sylvia Whitehorse stood tall in her uniform and ignored the blood on her pant leg and white shirt. It was not possible to get a rolling gurney from the ambulance up to Mantle Rock on a trail barely meant for foot traffic. The deputies were able to help the ambulance team maneuver the canvas stretcher down the hill, but it took six people to carry the weight.

Although relatively confident there had only been one shooter in the area, six men from the local tribe continued to search the tribal grounds, and Sylvia left two deputies at the base of the tribal land near the community building. The men out on patrol would report to Billy.

There was nothing to do now but wait.

Explanations

"Mommy, is Miss Bella coming over today?" Nora had just picked up her children from their outing to the library for story time.

"Mac, we can invite Miss Bella anytime. I think she and Grandpa had some work to do today, but we can call after you rest."

"If she can't come today, can she come tomorrow?"

"Mac, I don't know Miss Bella's schedule. You may ask her when we talk to her. Now, tell me about your trip to the library."

"Lilly held my hand and listened to the story."

"She did?" There was a sweetness in Nora's voice thinking about her two children learning to be friends as well as siblings.

"Yes. I don't think she was afraid; I think she just wanted to sit with me."

"I think she did too. I think you are a very kind brother and friend to your sister."

"But, Mommy, we aren't married."

Nora looked in the rearview mirror. *If you only knew how much you look like your daddy with that knitted brow and your squinted eyes; he has that exact expression when he's confused about something.*

"Mac, what is a friend?"

"Mommy, you know what a friend is."

"I would like to hear what *you* think a friend is."

"I think it's someone you want to talk to, do things with, eat supper with."

"Do you only do those things with friends?"

"No, we do them with family too."

"Right." Nora was trying to think how to reframe the question. She hadn't expected his answer. She thought he'd talk about people you weren't related to. "Is a friend a member of your family?" she said, hoping she had latched onto a better question.

"Yes, you and Daddy are best friends."

I should have quit while I was ahead. I should not have these discussions while I'm driving. It was so much easier when he was three.

As Nora drove down the hill towards the hospital, she heard the siren before she saw the blue lights. Fred was at the hospital, and she had planned to stop and say hello. He loved seeing her and the children when he could during the day. She knew an ambulance meant he wasn't going to have time to talk to them. She pulled over to the side of the road.

"Good job, Mommy. You stopped for the amb'lance."

"Yes, I did. We should always pull out of the way so the ambulance can get past. Why?"

"Because they need to get to my daddy so he can take care of them."

"Right. What if the ambulance is not in our town?"

"You mean like when we visit Grandmother Mary?"

"Yes, like when we go to Knoxville."

"You still pull off as far as you can."

"That's exactly right. What do you say we go to the Valley Store and buy the ingredients to make cookies?"

"Are we out of cookies?"

"I made sure there were two left for you and Lilly after you eat your carrot sticks."

"Okay, then we need more. Let's go." The enthusiasm in his voice melted her heart.

It's been a while since we've had an ambulance take someone to the ER. Wonder who's sick?

Nora pulled into the parking lot at the Valley Store, unbuckled Lilly, and put her on her hip.

"May I unbuckle now, Mommy?"

"Yes, you may. Then come out this way."

She took his hand and they started towards the door together. Carla was coming out of the store.

"Hey, Mac!"

"Hey, Miss Carla." He tugged on Nora's hand. "Mommy, it's Miss Carla."

"So I see. Hey, Carla."

"Hey, Nora." Carla rubbed Lilly's back. "Hey, little Lilly." She felt Mac's hand patting on her leg.

"Miss Carla, Lilly and I sat and held hands while Miss Dona read a book to us at the library."

"Aww, that's sweet, Mac. You're a fine big brother. My big brother looks out for me too."

"You have a big brother?"

"Mac," Nora said with a hint of admonishment, "you know Mr. James is Miss Carla's big brother."

"Oh, yeah. I forgot."

Carla bent down and was eye to eye with Mac. "It's okay. Sometimes I forget things too. How're you doing, Mac?"

"Fine as a hound dog asleep on the porch in the summer." Mac made it sound like a local.

"Sure doesn't get any better than that." Carla stood. She saw Nora was grinning. "No danger of losing our mountain sayings when kids learn 'em that young."

"That's for sure. How are you, Carla?"

"I'm well. Just heading home to make some supper." Carla wondered if Nora knew she was pregnant, but she didn't ask.

"That's great. Looks like marriage is agreeing with you."

"Sure enough. Well, I'll let you get on with your shopping. Have a nice day, Mac. Bye, little Lilly." She kissed Lilly on the head and looked at Nora. "See you soon."

"I hope so."

Nora walked into the store with her children and headed for the baking aisle.

The Plot Thickens

"Sergeant, you can go back now. Dr. Smith will speak with you, and he will stay with you if you want."

"Thanks. I'll be fine. Which way?" She was unsure if she was headed to the ER or to a patient room.

"Our guards were about to change shifts, so we had the one going off duty stay until you can arrange coverage."

"I have a deputy right outside." Sylvia pulled out her secure phone and called the deputy waiting in the parking lot. She told Ferguson to come in and the other to maintain a perimeter watch. "Thanks, Angela. Hope to see you at choir practice."

"You bet." Angela turned to walk off and stopped. "It was changed to Sunday afternoon for Christmas practice, right?"

Sylvia nodded. "Right, thanks." She pulled out her handcuffs and walked into the room.

Doc Smith heard the clink of the cuffs and glanced up.

"Already has on one set, Sergeant. I only had to use a local anesthetic, so he should be able to answer questions, but please keep them brief. He lost a considerable amount of blood." He turned away from the patient and looked at Sylvia. "As I see you are aware."

"Thanks, Dr. Smith." There was a light knock on the door. "That will be a deputy. He can step in, and we'll let you get back to taking care of the fine people in this valley."

"Fair enough, Sergeant. Fair enough."

The deputy entered, and Sylvia immediately read the man his Miranda Warning. "Do you understand these rights?"

"What's it to you?"

"Do you understand these rights?"

"Yeah. Nothing new."

She decided that was most likely true. "Do you wish to have an attorney present?"

"Nah. I'm good."

"I'm Sergeant Whitehorse." She turned towards the deputy.

"Deputy Ferguson."

"We are being recorded by my body camera. You are under arrest for trespassing on private property, hunting without a license, and not providing a gun permit." She walked over and put her cuffs on his right hand and the bedrail. She'd save the attempted murder charge until they had him at the jail—*and* had more information.

"Hey, pretty lady, I ain't going no place. You locked me to this bed before the doc could stitch me up."

"Yes, we did. State your name, home address, and date of birth, please."

"Roger Harris, 13135 Auburn Street, Detroit, Michigan. April 1, 1980." Practiced ease telling what may or may not be the truth. He didn't have any identification on him.

Sylvia was relieved Billy wasn't there; he wouldn't have been able to resist the April 1st birthdate. "What brought you to our mountains?"

"Friend of mine told me there was good hunting here."

"And what were you hunting?" She saw the smirk slide across his face.

"Hoping to snag me big game." He winked at her.

Sylvia made no response. She waited.

"Sorry about all the blood on your clothes. The leg apparently bled pretty good."

She did not move or respond.

"Any more questions?" He wiggled his wrists inside the handcuffs, causing them to clang against the siderails.

"Where's your Tennessee license to hunt this big game?" She was as smooth as spreading butter on a hot biscuit.

"Musta left it in my truck."

"Where's your truck?"

"Out there somewhere."

"Are you licensed to hunt in Michigan?"

He chuckled. "Lady, I grew up in the slums of Detroit City. I've been huntin' all my life."

Do you guys take lessons in answering without answering, or did you learn that in prison?

"That big game you were hunting, what kind was it? Be specific."

"Oh, I thought about a nice rack off a deer, but then I decided I like the big game that can stand on two feet."

Sylvia was pretty sure he'd claim he was talking about black bear if questioned on this in court. She changed tack.

"Travel here with anyone else?"

"Nah, I have some friends in North Carolina. They told me about this place."

"Good to have friends. Your friends have names?"

"Don't put much stock in names. You know they change from place to place."

I bet they do. Sylvia decided one more question for now. She'd try to get Doc Fred to send him to the jail before morning—interrogation could begin in earnest then.

"How is it you happened to be up on that *particular* mountain?" She wanted him to think she was a small-town cop and not too bright.

"A little bird whispered in my ear that it was *the* place to be to find good game."

"Thank you very much, Mr. Harris."

She turned to leave and spoke to Ferguson. "Deputy, you will be notified when we're ready to move Mr. Harris to the jail."

"Wait!" Harris tried to sit up.

Sylvia moved towards the door.

"Wait, don't leave me locked to this bed! At least take one of 'em off."

She walked slowly.

"I might remember the names of those boys in North Carolina." The handcuffs clanged on the bedrails.

She opened the door and walked out. Ferguson followed her.

"Bitc—" The word was cut off as the door closed.

She never even flinched.

Support

Nora had just shut the door of her SUV when her phone rang. "Hey, Daddy."

"Okay if I drop Bella off at your place?"

"Sure, could a little boy ask her to come by? Could go a long way in helping me out today."

"Is he there?"

"Yes. Here you go."

She reopened the door. "Mac, Grandpa would like to speak with you."

"Hey, Grandpa."

"Hey, my favorite grandson," Chad said, forcing himself to sound cheerful. "Someone here would like to speak to you."

"Okay, Grandpa."

"Hey, Mac."

"Miss Bella!" His head swiveled towards Nora. "Mommy, it's Miss Bella."

"Talk to her."

"Miss Bella, when may you … wait. Mommy, now I say 'can,' right?"

Nora nodded, trying not to laugh.

"Miss Bella, when can you come over to my house?"

"How about now?"

"Mommy, how about now?"

Nora nodded.

"Miss Bella, Mommy said you could."

"Thanks, Mac. See you soon."

"Okay. Bye." He handed the phone to Nora. She shut the door again, climbed in, and drove home. Mac clapped the entire way.

Chad and Bella were sitting in the driveway. Chad hopped out, took Bella's hand as she opened her door, and they walked towards the garage as Nora pulled in. He leaned in and kissed Bella. "Back soon. Just relax and enjoy the kids."

Mac hopped out as soon as Nora opened the side door. "Miss Bella." He ran to her.

Bella bent down and hugged him.

Chad looked over the top of them and mouthed to Nora, "Take care of her. I'll be back."

Nora nodded.

Conference Call

FBI Agent Bill Michaels told Billy Williams he was still at the local FBI office in North Carolina waiting on some information before he could return to Tennessee. He assured Billy he would be available as soon as they could do a conference call. Billy sent a text to the team to meet at 4:00 p.m. if at all possible. Billy's phone pinged with messages as Michaels and the others responded with "10-4."

Billy went to the front of the station to wait for Quinn and Sam to arrive. They came through the front door as Billy stopped to talk to the deputy on desk duty. "Might as well let these two in, waifs though they appear to be." He opened the door leading into the rest of the station as the deputy buzzed the release on the lock.

"You two look a little worse for wear. Shall I get you some towels from holding for a cleanup?"

"Hello to you, Mr. Clean Jeans. Afraid to get your hands dirty?" Sam threw quips at Billy as quickly as Billy did with anyone, at least when he wouldn't get in trouble with the sheriff.

"I'll be with you *boys* in a few minutes," Quinn said as she walked past them towards the ladies' room.

"Back in a minute, Billy. Need to wash my hands." He turned up his dirty and scratched palms.

"I'll meet you both in the conference room." He walked back to the deputy and asked him to call Cecelia to get someone from holding to bring a first aid kit. After a moment's thought, Billy also requested coffee and water. It was 3:50 p.m. and he wanted to double check the connections for the speaker phone in the conference room.

Quinn entered the conference room and shut the door behind her. "Don't run off after this meeting. We need to talk."

Billy looked over his shoulder at her. "Sure. Sure. Whatever you need. May I see your hands?"

She looked at him and raised her left eyebrow. "My hands, Detective?"

"Your hands."

"Afraid I didn't wash under my nails?"

"Concerned you might have been scratched by a poisonous briar while you were hiking around in the brush."

"How on earth would you know it was poisonous without the plant?"

"By how your skin is reacting to it. Now, please, Miss City Girl."

She rolled her eyes and held her hands out. She had no scratches.

He looked at her. "Wore gloves, did you?"

"Ahh, the detective at work."

"What's wrong with your sidekick? Too manly to wear gloves even in winter?"

Sam entered as Billy was speaking.

"No, too stupid to remember to grab them when I got out of my SUV holding my hands in the air so as not to get shot by your deputy."

"Whatever. Let's get ready for this call." Billy walked to the door when he heard a knock. Cecelia handed him the first aid kit. She followed him in with the water and coffee. Billy didn't remember ever seeing the cart she used. *Boy, we've needed an admin assistant for long time.* "Thanks, Cecelia."

"My pleasure, Detective. Need anything else?"

"Just for this phone to work."

"Would you like me to stay to make sure?" Cecelia said.

"Won't be necessary. I can actually work that piece of technology." Chad said as he walked in. They all turned to look at him.

"Sheriff," Billy said. "Pleased to see you."

"Not nearly as pleased as I am to be seen. Sergeant Whitehorse told me you were doing a four o'clock conference call with Michaels. I'd like the first five minutes."

"Yes, sir."

The Call

"Michaels here."

"Sir, Billy Williams. We are on a speaker phone in the conference room. Present are myself . . ."

"Sam."

"Quinn."

"And Chad."

"Sheriff, surprised and pleased to hear your voice. Sounds like some trouble might have come looking for you."

"Appears that way. May I have five minutes before you meet with these folks?"

"Sure. Want them in for this?"

"Absolutely. Thanks for the time. Now, for the record, I am officially on voluntary leave and I'm here only to provide a first-hand account of a man who is in our hospital right now. Sergeant Whitehorse is waiting to talk to him."

"Before you go on," Michaels said, "do we know who this man is?"

"Couldn't get him to stop screaming long enough to get his name, but I'm sure Sylvia will have it by now."

The door to the conference room opened and Sylvia walked in. Chad was not surprised to see she hadn't stopped to change; she was still wearing her blood-stained clothes.

"Agent, Sergeant Whitehorse has just joined us." He looked at Sylvia. "Bill would like to know if we have a name."

"We do, and we should have his rap sheet in short order. It's being pulled as we speak. Name is Roger Harris of Detroit. He seemed right proud of it." She gave his reported date of birth and address.

Michaels said, "Thanks. We're on it here too. Chad, you were saying?"

Chad filled them in on his perspective of the sequence of events from the time they heard the first shot. "Dr. Anderson has one of our deputies with her, and I'm about to go join her."

Agent Michaels said, "Any reason to believe this guy has backup there?"

Chad looked at Sylvia.

"Sir, I don't trust this man any further than I can throw him, but he seemed pretty sure of himself."

"Any lead on how he knew to go to that spot to find Chad or Dr Anderson?"

"I asked him why he was hunting on that particular mountain. Agent, do these guys take lessons in how not to answer questions?" Those around the table were surprised by her sarcasm; Sylvia typically only stated the facts, unless they were brainstorming an idea.

"What else are they going to do in prison? Now, what did he say about being on the mountain?"

"His exact words were, 'A little bird whispered in my ear that this was *the* place to be to find good game.'"

Chad was about to slip out when Michaels spoke.

"Chad, before you go, are you familiar with that phrase?"

Chad stopped before opening the door. "Likely not in the sense this guy used it."

"That's a pretty common phrase used to leave some negotiating room when the perp wants you to know someone is feeding him information but he's holding onto it to negotiate."

Everyone around the table nodded.

Chad's weariness crept into his voice. "We're not real sophisticated in big city ways here in these hills and don't get much of the prison lingo making its way back to us. I say thank God for that. Anyway, this is why *you* are in charge of this case. You've got good people, and so are the ones around this table. I need this wrapped up once and for all—and soon. Now, I will leave you where I tried to leave you yesterday to go be with my family. Thanks for your work." He didn't stop to speak or even look at any of them as the door clicked closed behind him.

Michaels said, "I want to run through any analyses that you have done since yesterday, then I'll bring you up to date on what we know here in North Carolina specific to the Anderson home. Questions?"

Billy looked around the table. "The only one here seems to be from me. Now that there's a possibility the events at Mantle Rock may be tied to the burning of the Anderson home in North Carolina, do we need to bring in the State Bureau of Investigation?"

"We certainly can call Elliott Nelson at the SBI. First, let's run through what we have here. Who wants to start?"

Sylvia slipped a note to Billy; she wanted to go last on the fire itself. He turned to Quinn to start off, and each of the team members reviewed the data they had been analyzing: phone numbers, earlier drug and prostitution cases, and motel properties.

"Anything else? Sam?" Sam shook his head at Billy. "Any questions, Agent?"

"Haven't heard from the sergeant yet." Agent Michaels said.

"Sir, I'm here. I wanted to hear the updates on prior activities because my report is specific to the fire."

"Go on."

Sylvia explained the information she used to calculate the probabilities of the fire starting from a typical fault within a house like bad wiring, a log rolling out of a fireplace, or a pot left on a stovetop. "Given the square footage and the construction materials, the only way to take that house to the ground in short order was with an explosion, such as a fuel tank, an ignited gas leak, or an accelerant which got the fire to the attic swiftly. There was likely an accelerant outside the home, yet to be determined, with high BTUs. It takes a very hot fire in the right place to do that much damage that quickly."

"Sergeant, have you seen any of the information gathered by the Statesboro fire department?"

"No, sir."

"Has anyone at that table seen a preliminary workup?"

"Sir, I am looking at the others, and none of us have. Is there a problem?" Sylvia tried to figure out where this was going.

"Take a stretch break, please. I've just been told there's a report being brought to me." As he waited, FBI Agent Bill Michaels tried to figure out why he always underestimated people because they didn't have the same ambitions he had. He had always believed that a mark of intelligence, and being the best at your job, was measured by which organization you were in and how high you climbed in it. *I've learned some pretty humbling things from the people in those hills.* He took the report that was handed to him and scanned it. "Sergeant, let me know when you're ready."

"Agent Isaacs will be right back."

"I'm here." Quinn said and shut the door behind her.

"I'm going to read the executive summary on the preliminary report, and please note it's marked 'very preliminary' by the Statesboro fire investigator."

He read the one-page summary which consisted of a short narrative and four bullet points. "Please note this wording: 'the preliminary observation is that this was an incendiary fire ignited by an unknown individual or individuals. There was likely an accelerant outside the house, yet to be determined, with high BTUs. Based on the V-pattern on the back wall, the ignition was aided by the vinyl siding on the rear, taking it to the attic.'" Michaels stopped. "Questions?"

The four looked at each other, shrugged, and Billy said, "None at this time, sir."

The FBI agent spoke, "The investigation has now moved to an arson specialist and, of course, the insurance company will have its own experts on it. Your analysis, Sylvia, will likely have you in high demand by fire chiefs everywhere."

"I'm humbled by your assessment, sir, but I'm a full-time sergeant here, and I love my community and my work. This report and the work of the law officers with you and around this table suggests we have to find the 'who.'"

"We do. I'll be back up there first thing tomorrow morning. I suggest you keep round-the-clock surveillance on the sheriff, his family, and Dr. Anderson."

"Done. What time do you wish to meet?"

"Eight a.m. too early?"

"See you then, sir. Drive safely."

Bill Michaels ended the call.

"Okay," Sylvia jumped right in. "Sergeant Douglas has taken the night shift. I'm going to go talk to the sheriff at his daughter's home. Amy Murphy is there now, but we'll need to increase surveillance there, the hospital, and the Anderson property up on the mountain."

"Sarge, I sent a deputy up to the Anderson property earlier today. I think we need to ask AD Nelson to send us some SBI backup. We're pretty thin to cover all this." Sylvia nodded in agreement to Billy's observation. He continued, "Maybe we should ask Doc Fred to send that bad boy over here now? A lot easier to keep a hold on him here than there. Frees up two deputies too."

"Good points, Billy. I'll let Michaels know we're calling Elliott Nelson; you call Doc Fred. Unless he says moving him could kill Harris . . ." She looked around the table at blank faces. Sylvia knew every one of them was thinking: *So what?*

She finished her sentence, "I want him in our jail." They all knew they needed to interrogate Harris, if nothing else to make sure there was no one else involved.

Quinn spoke up. "Okay if I go with you to talk to Chad?"

"Me too?" Sam had his index finger in the air.

"Give me ten minutes. Meet me in front and be ready to pull out when I come around."

Quinn and Sam left the conference room, and Billy was already on the phone to the hospital. Sylvia scribbled out a note and held it up for him to see: "I'll call you on how to brief Sargent Douglas after I talk to the sheriff. Then you need to go home and get some rest."

Billy was on hold, waiting for Doc Fred to pick up the line. He nodded and gave her a thumb's up. *As a child, we would cross our fingers behind our backs when we said something that wasn't quite true. Guess I've matured a little.* He'd wait to find out what Quinn wanted. With the sheriff and Bella in danger, he no more planned to go home than fly to the moon—and being an astronaut had never appealed to him.

Sylvia headed for the locker room to change uniforms.

CHAPTER 10

Yet how hard most people work for mere dust and ashes and care, taking no thought of growing in knowledge and grace, never having time to get in sight of their own ignorance.

John Muir

The Dark Comes Quickly

Chad saw the text from Sylvia as he arrived at Nora's. He went to the children's playroom to find them building with Lego blocks. Bella looked up from the floor and smiled at him. "Hey."

"Hey, yourself."

"Grandpa, come build with us."

"Will do. Give me a couple of minutes, and I'll be right back." He wanted to wash his face and hands. He had gone directly to the station after dropping Bella off from Mantle Rock.

"Oh, hey, Daddy, didn't hear you come in."

Chad eyed her. "Now, tell me why I shouldn't be worried about that?"

Nora's smile spread across her face. "Because one of the finest deputies on the planet is at my front door."

"Who I could have taken out without blinking an eye—do you understand?" He tried to pull back the harshness in his voice. He threw his arms around her. "I'm sorry. I just want you safe."

"Got it. Let me look at you."

"Hmm … none the worse for wear. Bella didn't say much more than you were up at Mantle Rock and there was an incident with a trespassing hunter."

"Pretty much sums it up for the moment."

"For the moment? Daddy, don't forget I'm the sheriff's daughter and pretty smart in my own right."

"That you are, Nora. That you are. I'm expecting company. Hope it's okay." He watched her face.

"The more the merrier. How about you tell me you and Bella are going to stay in my guest house?"

Chad raised his eyebrow. "Another psychic woman in my life?"

"Good intuition, perhaps, but psychic … never mind, I won't ask you to elaborate. I want you to go play with your grandchildren before your guests arrive. I'll welcome them."

"You know them. No problem. Love you, sweet daughter of mine." He kissed her on the head and went to wash up before settling into the playroom.

A half-hour later, Nora appeared in the doorway. "Wow! You guys built a whole Lego town. Time to wash up for supper, Mac and Lilly." The children got up immediately and Mac took Lilly's hand. "I'm going to feed the kids and then we can eat later. I assume your guests will be here soon?"

Bella looked at Chad. "Guests?"

"Yes, sorry—my colleagues. I'm on leave, so they aren't coming officially."

Nora shook her head and turned to walk off. "Daddy just can't stand to be out of the action." She decided this was a discussion where a couple didn't need a third wheel, especially the man's daughter.

Bella looked at Chad. "Maybe I should go back to your cabin." She didn't sound upset.

"Please, let me explain."

"Go ahead. "

"I will tell you whatever you want to know."

"Are you going to stay here—or are you going to work?"

"No, I'm not going to work. Sylvia asked to meet with me, but we can't and won't discuss the specifics of either investigation." He stopped. *Why did I say, either?* "Then they'll be on their way."

"Chad, I've already figured out that man wasn't a hunter."

"Right, on that note. . . we'll go to my cabin and get some things, but then I'm asking you to stay with me in Nora's guest house." He watched her face. "Just for a couple of days."

Bella looked into his gray eyes. She saw the pleading—he needed her to understand.

"Chad, I've told you before, your job was known to me when I fell in love with you. Choosing to be with you means I take you as you are. Whatever either of us does that proves an irritant for the other, I hope we'll talk about and see what we can do to navigate it. My question about you working was specific to your safety. We don't know who the man was on the mountain or why he was there or even if someone was with him, but the bet would be pretty good someone wanted one or both of us gone. If you don't trust the people handling the case, then get people you do trust." She leaned in and kissed him. "Now, I'm going to be with Nora and the children while they eat." She stood up and left.

Chad sat on the floor for a few minutes, looking at what they had built with the children. His eyes filled with tears. *Dear God, I have missed four years with my grandchildren. No more. And I don't know what I've done to deserve Bella, but thanks. Help me not mess this up.* He stood and walked to the front of the house. His secure phone rang. *Can I let myself not answer this?*

"Oliver."

"Murphy here, Sheriff. Folks at the door to see you."

"Be right there."

As Chad walked to the front of the house, he saw the sky was slipping into darkness. It fell quickly in these mountains in the winter.

Double Down

Chad let Nora open the front door to her home and welcome Quinn, Sam, and Sylvia. "You're setup in our home office just around this corner." She led the way, ushered them in, shut the door and returned to the kitchen.

The four of them walked into the office where Nora had left tea, coffee, and a plate of fresh cookies for them.

"Now that's service. Hope I get to thank Nora," Sam said as they all chose a chair.

"Before we start, I do *not* want to know a single detail about the investigation into the shooter or Bella's home in North Carolina. I just need to hear your plan to protect Bella and her cabin. I signed on for this, she didn't."

"Begging your pardon, Sheriff," Quinn looked at him, "none of us signed on for *this*. We signed on to serve and protect."

"And we intend to protect Miss Bella, you, and your family," Sylvia said.

Chad nodded. "Thanks."

"Billy suggested calling Elliott Nelson to get SBI agents to help cover the three homes again, as well as to be eyes for anyone who might come to do harm. I talked to him and agents are enroute."

"Thanks." Chad was relieved to hear the SBI was sending agents. He was convinced the loss of Bella's house, the shooter, and whatever else might come along would tie back to Zimmerman.

"Sir, did you hear me?" Sylvia said.

"Sorry, lost in thought. I apologize."

"Sir, every deputy in the department has been notified and all have pledged they will do whatever it takes to catch these folks—on duty or off."

"Please spread the word I appreciate everyone's concern."

Sylvia knew a "but" was coming.

"But I also need them to protect everyone in our community, so stay focused. I have every confidence this team will get this resolved."

Quinn made eye contact with Chad. "Didn't come to take up your time, Chad, just wanted you to know we're pulling threads, and together we're going to get this solved."

"Thanks, Quinn. Don't jeopardize your job doing it. If this doesn't have a thread in your bailiwick, you're not obligated."

"That's true. However, I have permission to engage, and if that changes I, too, can take leave."

Chad looked at her. He liked this young woman. She was well trained, diligent, smart, and had become a friend during the crime spree that had descended on the valley in the past three months. He nodded.

"Same here. I'm not as eloquent as my colleague, but the DEA is committed to the resolution of this. If that changes, I will never again forget these hills are my home, and you are a friend."

Chad wasn't sure how much more of this he could take. He knew for sure, though, that they meant it. They had no need to brown-nose him. Anyone who knew him knew that trying to do so was not going to end well.

"Anything else, Sylvia?"

"Not at this time. Sergeant Douglas is on duty now. Anything you need me to tell our folks?"

"Is my cabin covered already?"

"With our deputies, yes. Not sure if any SBI have arrived."

"Bella and I are going to my cabin to get some things before it gets too much darker. We'll stay here for a few days. That way you've got us all in one place. Thanks for handling this, Sylvia." He smiled at her.

"Hate that it has to be done, sir, but it's my privilege. We'll be leaving now. Stay safe."

"10-4." That was all Chad said as he walked them to the door.

Sylvia held back. "Sir, do you really need to go to your cabin? I could send a deputy to get your things."

He gave her shoulder a gentle tap. "Appreciate it. We'll be fine."

"Yes, sir. Talk to you tomorrow."

Chad saw Fred driving up as the others pulled out of the circular drive. He smiled that he would have the people he cared most about in the world under one roof tonight. *Well, at least we'll all be at the same address.*

What Not to Say

By the time Chad and Bella got to his cabin, there was an SBI agent and one of Chad's deputies on patrol.

"Evening, sir," the young deputy said.

Chad shook his hand. "Thanks for your work. Hopefully this surveillance won't take too long."

Chad recognized the young woman who had been assigned to his home the last time. He extended his hand. "Agent, I'm Chad Oliver, this is Dr. Bella Anderson. Thanks for coming."

"Yes, sir. I'm Mary Ann Duffy."

"We'll just be a few minutes and then we'll leave you to it. Not easy to get onto my back property, but not impossible either. I'll leave the front door open, and I suggest you take turns inside so you can warm up and keep an eye on the back." He thought he saw his deputy and the agent smile. It was December and, even with the snow melted, it was cold.

Once inside, Bella said, "Oh, Chad! Whoever's at Drellag Caban should be able to go inside too."

"If you're sure, I'll send someone up with a key, but they can warm up in their vehicle."

Bella shook her head and reached in her pocket only to realize she didn't have her keys.

"With your permission, they can take the key you left at the station." He smiled at her.

"I forgot there was one there now."

Chad sent a text to Sergeant Douglas. "Done. Now, let's get what we need for a few days at Nora's and get back for supper."

"Won't take me long." She kissed him and went to the back of the cabin to pack. Her mobile phone rang; she looked at the display and put it on speaker so she could continue to move about the room. "Hey, Joshua. What's up?"

"Just about to leave the store but I wanted to see how you're doing." He didn't add, 'after the fire.'

"I'm okay, thanks. Chad and I are going to stay at Nora's for a few days." Then she remembered he didn't know about the shooting. "Need some quality time with the little ones."

"I can understand that. Looking forward to those days myself ..." he hesitated, "even at my age." There was warmth and love in his voice.

"We'll spoil that baby rotten." Bella's voice was light.

"Thanks, Bella. I want to tell the whole world and can't yet, but it helps to know you and Chad can be supportive, especially for Carla."

"You bet. I'll do whatever is needed."

"I know. Thanks. Well, I'll let you get on with your evening. Regards to Chad."

"Give Carla a hug for me. Talk to you soon. Thanks for calling."

Chad walked in the bedroom. "That sounded like a nice, normal call."

"You're right. It was a normal call: brother-friend checking on sister-friend. I needed normal."

Chad pulled her into a hug. "I know. I want that for you. For us. We're going to talk about what 'our' normal is going to be." He pulled back but kept his arms around her and looked into her dark brown eyes. "And this chaos is not going to be it."

She kissed him then tightened the hug and said, "Who knows how to define normal? Let's work on today. I'll be ready in five minutes."

He kissed her. "Me too."

Arrival

Billy read the one-word message from Quinn: "Home?"

He responded with a pithy text of his own: "Work."

"Be there in 5."

"10-4."

Billy had been tempted to go back to holding when the ambulance arrived delivering Roger Harris on a gurney. *They sure took their sweet time getting him here.* He was ready to start the interrogation, but it wasn't going to happen before morning. He had promised Doc Fred he wouldn't put the guy in a wheelchair for twelve hours. So, he'd wait—at least until the early hours of morning. *What's magic about twelve hours? Might just show up here at 4:00 a.m. That'd be thirteen hours. One more than twelve for the judge and jury.*

"Williams here," he said into his desk phone.

"Agent Isaacs is here. Shall I send her back?"

"Tell her I'll meet her in the break room, please."

"Agent," Billy said as he met Quinn in the hallway.

"Detective." She fell in stride with him. "What's with the formality?"

"Just showing respect." Billy winked at her. "Thought you might need coffee."

"Had real coffee at the Oliver-Smith residence." She smiled and batted her eyes.

"Show off. I suppose you had cookies too?"

"We did." She smiled as she took the plastic bag out of her jacket pocket and handed it to him. "Nora even sent you some."

He took the plastic bag with a matching smile of his own and headed for the coffee machine. "What may I get you?"

"Water is fine." Quinn waited for him in the doorway.

Billy filled the cup, put money in the donation box, and waved the bag of cookies as he turned towards the door.

"Better put them away, Detective. They could disappear if you wave them in front of too many law officers."

Billy tucked the bag to his side, looked around like a skulking burglar, and said, "Quick, to the conference room—it's closest."

Quinn laughed.

Billy felt a tinge of disappointment that she didn't move to give him a kiss when the door of the conference room closed. Then he saw her looking up in the corner. *Of course, there are cameras in here, stupid.*

"Anything of significance I need to know from the meeting?"

"Didn't Sylvia call you?"

"She did. Just wasn't sure if there was something you wanted to share."

"Nope. Sheriff was his usual by-the-book self. Cordial, polite, and didn't want to know what was going on."

"Then what *did* you talk about?"

"He wanted to ensure that Bella and the Anderson property on the mountain are secure."

Billy nodded. "No surprise."

"Sarge told him it was your idea to have the SBI help out."

He looked at her. "That was nice of her."

"So, are you about to head out?"

"Yes, ma'am. I'm planning on being back here at four in the a.m. Buy you supper?"

"Happy to join you. Meet you at The Corral?"

"That works." He was disappointed again. *She said she'd join me. Meant we're still on duty. Oh, well. Better than not having supper with her.* He opened the door for her to leave the conference room, and they drove away from the station in their respective SUVs.

They met at the side door of the restaurant. Quinn had her hand on the door handle, and Billy realized she was holding it closed. She leaned in and whispered in his ear.

"Billy Williams, I am *very* taken with you, but I am very careful on the job. So, quit sulking." He turned his head and her lips brushed his cheeks. "Got it?"

"Yes, ma'am." He smiled and entered when she opened the door. He almost ran into Susan Thomas, the lead deputy for the sheriff's department. She was not in uniform.

"Evening, Billy, Quinn."

"Evening, Susan." Quinn said.

"Evening, Susan. Back from leave?"

"Officially back on duty as of midnight, but don't report until the morning shift." She read the look in his eyes. "How early, Detective?"

"Four a.m.?"

Susan looked at Quinn and rolled her eyes. "Always on duty, this one." She pointed to Billy.

"I *know*," Quinn said and winked at Susan.

"See you in holding. Night, Detective. Night, Agent. I'd stop and visit, but it appears I need to go home and get some sleep." Susan laughed and walked outside.

Quinn and Billy sat in a back corner, and Quinn immediately said, "Were you going to call her at three?"

"No, I didn't know I'd be lucky enough to have her for this interrogation."

"That good, is she?"

"The only one better is the sheriff."

"Better than you?"

"Both of them."

"You know what I just said to you outside?" He nodded. "Well, you just ratcheted it up another notch."

"How's that?"

Cheri walked up to them and put water on the table.

"Evening, Cheri. Work around the clock, do you?"

"No, Miss Quinn. Y'all will be my last table."

"Imagine it's taking some adjusting without Carla?" Billy said.

"We miss her, that's for sure. What can I get ya'll to drink?" They both pointed to their waters.

"I'll have that ham steak special I saw on the sign," Quinn said. "Separate checks, please."

"I'll do that too. Thanks, Cheri."

Cheri headed to the kitchen, and Billy looked back at Quinn. "I need lessons. How did I go up a notch?"

She leaned into the table. "I like a man with confidence. Confident men can acknowledge competence in others, like you did when you said Susan and Chad were better interrogators. I can never understand why so many men have to try and make themselves look like the best at everything. Law officers are some of the worst."

"Lesson learned."

"Don't think you needed it. Now, Detective, tell me what it was like growing up in this community."

His eyes looked into hers. "Well, I walked three miles to a one-room schoolhouse, uphill in the snow."

Quinn laughed.

The End of the Day

Lilly was sound asleep in Nora's lap, and Mac was fighting to keep his eyes open while sitting in Bella's.

Fred said, "Mac, go brush your teeth, please. Miss Bella and Mommy will meet you in your room."

Mac climbed down and headed to the bathroom.

"Leaves us to do the dishes," Chad said. He and Fred started clearing the table. Bella tried to help, but Fred said, "Go on, nothing better than putting two children to bed."

Bella followed Nora to Lilly's room and smiled when she saw all the animals, both stuffed and painted on the walls in muted colors.

Nora laid Lilly in her bed and leaned in and kissed her. "The angels will watch over you, sweet girl. I love you." She stepped away and nodded to Bella.

Bella walked over and ran her finger on Lilly's cheek. "Sweet dreams, precious child. You have the greatest gift on earth: you are loved."

Nora took Bella's hand and squeezed it, then she turned and checked the light on the video monitor. *You won't need this much longer, little girl.* They walked out of Lilly's room and shut the door.

Bella said, "I saw the video monitor in the kitchen, but I guess I never thought about how to monitor a child in a large home."

"I like the video monitor because I don't have to go in and run the risk of waking her if her noises are normal rolling-over noises." She smiled.

"Guess it's a miracle my generation survived childhood. Wonder what my parents would have thought about all the modern technology."

Laughing quietly, Nora said, "Go ask my daddy. He's a technology dinosaur."

"Mommy, what's funny?" Mac said from his bed.

"Mac, I'm so proud of you for getting your teeth brushed and into bed."

"Thanks, Mommy. I went to the bathroom too."

"Awesome. Miss Bella might be willing to read you a book."

"I have one." He held up one of his favorite books: *Dream Animals: A Bedtime Journey* by Emily Winfield Martin. He handed it to Bella.

"There are animals from long ago ..." Bella read softly. She watched Mac pull the covers up to his neck. "Sweet Dreams," she ended. She bent down and kissed him on the forehead.

"Miss Bella, will you sing with Mommy?"

"I'll try."

Nora began humming, and Bella smiled as she recognized the tune. She loved "What a Wonderful World." She joined in.

Nora and Bella finished the song and hugged each other. Mac was sound asleep, but Fred and Chad were standing in the doorway and clapped softly. Nora leaned in and kissed her son. Bella walked over and kissed Chad; they walked away as Fred joined his wife.

"I think it's time for us to give this lovely family some alone time," Bella said.

Chad took her hand and walked to the front room. "Agreed. We'll wait a minute and say good night." They stood together in front of the fireplace.

"What can I get you to drink?" Fred said.

Chad turned. "Nothing, thanks. We're going to give you some space. Thanks for having us, son. Sorry to bring danger to your door."

"Nonsense. We're grateful to all be together."

"Amen," Nora said. "You don't have to rush off."

"Long day for all concerned," Chad said.

"There's Fat Tire Ale and Kim Crawford Sauvignon Blanc in the fridge in the guest house. Do your deputies need anything?"

"They should be good. Thanks for feeding them and leaving the door open for them to have a break from the cold." He gave Fred a bear hug and kissed Nora on the cheek.

"Of course. I hope you can get some rest," Nora said as Bella gave her a hug.

"Thank you for sharing your family and your home. See you in the morning." Bella turned and Fred held out his arms to give her a hug. She hugged him. "Thanks, Fred. Goodnight to both of you."

Chad and Bella went out the kitchen door and across the portico to the guest house.

"Oh my, this is lovely." Bella scanned the room. She saw there was a fire in the fireplace in the open living, dining, and kitchen area. The walls were a pale, mottled tan, and the dark leather furniture was covered in bright throws and pillows in autumnal colors of yellow, red, and orange.

The smile on Chad's face was evidence of his pride in his daughter. "Nora has many artistic talents."

"Oh, I meant to ask, did she paint Lilly's room?"

"I think her words would be, 'I can see it, I just can't produce it.' She had Paula do the walls in Lilly's room and these; I think they look like leather."

"That's exactly what I was thinking. I can't wait for Paula to do the mural on the shed. Everything I see of hers is amazing."

"Very talented woman. Do you have ideas finalized with her?"

"Yes."

"Glass of wine?"

"Yes, please." She had left her boots at the door and was in her sock feet. She sat on the sofa in front of the fire and pulled her feet under her.

Chad handed her a glass of wine and set his beer on the wooden coffee table then sat next to her. He put his arm around her and pulled her close to him. "Going to tell me the design?"

She smiled. "Sure. It makes me happy you're interested. It will actually look like a continuation of the trees down the mountains, with a path leading down the hill. There will be two boys walking on the trail: my daddy and Mr. Joe." She turned from the fire to look at him.

"That sounds perfect—like the woman I love." He stared into her eyes. "I'm just sorry. . ."

"Shhh," she put her finger to his lips. "I love you too. Let's enjoy that we're together."

He clicked a switch on the remote and soft music started to play. Chad leaned his head on hers. "To us."

"To all of us." She raised her wine glass to his beer bottle.

CHAPTER 11

Deep Roots

The alarm on Billy's phone rang at 3:15 a.m. Wednesday morning. He got up to shower and have at least one cup of coffee before he went to the station. Billy didn't care how many times the man from Detroit had been in and out of prison and interrogated by big city cops. *He better think twice if he thinks he can outsmart us.* As he stepped out of the steaming hot shower, Billy decided to dress in jeans, a dark blue turtleneck, and a plaid shirt. *Might as well look like what he's expecting.* Billy even decided to put on his cowboy boots for effect. He couldn't remember the last time he had worn them, and his recent shoulder injury made it a struggle to get them on, but he grunted with satisfaction as he managed to squeeze his left foot into the boot.

A few streets away, Susan Thomas tried not to disturb her sleeping husband as she slid out of bed. After all these years, he pretty much didn't know when she left to go to work in the middle of the night; his sleep was rarely interrupted. He was an accountant and the only CPA on this side of the highway, though he had an office in Round City too. Waking in the middle of the night didn't come into play in his work.

She showered, put on a navy blue wool dress while hoping she wouldn't regret it if the yahoo decided to get out of hand. *I need him to think I don't know any better than to wear a dress into an interrogation—stupid woman.* She was smart enough to wear tights under her dress. She smiled in the bathroom mirror. *Yeah, you go right on believing I'm as dumb as one of the rocks in these hills.* She was out the door and headed to the station by 3:30 a.m.

Billy and Susan arrived in the back lot of the sheriff's station at the same time.

"Morning, Detective."

"If you say so. I kind of like that it's the middle of the night. I'll meet you in holding and bring you up to date on this guy."

"I read the report and his rap sheet."

Billy was not surprised. "Questions?"

"The sheriff and Dr. Anderson are okay, right?"

"Right as rain. We need to find out who this guy's working for. If it's Zimmerman, the Feds can have him with my blessing."

"Bring it on." She scanned her ID and Billy scanned his.

"See you in five, Detective."

Billy walked to the lab and scanned his ID at the door. There was a click as the door unlocked. He pushed it open and was surprised to see Elizabeth Alexander inside. "Alexander, it's the middle of the night. What are you doing?"

"Morning to you too, Detective."

"Morning. What are you working on?"

"The rifle, bullets, and rock from the big city guy." Elizabeth turned. "Did you hear some of the tribal members found his truck? Can't wait to get on that!"

"Where is it?" His voice was urgent.

"Out back in the garage. Went and took pictures before we moved it. Lucky we had his keys. I'm headed out back shortly."

"Call Thomas and tell her to meet me in the garage." He turned back around. "Please."

"On it. Can I come too?"

"Room for three. Let's move."

Billy pulled off his coat and threw it on his chair while Elizabeth called Susan. He grabbed the keys to the truck off the board by the door and headed out of the lab. He glanced at the Chevy logo on the keys. *I miss my Camaro. Chevy can't help it if bad guys buy their trucks too. I'll buy a Silverado to replace my Camaro so it evens the playing field.*

As they entered the evidence garage, each person grabbed a pair of latex gloves from the box by the door. Billy went straight for the cab of the truck.

He clicked the unlock button for the doors and the hard cover on the rear of the truck. "Deputy, see what's in the glove box. He didn't have any ID on him, so let's see if it's in here somewhere. Alexander, check the back end." Billy opened the driver's door. He looked through the papers in the pocket of the door.

"Glove box is locked. Got a key?"

"Here you go." He handed her the keys and continued to search through the papers. A small spiral notebook was tucked in amongst them. He pulled it and flipped the pages. He whistled.

Susan was looking for the right key for the glove box and stopped at his whistle. "What?"

"Later, keep looking."

Elizabeth opened the cover on the back end of the truck and called out, "You have to see this, Billy!" She bit her tongue. She forgot the lead deputy was there. *Hope Deputy Thomas didn't notice.*

Billy dropped the notebook in an evidence bag and moved to the back of the truck.

"Holy moly! Susan, come here."

She stared. "Anything he doesn't have in there?"

"Let's hope he doesn't have a bomb on a timer," Billy said as Elizabeth unlocked a wall cabinet and pulled out a camera.

They methodically took pictures and measured the highly organized armament in the back of the truck, along with enough ammunition to take out half a town.

"You have to be a real pro to care enough to have custom built compartments in the back of a truck for each and every weapon," Susan said.

"Looks like he's prepared for any job he gets," Billy said.

"I'll go check the glove box."

"Wait!" Billy grabbed her arm. "Key or no key, don't open it."

"Why? Most bombs are set for forced entry into a space, not with the key for the lock."

"Then why were his registration and his little black book . . . okay, his little brown spiral notebook, in the door?"

"So that he didn't have to make a cop nervous by reaching across to the glove box?" Elizabeth said.

"Good point, Alexander. Still, let's not take any chances. We've got enough to start an interrogation. Alexander, I don't want you working this truck until we get those folks you worked with at SBI here."

"Aww, Detective, do I have to share?"

"You do. I need you alive, and they have tools we don't. I'll give you the satisfaction of calling your buddy over there and inviting him to come have a look. How's that?"

"Can I tell him it's because I need his toys?"

"Yes. You do know he's likely going to want you to bring it to Knoxville."

"That's okay. Probably should anyway. They have lots more room. Should I just ask to do that?"

"Go for it. Download those pictures for me first, though. If he's willing, call Frank and he can put it on his truck and take it over. We have a criminal to go meet." He looked at his watch. It was 5:15 a.m.

"Be my luck the guy's an early riser. Really wanted to wake him up in the middle of the night."

"No worries, I had the matron wake him when we got here."

Billy gave Susan a high-five. "Way to go, Deputy!"

Early Morning

Bella rolled over and her arm fell across Chad's chest. He pulled her to him. He'd been awake since 5:30 a.m. She opened her eyes and looked at him.

"Shhh . . . go back to sleep." He kissed her on the forehead, closed his eyes, and tried to fall back to sleep himself.

"No use," she whispered. "I'm awake."

"Me too. Let's just lie here and enjoy that we don't *have* to get up."

"Lovely idea." She stretched her arm and inadvertently hit the lampshade. Startled, she sat straight up.

"Hey, it's okay," Chad said as the lamp crashed to the floor.

Bella lifted the lamp and tried the switch. Warm light filled the room, and she was thankful to see the lamp itself was metal; she hadn't even dented the shade. "Now I know why hotels put the bedside lamps on the wall. It's so people like me don't knock them off waking up in a new bed."

Chad was laughing. "Okay, Miss Everything-Has-To-Be-In-Place, it's no problem. What's the worst that could have happened?"

"Hmmm . . . that I took this rather heavy metal lamp and threw it?"

"At me?"

"Never." Now they were both laughing.

Chad pulled her down on the bed and kissed her; sleep and lamps were forgotten.

Changing of the Guard

Accustomed to early mornings, Fred and Nora were sitting at the kitchen counter when Chad walked in, kissed his daughter, and slapped his son-in-law on the back. "Morning, folks."

"Morning, Daddy. Nice to see you this hour of the morning."

"Really?" Chad squinted his eyes at her and turned down his mouth in a frown.

"Not like that. Reminds me of the faces you used to make when I complained about having to get up early for band practice before school."

"That's what I like—memories." He took the coffee mug she handed him. "Thanks, favorite daughter of mine." He sat down at the counter and turned to Fred. "Ashamed to say it, Fred, but I have no idea what time you usually head out in the morning."

"In about ten minutes. I try to make rounds at the hospital before I go to my office. Nora is kind enough to get up with me—makes the start to my day perfect."

"More than her mothe. . ." Chad stopped himself. He tried to never criticize his ex-wife . . . at least to his daughter. "True love. Glad to hear it."

"I'd say we're both lucky men."

Bella came through the door.

Chad stepped up and put his arm around her. "Amen to that, Fred. Amen to that."

"Amen to what?" Bella looked at the two men.

"That we're both lucky men." Chad winked at her.

"Tea, Bella?" Nora held out a mug.

"Bless you, Nora."

"Daddy, Amy Murphy told me she and the young deputy would be going off shift soon and there'd be two new deputies for the day."

"Murphy's a good deputy. I'd expect nothing less than her letting you know."

"I loved the part about not wanting to wake a sleeping bear. Could that be my daddy?" Her sass was on open throttle.

Chad stared at Nora. "She said what?" He tried to feign anger.

"Daddy, the day one of your deputies says anything remotely derogatory about you, I'm taking out a full-page ad in *The Tuesday Tattler.*"

Fred said, "Ha! I'll pay for a special edition."

"All right, all right. Flattery will keep you in the will." They all laughed.

"Duty calls," Fred stood and rinsed out his mug and put it in the dishwasher. He kissed Nora, shook hands with Chad, and gave Bella a kiss on the cheek. "And, Bella, don't let those little ones wear you out."

"The pleasure is all mine, I assure you."

Chad, Bella, and Nora moved into the comfortable chairs and sofa in front of the fire. It would be an hour or more before the children woke up.

The Interrogation Begins

Billy had taken pictures of each page in the brown spiral notebook. He printed out two of them and took the notebook in the evidence bag to the detectives' room. He was pleased that Jeff Coleman, the detective who had cracked the ownership of Zimmerman's by-the-hour motels in Round City, was on duty. "Any idea what these numbers mean?"

"Hot diggity dog! I get to play with numbers this morning. Let's see that." He pulled on latex gloves. "Got pictures?"

"Here are two to start. Alexander should be sending the rest to you any minute."

"Good, better not to handle the notebook. Did you get prints?" He saw the residue where they had dusted for prints. "Of course you did."

"One is a perfect match to the perp." Billy grinned from ear to ear. "Now, I need to go talk to the thug ... sorry, that fine gentleman from Detroit. We need to know what's here."

"Can't tell you where these numbers might lead, but these are probably offshore bank accounts, and this page is probably coded phone numbers."

"Can you break the code?"

The detective glared at Billy, "Do I *look* like I just fell off the turnip truck, *Detective* Williams?"

"No offense intended."

"You can't help it if you've been out of the detective bullpen up in that lab for so long."

Billy accepted the jab and let it go.

Coleman recovered and settled down. "Now, let me at this. Is it enough for you to know what these represent? Or do you need specifics?"

"I need the phone numbers as a priority. We can find his cache later."

"Do you have enough to hold him?"

"Long enough to find out if these are registered weapons." Billy showed him the photo of the guns.

The detective let out a long, low whistle. "Custom built storage. This boy's serious about his work."

"Looks that way. The phone numbers . . ." Billy headed out the door.

"On it."

Susan was walking towards the holding cells. "Deputy, wait up." Billy caught up with her. "You want to start?"

"Let me count the ways."

The matron had Harris in a wheelchair with his leg elevated and strapped to the board supporting it. His hands were loosely cuffed to the arms of the chair.

"Morning, Matron." Billy nodded at her.

"Morning, sir."

"Morning, Matron, room two?"

"Morning, ma'am. Yes, ma'am, room two. Shall I push the chair?"

"I've got it. Lead the way." Billy nodded to Susan.

She walked down the hall and unlocked the interrogation room. She put the recorder on the table, knowing full well the cameras were rolling and the matron would monitor them.

Billy rolled the wheelchair into the room and locked the wheels. He wasn't about to give this guy any kind of weapon, even rolling a wheelchair by rocking it back and forth. Then Billy leaned against the wall, bent his right leg, and put his foot against the wall. It wasn't as comfortable in boots as it was in his street shoes. He frowned.

"Sir," Susan wanted her voice to sound deferential. "The recorder is ready."

"You're learning. Get on with it."

"Yes, *sir*." Susan gave the date and said, "This is Deputy Thomas in interview room two with … please state your name …"

"Yeah, I know the routine. Roger Harris of Detroit, Michigan, April 1, 1980."

"And Detective Williams." Billy said it quickly to avoid guffawing at the guy's April Fools' birthdate.

Susan continued, "Mr. Harris, you have the right …" She knew he had been read his Miranda Rights at the hospital, but she didn't want some big city mob lawyer trying to pull a fast one on this interview and say he wasn't given the opportunity to have an attorney. "… if you cannot afford an attorney …"

"Could have saved you the trouble, lovely lady. Should have asked *me* to recite it for *you*."

She wanted to wipe the smug look off his face. "Do you wish to have an attorney present?"

"No need. I'm fine. You're mighty fine too." He winked at her.

Why do these guys think a law officer would be the least bit interested in them? She smiled. "Mr. Harris, what brings you to the mountains of east Tennessee?"

"Hunting."

"That's not surprising. We have many folks who come for our hunting season. What sort of game do you hunt?"

"Mostly those on foot."

"So, you don't hunt quail?"

He laughed. "They're on foot, ain't they?"

"Most of the ace quail hunters prefer to get them in flight." She smiled demurely.

"Good point. I could do that too. I'm a good shot."

"Is that how your leg got injured?"

"What the hell? I didn't shoot myself, lady." His temper flared, but he quickly got it under control.

She pulled out her notebook and pretended to read her notes. "No, I see that you didn't. Sorry. Since there was no one else hunting with you, I just naturally assumed your gun went off accidentally and caused that injury." She pointed to his elevated leg. "Does it hurt?"

"Listen, lady, this is a mosquito bite. Take a lot more than that to cause me pain."

"Good to hear." She smiled.

Billy liked watching Susan play the good cop. He was struggling not to jump in as the bad cop.

"How did you get to Tennessee?"

"Flew like those quail."

"Oh, and how did you get to our valley?"

"In a truck."

"Whose truck?"

"A rental."

"Rented where?"

"Don't remember."

"Oh, Mr. Harris, a smart man like you must surely remember where he rented a truck."

"Didn't say *I* rented it."

"So, someone was with you?"

"Didn't say that either."

Susan was trying to decide how long to let this guy string it out.

"Mr. Harris, do you own a truck?"

"I do."

"What make and model?"

"Chevy Colorado."

"Nice truck. Maybe you've heard our southern expression when someone is grumpy?"

"Can't say as I have."

"What's the matter? Chevy stop making trucks?" She laughed.

"Ha ha!" He said it without humor. "*Sounds* like a dumb southern expression."

"Yeah, we're just full of 'em. But I'm off track."

Billy stomped his foot on the floor. Susan and Harris jerked their heads towards him. The force of the heel on his cowboy boot sounded like a gunshot on the concrete floor. Billy tried to keep the look of surprise off his own face—he hadn't worn his boots to an interrogation before.

"Deputy, you're more than off track—you're in left field. Let me show you how to do this right." He grabbed the metal chair, turned the back towards them, and slammed it to the floor. *Might as well go for loud again.* He sat facing them, his arms folded on the back of the chair.

"Harris, you are under arrest for trespassing on private property, failure to produce a valid hunting license and special permit for large game, and failure to present a permit for the weapon you fired."

Harris smirked and said, "Noted." He knew even a lousy lawyer would have him off on those charges by the afternoon.

There was a knock on the door. Billy nodded to Susan. "Get that, Deputy! Make it quick! Remember do *not* leave this room without recording it." Billy rolled his eyes and shook his head.

Susan stood and straightened her skirt then went to the door. The matron handed her a piece of paper and a phone. She took it and handed it to Billy.

Billy snatched it out of her hand. "This better be important to interrupt this interview." As he unfolded the paper, it took every ounce of his self-control not to smile. He knew he had Roger Harris' phone and he was going to make a phone call.

Billy rolled his shoulders, leaned into the chair, and said, "Roger . . . okay if I call you Roger?"

"Never put much stock in names."

"Funny, I was just going to ask you about a name." Billy watched him carefully.

Susan made sure she was watching Harris too.

"Yeah, what name is that?"

"Doubt it's important."

"What name is that?" His agitation was starting to take over.

"Zimmerman."

Harris was clearly accustomed to interrogations, but he couldn't stop the slight jerk of his eyes. "No idea."

"Really? Let's see . . ." Billy lifted the phone. "I believe this phone was taken off of you at Mantle Rock. This note states that it has been verified as your number."

Harris smiled. He knew he didn't keep any numbers on his phone—it was always kept clean of contacts, recent calls, or voice mail. "Yeah. So what if it *is* my phone?"

"Any identifying marks on here that make you so sure it's your phone?" Billy decided to string him along a bit more. He knew it would all be over if the right person answered the phone. He turned the phone front to back so Harris could see it.

"Look, you already have my prints off of it, and it was taken off of me and photographed. *I'm* not stupid."

Billy resisted the temptation to say, "Is that so?" He entered the Zimmerman's home phone number, which Coleman had sent Billy on the notepaper. A woman answered. Billy didn't say a word.

"Roger, is that you? Did you get that stinking Sheriff Oliver?"

Billy clicked off the phone.

Harris started clanging his handcuffs against the wheelchair arm.

Billy was sorely tempted to show Roger the picture of his very own little brown spiral notebook pages, but he had what he came to get. The FBI could have this clown now.

"This is Detective Williams, and . . ."

"Deputy Thomas returning Roger Harris to holding. It is six nineteen a.m."

Billy pushed the wheelchair, and it took all the fortitude he had not to slam Harris' bad leg into a wall.

"He's all yours, Matron. Further instructions about his next location will be forthcoming."

"The only place I'm going is home, local yokel."

Billy turned around and looked at him. "Deputy, can't remember the last time we had a city slicker here, can you?"

"Nope. Sure can't. Been a coon's age, for sure."

"Thank God." Billy said and walked off. He was ready for the 8:00 a.m. meeting with FBI Agent Bill Michaels. He hoped that Michaels didn't talk about the deal the FBI would make with this jerk on the path to nailing Zimmerman. This was *their* sheriff this guy came here to kill.

CHAPTER 12

Come to the woods, for here is rest. There is no repose like that of the green deep woods. Sleep in forgetfulness of all ill.

John Muir

New Day in the Valley

Joshua and Carla were at the Valley Store at 6:30 a.m. Joshua checked the shelves for any gaps that needed to be filled while Carla made coffee and set up the storeroom to interview the candidates for the role of full-time cashier.

When Carla returned to the front of the store, she noticed Joshua seemed distracted. "Honey, are you nervous about the interviews?"

Joshua nodded. "Dad and I always relied on knowing folks. We never really did a formal interview. Guess we should have."

"Why? What you did worked for your needs, and you never had any full-time help. I'm accustomed to interviews because turnover in the restaurant was constant."

"I never thought about that. Guess I was always so accustomed to you being our server, it didn't occur to me how many employees you had, or had to interview, to keep a kitchen and restaurant going."

"Our full-time help has always been pretty consistent. It was the part-timers that gave us the turnover. The good news is that most of them were high school students, so they left to go to college or full-time work. It was always kind of fun seeing them grow into adults and find what they wanted to do in life."

"I suppose it was. Kinda like Melody and us. She's worked after school since she was fifteen. Before I knew that my parents had established a scholarship, I decided to have her help with bookwork to give her more hours at a higher wage. Her mama's been dealing with MS for quite a few years now, but Melody never complains. Think we can get a full-time employee like that?"

Carla smiled at her husband. "We talked about the personal traits we wanted, so I think we've got that covered. Besides, who would complain about working in a place where so many friendly people shop?"

"Except for those who aren't." Joshua laughed. "I'll get the cash drawers ready to go and bring them down and open up. It's almost seven thirty. Doug should be here any minute."

"I'll double check the coffee and tea on the service counter. Seems to be quite a hit with folks."

"Great idea. You did a nice job setting it up to look welcoming."

"Helps to know what it takes to meet health department sanitation requirements." She winked at him.

"Amen."

"Joshua, did we ever thank Chad for the idea?"

"Not sure I did. Let's be sure we do that."

Doug entered at precisely 7:30 a.m. "Morning, Miss Carla, Joshua. Little nippy out, but not too bad."

"I'm grateful the snow stopped and the roads are dry," Joshua said. "Appreciate you coming in to help out. We'll be in the back. I put a couple of chairs over yonder for the folks coming to interview."

"Sure glad you think you'll still need me some. Be good for Miss Carla to do all the bookwork and stuff you must have with this store."

"Yep, she's going to have her hands full, for sure." Joshua couldn't wait until he could tell Doug and Melody about the baby. "First person is supposed to be here in about fifteen minutes."

"Good luck," Doug said.

Carla did one last wipe down of the coffee counter and headed to the storeroom.

Conference Room

Sylvia was on day shift and in charge while Chad was on leave. She had debriefed with Sergeant Douglas and briefed the incoming shift; she now had a cushion of only twenty minutes until the meeting with the outside team. Sylvia found herself wondering how the sheriff juggled so many responsibilities in a day. She managed many small details in a day, but knew he had far more plates spinning.

Billy told Sylvia he'd call The Corral and order ham biscuits and a few plain ones. He'd been adamant when he said, "I want to make sure Susan gets some before they're all gone."

"Do a separate order for her, that's easiest."

"Thanks, Sarge."

She smiled; she liked it when Billy called her Sarge.

Sylvia was walking out of the conference room when she saw Quinn and Billy heading down the hall. They bypassed the door to his office in the lab, and he unlocked the door to the storage room. *Smart not to take an outsider, even one we can trust, into a lab with evidence.* Then a smile crept across her face. *Maybe they're dating. Good for them.* She stopped to thank Cecelia for preparing the conference room for visitors and was back at the front desk when FBI Agent Bill Michaels entered.

"Morning, Agent."

"Morning, Sergeant. Hope I'm not late." He looked at his watch and then the clock on the wall.

"Hard to keep that clock matched to any other timepiece. You're early." She shook his hand as he came through the door to the main area of the station. "Hoping for some good news today."

"Me too."

She didn't linger in the hallway but led him to the conference room. She didn't want him to see Quinn and Billy coming out of the sup-ply room, although he likely wouldn't know that's what it was. All the same—better he didn't see them. Sam caught up to Sylvia and Bill Michaels as they stepped into the room. He held up two paper bags.

"Told the guy from The Corral I'd save him the trip."

"And he trusted you?"

"No problem. I know him," Sam laughed. He glanced down the hall and saw Quinn and Billy coming out of a door that he knew was not Billy's office. He smiled. *Hope things work out for them.*

Sam set the biscuits on the counter behind the table and shook hands with Bill Michaels. "Morning, sir."

"Morning. Good man who comes bearing food, especially food that smells like that."

"Simply the messenger. These are on the sergeant, I believe."

"Well, the community fund actually, but the good deed was done by Billy." Sylvia had learned from her father, and from Chad, to give credit where it was due. She took the bag for Susan and stepped out to give it to her.

"Grab your plates, and let's get started," Agent Michaels said as Billy and Quinn entered.

When she returned, Sylvia was pleased to see that everyone had a biscuit and blackberry preserves on their plates—mountain food. She turned when she heard a knock at the door.

"Good morning, Agent Jackson. Glad you could join us." Bill Michaels stood and welcomed the agent-in-charge from the State Bureau of Investigation.

"Help yourself, sir," Sylvia pointed to the food and coffee.

"Hard to pass that up." He took a plain biscuit and coffee and sat.

"No introductions needed, so let's get started. First, any word on the sheriff and Dr. Anderson this morning?"

Everyone around the table looked at each of the others and shrugged.

Michaels started. "We'll assume, given there are deputies and agents out there protecting them, that no news is good news."

Everyone nodded.

"Unless anyone has reason to do otherwise, I'd like to go in the following order: update on things here in the valley, update on the fire in North Carolina, and update on the threads you've been tugging on with the Zimmerman data."

Everyone nodded again.

Sylvia looked at Billy. "Go ahead, Detective."

"About nine o'clock last night, some of our local tribe members found a truck registered to Roger Harris. Our forensic tech, Alexander, took pictures before it was moved. It's in our garage awaiting—" He saw Jackson raise a finger. "Sir? Something to add to that?"

"The truck is on its way to Knoxville. Agent Michaels agreed with Ms. Alexander that having it in our labs would speed up the forensic work. We are, of course, happy to have her join us. I believe she traveled separate from the truck."

"Thank you, sir. I tried to call her, but she must have been in a dead zone enroute. Lots of those here. But I digress . . ." Billy brought up the pictures of the truck bed on the screen.

"Son of a gun," Sam said.

"More than one," Quinn said. "Guy takes his weapons seriously, doesn't he?"

"Appears that way," Billy said. "Agent Jackson, given the early hour and lack of urgency, we were waiting on the truck to get to Knoxville before contacting the ATF."

"No need. They have someone headed to our labs too. According to Agent Michaels, the ATF was already on board regarding the fire in North Carolina."

"Any questions on the truck at this point?" No one spoke.

"We found the registration, insurance, and Harris' driver's license in the door pocket." Billy put them up on the screen.

"The unexpected find was this." He brought up a photo of the spiral notebook. All eyes were on the image. "Here are some sample pages." He scrolled through the individual sheets.

There was a hushed buzz of comment around the table as the numbers and codes flashed by.

"Go on, Detective," Michaels said.

"Where is Harris?" Sam asked.

"The attending physician approved moving him from the hospital last night. Dr. Smith's only stipulation was that we not put him under undue stress in an interrogation until twelve hours after injury."

"And did you?"

"No, sir. In fact, our lead deputy and I were here at four this morning, thirteen hours after his injury, but we didn't interrogate him until well after five o'clock. And I don't know if he ever experienced any stress."

Michaels nodded and made a note. "Did Harris cooperate?"

"It's all recorded, both audiotape and videotape. I rarely decide if someone has cooperated. I leave that to the DA. Jeff Coleman, our detective who traced Zimmerman to the by-the-hour motels, deciphered the code and sent me a phone number while I was in with Harris. I draw your attention to this moment in the interview." He had already cued up videotape of the phone call and brought it up on the screen.

They watched as Billy asked Harris about the phone and heard Harris acknowledge the phone was his. "Roger, is that you? Did you kill that stinking Sheriff Oliver?" Billy stopped the tape on Harris' face, just as his eye twitched. "I'll save you the handcuffs clanging. You can watch it all as you need."

"Good work, Detective. As soon as you called, I sent agents to pick up Mrs. Zimmerman. They got her an hour ago, and there are agents on their way here to relieve you of Harris."

"So this takes Zimmerman out of our hands?"

"Yes, should wrap up what we need from you. Let's take a stretch break, and we'll resume in ten minutes."

Folks stood.

Sam moved over by Billy. "Way to go, Billy. Nice work."

"Took Susan Thomas to make it work. I'll let her know."

Billy walked out by himself and went to the lab. He needed to calm down before they continued. He knew Harris would make a deal and there was nothing he could do about it. He wanted everyone to focus on finding anyone else who might be a threat to the sheriff.

Breakfast Together

Nora had bacon in the oven and the smell was wafting through the house. Mac went to his mother and hugged her leg. She reached down to pick him up then turned so he could see Chad and Bella. He slid down from her arms and fast walked over to the sofa, climbing into the space between Bella and Chad. He put his head on Bella's lap and his feet on Chad's.

"Morning, big guy. Nice to see you."

Mac rolled so he could look up at his grandfather. "Morning, Grandpa. Is it a special day?"

The question stabbed at Chad's heart. *The only time my grandson is used to seeing me when he wakes up is on holidays.* "It's the beginning of lots of special days, Mac."

Mac sat up and pulled his legs under him. "How many, Grandpa?"

Chad picked him up and put him on his lap. "Enough that seeing me in the morning won't be so special anymore." He hugged Mac and kissed the top of his head.

Bella slid her arm behind Chad and gently squeezed his neck. She smiled at him and then saw Nora taking a picture with her phone. She pulled her arm back so Nora could photograph the two without her.

"Mommy?" They all turned when Lilly came in the room. Nora picked her up and put her on the sofa. Lilly crawled into Bella's lap.

"Morning, sweet Lilly. Did you sleep well?" Bella stroked Lilly's cheek

Lilly nodded her head and pulled the corner of her small blanket up under her chin.

"I'm glad to hear that." Bella hugged her close. *What an amazing gift children are.*

"Five minutes and breakfast is ready. Mac, please come wash your hands and take a cloth to Miss Bella and ask her to wash off Lilly's hands."

"Mommy, you just did."

The adults all laughed. "That's my boy," Chad said, putting Mac on his feet. "Run along now and do as your mommy asked."

"I will, Grandpa."

Throughout breakfast, Mac focused his attention on Bella and Chad, but afterwards he turned to Nora. "Mommy, do we have school today?"

Nora looked at Chad. He shook his head slightly.

"Not today, sweet boy. Let's go put on Sesame Street and then you'll need to get dressed. Mommy, Grandpa, and Miss Bella need some grown-up time."

"Sure, Mommy. Come on, Lilly." He took his sister's hand.

Nora let them get down the hall before she said, "I pray to God they never lose that closeness."

"Nora, I haven't raised children myself, but I taught high school and saw the difference in teenagers whose parents taught them the value of love of self and others. Yours will be just fine."

"Equally as important," Chad said, "they *know* they are loved."

"They do, Daddy. Thanks to you." She kissed her father on the cheek and went to make sure her children were settled.

Chad and Bella took their mugs and went to the sofa.

"I love a fire in the morning."

"I love you, morning, noon, and night. The fire is nice, but loving you is way better."

"Listen to you, Mr. Flatterer." She hesitated. "I need to tell Nora I knocked off the lamp."

"No harm done. Forget it." He looked her in the eyes then kissed her. "Given that we are confined to quarters, what would you like to do today?"

"I'd rather not think we're confined. Let's think we have the whole day to enjoy ourselves in this lovely home. Do you think there's some way we could help Nora out today?"

"By relaxing." Nora had returned and was holding her mug of coffee. She sat on the arm of the large easy chair at the end of the sofa and looked at them sitting together. "Our home is your home. The internet works, there are books on the shelves, the children are occupied. Enjoy it."

There was a knock at the door. "I'll go." Chad stood.

"You'll get used to it, Bella. I don't know what magic you have, but this is the most relaxed I've seen my daddy in years ... no, ever. Love is an amazing gift."

Chad walked back to the great room. "I *am* trying to be on leave,"

"But," Nora said bluntly. It was not a question.

"FBI Agent Michaels would like to stop by around ten."

Bella sat up straight. "That's good news, right? He probably has some answers for us about the fire and the incident yesterday."

"Spill, Daddy. What *did* happen yesterday? You didn't agree to voluntary confinement over some stray hunter." She looked at Bella and hoped she had not upset her. "Sorry, Bella. Lots of years of pushing him when he thinks I'm still too young to hear the truth about the ugly side of life."

Bella smiled. "I told him some time ago that I would always listen, but I'd ask when I wanted to know more detail."

Nora jumped up and hugged her. "Oh, I knew the first time I met you that I would love you. You can hold your own against him."

"Does the subject under discussion get to speak?"

"In a minute," Nora said. She turned and kissed him on the forehead. "Okay, now."

"Right now, I am piecing together what I *do* know. Someone took a shot with a rifle and was clearly trespassing. The shot was too close to be a typical deer hunter. We waited for over a half hour ... in a standoff, I guess you'd say." He looked at Bella. She nodded.

"What I know at this point is that Sergeant Whitehorse threw a rock to let me know they were up the mountain and hopefully to draw fire."

"She what?" Nora sat up straight.

"Our position was obvious, given the angle of Mantle Rock. I think the shooter was hoping we'd get tired and step out. Sylvia is a good aim, and she threw the rock so that it hit almost directly in front of us. He stepped out and shot at the movement, and I was ready. Hit him in the leg."

"Daddy," Nora started slowly, "I was always proud you won so many marksman competitions, but I don't think I ever really thought about you shooting to hit someone."

Chad's voice was heavy. "I never wanted you to think about it." Tears welled up in his eyes. He stood up. "Now you know everything I know. Anyone need a refill?"

Nora stood and hugged her father. "Sorry I forced you on that one. It wasn't fair."

"Maybe I'm the one who hasn't always been fair with you." He took her hand. "How about we make fresh coffee?"

Next Steps

The team reassembled and Agent Michaels asked if there was anything else Billy had to share.

"Not at this time."

"The detective in Statesboro called me this morning, and the arson specialist and insurance arson specialist are to be on scene today. It was definitely an incendiary fire. They will have the report from the arson dog sometime today."

Billy started laughing. "Wait a minute. No disrespect, sir, but an arson dog?"

Michaels knew some of the laughter was a tension reliever. He didn't take offense. "Just like bomb and drug sniffing dogs. They train the dogs to sniff for the chemicals that might have been used to ignite or accelerate the fire."

"I haven't worked any fires, Agent," Quinn said. "How do the dogs differentiate with all the chemicals in a home?"

"The dogs are trained to sniff for hydrocarbons, the most common fuels used as accelerants. Things like gasoline, kerosene, and diesel fuel.

In fact, the only way the dog eats each meal is to correctly identify an accelerant from his or her handler. The combination of the dog's nose with the investigative training of the fire investigator help to seek out possible accelerants at a fire scene. To ensure destruction of a property, either the amount of accelerant used by an arsonist, or the accelerants in or around a home might be atypical. The dog can help the investigator identify the best place to take samples to send to the lab."

"My work in immigration isn't as likely to involve me in a fire investigation, but I can see I have some training to do." Quinn sat back.

"Me too," Sam said.

"Anyway, the detective is not concerned about the reports by the various arson specialists. We have to find the humans involved."

"We?" Billy said.

"We're a team, Detective. There are FBI agents and North Carolina's state police involved now. Outside of the FBI field teams, this team has the most in-depth information on Zimmerman at this point. Let's hear what threads Isaacs and Nations have found."

"I was going over the phone numbers we received when Dr Anderson had the threatening phone calls. Sam and I were working our way through the numbers used to call the Anderson cabin." She looked around the table. "I was concerned that once the guys who ran Billy off the road were arrested, no one bothered to look at the numbers for a pattern."

"Fair assessment that it would have dropped down the priority list, but it would not have been ignored." Michaels was all business.

I could have said that better. "Yes, sir. I believe that." She looked back at her paper. "There is one number that was used during the earlier threats that rang her on Monday of this week."

"Do you have the number?" Michaels had his pencil poised over his paper.

"313-542—"

"9896," Billy said.

Quinn looked at him. "I didn't tell you that number."

"No, you didn't. It's the number of Harris' phone."

Michaels looked at him. "You sure?"

"As sure as snow in the winter on top of these mountains."

"Where's the phone now?"

"Back in the evidence locker unless your agents have picked Harris up."

"Call and see," Michaels said.

Billy called the matron. "He's still here."

AIC Jackson remained quiet as he got up to speed on what had happened. "I can get a chopper here and have it back in Knoxville in short order."

"Do it," Michaels said.

Sylvia spoke up, "Probably best that Billy signs out the phone and hands it over to the agents who arrive. One less person's name on the chain of evidence."

"Excellent point, Sergeant."

Jackson stepped back in the room. "Chopper was in Gatlinburg and it will be here shortly. Pilot said the best place to land was the high school football field. Can we make that happen?"

Sylvia took out her phone and hit speed dial for the high school principal. "Dr. Bennett? Hey, Sylvia here. Need to land an SBI helicopter on your football field in less than thirty minutes. Possible?" Sylvia nodded. "Okay, thanks. I'll let you know when we have an ETA."

"Not to doubt the integrity of your high school principal, but does she know SBI and ETA?" Jackson said.

"Yes," Billy, Sylvia, and Sam answered in unison.

"Sir," Sylvia said, "she's a smart woman in her own right and her husband is a deputy on our force."

He nodded. "Got it. Tell her fifteen or twenty minutes. Best if no one is outside."

"Knowing Amanda," Billy said, "she'll make it a drill that puts everyone in lockdown."

Michaels looked surprised.

"This woman doesn't waste learning time. If there are going to be distractions, she'll find some way to make it educational."

Sylvia looked down the table at Billy. "Detective, you need to go. Take Thomas with you for corroboration on chain of evidence."

"10-4." Billy stood and left the room.

"Sam, do you have anything to add?" Michaels looked at him.

"Thought I might have a lead tying the drugs from the powwow back to Zimmerman. I'll pass on the details so your folks can double check it, but I don't see how it's relevant to the fire or the shooting."

"Very well. Thank you for your work. Quinn and Sam, if you have time to hang around in the valley, I'll touch base with you after Agent Jackson and I talk with the sheriff."

Quinn and Sam looked at each other. "Want to hang out at The Corral?" Quinn smiled.

Sam nodded. "Sounds good to me."

"We're adjourned. Again, everyone, good work."

Chapter 13

Help is on the Way

Joshua returned to the storeroom after walking the last interviewee to the front door. He wondered how Carla would want to discuss the candidates. *It's not like we need a rocket scientist.* He walked through the swinging doors to find Carla busy writing.

"Glass of tea, honey?"

"Sure, thanks. No, on second thought, glass of ice water would be great."

"Good for you. I should have offered."

"Sure, live dangerously. I hate water!"

"You do?"

"Too much tea in my lifetime." She laughed, "Nah, I'm getting used to it. Doc said it was important to drink plenty of fluids."

"*Preferably* water. I was the guy there with you, remember?" He handed her the water and kissed her on the forehead.

"Thanks." She tapped the paper in front of the chair where he had been sitting. "Write the name of the candidates in order of your preference. If there's one that's a no go for you, leave it off. I've done mine. Then we'll talk about them."

Joshua looked at her. He was both surprised and tickled at her very formal approach to the task of hiring a full-time cashier. After all, they were a small-time, privately owned local grocery. They could hire whoever they wanted. He sipped the glass of tea he had poured himself and wrote the first name immediately. He wrote two more and put down his pen. "I'm ready."

"First let's talk about strengths and concerns for each one and then we'll share how we ranked them."

"Fine with me. Can we see if we both eliminated one?"

"Sure, you have a say in how we do it. I should have asked that. Who did you eliminate?"

"The last one."

"Me too." She smiled. "Done."

Twenty minutes later they had discussed the remaining applicants. Joshua hoped to let Carla have first pick, so he said, "Who's your first choice?"

"Chuck."

"Really?" Joshua was surprised she hadn't picked one of the women. "Why?"

"For all the reasons we outlined specific to the job but also because we can train him to do propane deliveries. Time you stopped trying to do everything." She waited. "How about you? Who's your first choice?"

"Hannah." He watched her face. "I was thinking we could hire Chuck to do stock work and drive the propane truck, that way we can keep him year-round. I'm not opposed to training Hannah to do propane deliveries, but it just doesn't seem a good match for her."

"I agree. Are you sure about hiring both of them?"

"After our review of the store's finances, I'm confident we can handle it. Dad had a salary, and we'd pay the cashier less than that. I'd already worked out the numbers for a full-time bookkeeper, but you and I can do that. I don't want to be on the road doing propane deliveries when I can be with you and our child. So, what do you think? Two new people?"

"Not sure why I didn't think about that when we were strategizing. I liked Hannah, and I think she'll have the skills we need and the personality too. Friendly but not too chatty. Since her sisters worked at The Corral a few years back, I know we can trust her with the store if we're both out."

He raised his hand to high-five her. "Then let's do it."

"I'll get them in for paperwork, and we'll be ready to go. One more thing, Andrea told me that they appreciated the offer we made to Natalia to work part-time, but asked if we could wait until summer. You okay with that?"

"Absolutely."

"Thanks, husband." She loved calling him 'husband.'

"Thanks go to you, my beautiful wife. I love you! I love that you are smart and are helping me to remember that I actually did learn something from my UT business school days."

"I love you, Joshua. Thanks for being willing to dream with me."

"Pleasure is all mine. Now, I need to relieve Doug and you—"

"Need to go rest. Don't remind me."

They stood and hugged.

Carla teased him, "We're at work, remember?!"

"Got it." He gave her a light kiss on the cheek.

Visitors

"Sir, Agent Michaels and Agent Jackson are here. Credentials verified." Chad remembered this was the deputy who had hesitated coming out of the back door at the station recently when Chad walked up. The young man had waited on the sheriff to scan his ID. Chad valued deputies who understood that all these processes became more and more important as their little corner of the world grew with new residents—and with crime.

"Thank you, Deputy. I'll be right there."

He clicked off the call and looked at Bella. "You okay?"

She nodded. "If I miss a cue that I should leave the room, tell me. If it's about my property, I want to know."

"Fair enough." He gave her a kiss and said, "Time to let our visitors in to warm up."

"Morning, gentlemen. Come in out of the cold." Chad shook hands. "Bill. Ralph. Welcome to my daughter's home."

"Nice compound she has here," Bill Michaels said. "Pleased to see there was a gated wall."

"Her daddy's the sheriff," Chad said. "He's funny that way. Couldn't convince her and her husband to run that wall completely around their property, but I'm satisfied they're safe as they can be here."

"You too." Ralph Jackson said. "Thanks for letting us intrude."

They entered the great room. Bella stood and Chad made introductions. "I couldn't remember if you two had met. Please have a seat."

Chad was well prepared for him and Bella to be the center of discussion, so he had made sure they were seated on the sofa. The FBI agent took the comfortable leather chair at the side of the coffee table, and the SBI agent chose one of the wingback chairs Chad had pulled up. He was directly in front of Bella.

"Coffee, tea, water?" Chad asked. Both declined. Chad sat back on the sofa and waited.

"Dr. Anderson," Bill Michaels started.

"Please, call me Bella."

"Very well, Bella. I want to start with offering our sincere sympathy at the loss of your home in North Carolina. While there are no words to address the loss of personal items or memories, I am here to inform you that we have multiple agencies working to find who's responsible."

Bella tried to stop the gasp, but it escaped. All three men watched her. She recovered quickly.

"Am I to understand that the fire was arson?"

"Yes, ma'am. It was definitely an incendiary fire, but that will be finalized once the arson specialists have completed their work."

Chad noticed that Ralph Jackson watched Bella the entire time. *You can watch her all you want. She had nothing to do with this. It's all on me.*

"You'll excuse me, Agent . . ."

"Bill, please." Michaels returned the courtesy she had extended.

"Bill. You'll excuse me." She turned and nodded at Jackson. "On the one hand, it's a relief that the fire was not a result of some maintenance left undone on my part. On the other, I have no idea why someone would want to burn down my home." She saw his involuntary glance at Chad.

"Ma'am, we have the FBI, the State Bureaus of Investigation in Tennessee and North Carolina, the ATF, and the local team all working to track down the person or persons responsible. We will do everything in our power to find them."

"Thank you. May I ask why you're telling me this without first interviewing me as a potential suspect?"

Michaels and Jackson looked at her with surprise. Chad had to keep himself from smiling.

"Important question. There may be questions for you at some time in the future, but at this time we have corroborated evidence that you were here in Tennessee at the time of the fire."

"Ma'am," Ralph Jackson said, "one of the challenges of this type of investigation is that what may appear obvious may not be what it seems."

"Agent Jackson, I believe that holds true for many things in life. For what it's worth, I'm devastated by the loss of my home. While I have the memories of my life there, the personal effects of my family are gone forever. I don't know how you explain that to someone who hasn't experienced that kind of loss." She fell silent.

Chad was struggling not to take her hand or put his arm around her to comfort her.

"If you have nothing else for me, I will leave you gentlemen and wish you a good day." She stood.

All three of the men stood too.

Bella debated about whether to go to the guest house or the playroom—she opted for the children and Nora.

Chad poured himself a cup of coffee and held up the carafe. Both men accepted the offer.

"Sorry, Chad. Better she hears it from us than from you."

"Hey, I'm on leave. I would not have expected to know before she did. Thank you for being the ones to come and tell her."

Bill Michaels said, "We do not have any reason, at this time, to suspect Dr. Anderson of any involvement and, as a courtesy to you, we have not felt it necessary to question her. However, you and I ... we," he nodded to Ralph Jackson, "know that should any line of inquiry lead back to her, we will interview her and you will not be part of it."

"I'd expect nothing less."

"How much do you know about the shooter?" Ralph said, looking directly at Chad.

"I know he trespassed on tribal property, which is clearly marked with purple paint on the trees, and he shot towards Mantle Rock where Bella and I were having what I had hoped would be a restorative walk following the loss of her home." He explained the stand-off and subsequent showdown that resulted in the suspect's injury. "And that's all I know."

Ralph did not believe Chad would have asked for information, but he had to ask the question. "Have any of your staff spoken with you about the case since the shooter was taken to the hospital?"

Chad's gray eyes flashed. He started to lean forward and put his elbows on his knees before he caught himself. "Agent, I will sit for as many interviews as you want. I will take as many lie detector tests as you can devise. However, I will kindly ask you not to insult me in my daughter's home. My staff are all highly competent and they know that my personal relationship with Dr. Anderson is the reason I have recused myself from the investigation into the fire at her home. None would even consider talking to me. I want to ensure that the person or persons responsible for destroying Dr. Anderson's home, as well as the man and any accomplices to the shooting yesterday, are caught and prosecuted to the fullest extent of the law. I would never do anything to jeopardize that." He sat back and counted slowly to three. "And, if one of my employees tried in any way to get information to me personally or through someone else, they would pick up their last paycheck and be gone. I *cannot* be more clear than that." He knew they had to ask. He didn't know why he was so vehement in his response.

Bill Michaels said, "Understood, Chad. Ralph had to ask."

"I know. I know." He stared at the fire in the fireplace.

"For the record, your Detective Williams and Deputy Thomas aced cornering Harris." Michaels hoped that would redirect them.

Chad looked at him. He assumed Harris was the name of the shooter. He wondered if he'd get told anything else.

"Apparently, your Detective Coleman decoded a list of phone numbers Harris had in his truck and one belonged to Mrs. Zimmerman."

Chad bit his tongue to keep from asking questions. He didn't want to be accused of interfering, and he knew that sooner or later he'd get the whole story. He continued to stare into the fireplace. *Coleman did it again.*

"SBI agents have his truck in Knoxville with your forensic tech, and Harris is on his way out of here with FBI agents." Michaels watched Chad and saw an almost imperceptible nod of his head.

"Last, but far from least, we are still tugging on threads that may connect Zimmerman, himself, in the arson and shooting. The North Carolina SBI are working different angles there as well. Questions?"

"No, not on what you've shared. Thank you for this much. I would like my community to get back to normal as soon as possible. Will you pull your people?"

Michaels looked at Jackson.

Jackson shrugged. "Do you need them, Chad?"

"I'm grateful for the support and service, Ralph, but I think we're good. I'll ask Bella to stay in the valley until the weekend, and then we'll try to go back to a normal life."

"Well, I could sure use lessons on how to make that happen," Jackson said and smiled at Chad.

"I plan to be away for a day or two, but you can reach me. All that has happened is on me. This amazing woman, who is as important to me as my family, needs a break. I'm going to try and convince her to hop on a plane and go to the beach."

The two men stood. "Thanks, Sheriff. You have a pretty awesome community here in these hills. Privilege to work with you." SBI Agent Ralph Jackson extended his hand.

Chad took it. "Thank *you,* Agent Jackson. As I told you before, you're welcome here anytime. We still do Friday night jamborees. Bring that dobro and join us."

Jackson nodded. "One of these days."

Michaels extended his hand. "Thanks, Chad. I think you're safe to go back to life as normal, at least as far as the shooter goes. We'll leave the agents one more night and then just call if anything changes. I'm going back to meet with your team, and then we'll send Ralph on his way to the big city."

"Thanks, Bill. Been a huge relief for me to have you two work to bring this whole Zimmerman thing to an end."

"Working on it," Bill said as he opened the front door

Reflections

Chad thanked the agents again at the doorway and nodded to his deputies on patrol outside Nora's house. He stepped back inside and went into Nora and Fred's office, closing the door behind him. He sat down and stared out the window towards the side yard and the playground equipment his grandchildren loved. Warm tears fell on his cheeks. *I almost cost Bella her life yesterday, and it's highly likely revenge directed at me cost all of the ties she had to her family. Nora and her family were targets in all this too.* He heard the office door open but did not move.

"Daddy?"

He put his arm out from the side of the wingback chair. "Here, sweet girl."

Nora walked over and sat on the arm of the chair and faced him. She leaned in and rested her forehead on his.

Chad hugged her. "I don't deserve any of you, you know?"

Nora bit her lip. "Shhh … shhh …" As much as she wanted to shake him, she knew it was sadness and grief talking.

Chad pulled himself together. He couldn't remember a time he had cried in front of his daughter, even when his parents passed away. He saved tears for his bedroom. He always believed he had to be strong for her. "I was wrong, Nora."

"Wrong about what, Daddy?"

"Always thinking I was the only one who could protect you. Keep you safe."

"Maybe you *were* the only one and *maybe* you were wrong, but I love you no matter what. You grew up with a father who held the law above all else. You complemented his law practice with your belief you could lead law officers to ensure a safe community."

He pulled his head back against the chair and looked at her. "How'd you get so smart?"

"A little bit of my mother and a whole lot of you. Now, you need to listen to me. There is a very lovely woman sitting by my fireplace who is smart, talented, and in love with you. She needs you to be *you*—not her superhero. You need to go be with her."

"I'm going to take her away."

"What?"

"I'm going to ask her to go to Knoxville, buy tickets on the first non-stop flight to one of the oceans, and go walk in the sand."

Nora started crying. "Oh, Daddy, go. Get up off this chair and go." She stood and then stopped to look at him. "Is it safe?"

"It is. I think you'll be fine. Go about your daily routines. I'll keep a deputy around you, but out of sight until we get back. Okay?"

"Go. She's waiting." She pushed him out the door, shut it, and hurried to her computer.

Bella sat in front of the fire with a book open in her lap. She found she couldn't focus on the words. She felt Chad's hands on her shoulders before she even realized he was there. She put her hands on his—and looked up at him. He took her wrists and gave a slight tug. "Let's go."

"Go where?"

"The ocean."

She stood and faced him. "Did those agents slip something in your coffee?"

"No." He leaned across and kissed her. "I fell in love with a highly intelligent, beautiful woman who has been more than patient with the slowness of my awakening."

She raised her left eyebrow and looked at him. "Meaning?"

"Meaning, in the last twenty-four hours, give or take, I have realized how much of my daughter's life and my grandchildren's lives I have missed, thinking I was the only one to keep our little corner of the world safe."

"Which you have done admirably."

"Kindness is just one of your many traits. I'm not the only one who can keep this community safe. I want to talk to you without my job hovering over me. I want to understand what you need to navigate the loss you just experienced. I want to walk hand in hand with you on the beach. Shall we?"

"You mean go to the airport, buy a ticket, and go?"

"Exactly. If you prefer, even this tech dinosaur could figure out how to buy a ticket online."

Bella saw Nora out of the corner of her eyes. She was grinning and waving a piece of paper.

"Two tickets, open return, leaving Knoxville at four forty this afternoon and going to Destin, Florida, courtesy of the Oliver-Smiths. I'll have your accommodation booked before you get to the airport. Now, go."

They both looked at Nora and then at each other.

She said, "Get moving. Time's a wasting."

Bella said, "Why not? Can't imagine anyone I'd rather go to the beach with . . . other than the Oliver-Smith family."

"Next time," Nora said.

Chad picked Nora up and swung her around. "I love you, my very special daughter."

"Yeah, yeah. Go hug your grandchildren and get out of here."

Chad took Bella's hand as they did Mac's quick walk down the hall to the playroom.

The Corral

Quinn and Sam had arrived at The Corral a little before 10:00 a.m. and sat with their coffees, talking about what they thought would happen next.

"I would love to be a fly on the wall to hear what the FBI and SBI say to Chad."

"Of course you would, Sam. Heck, you could probably even learn something."

"Ouch! Am I in for a lifetime of harassment from you for my cruel ways in college?"

"Time will tell, won't it?" Quinn saw a text pop up on her screen. She picked up her phone and typed "Join us @ TC."

The reply, "10-4!"

"Is that your new beau?" Sam winked.

"Beau? Sam Nations, are you kidding me? Beau? I have *never* in the fourteen years I've known you *ever* heard you use the word 'beau.'"

"Think I'm incapable of new vocabulary, Agent Isaacs?" He tried to keep a deadpan look.

"Oh, Sam, for the disappointment I think we both felt when we knew we weren't going to make it as a couple, I am eternally grateful for your friendship and for the chance to work with you. I have never, in all of it, doubted your ability to learn."

"Back at 'cha, Quinn."

The side door opened and Billy stepped in.

"Did you fly?" Quinn said.

"I was at the high school, remember? Didn't you hear the helicopter?"

"No. I guess the music drowned it out."

"Really?" He looked from one to the other. "Sure you weren't sitting here scheming how to get revenge on the local detective who stole your thunder?" As hard as Billy tried to keep a straight face, he couldn't.

All three started laughing. He sat down in the booth next to Quinn.

"Any word on what the agents said to the sheriff?" Sam said to Billy.

"I haven't talked to anyone." His secure phone rang. "Duty calls." He stood and walked to a quiet corner to take Sylvia's call.

"Got your message. Michaels would like us back at the conference room for a brief meeting in fifteen. Where are you?"

"At The Corral with Sam and Quinn. We're on our way."

He walked back to the table. "Pay your bill and be sure you tip Cheri well. We take care of our folks around here. Michaels wants us in the conference room in fifteen."

Sam took the last swig of his coffee, put a ten-dollar bill on the table, and said, "Good enough?"

"Expect nothing less of a local." Billy slapped him on the back, and they left.

CHAPTER 14

When the last tree is cut down, the last river poisoned, the last fish caught, then only will man discover that he cannot eat money.

Cree Indian Wisdom

On the Road

"Do you need anything from my home, or can you travel with what you have here?"

Bella shrugged. "I have no idea what I need. Impulse decisions about travel have not been frequent in my life."

"Uncomfortable with them?"

"Don't think so, just not a lot of experience. How about you?"

"Scared to death." Chad smiled at her. "But there's no time like the present to learn."

"What if we want to go swimming?"

"Likely no better place to buy a swimsuit than Florida, right?" He wiggled his eyebrows. "Maybe even a bikini."

She laughed. "I look forward to seeing you in a bikini. I will be in a one-piece."

"Okay, then we don't need to go to my house. I'm going to put our things in the Jeep. Would you please go tell Nora we're leaving?"

"Tell Sylvia I'll be sure you get back." It was said without rancor. She knew he wouldn't go without telling his sergeant, even though he was on leave. She kissed him and headed across the courtyard to the kitchen door.

How did she know I'd call work? Chad couldn't believe that Bella could speak so easily when it came to his job. *I didn't even take her comment with the anger I always felt with Mary.* He picked up their bags and walked to his Jeep, promptly forgetting his ex-wife. He dialed Sylvia on her secure phone.

"Whitehorse here."

"Hey, Sylvia. Bill Michaels left here a few minutes ago and is headed back your way. Thanks for all you've taken on."

"Here to serve, Sheriff."

"Thank you. We are a better community for it. I'm going to take a day or two more of leave if it works in your personal life."

"We're good on this end, sir."

"Not advertising this, but Bella and I are headed to Knoxville to fly to Florida. I want to walk on a beach." He waited to see what she'd say.

He couldn't see the smile on Sylvia's face, but it came across loud and clear over the phone. "Sounds like good medicine to me. We'll see you when you get back."

"I'll just be a phone—"

"No calls. We'll handle it. I'm sure it won't be with the ease you have, but I promise the station will still be standing when you return."

"No doubt, Sylvia. No doubt. See you soon. Thanks again."

He dialed Doc Jim's number to make sure the retired vet was good with keeping Wizard for a few more days.

"Whatever Bella needs, Chad. Wizard is good company. Tell her not to worry—even the cats like Wizard."

Chad turned as the front door opened and Bella and Nora walked out. Chad opened the car door for Bella. He kissed Nora on the cheek as she handed him a piece of paper.

"What's this?"

"Your accommodations: address, directions, and keycode access provided. Rental car is in your name."

He looked into his daughter's eyes. "I love you, Nora Oliver-Smith. Take care of yourself, Fred, and the kids. See you in a couple of days."

"Take your time. You deserve it." She stood on the front lawn and waved as they drove off. She saw the deputy standing off to the side.

Looking for Answers

The three SUVs pulled up at the sheriff's station, and Billy continued through the gate to the back. Quinn and Sam parked in front and were in the conference room when Billy arrived.

"You may be a good problem solver, Williams, but you're not very fast."

"Stopped to ..." Billy looked at Sam. Billy was so accustomed to teasing others that he didn't always pick up on being teased himself. He shook his head and sat down.

Bill Michaels looked around the table. There were two local law enforcement officers, two agents from different federal agencies, and a state bureau agent at the table. He felt there was friendship here that came with today's young people understanding something his generation was figuring out late in life: a job is a job, not your life. "Let's talk about next steps."

Quinn looked around the table. When no one else spoke, she said, "Is there any evidence that Harris had accomplices here?"

Ralph Jackson answered, "I had a call from the lab in Knoxville just before this meeting. A preliminary report indicates that there are no prints in his truck but his."

Sylvia waited to see if anyone else was going to speak. "The tribal members who found the truck are good trackers, and there was no evidence of more than one vehicle or set of footprints."

"Anything else on the truck, Ralph?" Michaels said.

"Not at this point. They will be very thorough with it, but they'll need time, especially with the arsenal he had in the back. I'll keep you and Sergeant Whitehorse updated."

"That works. Anything else from DEA or IEA?"

"Nothing on this matter from DEA," Sam said.

Quinn shook her head.

"Update on the North Carolina investigation is that the incendiary fire is confirmed and agreed by all specialists, but the accelerant is still under investigation. Samples were collected as evidence and will be confirmed in the lab. The detective from North Carolina told me they were fortunate that the lower part of the basement wall had not collapsed. It allowed them to find the V-pattern up the back where the fire started."

"Any word on possible suspects?" Billy said.

"Not yet, but fortunately it seems almost everyone in the area has some sort of camera system. The neighbors are being very cooperative and offered their videos willingly."

Sam nodded. "I'd assume you have a camera to make sure your property's safe, so makes sense you'd want your neighbors to cooperate for you."

"Besides that," Billy said, "seeing a completely demolished home would be a pretty good motivator."

Agent Michaels continued. "They will look for any individuals they can piece together from various videos and try to establish time patterns as well. I'm sure the North Carolina SBI is being diligent on this, and I'll let you know as soon as we have anything to share." He looked around the table. "Any questions?"

"What's your assessment of concern for the sheriff and Dr. Anderson?" Sam asked.

"I'm not a betting man, Sam, but it appears to me that these two events could be coordinated, just not by the people doing the damage. They were hired by someone and a timeline given, or they are two completely random acts. It appears Harris was alone, so I think life can return to normal here."

Sam wanted reinforcement of what Sylvia had asked earlier. "So looks like Zimmerman and his cronies are no longer the valley's concern?"

"May need some information, but nothing left for them to investigate."

Everyone around the table nodded.

"Be good to have the sheriff back," Billy said. Then he looked at Sylvia, "No offense, Sergeant."

"I agree completely. However, I have spoken with the sheriff, and he is going to stay on leave for a few more days. I will let you know when he returns."

"Good for him," Quinn said. "Well, Sergeant, gentlemen, if there is no further need of my assistance, I have other work needing my attention. It's been a pleasure, as always, to work with you."

They all stood, exchanged comments of appreciation, and started to drift out the door.

"Agent Michaels," Sylvia said, "may I have a word?"

"Certainly."

"On behalf of the sheriff and our community, please accept my thanks and appreciation for your quick response and your leadership. I'm fully aware that there are still loose ends on the fire and Zimmerman, but we'll wait on direction from you if our help is needed."

"My pleasure. Pretty special place you have here."

"Come back anytime. Better yet, move here. We like neighbors who are law abiding and civic minded."

He laughed. "Don't I wish! Maybe in retirement—if I can get my wife to leave the city."

"Just know you're welcome anytime." She shook his hand as he walked out the door.

North Carolina

Detective Burton was at the North Carolina state forensic lab reviewing the videos from the camera systems around Bella's home. Some of her neighbors had a high dynamic range toggle, which helped clarify the daytime images.

"We count on criminals having patterns of behavior," said the forensic tech.

"Like scouting the property during the daytime?"

"Exactly. The perp counts on people being busy or absent from home during the day and tries to get a sense of the property of interest. Middle of the night is a great time to start a fire. Even if the resident is home, most people are asleep. Who knows if the perp considers if there's anyone inside at night . . . unless, of course, he wants to kill someone."

"I've read profiles on arsonists, and there just doesn't seem to be a pattern that can lead to identifying an arsonist before they act," the detective said. "Is that your experience?"

"Well, sir, my work is in reviewing the elements we have from the fire, including videotapes. The research I've read generally indicates it's hard to pinpoint who will set fires."

"No surprise, given that less than twenty percent of fire setters are ever found."

"Exactly. Now, look at this. Patterns are important in my work, and here's one based on the video from neighbors across the road and the two on either side of the property."

Getting Away

Chad settled into his seat in the airport lounge. "Look at this information Nora printed out about Destin, Florida. Ever been there?"

"I haven't been to the panhandle at all. You?"

"Never. Only been to Florida once and that was to take Nora to Disney World years ago."

"So, why the desire to go walk a beach?" She watched his face.

"Several reasons, really. Most important is getting you out of the unsettling events of the last few days." He smiled at her. "I think the beach occurred to me because Joshua talked about wanting to see the ocean and never doing it. He seemed to have real regrets after Jan passed away and then the loss of his dad, too."

"Regrets are often a part of grieving. Matt and I ..." She turned away.

"Bella, I told you, you don't have to apologize for saying things that involved you and Matt. I'm glad you had a good marriage and a loving companion. No apologies. Okay?"

"Thanks. Although we lived in one city all our married life, we traveled extensively. I've seen a great deal of the world. The difference is we always planned it. We used to joke about what we'd do if we won the lottery."

"And?"

"Hire a private plane and fly to New Orleans for dinner the first night. Of course, first you'd have to play the lottery." She laughed.

"Got it. Next time a private jet."

Bella leaned over and kissed him. "No need." She pulled back. "Oh no, Chad, I totally forgot."

"Forgot what?"

"To check with Doc Jim about Wizard." She had her phone out.

Chad reached over and put his hand on hers. "Done. He said to tell you to take whatever time you need. Something about Wizard being company even his cats like."

"He told me once that Wizard was much better company than his cats. Since I'm allergic to cats I've never had one, but my friends always talk about how independent they are."

"Time for our flight. Let's leave the mountains and cold behind for a day or so. Ready?"

"Ready. By the way, how long is the accommodation booked?"

"Two nights: Wednesday and Thursday. There's a note that we can extend it. I suspect it tells you my daughter either knows me too well, or she decided to give us some choice."

"Maybe both." They walked towards the gate holding hands.

Not Quite Satisfied

Quinn sent a text to Billy: "Meet at ur place"

"20 mins. 10-4."

"10-4."

Billy arrived to find Quinn sitting on his small front porch. "You'll freeze to death."

"Hardly. Used to working out in the cold, Mr. Detective. Illegal immigrants tend to be on the move."

"Fair enough. Come on in." He unlocked the front door. "I can give you a key so you can crash here anytime."

"Thanks for the offer. Better to keep personal life and work life separate. Right now, my time over here always involves work."

"Just let me know if you change your mind." He smiled at her. "It's lunch time. Want to eat bachelor fixings?"

"I'd be delighted. Seems to me the last time I ate here was when I was cooking for you after you decided to take a flying leap off the highway."

"Not sure I *decided* to do that, but I did take a flying leap." He washed his hands in the kitchen sink and walked to the fridge.

Quinn's eyebrows lifted when he took lettuce, tomatoes, cucumbers, celery, broccoli, and ham steak out of the fridge.

"We can have a salad, and I can warm up the ham steak in the iron skillet, or we can have salad with ham chopped into small pieces. What's the lady's pleasure?"

She stepped up to him and kissed him. "I'd like this to be my pleasure, but I have to get to the office."

He pulled her into an embrace. "Your choice: visit with or without lunch."

"Sorry, fella, lunch wins out today."

He nodded and started chopping the veggies. She took a knife and chopped the ham.

"What's so important, without divulging federal secrets, that you have to get to the office?"

"I'm trying to figure out a situation between a senior agent and a young agent."

"Want to talk about it?"

"Not right now. I need to think this one through on my own. Maybe I'm suffering from the ten-year itch."

"Come again?"

"Well, most folks talk about the seven-year itch . . ."

"I thought that was about marriage. Of course, I wouldn't have a clue since I've never been married."

"Likewise. But some people talk about ten years in a marriage, or a relationship, or a job as the time when most folks are itching for something different."

"Are you?"

"I don't think so. I'm pretty good at what I do. I like the work when I can really help people who are just trying to improve life for their children and family, but, like you, most of what I encounter is not so pretty."

"True. The fun in being a detective is the problem solving. Although it involves people who often lie about their activity, putting all the pieces together is what I enjoy."

They sat at Billy's grandmother's dining room table. He rarely used it, but enjoyed the memories made around it when he was a child.

"There are pieces to put together in my job too. I also like the variety of things I get to do. I think what I'm struggling with right now is the lack of leadership . . . well, maybe some lines are being crossed that could prove difficult down the road, if not dangerous."

"Well, just know that if you need help, I'm here."

"Thanks. I'd already figured out you're one of the good guys—and I'm intrigued."

"Flattered, I am. Thank you. I'm pretty taken with you too."

"It's about that puzzle solving. Our lives bring their own brand of puzzles."

"Like?"

"Like what if I ended up supervising a case and you were on a joint task force?"

"Think I'd have trouble separating out my personal life from my work?"

"No." She hesitated. "I don't. The problem with being burned is you're reluctant to touch that same brand of conflict."

"Is that what happened to you and Sam?"

She looked at him. She didn't know he knew she had dated Sam in college. "You figured that out?"

"Quinn, I'm forty-two years old. I've been single all my life and, on the job, since I graduated from college. I made detective faster than anyone on the force ever has, including the boss. I live in a small community, which I happen to love, but the opportunity to meet intriguing, intelligent women doesn't come along every day. Despite my reputation as a prankster, one of my strengths is that I'm a really good observer of people. You and Sam have a tension that doesn't generally exist on the job unless you've been romantically involved."

She lifted her glass of tea. "And pretty good deductive powers too, I see."

He leaned in towards her. "I like being with you, and I would like to be friends—very good friends." He stared into her eyes. "I'm also patient. I'm not going anywhere, and I won't push you. Fair enough?"

"Fair enough. I need to sort out the job first. Okay?"

"I can keep secrets too. So, when you need an ear or want to bounce puzzle pieces off someone, I'm available. In the meantime, I hope you'll come to the jamboree on Friday night this week. It will be the beginning of the holiday season, and the Fridays leading up to Christmas always draw a crowd. We love the holidays in these hills."

"I'll come over. I'll check with Joshua and—"

"I have a guest room." He smiled but was not forceful in his comment.

"—see if Joe's house is available. Thanks though."

He lifted his glass. "Here's to some foot stomping and early Christmas carols on Friday."

They talked about their families as they ate lunch, and Quinn was surprised how fast the time disappeared. She realized two things as she helped clean up and load the dishwasher. First, she was no closer to solving the problem at her office. And second, Billy was the first man she was interested in getting to know personally in a very long time.

At his front door, Billy put his hand on the doorknob and one around her waist. "A kiss for the road." He kissed her lightly and she responded with more interest than he had expected.

"Thanks for giving me space. Talk to you soon."

He opened the door and she went to her SUV. "Text me when you get there," he called.

She nodded, waved, and drove off.

Billy wondered if he truly was capable of being patient when it came to love.

Afternoon at the Valley Store

"How's it going, Hannah?" Carla had been up in the loft office working out a schedule for propane deliveries.

"So far so good, Miss Carla. The cash register was easy to learn, and making change is easy enough. The hardest part has been questions on where things are located in the store. I've found everything that's been asked for, and I walked the aisles during my lunch break. I'll learn it in a day or two, I promise."

"No doubt. Does the paper with the aisles and products help?"

"Yes, ma'am. It's just that I'd like to be able to say things like, 'We have two brands of canned tomatoes.' You know, things like that."

Carla was pleased. "You'll do just fine. Keep up the good work." Carla headed to the back of the store. She felt her assessment of Hannah had been correct, and either she or Chuck would have been a good choice for cashier. She also thought Chuck was a good choice for stock and propane deliveries. She had noticed on his application that he had a Class B CDL driver's license. *Why didn't I think about him for the propane truck from the beginning?*

She heard the bell above the front door jingle.

"Hey, Quinn."

"Hey, Carla."

"Hello," Hannah said.

"Hey, I'm Quinn Isaacs. New here?"

"Yes, ma'am. I'm Hannah."

"Nice to meet you." She smiled at the young woman. "Just stopped to see if Joe's house is available Friday night."

"Coming to the jamboree?"

"Hope so."

"I'm pretty sure it is, but let's check with Joshua."

The two women walked to the back and reached the swinging doors just as Joshua opened them.

"I was just coming to tell you I'm headed out . . . Oh, hey, Quinn."

"Hey, Joshua. Won't take your time, just wondered if I could use Joe's house on Friday night."

"Of course. Happy to have someone in it."

"Please let me pay—"

"Nonsense," Carla said.

"We're happy to have someone in it from time to time."

"Thanks. I'll see you Friday." Quinn smiled.

"See you then," Joshua said, waving as she walked out the door. He looked at Carla. "You look lost in thought. Problem with her staying there?"

"No. Not at all. I was just thinking about our new hires. I think Hannah's going to work our great. I haven't had a chance to tell you

I called Chuck to offer him the position, and he told me he had received his clearance from the TSA and was finalizing his license endorsement for hazmat."

"That's great news. He doesn't *have* to have the hazmat endorsement, but I would have asked him to get it."

"Apparently, he's being trying to get it for a while. Seems the biggest delay is in getting TSA clearance. He can start next week. That work for you?"

"Sounds good to me. Speaking of propane deliveries, though, I need to make some and will be back around four."

"Be careful out there. Glad the roads are still dry."

"Me too. See you soon." He kissed her and headed towards the back door.

"Lock this door, please."

"Yes, boss." She winked at him and locked the door as he went out.

Sunset on the Gulf of Mexico

Chad squeezed Bella's hand when she splashed water up on his legs.

"Oh, you want to play games?" He started running—gently pulling her with him.

She dropped his hand and took off. "Last one to the house..."

"Decides how we spend the rest of the evening." He called after her as he laughed and slowed down.

She stopped and turned around. "Now, who's being playful?" This playful exchange had happened more than once up on her mountain. She turned and waited for him to reach her. She held her hand out.

He stepped up, took her hand, and pulled her into his arms. "I love you, Bella Anderson."

"I love you, too, Chad Oliver." She turned and looked out over the gulf. "I don't want to do my bad list and good list tonight."

He waited.

"I just want to tell you here, under these stars and over this vast body of water that I am the luckiest woman alive. Thank you for loving me, for sharing you family with me, and for keeping us all safe."

He shuddered. *You will never know how unworthy I feel of all of that.* "I think that's a good note on which to end. I will just add that I love you, love that you love my family, and promise that keeping all of you safe is something I will always try to do." He kissed her on the forehead. "Now, let's go have a drink on that porch and call it a day."

"Lead the way."

CHAPTER 15

*The morning stars still sing together, and the world, not yet half made,
becomes more beautiful every day.*

John Muir

In the Valley

Fall visitors, who came for the painted vista the colorful trees provided each autumn, were long gone from the valley and surrounding mountains. Sylvia was thankful winter visitors chose places like Gatlinburg where they could ski among the beauty of the Great Smokies. *That's one less thing to worry about right now.*

It was early Thursday morning as Fire Chief Mike Smallwood beamed at his wife across the breakfast table. "I'm proud of you, Sylvia. I hope you know that."

"The feeling is mutual."

"I was specifically referring to your work on identifying the likely incendiary nature of the fire on Bella's home in North Carolina."

"It was the only thing that made sense. Now we need to figure out who started it."

"Not your job." Mike watched to see how she would react.

"True, on the one hand . . ."

"But on the other hand we have five fingers?"

Sylvia nodded and wondered where he was going with this.

"Then tick them off for me."

She lifted her index finger. "One, Bella is a member of our community. Two, this may well be tied to the illegal activities of Zimmerman and the former DEA Assistant Director. Three, we figured out it was incendiary before the North Carolina local police did and we hadn't even seen the house." She started to list four, but he raised his hand.

"Got it. *You* figured out it was incendiary before you *knew* they had. Give them some credit. You would expect the same courtesy."

"You're right. That one wasn't fair."

"One of your great strengths has always been that you do not seek credit, and it may also be a blind spot you have about others." He paused a moment. "I'm not sure you realize how naturally you solve problems—it's a rare gift. You also have a deep and abiding love and loyalty to the people in these hills; all that makes you pretty amazing."

"And you're more than a little biased." She threw him a kiss across the table.

"Admittedly. I know you'll figure out the role of the sheriff's department in all of this. In the meantime, how's it feel to be in charge with the boss really out of town?"

"Strange. Even when he goes to meetings in Nashville, I have always known he was a phone call away and would come back here in a heartbeat if he was needed."

"And now?"

"I'm glad he has finally taken time off after all these years. I just want to do the best I can to keep things on an even keel and keep everyone going about their business as usual. I'm also glad we're beyond summer and leaf season."

"I'm sure there's nothing you can't handle. Chad Oliver would not have left you in charge if he thought otherwise. So, have fun because you won't get the pay raise." He picked up their plates and kissed the top of his wife's head. "Let's go stomp out crime and prevent fires. My work, unfortunately, picks up this time of year with faulty heating systems, untended fireplaces and candles . . . the usual."

Sylvia stepped to the sink where Mike was putting the dishes in the dishwasher. She put her arms around him. "Sometimes I forget what you go through. You keep your own counsel much better than I do."

He turned his head and kissed her. "You keep your own counsel just fine. Here's to another beautiful day in our special place in these mountains. See you tonight. Love you."

"Love you too. Have a safe day."

Sylvia pulled into the back lot of the sheriff's station. Even though it was very dark at 6:00 a.m. this time of year, she loved the solitude of this time of day and the clear, crisp sky above the mountains. She was stepping out of her SUV as Billy Williams pulled in.

"Morning, Sergeant."

"Morning, Detective. Sorry, I haven't asked recently—how's the arm doing?"

"Finer than dew on a summer garden, thanks. The physical therapist was pleased with my recovery, and after the last scan Doc Smith said I was, and I quote, 'fit as a fiddle.'"

"Guess it doesn't get any better than that. Glad you're doing well. Anything that needs to be addressed this morning?"

"Alexander is still in Knoxville working with the SBI team on the truck. I need to run a couple of things that came in from a local B and E on a vacant cabin. Neighbors saw a light in the cabin and knew the owners weren't in the area. Deputies caught the guys who did it. Just working through the jewelry we found on them."

"No injuries then?"

"None."

"Glad it was only property and not people. Let me know if you need anything."

"10-4! Have a good one!"

Sunrise on the Beach

It was 6:50 a.m. The sun glinted off the glassy water as the gentle swells in this part of the Gulf of Mexico lapped against the shore. Chad and Bella had been walking for more than thirty minutes, and they stopped for a moment to look back at the trail of footprints stretching behind them.

"I wonder if I could get used to being a beach bum?" Bella said.

"We could tempt fate."

Bella squeezed Chad's hand. "It's been a while since I've seen the sun so early in the morning. It's so different from the mountains where the first hints of light don't really arrive before eight and the full sun two hours later."

"Guess normal is whatever your day-to-day life is. Let's turn around and go eat breakfast at the café we passed earlier. Sign said they open at seven."

"Sounds like a plan."

They arrived just as the doors opened, and Chad chose a table in the back corner. He chuckled.

"What's funny?"

"Old habits die hard. I'm so used to sitting in the corner at The Corral, I just naturally gravitate to a corner. Would you like to sit someplace else?"

"I'm good." Bella looked up at the server. "Hot tea, please."

"Earl Grey or green?"

"Earl Grey is perfect."

"Sir?"

"Black coffee, thanks."

Their orders for breakfast taken, Chad reached across and took Bella's hands. "Thank you for coming away with me."

"My pleasure. And thank *you*. This is a lovely place, and it's nice to have time together without the other activities in our daily lives."

Tears sprang up in Chad's eyes. "My job, you mean."

"Chad, please don't apologize again for what you do. How many times do I need to tell you I fell in love with you, and I knew from the beginning what you do? If *you* are struggling with what you do, then let's talk about it." She slipped her foot out of her sandal and ran it up and down his bare leg.

His gray eyes softened and the tears retreated. "Well, it did get us out of the mountains for a few days."

"I told you last night that no matter how the destruction of my house turns out, it isn't on you. It's the responsibility of whoever did it. The same thing is true for the guy who shot at us."

"If I weren't the sheriff, it wouldn't have happened."

"You don't know that. On any day, at any moment, someone determined to alter someone else's life can act. And, albeit my experience is limited on out-of-the-ordinary events, I read enough to know that most of the time people do heinous acts with very little planning."

"Been reading criminal profiles, have you?" He tried to lighten the mood.

"Yes, as a matter of fact—especially when I was so certain I wanted to write a mystery novel."

"Wait. You don't want to write?" The stricken look on his face stunned her.

"Whoa, I didn't say—" she stopped as the server appeared and put their food on the table.

"Get ya'll anything at the moment?" They both shook their heads. "Okay, enjoy."

"I didn't say I didn't want to write. Let's just say I'm rethinking the novel. I'm pretty good at writing short stories, and I'm thoroughly enjoying my work with Chief Whitehorse on his stories. Maybe I'll stick with that for a while. I'm also thinking about holding writing retreats once Solasta Caban is finished. So, let's see what happens. For now, let's eat!"

As they were finishing their breakfasts, the conversation shifted to what they wanted to do and whether they wanted to stay longer.

"If it's all the same to you, and we can get a flight, I'd just as soon go home tomorrow. It'll be Friday night and there'll be a jamboree. I promised a young man who has shown a lot of interest in me that if it was held, I'd try to be there."

"That kid is at it again. Four-years-old or not, he better tread lightly." They both laughed. "I'll check with the airlines, and then we can do whatever we want to do until tomorrow."

"I was reading about the area, and one of the two almost perfectly round lakes in the world is in a place called DeFuniak Springs. There are some lovely Victorian Houses around the lake which makes it sound like a nice place to walk. Feel like taking an hour's drive?"

"Sounds perfect. We can probably find some place there to have a late lunch and then come back and watch the sunset on the beach."

"Perfect. I'm ready when you are."

Chad paid the bill, and they walked back to the house Nora had rented for them on the beach.

"Let me call the airlines, then we'll head out."

Bella sat down on the front porch facing the gulf. "I'll be right here."

Chad made an early reservation for Friday morning and sent a text to Sylvia to let her know they'd be home before mid-day. *Good job, Chad, you didn't call her.* He walked out on the porch and said, "Let's go for that drive."

Updates

"Sergeant Whitehorse speaking."

"Sylvia, Bill Michaels here. Have a bit of an update if you have time to talk."

"Absolutely. What's up?"

"Just heard from the detective in North Carolina. He's been with their SBI forensic folks, and it seems they have some potential evidence from the neighbors' cameras. They're doing a composite from three cameras that might give something a forensic artist can render to a reasonable likeness."

"How long will that take?"

"They're hoping to have something by tomorrow. Once they do, they'll verify with the neighbors to see if anyone can identify the person."

"Can you get a copy to me? It may be connected up here somehow, and we should have Dr. Anderson look at it too."

"As soon as I have it, you'll have it. Anything new on your end?"

"Had a message from the sheriff, and he'll be back mid-afternoon tomorrow."

"Does he *know* how to take a vacation?"

"It's been many years, so I suspect he's a bit rusty. But we'll take this break as a good sign. Thanks, Agent Michaels. Appreciate your help to get this solved."

"Let's get it done."

Sylvia leaned back in her chair and looked up at the ceiling. A few minutes later she picked up the phone and called Billy. "Got a minute?"

"Sure, be right there."

"I'll come to you."

"10-4."

She took another couple of minutes to process her thinking, then she refilled her coffee mug in the break room and headed to the lab. She scanned her card and walked in.

"What's up?"

"Ever think about how easily we only adopt the technology we can afford? Or whatever the state gives us as earmarked money to spend on what *they've* decided we need—like these ID scanners?"

"Think I'd be lying if I said I gave it much thought. I have no doubt you are far better informed on technology, as well as the funding matters, than I am."

She told him about the video footage being examined in the North Carolina SBI lab from the neighbors around Bella's home. "We don't have a lot of folks in these hills who have cameras, except in the gated communities."

"Whoa, Sarge, more and more folks are getting them. Mostly it's about the bears and deer. Folks are careless with their trash, and we've taken so much of their habitat that the critters are getting bolder and bolder. Folks don't like being surprised by a bear when they go outside on the porch."

"Fair enough."

"And speaking of wild bears and other things in the night, Elizabeth isolated the poison that was killing the wildlife near The Mountain Villages. Park rangers set up a night camera and caught the culprit; he's a resident of The Mountain Villages and he's under arrest."

"Good to know. Always happy when we wrap up a case. Now, I wanted to tell you what Agent Michaels told me, but I also want to ask if you think we do enough to help our deputies understand how technology is being used today? It can be their ally and their enemy."

"Seems to me it's been a while since we did any training on the effects of phones and other recording devices at crime scenes. Guess we've not encountered as much as city folk do."

Sylvia leaned against the lab table. "And we didn't use to have drugs running through here, formalized prostitution, and someone trying to shoot the sheriff."

"Fair enough. I say let's add it to the next leadership team agenda."

"Good idea." She stood up straight and turned for the door.

"Got a minute?" Billy spoke slowly.

"Sure." She turned back to him.

"What do you think about me looking into what we'd need in order to do our own video analysis? The SBI and FBI have the heavy-duty stuff, so the cost for general equipment is probably not as much as we might think."

"Good idea, Billy. Look into it. I suspect Alexander has some thoughts on it too."

"No doubt. Speaking of which, they've cataloged all of Harris' guns and ammunition. Our very own Elizabeth Alexander was feeling pretty good about the work. She expects reports to be finished up today, and she'll be back tomorrow."

"Think we'll lose her to the SBI or FBI?"

"If you had asked me that several months ago, I'd have said, 'For sure.' Now, I'm not as convinced. She's had a taste of the big leagues, and I think she might like running her own show here. I think if she can follow up on cases with the SBI like she's done with the guys who ran me off the road and this case, she might find she can have the best of both worlds."

Sylvia nodded. "Hadn't considered that. Never want to stand in any-one's way, but I like the team we have here in our little corner of the world."

"Me too, Sylvia, me too."

Observations

Quinn was replaying the events of Wednesday afternoon. Her mind switched from thinking about Billy to the situation in the office. It was foremost in her mind when she arrived at the IEA offices Thursday morning. She was totally absorbed in replaying the exchange.

"Afternoon, Agent Isaacs." Okay, her normal perfunctory greeting.

"Good afternoon to you. Lovely day in Round City." I've been in this office almost ten years and the greeting has rarely changed.

"If you say so." Might as well have been a recording. The answer was always as routine as her greeting. Why do so many people stay in a job they seem to hate. I ignored the comment as usual, didn't I?

This morning, it was the early morning phone call gnawing at her. She replayed the conversation in her head.

"Isaacs here."

"Oh, didn't expect to catch you in." The young agent had sounded startled. Why?

"How may I help you, Agent?"

"Uh, well. I was just going to leave you a message."

"And that would be?"

Why did he blurt out? "The director . . . oh, sorry, have to take this other call." *He hung up on me. HE HUNG UP ON ME!*

She stopped on the steps into the IEA offices. *That's the curious part. I doubt he had another call. Why did he hang up and never call back?*

She devised a plan for what she would do if she ran into the agent, even if he was with the director. She unlocked the front door since the receptionist wasn't due in until eight. The space seemed eerily quiet. *Director must be out of town; his blinds aren't drawn yet.* Quinn continued towards her office and was about to turn the corner when she heard the click on the door to the storeroom and it opened towards her.

Then she heard the director's voice. "Of course I love you. Now, wait a few minutes and then come out. No one here yet to worry about."

She decided it would be more awkward to turn and go back, so she tried to keep walking. However, she couldn't help hearing a loud whisper: "I love you too." She didn't know who it was—and she didn't care.

The director turned and almost knocked her down. They were face to face. "Oh," he looked over her shoulder. "Good morning, Quinn." He studied her face. "You're in early."

"Morning, sir. Have some work to catch up on after all the events of the past week." She stepped around him as he closed the door. "Have a nice day, sir."

"You too, *Quinn*." She thought his voice was louder than necessary.

She unlocked her office and shut the door. She took several deep breaths and let them out slowly. She thought she had brought herself under control, but she almost jumped out of her skin when her mobile phone rang.

"Morning, Agent Isaacs. This is your friendly detective from the valley."

She took a deep breath. "Morning to you, Detective." She had to check whether he had called her on her personal mobile or secure mobile phone; she hadn't even looked. It was her personal phone. "As much as I appreciate the call, unless it's urgent, may I call you back this afternoon?"

"Sure. Just wanted to remind you I'm here if you need a friend."

"Thanks. I do. I mean, I do know that you told me that. I'll talk to you later. Have a nice day."

"10-4."

She realized her hands were shaking. She closed her eyes trying to sort out her reaction. *Would I have been startled if I had run into any-one because the closet door opened in my face? Yes. I've always hated that I had to turn that corner and risk running into the door, much less some-one coming out of the storeroom. Awkward. Or was it the fact that it was the director, even if I hadn't heard what he said? Am I upset that he spoke endearments at work? Not particularly. After all, Billy and I stepped into a storeroom at the sheriff's office.* She chuckled, realizing small store-rooms were the least likely places to have cameras, even in a law en-forcement agency. She tried to let go of the encounter. *Am I upset that this was the director? No. He's single and free to do what he wants. Then what's the problem?*

She decided to concentrate on her normal routine: she turned on her computer and desk lamp, then put on her music playlist. She opened the Zimmerman file and started reading the immigration-related violations on which he was being held. She knew focus would clear her head. She'd figure out what bothered her in due course.

The Sun Sets

Back from their drive, Chad poured the Kim Crawford Sauvignon Blanc into a glass and took it with his Fat Tire Ale out to the porch where Bella was already sitting in the porch swing with her feet up on the railing. She had tried to talk him out of getting her wine when they stopped in a shop in DeFuniak Springs, but she agreed when she saw they had the 250 ml cans.

"Glad I won't be wasting good wine."

"We could have stayed a few more days for you to drink the standard bottle."

"And disappoint a four-year-old?"

"Absolutely not. I'm even learning to tame my jealous streak when it comes to him being in love with you."

"That shows a surprising maturity for a grandfather."

Chad laughed. He held up his beer bottle and said, "Here's to us and four-year-old grandsons."

"And two-year-old granddaughters and daughters and sons-in-law." She looked at him. "That sounds nice, doesn't it? Maybe *I* have a little jealous streak—about your family."

"No need. I know how to make them yours officially." He put his arm around her.

Bella did not turn and look at him; she stared out to the fading sunset.

He didn't say anymore.

"I've been thinking about Joshua and Carla. They're so happy together, and Joshua is going to be a father. I'm thrilled for them. We never talked about the fact that Matt and I didn't have children and he and Jan didn't have children." She continued to stare out to sea. "I prayed Carla would never ask me about children. I could *not* have told her what it was like to have two miscarriages."

Chad stopped rocking. He turned, pulled her to him, and held her. Being quiet had always been one of his strong suits.

Tears ran down her cheeks. "There is nothing I would like more than a family." She looked up at him; her deep brown eyes showed the pain of many losses. "I've probably been as impulsive as I can be for a while just coming here. Will you wait for me?"

He kissed her tears and then her lips. "Forever."

Get the Picture

"Burton here," the Statesboro detective answered the phone on his desk. He knew the number was from the North Carolina SBI.

"Detective, our lab tech has that video composite ready for you. Our forensic artist is working on it, but you said you want your gal to do a sketch too. Did I understand that right?"

"I do. Can you send it to me?"

"Should already be in your secure folder. Wanted you to open it so I can point something out."

"Give me a minute." Burton went through the steps for entering the secure electronic folder and saw the file from the forensic tech. "Opening it now."

"If your artist needs a better resolution than she can get on your system, she's welcome to come over to our lab."

"Thanks. I'll let her know. Now, what do you want to point out to me?"

"Look at the fourth image."

"Okay. Doesn't look that much different to me."

"Exactly. You'll lose clarity, but if you zoom in and look at the left side of the neck below the ear—"

"Son of a—"

"Right!"

"Is that part of a ponytail?"

"Probably. And do you see anything else?"

"Some kind of birth mark?"

"Close." The forensic tech told him what he thought it was. "Let's see what the artists come up with."

"Stay in touch. And thanks. I'll call you as soon as she finishes her sketches."

"10-4."

Burton hung up the phone and looked at the picture again. He had to make sure not to influence the artist. He dialed her number.

CHAPTER 16

There is the world of the flesh and there is the spirit world. When the flesh is gone, the spirit forever remains. Their voices speak to those who know how to listen. Wisdom is born in the heart, and then spoken.

Wolf Clan Song

A Journey Begins with a Single Step

Bella and Chad started Friday morning at sunrise with a walk on the beach, sandals in hand, as they dug their toes into the warm sand.

Chad lightly squeezed her hand. "Sam would be proud of us for taking off our shoes and truly connecting with the earth."

"I think Chief Whitehorse would approve too." Bella hoped to have a long conversation with the chief about spiritual connections to the earth the next time they got together.

"Are you enjoying working with the chief?"

"Oh, Chad . . . it is an *honor* for me. He is one of the wisest men I've ever met."

"He is that. I have come to appreciate the sparseness of his words when dispensing that wisdom. It feels to me that he doesn't tell you *what to do,* rather his words guide you to figuring out for yourself what you *need* to do. That's a gift."

"I agree. I always thought we should teach students how to take the wisdom of the ages and apply it in their own lives. For example, the verse from Ephesians that says to be truly humble and gentle. Why don't we teach students to share what that would look like in their lives?"

"I don't know. Why don't we, as adults, talk about those things and ask ourselves those questions?"

"Maybe because we weren't taught *how* to apply the wisdom: we were genrally just told to 'do it.'"

Chad swung their arms high in the air. "Bella Anderson, I love you more than air, but I have to say this is pretty heady stuff for this hour of the morning."

"Maybe it's the best time—clear head, rested body, and energized soul walking along the shores of one of God's great creations."

"Amen." Her hand firmly in his, they walked back towards the rental house. "Do you want to eat before or after we dress for the cold weather of our mountains?"

"We need to leave by eight, right?"

"Should give us plenty of time to return the rental car and check in. Short flight and we'll be in Knoxville by 10:30."

"Then let's eat first and enjoy the comfort of shorts and sandals a little while longer."

"I like that idea. Same place or somewhere new?"

"Oh, let's live dangerously and try something else. Much as I love The Corral, we don't have other choices at home."

He smiled when she said "at home." *I doubt if she expected the journey to making the mountains her home would happen quite the way it has.*

The Valley Store

Joshua was surprised to hear a knock on the front door of the store at 7:00 a.m. He saw Hannah standing there. "Morning, Hannah, you're here early."

"Miss Carla told me she wouldn't be in today, so I didn't know if you needed help. I was up and thought I'd spend some time studying the aisles so I could be more helpful to customers." She saw his eyes grow wide. "You don't have to pay me for the half hour. It's okay." She smiled at him as she pulled off her coat and hung it on the hook under the loft office.

"Of course we'll pay you. I'm thrilled you want to know the products and location well enough to help the customers. I'm sure it will help me too. You might see ways we can display something better or put some items together in a way I've never thought about. Happy to have you."

"Thanks, Mr. Joshua."

He saw her take a small notebook and a pencil from her pocket and start down the produce aisle. *Looks like we made a good choice, Carla. Hope she likes working here.* He turned when he heard the silver bell above the door jingle and saw Billy Williams.

"Surprised the door was open. I was going to knock."

"Shady character though you are, I would have let you in." Joshua slapped Billy on the back. "What's up? Need something before work or just here to get the free coffee?"

"Free coffee? Where? When did you start that?"

Joshua pointed to the counter, pleased he had put the coffee on first thing after getting the cash drawers ready. "Chad's idea. Carla's execution."

"Does it mean I have to buy something?"

"Read the box, Billy."

"Oh, great idea. I suspect most of our folks will gladly contribute to the scholarship fund and hopefully feel obliged to buy something. So that works for you and our community. Smart move." Billy put a ten dollar bill in the box.

"Thanks."

"How do you like serving as a commissioner? Been to enough meetings yet to give up politics?"

"Actually, I'm learning . . ." Joshua hesitated. "Well, maybe learning more than I ever wanted to know about our community and about the rules and regulations that get pushed down from Washington and Nashville. Some of them are good for us, but some are getting a little too much like Big Brother."

Billy nodded.

"The ones that get my dander up the most seem to come from state legislators telling us what to do, and then telling the world that Washington can't tell them what to do."

"I hear you. Well, glad you agreed to serve—hope you'll stand for election. We need you."

"Whoa, not so sure about that. Don't go spreading those rumors."

Billy laughed. "No problem. No problem."

He took his cup of coffee and headed for the aisle with the protein bars. He almost tripped over Hannah, who was bent over looking at the bottom shelf. "Oh, hey, Jeanne."

She looked up. "No, sir. I'm Hannah. Jeanne's my oldest sister."

"You sure are the spitting image of her."

"Guess most folks think so with our red hair. You're the detective that went to school with Jeanne, right?"

"I am." He extended his hand. "Billy Williams. Please tell Jeanne I said, 'hey.'"

"Sure will." She shook his hand. "May I help you find something?"

"You working here?"

"Yes, sir. Just started."

"Well, good for you."

He pointed down the aisle. "Need to fill up my protein bar stash."

"Yes, sir, they're just halfway down the other side of the aisle."

Joshua had been listening and he beamed.

"Detective Williams, I'll check you out whenever you're ready." Hannah started towards the front.

"Be right there."

Can You Control Pixels?

"Did you work through the night?" Detective Burton stood up as the forensic artist for the Statesboro police entered his office.

She stifled a yawn. "Most of it."

"Are you going to keep me waiting?"

"First, I want to explain to you that even with the fancy footwork, well, fingers on a keyboard at the SBI, there's only so much you can do with a composite from even high-quality home cameras. When you try to get down to facial recognition from someone walking on a street in uncontrolled light . . ."

She paused for a breath. Burton was anxious to see the picture she had drawn but also appreciated that she spent a lot of time by herself—besides he always learned something from her.

". . . you aren't going to have great resolution," she continued. "Right now, you can't add pixels to the image, although someday someone will probably figure out how to do that too."

"I know you've told me this before . . . what are pixels?"

"They're the tiny dots that make up an image on a photo or a computer screen."

"Right, got it. The numeral one on a Word document is made up of thousands of tiny dots."

"You *do* remember. Okay, so you can't add any more dots when you have a low-resolution picture to make it more distinct. With a high-resolution photo . . . meaning what?"

"Lots of pixels." He smiled.

"A-plus. With lots of pixels, you can reduce or enhance a photo and not lose clarity. So, here's my best shot."

Burton always flinched when she said that. She didn't work in the part of the police department where "my best shot" meant hitting a bull's eye on a target or an out-of-control junkie with a gun. He waited.

She opened her portfolio.

He gasped. "Don't get insulted. Promise?"

"Promise." She held up crossed fingers.

"How likely is this drawing accurate?"

"I'd go with seventy-five to eighty-five percent."

Burton stared at the picture. The woman in the picture appeared to be in her late twenties or early thirties. She had light hair, and the artist purposely made the appearance of the eye color light but indistinct. He knew the drawings were charcoal or pen so as not to prejudice those who viewed it by assuming the suspect was blue-eyed or blonde as opposed to having light brown hair and hazel eyes. He tried not to rush to see if there was anything drawn on the neck, but he couldn't help himself. He pulled out his chair and sat.

"Something wrong, Burton?"

"Why aren't you out painting church ceilings or fine art for castles? How do you do this?"

"Very carefully, sir. Oh, and as to your question, no matter how good you are, the chances of being noticed are slim to none. I like this work. It pays the bills, and, who knows, maybe the stuff I dabble with at home in my studio will sell some day."

"I'll buy a painting from you sight unseen."

"Flattery will work again when you need me to work all night."

"Again, no insult intended, but you're sure it's a woman?"

"She's very fit and the bone structure is well defined, relatively speaking. *Could* it be a male? Yes. We only provide you with faces. The video had the whole person. Based on the rest of the body I saw; it's a woman."

"Are you confident enough for me to share this with the SBI?"

She handed him a thumb drive. "Here are the high resolution . . ."

She raised her eyebrows and looked at him like a stern teacher.

"Lots of pixels."

"Correct. Yes, high resolution digital photographs. Send away. And, if you're finished with me, I'm going home to bed or, who knows, to paint the Sistine Chapel."

"There'll be a note in your file on this one. Great work. Thanks again."

"Later, Detective." She gave a slight wave as she left his office.

The detective sat and stared. He was not so much taken with the image of the young woman as the tattoo on her neck.

Homeward Bound

"For all the flights I've had go awry in my travels, I'm grateful both of ours were perfect. We're even back in Knoxville early which almost never happens."

"Haven't flown a lot myself. I've been to a few meetings in D.C., but this has certainly made me think about the possibilities. I think we should plan a real trip."

"Might just do that if you're willing to go somewhere warm when the ice is headed our way."

"In a heartbeat. I've lost more leave in my life than I've taken. You think about where you'd like to go and when—and we'll make it happen."

She leaned across the console in his Jeep and kissed him on the cheek.

"No fair distracting the driver." He reached over and took her hand.

"I think you're mature enough to handle it—and maybe even appreciate it."

He laughed loudly.

"What's so funny?"

"I have thought so many times how naïve and stupid I was when I dated Mary in my teens. Everyone else had the wedding set before I even asked her."

"Well, I think teenage love and hormones don't often connect with the brain." She kept watching him as he focused on the road.

"True for most, I think. Okay if I change the subject?"

"If you can't stand the heat, get out of the kitchen, is it?"

"I can talk with you now, or anytime, about my bad decisions as a teen based on whatever may have been the cause, but I don't think you really want to hear that right now. So, let's talk about whether you need or want to go to Drellag Caban on our way into the valley."

She thought for a few seconds. "I think that's a good idea. I can get my Jeep and touch base with Arthur. If it's okay with you, I'll stay in the valley tonight."

"You can stay as long as you like—forever. At some point I have to make a decision about going back to work. We can talk about that too. Okay?"

"Sure. I just assumed you'd go back when we get home."

"No plans. *We'll* talk about it and decide together. Want me to stop and get Wizard?"

"Oh, that would be great. I'll talk with Arthur. I have some food in the fridge that I'll bring down, and we can make supper."

"Sounds like a deal. As much as I appreciate The Corral, it will be nice to have a home-cooked meal on the back of the rich food we had at supper last night."

"Well," she said in her best southern drawl. "Maybe, maybe not. Unless you're the cook, of course."

"We'll figure out something, I'm sure." He turned off the highway onto Route 54.

"Chad, could we stop at the lookout?"

"Absolutely. What are you thinking?"

"I'm thinking I want to take in the valley and the hills with a new lens now that this is my *only* home."

"I love the view too." He smiled when she reached over and inserted a disc into the CD player of Nora singing. He drove on in silence as Bella hummed along. They made the turn off the highway and climbed up the hill to the lookout. Chad parked the SUV and opened the passenger door; Bella's gaze was already distracted by the view below them.

As they settled on one of the benches, Bella's gaze soaked in the scene: the Valley Store, The Corral, the elementary school, the middle-high school, the library, and the hospital. "I can even see the sheriff's station." She pointed.

"Pretty compact community, aren't we?"

"I've always been drawn to this place as my ancestral home, and I was seriously considering whether I could live up here full time." She looked over at him. "Although I'm not a fatalist, I do believe things happen for a reason, even when we can't understand it at the time. With the work on my property, I might have been close to deciding to stay …"

His mouth was downturned and his eyes begging.

"Now, that's a hangdog look if I ever saw one. Here, let me throw you a bone."

Chad pulled his arms up in front of him like a dog and started panting with his tongue out.

She playfully tapped his arm. "Enough already. If you had waited a minute, I was going to say falling in love with you was a major part of my thinking about staying."

He threw his arms around her and kissed her deeply. "Good. I was afraid I'd have to retire and move to Statesville." He stopped. He watched for her reaction. "Sorry, that was really thoughtless."

"No, it was a normal, everyday response. We just haven't had a normal, everyday week." She kissed him. "Thanks for stopping here. I just wanted to really take in home." She stood and reached for his hand. They walked back to his SUV their hands swinging in the air.

Pictures

Detective Burton decided to drive to the regional SBI offices to deliver the thumb drive with the drawings by the Statesville Police forensic artist. A disembodied voice came over the speaker at the locked door where he presented his credentials.

"Yes, he's expecting me." Twenty seconds later the door latch unlocked. He walked in.

"You know where to go? Down one flight and to the back."

"I do, thanks."

He was met at the lab door by the forensic tech. "Sorry I couldn't come up and meet you. I had something running on a machine that needed to be removed as soon as it stopped."

"Take your time."

"No, I'm good. What 'cha got?"

"I have a thumb drive for you to download, but I wanted us to put the drawings by your artist and our artist side by side and look at them together at the same time."

"Sure. Sounds like fun. Let's go over to my worktable." The forensic tech picked up a portfolio from his desk and put it on the table.

Detective Burton set his down far enough away for the flap of the SBI portfolio to open and not cover the other drawing. "Shall we do the countdown to launch?"

"Sure, three … two … one …. open."

Each flipped back their respective portfolio covers. They stared.

"Son of a gun! Both of them saw the critter on her neck that I did."

"Now we just have to hope it's a permanent tattoo and not one of those you can rub on. I called Bill Michaels, the FBI agent, and he would like to take a copy to the sheriff's department up in the mountains and have the homeowner look at it before we put it out."

"Hey, putting it out is up to you. We just do the work. You're in charge of it."

"As a courtesy, I'll touch base with your agent who worked with us, but I agree with the FBI agent. Let's see the reaction of the homeowner first."

"Are you running it through facial recognition software in the meantime?"

"Haven't yet, but it will run through your database anyway. Your system is more complete and faster than ours."

"We run most of the big cases. I'll get started on it. I'll let you know if we get a hit. Someday, with all this artificial intelligence, you won't have to have been arrested to be in our database."

"Well, we could spend hours debating the wisdom of everyone on the planet being identifiable. Pretty much my experience after twenty-five years on the force is that our view of humanity gets distorted when all you do is chase criminals—everybody starts to look like one."

"I hear you. I'll let you know if we get a hit. In the meantime, let's get that FBI agent on this."

"He's already enroute to the valley in the mountains where the homeowner is. It's apparently not very far from Knoxville as the crow flies, but mountain roads take about eighty minutes he said. He'll call me and I'll send him the image. I'll let you know if we learn anything."

"10-4!" A loud beeping sound caused the forensic tech to turn his head. "Duty calls. Machines don't wait. Catch you later."

"Thanks for your help." Burton waved as he left.

Detective Burton had already calculated that given his twenty-minute drive each way and the time with the tech, he'd be back at his computer about the time the FBI agent got from Knoxville to the sheriff's office in the Valley.

CHAPTER 17

*Great Mystery, Teach me how to trust my heart, my mind, my intuition,
my inner knowing, the senses of my body, the blessings of my spirit.
Teach me to trust these things so that I may enter my Sacred Space
and love beyond my fear, and thus walk in balance with the
passing of each glorious sun.*

Lakota Prayer

Home

Chad pulled up to the crest in the road to Drellag Caban and stopped. They both stared at the natural funnel formed by the new cabin and the shed that drew the eye out to the hills beyond.

"Oh, Chad. Having the outside of Solasta Caban finished and the sun at this angle, I feel like I can see forever." She looked across Chad and out the window, trying to mark the location where they stopped so she could recreate this exact image next time she came up the road.

"The first time I saw this view, I marveled at the serenity of it." He turned to look at her. "When you started Solasta Caban, I wondered if it would ruin the view. Now I think it has enhanced it. It brings the settling of humans on this land into alignment with the beauty of the creation of it."

Bella leaned over and kissed him. "Do you know when I first started to fall in love with you?"

"Do tell."

"You came up here after the ATV wrecks, and I was eating my peanut butter sandwich while leaning on the shed. You commented about the 'painter's palette of color' I would have here in the autumn."

"So, I impressed the professor with my alliteration?"

She laughed. "Maybe a little. More so, though, you impressed me with the care you have for your community, for your staff, and for our land. Those things matter to me."

"And you, lovely lady," he waited a second, "had me when you called me out for talking about what was happening on your land with Joshua and excluding you. I knew then you were your own person. I just hope Nora never finds out I did that—she'd thrash me worse than you did."

"I love you, Chad. I love your sweet family, and I know your daughter is the strong woman she is because of you."

He stroked her cheek with his finger. "I love this mutual admiration society we have going here." He leaned in and kissed her. "By the way, I can see your idea for the mural. It will be perfect." He put the Jeep in gear.

Bella gently squeezed his arm. "Thanks. I'm glad you like it."

Arthur Gillett waved when he saw them. Chad pulled up close to him and they got out.

"Hey, Arthur."

"Greetings, folks."

"Arthur," Bella said, hurrying around the SUV. "Everything looks amazing. I love the Solasta Caban sign. It's perfect." She turned and looked towards the new connecting walk and dog run between Drellag Caban and the shed. She started walking towards it.

The two men joined her.

Arthur pointed to the bump out they had made for Wizard to relieve himself. "The low-wattage heat installed in the concrete works perfectly. The solar panel on the roof of the shed should generate enough electricity to run it and keep you from slipping on ice going out to the shed or for Wizard to his own little corner." Chad was nodding his head. "Arthur, your design turned out great. You can make a fortune with it, especially in those fancy gated communities along the highway." He looked at Bella. "No offense."

"None taken. Happy to be the prototype."

"Miss Bella," Arthur said, "I'm going to ask you to wait until at least tomorrow before going in Solasta Cabin. We put the final coat of polyurethane on the floors yesterday morning. Even with some heat on, it needs a little longer to cure this time of year."

"I'm just picking up a few things. Are you going to the jamboree?"

"Yes, ma'am. Plan to be there with my family."

"Great. I'd love to meet them."

"Sure thing. I'll make it happen."

"Thanks for your fine work, Arthur. You've been a blessing to me." Bella shook his hand.

Chad nodded to Arthur.

"Pleasure's mine, ma'am. My crew appreciates the work this time of year too. Well, if you don't have any questions, I'll let you get on with your day."

Bella headed towards the cabin.

"Thanks for taking good care of this," Chad said as he extended his hand to shake with Arthur.

"Yes, sir." Arthur heard Bella shut the screen door. "Chad, hope I'm not out of line here, but I've known Miss Bella for about ten years now, back from when we repaired and made Drellag Caban a four-season cabin." He hesitated. "Well, I've always thought highly of both of you, and I just wish you both lots of happiness."

Chad slapped him on the back. "Bella's brought a great happiness into my life. Thanks for the good wishes."

Arthur turned and headed to help his crew clean up debris outside the new cabin.

"Hey!" Chad stepped into Drellag Caban.

Bella stepped out of the bedroom. "Would you please check the messages?"

Chad had just seen the blinking light. He turned down the volume on the answering machine; he wished he had thought to turn off completely. There was only one message and it was from his grandson. He rewound it and called Bella to the kitchen.

"Listen to this." He saw the worry on her face. "No reporters." He pushed the "play" button.

"Hey, Miss Bella. Mommy said I could leave a message on your machine so you would smile when you came home. We miss you. Bye now."

"Oh, sweet little Mac." The smile spread across her face. She kissed Chad. "Thanks."

"Thank Mac… and Nora."

"I will."

"Give me your keys and I'll make sure the Jeep is running."

"They're in my purse on the counter."

"Anything in there that will bite me?"

She glared at him. "Only me if you don't stop acting like a—"

"Man?"

"No! An idiot." She reached in the outer pocket of her purse and threw him the keys.

"Touché!"

"Next time it will be swords at dawn." She moved her hand in a zig-zag pattern.

"I'm headed out to check the Jeep before I fall further behind your quick wit."

She laughed and shooed him out the door.

After Chad was satisfied that there were no problems with the car, he bounded back into the kitchen. "Bella, the Jeep started right up and seems good to go." He began to walk towards the bedroom then stopped. He heard muffled crying.

"I'm here." She stood and walked to the door of the second bedroom. She held the picture of her and Matt on their 25th wedding anniversary. "It's stupid," she said.

He held out his arms, not sure whether to go to her or just be there. She walked into them, the picture frame between them. "Nothing's stupid," he whispered to her. "You've had a huge shock and another big loss. I suspect you hadn't told Matt yet."

She stepped back and looked up at him. "No. No, I hadn't. Do you think I'm crazy?"

"No. I think I'm envious."

"What?"

"Until I met you, I have never known what it is to love a mate so deeply that you could find comfort in sharing. I wish I could have known Matt. Would it help you to know in this moment that just as you must feel some conflict in loving him and loving me, I feel some guilt in taking you from him—emotionally?"

She hugged him tightly. She kissed him and laid her head on his chest. She started humming a song then sang the words.

"What's that from? I can't remember."

"*Sound of Music*. It's one of my all-time favorite movies."

"Then we'll have to watch it together. I saw it once with Nora. She'd probably enjoy seeing it with us."

"I'd like that. Thanks for saving me from myself. Now, how about you go get Wizard, and I'll be down shortly? I'll meet you at your place."

"You sure? I can put your things in my Jeep and have them all put away by the time you go get Wizard. He'll be happy to see you. I think Doc Jim will be too."

"Thanks." She smiled and kissed him. "I *would* like to thank Doc Jim. If you'd get the cooler out of the shed, I'll get the food out of the fridge."

"Done." He took the key off the hook by the kitchen door and headed out.

That Nagging Feeling

Quinn had been working all morning on any clues that could lead to who was responsible for hiring the shooter. She decided to take a break and go home and get some lunch. She liked puzzles, especially when they were on an active case—too much of the job was reviewing old files for some missed clue. She stood up and realized she was still skittish about going out in the hall after her encounter with the director. *With my coat on, I can move with purpose right out of the building.* She turned off her desk lamp, sent a pink note to the receptionist saying she'd be back at two, and headed for the front door. She almost made it.

"Agent Isaacs." She was surprised to hear the receptionist speak to her on her way out.

"Yes."

"Oh, never mind. I see now this question is for the new agent. Sharp young man, isn't he?"

"Then I'm sure he'd rather you not deliver it to me." She kept walking. Quinn made a beeline for her SUV. *We've been in this office for ten years together. You have never made a comment like that. Is the young agent kissing up to you, too?* She slammed her door so hard without paying attention she could have caught her foot in it—she didn't like being distracted. She pushed the phone button on her steering wheel and told the insipid voice to call Billy.

Billy said, "I like early afternoon. The sun is shining ... Oh, hey! Were you calling me?"

Quinn smiled. One of the things she liked about Detective Billy Williams of the Valley Sheriff's office was his sense of humor. "Psychic, are you?"

"Depends. What do you need to know?"

"Did you *know* when you answered that I needed a tension breaker?"

"Goes with the job, don't you think? I manage to get in trouble with the sheriff from time to time because I'm too glib, but he does cut me slack because he knows it's about tension on the job." *Wonder if he knows I know he cuts me slack? Hmmm . . .*

"Good boss you've got there."

"What? Yeah, amen to that. Where are you?"

"Headed to get some lunch. Where are you?"

"Well, as luck would have it, I'm off today. So, I'm in Round City doing a little shopping that I can't do in our fair valley."

"Great. Time to meet me at my place for lunch?"

"Sure."

"See you soon." She disconnected the call.

She jumped when her phone rang. When she saw it was Billy, her voice became contrite. "Guess it would help if I gave you my address?"

"I have my ways but, at this moment, it would be more expedient."

She gave the address.

"Be there shortly. *Now* you can hang up." He laughed and entered the details into his GPS.

Billy pulled in just as Quinn got out of her SUV.

"Where were you?"

"Actually, just down the street and around the corner. I had to drop off some papers at the funeral home."

She cocked her head. "The funeral . . . never mind, come in." She unlocked the door and stood back for him to enter.

He gave a low whistle. He'd been surprised when he pulled up at the white brick home. The generous gardens were flanked by evergreens and deciduous trees that fanned out to welcome visitors to the screened arches across the front porch. He imagined the seating area was lovely in warmer weather. It was at least a double lot and the front looked out onto a park across the street. *Don't know what I would have pictured as her home, but not this.*

"Nice place."

"Thanks. I call it home." She threw her coat on a chair and walked through to the kitchen. "Come on back."

He walked through the dining room into the kitchen, which opened onto a large great room with a fireplace. "Lived here long?"

"My mother's mother gave it to me when I managed to stay in Tennessee with my job. She was so afraid I'd be sent to what she always referred to as 'that awful city, D.C.,' that she bought me a house. Sadly, she passed away a year after I moved in. She never got to see the finished product."

"Well, I'm guessing she'd be very proud. It's lovely."

"Thanks, kind sir." She looked at him, stopped herself from kissing him, and said, "Ham sandwiches work?"

"Any day of the week. How may I help?"

"Seriously? Mr. I-Can-Open-a-Can is offering to help?"

"I didn't offer to cook. I can get the plates without breaking them and fill glasses with ice and water or tea. Heck, I've even been known to occasionally make a half-decent cup of coffee."

"That one." She pointed to the coffee machine.

He looked at the modern coffee maker with the coffee premeasured in small cups. "Yeah, well, about that ... didn't you notice I have an old-fashioned drip coffee maker?"

She leaned against the counter and looked at him for a moment before moving over to kiss him.

He responded.

She pulled back and said, "My, my, a Neanderthal. And here I thought they were extinct." She winked at him. "Need to fix the sandwiches."

"How about water?"

"There's tea in the fridge. No southerner has ever turned down a glass of iced tea even in the dead of winter."

"On it!" He started opening kitchen cabinets. He had never seen such fine crystal and china except in a store. His own family was middle class, but his parents had been happy with simple cabin living.

"Don't be shocked. I didn't buy them. They are inherited from my mother's family, and what wasn't inherited she fleshed out. It's her thing. I humor her. She's a great mother and a very elegant lady. The things I bought are here." She pointed to another cabinet. "Mother knows to save herself the anguish of opening it."

He opened the cabinet and found stoneware in teal and beige. He liked the dishes. The hobnail glasses looked like the ones he grew up with. He took out two. "No offense meant here, but I think my mom got these same glasses from my grandmother. I think she got them with some kind of stamps she saved."

"Probably did. They were called "S & H" green stamps. I'd save those stamps if they were still giving them—*My* mother—not so much. Okay, let's eat."

Billy looked at the plate. "Dill?"

"Billy Williams, are you *from* these mountains? There are two kinds of pickles: dill and everything else. Okay, I know some folks eat bread and butter pickles. Got something against dill pickles?"

"You've made my day."

"Long been my goal." Her sarcasm was tempered with a smile.

They sat at a table overlooking the back yard. "You could forget you lived in town here. The backyard is a paradise."

"Thanks, Billy. I needed to be reminded I have this place because of my grandmother. I sure wouldn't be here on a federal government salary. Unfortunately, I'm guilty of taking it for granted. Nice to have fresh eyes see it. So, what great shopping brings you to our fair town?"

"I needed a couple of blades for my lathe, and I don't care for the ones I can order online. There's a guy here who makes the blades and the hand tools. It's fun to visit with him."

"Wait a minute. You have a lathe?"

"I do."

"Where?"

"In my walkout basement. My cabin sits on a block foundation with a walkout basement. I designed it to have a place to do woodworking."

"Williams, you've been holding out on me."

"I don't think we've had a lot of time to talk about anything other than crime and, oh yeah, nursing me back to health—which I appreciate." He grinned at her.

She nodded her head. "You were pretty high on my list of cool guys, but you just vaulted over the top with that little bit of news."

"Done any woodworking?"

"None. Want to teach me?"

"Anytime." He looked deep into her hazel eyes. "Now, quit procrastinating. What's going on? There's something bugging you and I don't think it's a case."

She pushed her chair back from the table. "What clues do you have?"

"Rushed off yesterday muttering about a young agent and the director, tripped over your tongue today about needing a friend, need more?"

"Attentive, aren't you?"

"Detective. Remember?"

"Fair enough. I surrender." She told him about this morning's incident on top of the phone calls from the new agent.

"You're a senior agent, I assume. Why not just ask him what his game is?"

"The direct approach. I like that. But no."

"Why not?"

"I have a strong feeling that there's something more than work between the young agent and the director."

"Dating?"

"Nah. If it was that, I'd think the director was stupid for dating someone he supervises, but even in the federal government no one is going to get too bent out of shape over a gay couple. Being a supervisor, that's different. But it just doesn't feel like that's what it is. It's more than buttering up the boss. Heck, it's more than deferential. It's like awe ... or a hero worship kind of thing."

Billy waited to see what else she'd say.

She started nodding her head. "Yeah, that's it. It's hero worship." She sat back.

"Nothing wrong with hero worship. Is it interfering in the job?" Billy watched her face.

"Maybe not. May just be the coincidence of his newness in the IEA and his adulation of the director."

"Does that help? I mean, figuring out that you have a young agent caught up in hero worship?"

"Yes and no."

"Tell me more."

"Investigating, are you?"

"No, just trying to help a friend who I find very intriguing and would like to get to know a whole lot better."

"A-ha! That's it."

"That's what?"

"That's what the young agent is doing. He's trying to get to know the director. Why couldn't I see that?"

"Because he annoys you?"

"Probably. Thanks, Billy. I have perspective now. Not sure why a new agent would be so taken with the director of a small regional IEA office, but hey, to each his own."

"Maybe he's just a poor boy from some backwater place?"

"Could be. Now, what will you do with the rest of your day, sir?"

"Planned to go home and play with some wood til time for the jamboree. I'm easily distracted, though, if you had something else in mind."

"I might. There's nothing at the office I can't take care of tomorrw. I'll take leave for the rest of the day. Want to show me what you do with those tools you came over here to buy?"

"Requires going back to the valley."

"I think I know the way. I'd set to stay at Joe's house tonight after the jamboree. I'll be there by three. You figure out supper." She kissed him on the cheek then gathered up their dishes.

"I know a dismissal when I hear it. See you there." He walked towards the front door. "And, Quinn, I'm glad you're coming over." He started whistling and walked out the front door.

Down the Mountain

Chad put the food and the small bag Bella had handed him in his SUV. He watched her lock the door to Drellag Caban and head to her Jeep. He honked, waved, and headed down the mountain.

Lost in thoughts of Bella, Chad was startled when his secure phone rang just as he passed the switchbacks.

"Oliver."

"Sir, Whitehorse here. Sorry to disturb you. Are you still in Florida?"

"No problem. Just got back, as a matter of fact. Headed towards home now."

"Can you speak freely, sir?"

"Yes." Chad sat up a little straighter.

"Agent Michaels is on his way here from Knoxville. Seems they have an artist's rendering of the potential arsonist."

"They do, do they? Who did the drawing?"

"Not sure. I know he's been working with the detective in Statesboro. Sir, the reason I'm calling is they want Dr. Anderson to be the first person to see it."

Chad almost slammed on his brakes. He looked in the rearview mirror and saw Bella making the last curve on the switchbacks.

"Okay. Let me think about where to do that. I don't want her to have to do it at the station. And—"

"Sir, sorry to interrupt. But may I suggest you reconsider?"

"I'm listening."

"If she does it anywhere other than here, she'll always associate it with the place where she sees the picture. While I'm sure we'll always welcome her here, it *is* a sheriff's station."

"Yes. *My* station." Chad's voice was flat. He was thinking about what Sylvia said. "You make a good point. Thanks. I'm headed home. I'll think about where to do this and talk to Bella. I'll call you in less than half an hour. If Michaels gets there before that, just show him our fine hospitality. Thanks, Sergeant."

"Sure, sir. I'll wait for your call."

"10-4." Chad disconnected the call and headed for his cabin.

Woman's Best Friend

Bella pulled up in front of Doc Jim's and was not surprised to see him sitting on the front porch. She was glad to see he had a lap rug draped over his legs. The temperature was nearing fifty degrees, but it was cool enough to need warmth in the shade. She hopped out and headed up the sidewalk.

"Your call gave me a chance to get out and enjoy this fine day. You sure you want this boy now? Aren't you going to the jamboree?"

"I am, but he'll be fine by himself for a few hours. I've missed him." Wizard sat on his haunches, his tail wagging; he was waiting for her. She kissed Doc Jim on the cheek then squatted down next to Wizard. She was nuzzling his fur when she blurted out, "I don't know if Chad told you, but my home in North Carolina burned to the ground early Monday morning; it appears to be arson."

"Oh, Bella. I'm sorry to hear that. You know I'm glad to have Wizard anytime, and if I eased your burden a bit, I'm happy I could help."

Bella stood and hugged him. "Doc, you're the best." She looked at him. "Are you warm enough out here?"

"Just fine, missy, just fine. Tell me how I can help you."

"You already have. More than you can know. My new cabin is almost finished and the dog run is complete. Maybe you'd let me come get you one day next week, and we'll take a ride so I can show it to you."

"That would be a mighty fine outing for me. I'll look forward to it."

"Then it's a date. I'll call you to set a day that's good."

"Any that works for you. Come on, Wizard. Bella needs you now. You go and be a good boy."

Wizard's tail wagged and he nuzzled Doc's leg as he passed him. Doc Jim scratched his ears.

"You take care now, missy. I'm here whenever you need me."

"Thanks, Jim. Thanks for everything."

He smiled and waved as she put Wizard in the back of her Jeep and drove off.

Bella started talking to Wizard. "Wait until I tell you about going to the beach. You'd have loved running in the waves. Maybe we'll take a road trip one of these days."

She pulled up in the driveway and on to the concrete apron to the side of Chad's garage. He was waiting on the porch for her.

CHAPTER 18

Nature is ever at work building and pulling down, creating and destroying, keeping everything whirling and flowing, allowing no rest but in rhythmical motion, chasing everything in endless song out of one beautiful form into another.

John Muir

The Valley Store

Billy pulled up in front of the Valley Store to pick up something he could have for supper with Quinn. He took the steps two at a time and opened the door with more force than he intended.

"Afternoon, Detective. Did you eat all your protein bars?"

He smiled at the quick humor of Hannah. *We all miss Joe, but she'll be a real asset to Joshua and Carla.* "More like I decided I need to expand what I have in my pantry."

"Any way I can be of help?"

"Where's Joshua?" Billy looked around. He had hoped Joshua could advise him.

"Oh, he had to do a quick propane delivery. He'll be back shortly."

"Hmm . . . well, then . . ." he hesitated. "Any suggestions for fixing a supper for a guest when you don't know how to cook?"

"Yes, sir. I know just the thing. Right this way."

"Really? Do I have to do a lot of preparation?"

"All you'll need is time, a good oven, and the ability to put a salad in a bowl to go with it."

"Could be right up my alley."

They stopped at the refrigerated section. Hannah took out a packaged salad mix and handed it to him. "We'll stop and get a fresh tomato. Do you have salad dressing at home?"

"That I have." He had a tomato, too, but he wasn't about to say so.

"Okay." She moved further down the refrigerated section.

"Diane's Home Cooking has started making these meals for us. You only need to put it in the oven and heat according to the directions. Do you want chicken pot pie, beef stroganoff, or macaroni and cheese with ham?" She looked at him while pointing to the trays of food.

"Hannah, Joshua and Carla are going to have to expand this building with you and Diane's Home Cooking here. Lots of folks like me who don't cook will be grateful for something we can fix at home without having to try and read a recipe. I'll take the chicken pot pie. Seems like a good day for it."

"I've had it, and there's lots of chicken and vegetables. Hope you like it." She headed to the produce aisle and picked up a tomato. "I've got this. Do you want bread with it?"

"No, I think I'm good."

"What about wine?"

They did not hear Joshua come in the back door. He stopped when he heard Hannah speaking. *Did she just offer a customer wine to go with a meal? How did Carla find her?*

"Sure. I guess white wine, right?"

"Yes, sir. Lots of the ladies like this Kim Crawford Sauvignon Blanc."

Billy looked at her. He had not said who was coming to supper. "Then I'm sure I'll like it too."

"Oh, no offense. Didn't mean to imply your guest was a lady. Just wanted you to know."

Joshua came up beside them and saw the salad and chicken pot pie Billy was holding.

"Relax, Hannah. Hard to offend Billy. I promise you he wouldn't be cooking for the guys. Besides, they'd drink beer." He slapped Billy on the back and walked to the front.

"And I thought *I* was the only detective here." Billy shook his head.

"I'll check you out." Hannah hurried to the register.

Joshua held the door for Billy. "Guess you're eating in since the jamboree is postponed to tomorrow night. Enjoy your dinner." He winked at him.

"Hannah was very helpful. Good hire—don't run her off." Billy headed to his SUV. *So, we can have the whole evening. Hot diggedy dog.*

Joshua turned to see Hannah wiping down the counter.

"Hannah, I heard part of your sales pitch to Billy. Good job. My dad was good at that with folks. Just isn't my strong suit."

"Mr. Joshua, I'm sorry if I was—"

"You were just fine. Another way you could ask might be, 'Would your guest prefer wine or beer?'" Joshua was proud of himself. After all these years, his degree in business and his continued reading of the trade magazines were giving him the skills to supervise a full-time employee.

"Sure. That's a good way. Maybe then they'd say what kind of wine or beer. Or they could ask me what most men drink, or what a lady would like. Thanks. I'll remember."

"I have no doubt. Keep up the good work, Hannah. Glad you're with us."

"Me too, Mr. Joshua. Thanks."

Next Steps

"Whitehorse."

"Sarge, Agent Michaels of the FBI is in the front lobby. Shall I send him back?"

"By all means, I'll meet him on his way to the conference room. He knows where it is."

"10-4."

Sylvia tucked the small notebook in her pocket and headed out. She was almost to the front entry when the desk deputy buzzed Michaels through.

"Agent, welcome back. Too bad it's not tomorrow; our jamboree got moved to Saturday night: you could join us."

He extended his hand to shake. "Couldn't do it this week anyway, but I'll get back here one of these days."

"You're welcome anytime." She opened the door to the conference room. "How was the drive?"

"Easier this time of year without the leaf-lookers; isn't that what you call them out here?"

"We do. What do you call them in Knoxville?"

"Revenue."

"Fair enough. Fair enough." Sylvia laughed. "We forget they help our economy out here, too. Sometimes a fine line between trying to protect our special little corner of the world and having work for people to survive. Anyway, that's not what brought you to the valley."

"No, it's not. As I mentioned on the phone, Detective Burton called. They had a North Carolina SBI forensic artist and one in the Statesboro department render a composite of a possible suspect. They had video from three cameras near the Anderson property."

"Get anything?"

He nodded. "They are remarkably similar, and there is a mark on the suspect's neck. They both drew an almost identical rendering of it."

"Birthmark or tattoo?"

"Tattoo, no question. The only question is whether it was permanent or one of those temporary ones." Michaels paused. "Is Dr. Anderson in town?"

"Yes, sir. I've spoken with the sheriff, and he will tell her we have something for her to see. I told him I'd let him know when you arrived."

"Go ahead. I'd like to get the folks down there on it if she can identify the subject."

"Is it likely she will?"

"The North Carolina SBI is running it through facial recognition but the last I heard, no hit. There are a couple of things that make me think Dr. Anderson might know the suspect."

"Oh?"

"The photo suggests it's a young woman."

"And?"

"Let's look at the photos with Dr. Anderson." Michaels was quick but not brusque; he didn't mention the tattoo.

"Certainly."

Sylvia took out her phone and dialed Chad.

"Sir, Whitehorse here. Agent Michaels is in the house."

"10-4. I'll call you back in a few minutes. Offer him coffee. Thanks, Sylvia."

Fire in the Fireplace

Billy knew they would be in the basement to turn wood for at least an hour, but he lit the fireplace so he didn't have to deal with it later. He read the directions on the pot pie and saw it needed to come to room temperature, so he put it in the oven, read the manual on how to start the oven automatically so it would be ready at 5:00: he hoped for the best. He cut up the tomato—a skill he actually had—and then tossed the salad in the wooden salad bowl he had made for his mother. He stuck it in the fridge and decided to set the table while he waited for Quinn.

Satisfied things were ready for supper, he went to change into his work jeans and chambray shirt. *As much as I love wearing my plaid shirts, they're a magnet for wood shavings and sawdust.* He'd made the mistake of wearing a wool shirt to turn wood one time too many. He pulled out another chambray shirt he could offer Quinn to put over whatever she wore. He heard the doorbell ring.

"Welcome to my lair, said the spider to the fly." He opened the door widely.

"Actually, I think it's 'Will you walk into my parlour?'" Quinn said.

"Great. I'll try again, 'Will you walk—'"

Quinn put her finger to her lips and shook her head. "Best quit while you're ahead."

"Right. May I take your coat?"

"That's better." She smiled and kissed him on the cheek. "Thank you."

Billy took her coat and hung it in the small closet by the front door. "What would you like to drink? I made coffee, and we also have tea, water, wine, beer ..."

"Water is fine for now." She wiggled her fingers. "Need to keep all ten of them."

Billy squinted his eyes. "Oh, right. The lathe."

"Yes, Mr. Detective. I came to learn about turning wood on a lathe."

"Absolutely." He picked up the chambray shirt off the back of the sofa. "Might want to cover up that nice shirt. We'll put on aprons when we get downstairs. Hope you're not allergic to sawdust and wood shavings."

"No problem. Let's go."

Billy led the way across the living room to a door, opened it, and flipped on the switch. "I'll grab two waters and be right down."

Quinn went down the stairs. As soon as she turned from the bottom step, she whistled. "Williams, you've been holding out on me *big time!* You have a full-blown workshop here. I know you told me you helped build this cabin, but I assumed you hammered nails or something." She stepped towards his work bench. "Are these Adirondack chairs?"

Billy moved one of the chairs he was building and turned it around. "Yes, ma'am. Figured it was about time I quit sitting in plastic chairs out back." He pointed beyond the table to the sliding glass doors.

Quinn walked over and looked out. "Wow! And you thought my view was nice? I had to create mine, but you got the real deal."

"It's not the view folks have high up on the mountains, but I was already on the force when I built this and it's not practical to live up high and make it to work in this job."

She nodded her head. "I know. My parents thought I could commute from Knoxville. Afraid it was during my tantrum days, and I think that's why my grandmother bought the house for me."

"Because she knew you were right?"

"Ha. Because she always tried to placate me."

"Still throw tantrums?" He cocked his head and raised his left eyebrow.

"Not so much. Growing up can help you realize what bad habits you develop when you're an only child with indulgent parents and a placating grandmother."

Billy laughed. "A tantrum in my house would have gotten a switch on the legs from my mother."

"And your dad?"

"Smart enough not to throw one in front of him to find out."

"Good for you. Well, I see your wood working talents far exceed my expectations, and I am really interested in turning wood. Shall we?"

"Shirt on, here's an apron." He handed her one as he put on his. "Not that they help much, but there's a vacuum over there to get the rest of it."

She laughed. Tension drained out of her, and she tried to forget the director, the young agent, and the change in the receptionist's behavior.

Take My Hand

Bella let Wizard out of the back of her Jeep. He ran to a tree and then straight up the porch stairs to Chad.

"Hello, buddy. Miss us, did you?" Chad whispered in Wizard's ears while he scratched behind them.

Bella locked her Jeep and headed up the stairs. "Sorry, it took longer than I thought. Visited with Doc Jim for a few minutes." She stepped up on the porch and kissed Chad. "Lovely afternoon, isn't it?"

"Pretty nice for December. Starting to cool off with the sun moving behind us."

"Guess I'm still warm from the heater." She sat down in one of the rockers. "Do you move your rockers inside in the winter? Or put covers on them?"

"I put them in the back of the garage. Should have already done it. Guess I've been distracted." He reached over and took her hand. Wizard walked up and put his head on Chad's lap.

"Well, that's a fine howdy do. He hasn't seen me in three days and you're the one he favors."

"That's 'cause you didn't see me give him a treat." Chad leaned over and kissed her.

"Sneaky."

"Not really. Not my style."

Bella heard his voice turn from carefree to more serious.

"What's up? I think I hear the precursor to news, and I have a feeling it might not be good news."

"Or it could be." He rocked slowly.

"Tell me."

"I had a call from Sylvia on the way down the mountain. The detective in Statesboro has a composite of someone who may be a suspect in the fire."

"Really? Have they found him?" She stopped. "Or her, them? Listen to me. I correct other people about gender bias statements and I just did it." Her words flew out of her mouth.

Chad thought she sounded like she was on a mission to get something accomplished—maybe she was.

"I don't think so, Bella. Agent Michaels of the FBI in Knoxville has the composite. They want you to be the first person to see the drawing." He studied her face.

She looked at him from the side of her eyes without turning her head. "Why me? How likely am I to know the person who did this?"

"It's routine. Always easiest to solve a case if the victim knows the perpetrator."

"Sure. I should have considered that. Okay, when will he be here?"

"He's here. I need to call Sylvia. First, I need to ask you something."

"Did I hire someone?" She tried to make it sound like a joke, but he heard the sarcasm.

"Bella." He squeezed her hand. "I don't think anyone suspects you of being involved. If I did, I would tell you. Hell, if I thought you were . . . I'd struggle with whether to arrest you myself or take you to a South Sea island where no one could ever find us."

"Chad, I love that you are trying to protect me. I need to see this picture. If by some weird chance I know the person, I want them caught. I honestly don't know how it's possible for me to know them, but I guess we'll find out. Is he coming here?"

"I think it's best if we go to the station—"

"So it's easier to arrest me." She knew the sarcasm was evident this time.

"No."

She finally turned and looked at him. He had not let go of her hand.

"Because if you do know the person, and it turns out to be the person who committed the crime, I don't want you to associate it with someplace you'll spend time."

She leaned back in the rocker. "And you still love me in spite of my less-than-gracious self?"

"I love you, period. I may never be able to show you how much."

"Not wanting me to have the possibility of associating a place with the horror of losing my North Carolina home is right up there in my book."

"Can't claim credit."

"Oh?"

"I didn't want you to go to the station for the very reason to which you reacted. I don't think you had anything to do with the arson, and I didn't want you to feel anyone else did. It was Sylvia who said, 'If she does it anywhere other than here, she'll always associate it with the place where she sees the picture. While I'm sure we'll always welcome her here, it *is* a sheriff's station.' I'm sure she meant you aren't likely to spend a lot of time there."

Bella rocked. Wizard was now at her feet with his head on her lap. She scratched his ears. "Wizard, I don't know what we did to be so lucky to have this fine man in our lives. I need you to be a good boy while we're gone." She stood up. "Call Sylvia. I'll be ready to go when it's time." She kissed him and walked into the cabin to change clothes.

Chad watched her go inside, his chest tightening at the love he felt.

Wizard rested his chin on the now-vacant rocking chair and watched as Chad took out his phone and dialed.

The Goblet

"Ever done any work on a lathe?"

"Never done work of this kind at all. I'm assuming the same rules I know about kitchen knives applies to these tools: keep the sharp blades away from your body, fingers, and limbs. How am I doing so far?"

"Smart lady. It's important to wear goggles, no jewelry, no loose sleeves, and hair pulled back." He looked at her. "You pass that test. Here are the goggles." He handed them to her. "This part of the machine is called the tool rest. I'm sure you're going to want to know the names of all the parts of this machine, but you'll be more motivated to learn them once you've experienced turning a piece of wood. So, will you trust me on that?"

"Sure, teacher. I'm reasonably compliant."

"Counting on it. We have an added dimension here: movement. The block of wood will be moving, but you have to move too. You need a controlled sway, like this." Billy moved his shoulders from his waist without moving his feet. "Questions?"

She swayed. "Think I have it."

"Once I show you how to put the block on the machine, you'll place this roughing gouge," he handed the tool to her, "on the tool rest. You need a firm grip, but not white-knuckled." He had not turned on the machine. "Show me that much."

Quinn took the tool from him and placed it on the tool rest. "This way up or this?"

"Good question. Open side of the U-shape up." He took her hands and placed them in a good grip position.

"I'll show you one run, and then it's all yours."

"Where are you going?" It seemed more a question of curiosity than concern.

"I'll be right here by your side. Something tells me you'll be a one-trial learner."

Quinn stepped back from the lathe. "Hope I don't disappoint the teacher." They stood looking at the carved piece of hickory she held in her hand. "I like the goblet shape, but how do I hollow out the center so I can drink wine?"

"Ahhh, that my fine student, is lesson number two."

"So, this is how the spider gets me back to the lair?"

"Well, you can hardly call this a parlor!"

They both laughed as they brushed sawdust and wood shavings off their clothes.

"Food will be ready in twenty minutes. I'm pretty serious about keeping a clean workspace, so if you want to vacuum off your clothes over there, I'll clean up, and we can go wash up for supper."

"I made the mess; I can clean it up."

"First time is on the teacher. Now, go get as much of that off you as you can." He waved the palms of his hands as if shooing a child out to play.

"On it." She vacuumed off the shavings and then took off the apron and chambray shirt.

Once the area was cleaned and Billy free of shavings and sawdust, they headed upstairs.

"Wow! It smells great up here. Did someone sneak in and bring supper while we were working?"

He bowed. "The cook at your service. I believe you know where the guest bathroom is. I'm off to the kitchen. By the way, wine or beer?"

"White wine if you have it."

"Kim Crawford Sauvignon Blanc work?" He was all but gloating.

"Hmmm ... Must be a detective!" She raised her left eyebrow. "Been snooping in my fridge?"

"I was *not*. But, if I had been smart, I would have!" Quinn shook her head and chuckled before heading down the hall.

Billy washed his hands then lined up the wine, a Guinness Golden Ale, the salad, and the salad dressing on the counter. He saw a text to all deputies; the jamboree had been moved to Saturday. *Joshua was right.* He poured his ale into a mug and was decanting the wine when he heard a low whistle. He turned.

"That bowl is a piece of art. How old is it?"

"This?" he pointed to the salad bowl. "I made it for my mother when I was in high school."

"Now things make sense. You have a natural talent. Billy, it really is gorgeous."

"Thanks. Mom loved it. Always makes me think of supper with my folks when I use it."

She took the glass of wine he offered her but set it on the counter. She put her arms around his neck and kissed him—deeply.

He followed her lead while trying to keep himself from picking her up and walking down the hall to his bedroom. The timer on the stove rang.

"Well, there's a mood changer for you." He stepped to the stove and turned it off. "Ready for supper?"

"Sure, why not?" She smiled at him as she picked up their drinks and walked to the table.

"Have a seat. Be right out." He found his grandmother's small glass milk pitcher that she had used for salad dressing and poured some in. He took the salad bowl and dressing to the table. He returned to the kitchen and brought out the chicken pot pie.

"What was all the rustling about?"

"I'm sure my mother or grandmother had a basket they used to put dishes like this in, but I couldn't find it. You'll have to accept bachelor aluminum."

"No need to stand on ceremony for me. You pass the supper test just for having it made and ready. I'm impressed."

"Great. I could have done without you telling me I was being tested."

"Not to worry. It would take a lot for you to drop from the A-plus you have at the moment."

He kissed her then lifted his beer and said, "Then here's to making the mark. Thanks for spending the afternoon with me, and here's to a lovely evening by the fire."

She clinked glasses and smiled at him. "The fire sounds tempting, but I thought we were going to the jamboree."

"Got word it's moved to tomorrow night."

He set down his beer mug and served the salad.

CHAPTER 19

Any fool can destroy trees. They cannot run away.

John Muir

What Do I See?

Chad read the text about the jamboree being moved, but decided to wait and tell Bella later. He called Sylvia.

"Whitehorse here."

"We'll be there shortly."

"We're in the conference room, sir."

"10-4."

Chad took Wizard for a short walk before returning to the cabin. "Water. Food." He pointed to the bowls in the kitchen. Chad still marveled at how quickly Bella had trained Wizard. He left the pup eating and went to change clothes. As he left his bedroom, he found Bella sitting in the wingback chair in the guest room.

"Doing okay?"

She nodded. "I'll be fine. I suppose it's normal to try to run through all the people you've known in your life—not easy when you were a teacher. I just can't imagine why someone would want to burn down my house."

He took her hand and squeezed it. "I'm ready when you are, but we can take all the time you need."

She returned the squeeze and stood up. They walked to the living room, where Wizard was just curling up on his bed by the fire. "You stay here by the fire. We'll be back soon." She reached out and petted him as she walked by. She turned to Chad. "I'll meet you out front." She walked out the front door, closing it behind her.

Chad realized she didn't want to see him put on his sidearm. He armed himself, then turned to Wizard. "Take care of the house, boy." He stopped the SUV on the driveway and struggled with not getting out to open the door for her, but somehow he knew she'd prefer to get in herself. She did.

Chad pulled in the front of the station and hopped out; Bella was already at the front of the SUV before he could make a move for her door. He fell in step beside her but did not touch her. He sensed she needed to gather her own strength.

"Afternoon, Sheriff. Well, I guess it's almost evening." The deputy on the desk pushed the button for the door into the secured area.

"Afternoon, ma'am." He nodded at Bella.

"Afternoon, Deputy. Sergeant Whitehorse is expecting us in the conference room."

"Good to see you, sir."

"Likewise." Chad pulled the door open and stood back for Bella to walk through. She did and stopped.

"We're headed right over there." He pointed to the conference room. "Do you want tea?"

"No. I'm fine. Thanks."

"There should be water in the conference room. I'll get one for you."

"Thanks."

He opened the door. Bill Michaels and Sylvia stood, and the group exchanged greetings before Agent Michaels pulled out a chair. "Have a seat. Would you like . . . " He was going to offer her water and he saw Chad put a bottle in front of her. "Dr. Anderson, would you like Sheriff Oliver to stay?"

Bella looked from Michaels to Chad to Sylvia. "Is there a reason he shouldn't?"

"No, ma'am. This is his station and he's welcome to stay as far as I'm concerned."

"Then I'd like him to stay."

Chad let out an inaudible breath. He hadn't been sure Michaels would want him there.

"Dr. Anderson, you are here voluntarily and you are being questioned in an effort to solve the crime that destroyed your home in North Carolina. I am asking your permission to record this session."

"Certainly."

Chad heard the formal voice of the professor. He was not surprised.

Sylvia started the recording. "This is Sergeant Sylvia Whitehorse of the valley sheriff's office."

"Agent Bill Michaels of the FBI Knoxville office."

"Sheriff Chad Oliver of the valley sheriff's office currently on voluntary leave." He turned to Bella.

"Bella Anderson of . . ." she gave her North Carolina and her Tennessee addresses.

Michaels gave the date, time, and location of the interview. "Dr. Anderson, would you please tell me your whereabouts from Friday of last week until today?"

Bella had been staring at the whiteboard at the end of the table; the word "owner" under "arson" glared at her. She turned to Agent Michaels. "I was at Drellag Caban, my home here in the mountains, until Monday afternoon of this week when I came to the valley. I was at the home of Dr. and Mrs. Smith until Wednesday afternoon when I went to Knoxville, caught a plane, and went to Destin, Florida." She knew she omitted staying at Chad's Monday night, but she hadn't lied either. "I returned today. I've been back in the valley since about two this afternoon after stopping at Drellag Caban. I picked up my dog and left him at the home of a friend. Now I am here." She smiled and studied his face.

"When did you learn of the fire at your property in North Carolina?"

"I learned of the fire that destroyed *my home* in North Carolina early on Monday from a detective in Statesboro. He called me at Drellag Caban." The three law enforcement officers did not miss the emphasis on "my home."

"Thank you. Does Drellag Caban mean something special?"

"Yes, Drellag is Scottish for dragonfly and Caban is the Welsh word for cabin. Both cultures are part of my heritage."

Chad noticed Michaels' eyes dart around the table when she said dragonfly.

"Do you have any reason to suspect anyone of wanting to destroy your home or get back at you for something?"

"Agent Michaels, I can't imagine why *anyone* would burn down my home."

"Technology in today's world can often provide us with clues that were not readily available even a few years ago. Your neighbors voluntarily shared the video from their home security cameras, and the Statesboro police and North Carolina State Bureau of Investigation were able to create a composite of someone who advanced onto your property and is likely a suspect in the fire that destroyed your home."

Bella kept her gaze on him.

"I am going to show you both drawings, which are almost identical, and ask you if you recognize the person in the rendering."

"Fine." Bella sat a little straighter in her chair.

Michaels was sitting to her left; he slid the first closed portfolio in front of her. "Ready?"

"Yes, sir."

Michaels flipped back the cover.

Bella gasped.

Quiet Conversation over Supper

"First, you hadn't told me about the fine wood working you do, now I find out you can cook. What's with all the false modesty?"

"Ah, fair maiden, 'Beyond the sunlit dappled forest ground.' I even remember some Shakespeare. I always thought the meaning of that sonnet was things are not always what they seem. I never won that argument with my professor, but *c'est la vie*."

"Sonnets and French too. What *is* going to be the downfall of this man?"

"My mouth."

Quinn laughed then leaned over and kissed him. "Seriously, I can deal with a bit of sarcasm from time to time. Unless, of course, it's directed at me."

"Fair enough."

"Now to this delicious chicken pot pie …"

Billy threw up his hands in mock surrender. "I confess. Made by Diane's Home Cooking and baked in the oven by yours truly."

"That works. I cooked a stir fry for you that someone else made. No apologies needed." She sat up straighter in her chair and turned towards him. "I am deeply fascinated by all things Billy Williams. I am also scared to death of getting into a relationship when I am unsettled at work."

Billy's smile disarmed most people. He didn't flash it often, but when he did it shone through his eyes too. He rested his hand on her arm. "Quinn, I am beyond intrigued by you. I want to get to know you. I am also a patient man—" She interrupted him.

"Good detective skill." She smiled.

"If I can help you sort out the feelings you have about work, I'm here for you. When you want company, I'm here for you. I will not ignore you, but I won't bug you. That work?"

"Do you have to make it more difficult? I didn't expect you to be so gracious. I was prepared for a typical male response …"

"Which would be?" He cocked his head.

She tried to drop her voice an octave. "*Fine*. You call me. I might or might not be available."

"I'll store that one away for my next investigation of a love affair gone badly. Sorry to disappoint. I, too, have a big job that keeps me very busy, and I love it." He leaned in so their faces were almost touching. "But I never expected to meet a woman who would fascinate me the way you do; one who makes me realize I need to find some time *not* to work." He kissed her. "I look forward to an evening getting to know you better, I'm glad you're staying at Joe's tonight and I'm sure you can extend it for the jamboree tomorrow night."

"What? No jamboree tonight?"

"They had to move it." He stood and pulled her up from her chair into a long, deep kiss and held her tight.

She leaned back and looked at him. "Billy, you really are special. . ."

"I hear the 'but. . .'"

She nodded, "But I have some reading I must do. I had already decided I couldn't stay long at the jamboree. I got a text on the way over about another caravan headed this way. I have to read the field reports. I promise I'll do it at Joe's and go home in the morning. Sorry."

"Don't apologize. You'll figure out the office thing, and I'll be here when you're ready." He stepped back, took her hand, and walked towards the front door. He took her coat and held it for her to put on.

Quinn stood looking at him. "Why couldn't you be a jerk?"

"You wouldn't be interested if I were. And I wouldn't be interested if you weren't who you are. Go forth and do good work. Then come back and we'll finish that wine goblet." He kissed her and opened the door. "Text me when you get to Joe's, please."

She kissed him. "I will." She hurried down the stairs. As she reached her SUV, she turned back to look at him and wave before driving off.

Billy sat down in front of the fire. *Careful, Billy, hearts can be broken.* He stood up to clear the table and put away the rest of the dinner. *Wonder how you reheat pot pie?*

The Tattoo

All color had drained from Bella's face. Chad opened the bottle of water and handed it to her. He rested his hand on her arm. Bella started to touch the drawing, her fingers hovering over the tattoo on the woman's neck. She drew her hand back like it was on fire.

Michaels wondered if it was the dragonfly that caused her reaction, or the face. Did she know the woman? He waited.

Bella took several deep breaths and let them out slowly. She turned to Chad, who saw the anguish in her eyes.

"It's okay, Bella. If you know who it is, tell us." Chad's voice was soft and caring.

"Jocelyn Walters." They watched her. "She was a graduate student of mine." She looked around the table. "You'll have to excuse me. I'm trying to figure out how she would be able to do this much damage."

Chad's voice remained calm and reassuring. "It's easy enough to learn how to set a fire. Having the destructive nature to do it is something else. What else do you know about her?" He noticed Bill Michaels had started a text as soon as Bella said the name.

"Is it okay if I stand up for a minute?" Bella's eyes held a plea; it almost broke Chad's heart.

Chad turned off the recorder and pulled out her chair. "Do you need some time?"

"I just need a minute to process this."

Chad didn't care who was in the room or that the video camera was likely recording. He pulled Bella into an embrace and whispered in her ear. "I love you. We will get through this together. You just need to tell us what you know so we can find out if she was involved."

Bella stood for a moment then let go of Chad. She walked over to the counter, turned around, and walked back. Then she turned and walked back again.

"Do you want to go out and get some fresh air?" Agent Michaels gave her a slight smile.

"I'll be okay." She sat down and the others followed suit. "I have been racking my brain for the last couple of hours … do you want to turn the recorder on?"

"Only so I don't miss any details that can help us. Are you okay with it?"

"Yes. I want this resolved too."

He turned on the recorder.

Bella sat back in her chair and took a sip of the water. She turned to the FBI agent but reached for Chad's hand.

"Jocelyn is a bright young woman who was a master's student of mine. It's not unusual for students to be attracted to a professor. Some want to be your best friend, some want your counsel like a big sister, some interests are romantic." She took another sip of her water. "I don't know exactly how old she is, but I'd guess early thirties. When she enrolled in a third class with me, I told her she needed to follow the curriculum that had been set for her and not waste her credits on classes with me. She talked with me about chairing her thesis." Bella looked at Sylvia, who smiled and gave her a slight nod.

"I told her it was too early in her program to be making that decision. Then she fell apart and told me she was in love with me." Bella's voice was barely above a whisper. She straightened up and looked around the table. "I am not unaware that students fall in love with their idealized version of who they think the professor is. Sadly, in my opinion, some professors encourage that behavior from students. I do not and never did. I tried to be gentle with her, but I told her that I do not have relationships with my students beyond that of instructor and student."

"At first, I thought she assumed I said it because I wasn't interested in another woman. Although I am not attracted to other women in that way, I would never have a romantic relationship with any student. She stopped coming to class but did not withdraw, so she received an F. That is almost always a death knell … uh, dismissal, from a graduate program. Some masters students don't realize that fact. They can appeal dismissal from the program. She did not. She just disappeared. I am sorry to tell you I never gave it any more thought." She took a deep breath and then sipped her water. "Oh, timelines might be important to you. This happened in the fall semester before my retirement this past summer." She looked at Chad.

Chad smiled at her and nodded. "Up for any questions?"

"I'll try."

Agent Michaels said, "I'm sorry for you to have to go through this. Did she reach out to you at all after she left your class?"

"No."

"Did she have the dragonfly tattoo when she was in your class?"

"Not that I recall. I think I would have noticed since I love dragonflies."

"It's not unusual in situations like this for an individual to choose something which ties them to the victim." Michaels watched her face. "Often, they will steal something from the person's home or office or unlocked car. A keepsake. A memento."

Bella nodded her head in understanding.

"Dr. Anderson," Bella turned towards Sylvia. "Does this young woman have any ties to your house sitter . . . Victoria, is that her name?"

Bella slowly shook her head. "I honestly don't know. I don't think they were in *my* class together, but that doesn't mean they didn't have *a* class together."

Sylvia continued. "Would she have known Victoria was house sitting?"

"I don't know. I suppose if she knew where I lived, she could have seen Victoria there."

"Would she have known Victoria was away at a conference?"

Bella caught a sob before it escaped her throat. "Oh, Sylvia. Victoria. I haven't actually spoken to Victoria. Chad . . . Sheriff Oliver did. In her text, she said she was fine. She lost whatever she had in my home." Bella couldn't hold it back any longer. She didn't make a sound as tears flowed down her cheeks.

Agent Michaels turned off the tape recorder. He and Sylvia stood up and left the room. Chad put his arms around Bella and held her. He didn't speak.

Finally, Chad went to the sink in the conference room counter; he wet a paper towel and took it to her. "Not the finest cloth in America."

She looked up at him—her eyes red and her face pale—but she still smiled. "Thanks." She took the paper towel and wiped her eyes.

"Chad, what if Victoria had been in that house?"

"Bella, she wasn't. If this woman is responsible, it would appear she probably knew Victoria would be gone. Let's be thankful for that. I'm not a psychologist or psychiatrist, but I've read FBI profiles on arsonists. As hard as this may be to make sense of, these kinds of acts are often not to destroy the property of someone they believe has spurned them, but to get their attention."

Bella gave a bitter laugh. "Well, it certainly got my attention ... as well as the police, the FBI, and you." She leaned her head on his shoulder. "Can we see if Agent Michaels needs anything else? I'd like to go home."

Chad kissed her and went out into the hall. He found Bill and Sylvia in her office. "She's ready if you need her."

Sylvia watched Chad's face. She hadn't known much about him during his marriage, but she saw the aftermath of the divorce when she was a deputy. The sheriff had always kept to himself, done a bang-up job as sheriff, and was widely admired and respected. She valued that. But she was also happy for him and Bella and hoped this would be the end of the crime spree affecting her—and him.

Bill Michaels spoke up. "Chad, the detective in Statesboro is on this. Folks are likely already at her door and the picture is out with an APB. They'll find her. I don't think there's anything material that Dr. Anderson can give us at this time. I assume she's going to stay in the area?"

"As far as I know. You might want to ask her yourself."

"Need me, Agent?" Sylvia asked.

"Just to keep the recording clean. Let's go wrap this up."

Sylvia and Chad followed Michaels into the conference room. Michaels turned on the recorder.

"Dr. Anderson, I am resuming the recording with . . ."

"Sheriff Oliver."

"Sergeant Whitehorse."

"Agent Michaels." He turned to Bella. "Are you okay with us wrapping this up for now?"

Bella looked at him. "Agent Michaels, I will answer any questions you have, if I can. I don't know what else I can tell you. Jocelyn took two classes with me in the fall semester of last year and signed up for the third one in the spring. That is when I spoke to her about the need to follow her curriculum."

"Did you see her in the spring semester?"

Bella sat for a moment. "Not that I recall. No, I don't remember seeing her in spring or summer terms. Many of the full-time students don't take summer classes unless they are on a fast track to get finished. Some have an assistantship, so they don't take coursework in the summer. It varies."

"Anyone else have a question?" Michaels looked at Sylvia and Chad. Both shook their heads. "Do you have any questions for me?"

"Is there anything I will have to do? Do I need to go to North Carolina?"

"Would you like to go to North Carolina?" Bill Michaels' voice was calm and gentle.

She shrugged. "Part of me needs to go see for myself that everything really is gone. Part of me wants to remember it the way it was. Right now, I think I would only go if I was needed."

Chad had been watching her carefully, and he saw panic rise on her face.

"Will I have to testify?" She looked wide-eyed at the FBI agent.

"That's a long way off, ma'am, if ever. Let the system work and catch the suspect, then we'll go from there. We'll keep you informed."

He looked around the table. "If no one has anything else, we're finished here. Thank you for your cooperation, Dr. Anderson. If you have plans to leave the area, just let Sergeant Whitehorse know where you can be reached. I'm sorry for your loss."

"Thank you." Bella stood as Michaels did. She extended her hand. "Oh, one other thing. Could I see the other drawing?"

Michaels looked at Chad, who was standing behind her. He nodded.

"Certainly." He set the second portfolio down and opened it.

Bella stared at it for a moment and said, "I hope the tattoo is one of those temporary things." She turned and walked out into the hall.

Chad extended his hand to Michaels. "Thanks for everything. I'll be in touch."

He went out the door, put his arm around Bella's shoulder and walked her out to his Jeep. He opened the door for her. "Bella, I received a text about the jamboree; it's been moved to tomorrow night. So, what would you like to do?"

"Chad, let's go by the Valley Store. I don't think either of us feels like cooking and we can get a pizza. It would be nice to see Joshua and Carla."

"Your wish is my command."

Friends

The jingle of the silver bell above the door made Bella smile, and the smell of coffee permeated the air as they stepped inside.

Carla rushed over to hug her. "Bella, it's great to see you." She pulled back and said, "How y'all doing? Can I get y'all some coffee? Sorry, tea?"

"I'm surprised to smell coffee." Bella looked around and saw the new counter. "What's this?" She walked over to investigate then cocked her head to the side and smiled. "There's music. I love it. What a great idea!" She poured herself a cup of hot water and took a bag of Earl Grey tea. She pulled her wallet out and put a twenty-dollar bill in the box. "Scholarship fund. That's great." She turned and saw the three of them staring at her.

Carla jumped in. "The coffee was Chad's idea." She turned to him. "Don't think we thanked you properly for that." She kissed him on the cheek. "The scholarship fund was mine and Joshua's." She took Joshua's hand. "Oh, and Bella, I don't think you've met Hannah. She's our new full-time cashier. She's about to leave for the day."

Bella saw the redhaired young woman come out from the back of the store. Introductions were made. "So nice to meet you, Hannah. I hope you enjoy being a part of this fine family store."

"Yes, ma'am. I already love it. Well, I told my mama I'd be home by six. Better step on it."

"Thanks for everything, Hannah. See you tomorrow." Joshua held the door open for her.

The four stood near the cash register; the store was otherwise empty. There was an awkward silence.

Chad tried to bring the conversation back to the scholarship fund. "Joshua, do you know why your folks wanted the scholarship to go to a girl?"

Joshua didn't want to say he thought his parents had lost a girl child, and the silence began to deepen.

Never one to be deterred, Carla blurted out, "Did you hear my brother misses me? Can't keep a schedule straight." She laughed. "He scheduled a get together for a family in the community room for tonight, so the jamboree is tomorrow night." She took a quick breath and continued. "And, guess what we had our ultrasound and everything is fine with the baby."

"Oh, Carla, that's great news." Bella laughed, "Not about the jamboree but I'm so happy for the baby and for both of you ... all of us!" She gave Carla a hug.

"The best part is that we can tell people now." Joshua beamed.

"Yeah, Doc Smith said he thought it would be fine if we wanted to share the news. We were going to wait until four months but, heck, that's almost half the time gone and no one else knows—except for you two and James, of course."

"Won't be putting up any banners," Joshua said with a big grin, "but we'll let folks know when it's right to say anything."

Carla poked him with her elbow. "My right proper husband here." She smiled.

"It's yours to tell. Do it however you want. We're happy for you."

"That we are," Chad said. "I'll just grab a pizza, then we'll get out of your way. Have you started closing at six yet?"

"This time of year, it's usually six thirty, but we'll see how the traffic is." Joshua pointed towards the section where the fresh pizzas now resided.

"Been slow, but it's that time of year," Carla said.

Chad walked with Joshua. "Glad things with Carla are going well."

"Me, too. Bella doing okay?"

"I think she will be. Been a rough few days."

"Tell us if we can do anything. You know, she's the closest I'll ever have to a sister."

"Means a lot to both of us." They were back at the register. Chad paid for the pizza.

The couples exchanged hugs and handshakes, and the bell jingled as Bella and Chad left.

Carla turned to Joshua. "I didn't ask her how she was holding up. I didn't know what to say."

"Carla, I think sometimes folks don't need to say or hear anything. They just need to know their friends are there for them."

"You're right. Guess I'm so used to the chatter in The Corral that I haven't totally adapted to the quieter nature of a grocery store."

"Problem for you?"

"Welcome relief." She kissed him on the cheek. "Let's get things finished up here and go home."

"Works for me." Joshua headed to the back of the store to finish the stock work and lock up. *Next week Chuck will be here to learn this.* He quickened his pace.

CHAPTER 20

How narrow we selfish conceited creatures are in our sympathies!
How blind to the rights of all the rest of creation!

John Muir

Night Shift

Quinn knew Billy would be disappointed to learn she drove home, but she had called Joshua and changed her time to tomorrow night. She pulled up to her home in Round City and called him—after convincing herself a text was the chicken's way out.

"Hey. Just wanted to let you know the roads were dry and I decided to come on home. Thanks for the wood turning and supper. I promise I'll stay over after the jamboree."

"Appreciate the update. Glad the roads were dry. Hope you can get your reading done and get an early night. Thanks for coming over."

"Pleasure was mine; I assure you. Talk to you tomorrow. Good night, Billy."

"Good night, Quinn." He hoped it was wistfulness he heard in her voice.

She smiled. She had spent the entire drive home trying to sort out who this complex yet simple man was. Intruding on her thoughts, though, was a younger man: the new agent in her office. She parked in her garage and walked into the kitchen still puzzling over the emerging office dynamics. After closing the drapes on her front and back windows, she decided to shower before she dug into the reading she needed to do. *Maybe I'll make tea. It will keep me alert, but not awake half the night.* She put on the kettle to boil and headed for the bathroom.

Day Is Done

Billy watched the fire; his personal phone rang again. He answered without looking, thinking it was Quinn. "Hey!"

"Guess you were expecting someone else?"

"Just being friendly ... mostly. What's up, Sarge?"

"Wondering if I could stop by for a few minutes on my way home?"

Billy sat up straighter. He only remembered Sylvia coming to his home during his recent injury and once a few years ago when he had the flu soon after his mother passed away. "Sure, anytime. See you shortly."

"Headed your way."

Billy stood and looked around. He had cleaned up the dishes and put the leftovers in the fridge. He shrugged. *What did I expect to find? Okay, maybe I was holding onto dreams of a romantic evening.* He turned when he saw the lights of Sylvia's SUV through his front window. He walked to the door and opened it.

"What an unexpected pleasure. Welcome."

"Thanks for seeing me, Billy." She walked in unbuttoning her jacket. He noticed she didn't have on an overcoat.

"Come in, come in. I have some left over chicken pot pie and salad. Hungry? I know how to heat it up. Well, not the salad." He laughed.

"Mike's at work; I could use a bite and a listening ear if you have time."

"Nothing but time. My day off."

"Sorry. I forgot that."

"Sylvia, you know full well that has never made a difference even when I was out of town."

"I know. It doesn't stop me from feeling guilty, though."

"A wise man I know once said, 'Whose problem is that?'"

"Yeah, he's told me that, too. However, he usually adds a little more when speaking to me."

"Really? That's the only part I ever heard Chief Whitehorse say."

"That's because you're not one of his children. He expects us to acknowledge that guilt is something we do to ourselves."

"Yeah, so? I assumed that was the point."

"To us he says, 'So why are you making it everyone else's problem?'"

"Arghh! Yeah, glad he never told me that part. Although glad to know it. Thanks. Get you something to drink? Wine? Beer?"

"Tea, if you have it."

"You are tired. Who doesn't have tea?"

"I was thinking hot tea."

"No problem. Come sit and talk at me while I work miracles with a microwave. Don't faint, but I actually looked up how to reheat chicken pot pie. It hasn't had time to get cold yet, so it should heat up fine." Billy put the kettle on then took out a box of tea bags. He hoped they hadn't expired since he had no idea how long they'd been in his cupboard. He put some of the pot pie in a small stoneware tureen and placed it in the microwave. He added salad to a bowl and was glad he had not bothered to put the salad dressing back in the bottle. He looked at Sylvia standing in the doorway.

"Okay, don't sit. Where would you like to eat? Here? Or the dining room table?"

"Counter is fine." She pulled out a stool and sat.

Billy grabbed a stool and put it on the opposite side of the island. He pushed the salad towards her and moved to take the kettle off the stove. It whistled at the same time the microwave beeped. "Okay, this might push the limit of my cooking skills. Pot pie first, right?"

"Sound decision." She chuckled at him. "No offense, Billy. This is relieving the stress of my day."

"Glad I can offer some amusement."

"You don't understand. I can't do this much when it comes to cooking. If Mike isn't home to cook, I eat cereal."

Billy roared with laughter. "My kind of cop." He put the pot pie in front of her.

"This smells delicious."

"Thank Joshua and Carla for carrying Diane's Home Cooking. You've seen the limits of my skills." He poured hot water in the mug, added the tea bag, and put it front of her. "Best I can do."

"This is great. Wasn't counting on eating." She had already eaten three bites of the pie.

"Sorry I wasn't there today. Sounds like a rough one. You could have called me."

"No. It was okay until an hour or so ago." She took a bite of salad.

Billy stood up and got a beer out of the fridge. He wasn't on duty or driving and a second one wouldn't do him in.

"It's the sheriff." Sylvia said it without any preamble.

"Say what? Is he okay? Where is he?"

"Slow down. I could have said that better. I'm worried about the sheriff and Bella."

"Okay, that's better. We all are. What's new? Where is he?"

"He's at home." She had not told anyone the sheriff had gone out of town—she kept confidences.

"Anything new from North Carolina?"

"Yes. That's what's got me concerned."

Billy sipped on his beer and waited.

"The folks down there were able to get a composite of the likely suspect."

Billy set his beer down and leaned in on his elbows. "Really? Have you seen it?"

She nodded. "So have the sheriff and Bella." She took another bite of salad.

Billy was trying to let her eat, but he wanted to know more.

Sylvia started to cough as if she were choking.

Billy jumped up, ready to do the Heimlich maneuver. She put her hands up and shook her head. He grabbed a bottle of water out of the fridge, annoyed he hadn't poured her a glass.

Sylvia took the water, sipped it, and finally said, "I'm fine. Sorry about that. Just went down the wrong way." She coughed again and sipped more water.

"Look, just finish eating, and then we can sit and talk about this."

"No, no. I'm fine. I'm the one barging in on your day off."

"You're welcome anytime. Not sure why we haven't spent more time together over the years."

"Too busy working."

He laughed. "That's the truth." He decided to talk and let her eat. "I've only ever had one boss—our Sheriff. Sometimes I wonder if other people work as hard, or not as hard, as their boss. He sets such a high bar, it's a full-time job to keep up."

She nodded. "Good question."

"I talked to him about it one time. You know what he said?"

She shook her head.

"He told me he doesn't expect other people to work as hard as he does. Said it's his own expectation of himself." Billy paused. "I told him that other people see how hard he works and feel like they have to as well."

"What did he say?"

"Said he'd think about it and try to be more aware of how his behavior affects others."

"Do you think he has?"

"Well, up until this week when he actually took leave, I'd have said, 'Maybe, a little.' But now? Wow! I never thought I'd see the day he was not at work for one day, much less two."

"He told me the earliest he'd be back was Sunday."

"That work for you? I can help cover. I haven't totally forgotten what it's like to run a shift."

"I'm good. It's Mike's busy time of year. You'd be amazed how fast fires increase in the winter."

"No doubt. Want some more?" He saw her plate was empty.

"No thanks. I appreciate it though."

"Let's go sit by the fire. I can get these dishes later. Grab your tea and come on." He nodded towards the living room.

Sylvia sat in a leather side chair and set her tea on the coffee table. She leaned forward with her elbows on her thighs. "Bella knew the suspect."

"Say what? She knew him?"

"Sexist language, Detective."

"Right." The surprise spread across his wide eyes and raised eyebrows. "What? It was a female?"

"Look how skilled this detective is." She gave a slight smile. "Yes, she is a woman." She told him about the drawings and indicated the woman was a former student. "Michaels sent the name to North Carolina as soon as she said it."

"Did Michaels leave right away?"

She gave a slight shake of her head as she sipped her tea. "I think he felt sorry for Bella. Either that or he's taken a shine to our little corner of the world."

"Could be. He plays dobro, right?"

"No, the dobro player is Agent Jackson from the SBI. I love the sound of a dobro. I heard Chad encourage him to come play at our jamboree."

"Yeah, now I remember. Well, back to the case at hand. How'd the sheriff handle it?"

"He was textbook Oliver until she began to cry. That's when Michaels and I left the room." Sylvia almost choked on the words.

"Whew, glad I missed that one."

"Yeah, Williams, you'd have a hard time facing her after seeing her lose her composure. I get the reaction, and I'm struggling with it. This woman came here to the mountains, to her ancestral home, to enjoy retirement and think about making this her home full time. How much more does a soul need in the space of three or four months?"

"It *has* been pretty rough for her." Billy started to use his fingers to mark off each event. "Trespassing ATVs *and* property damage. Mr. Joe getting killed. Threatening phone calls. Now she finds out her home was torched by a student?" He held up his outstretched palm; it was a full hand's worth of misfortune.

"Billy, I'm not one much to talk about people's lives and certainly not about our sheriff..." She hesitated. "He's in love with Bella—"

"Big time!" Billy interrupted her.

"Okay, big time. And it's pretty obvious she's fallen in love with him. Seems to me they both deserve a break. Here's what I wanted to talk to you about."

Billy sat back on the sofa and looked at her. He assumed she had just come to catch him up and unburden herself since Mike was working. He was fine with that. Now he wondered what she wanted to discuss.

"I don't think the sheriff will take time off right away because he's going to want to make sure things are back on an even keel here."

"Agreed. Although I think we made a good start getting the leadership team up and running with our planning session and moving Cecelia into an administrative assistant position, he hasn't even had a chance to know what it is to have her help."

Sylvia nodded. "That's true." She sat for a second then said, "Well, here's what I wanted to ask. I have to be with my family for Christmas Eve. My dad's getting up in years and not in the best of health."

"Stop right there. I can cover whenever. No problem. None at all. I can see where you're going with this. Remember? I'm a detective."

They both started laughing, then each picked up their drinks and did a mock salute.

"Okay, you figured it out. Maybe if we both sit him down, we can work out a schedule so that he can take a week off at Christmas through New Year's and see how the rest of the world lives."

"It's a deal. He said we were having a leadership team meeting on Monday, right? Shall we do it then?"

"Perfect." Sylvia stood. "Thanks, Billy. For supper, for being one of the good guys, and letting me get this out of my head so I can sleep tonight." She was at the door. "See you tomorrow."

"I'll be there. Thanks, Sylvia. Come back anytime." He shut the door behind her. *Mom, you'd be proud of me tonight. One woman tells me I'm one of the good guys. The other tells me I'm really special.* He watched Sylvia's taillights fade into the night. *I'm still going to bed alone—guess you'd rather I didn't tell you that.* He locked the front door and turned off the porch light before cleaning up the kitchen and heading to bed.

Night Has Fallen

The pizza was long gone, eaten off of paper plates at the kitchen counter. Bella and Chad settled themselves on the sofa in front of the fire.

"Oh, Chad. My brain is so scattered. Did you let Nora know we're back?"

"I did."

"It was beyond generous for her to organize us, she didn't need to pay for it. Will I insult her if—"

"Don't say it. We both need to work on letting others do for us, don't you think?" He tightened his arm around her shoulder.

"I need to work on being more gracious. I have a lifetime of doing for others, but it isn't easy to let others do for me."

"My very wise daughter told me not too long ago that accepting a gift is a gift in itself."

Bella nodded. "She is a wise woman. Smart and talented too—like her father."

"Well, as much as I'd like to take credit for it all, she's always been her own person, and I'd say she made the best of her two gene pools.

Sometimes I can grudgingly acknowledge that Mary had some positive influence on her."

"I'm sure she did." She stared into the fire. "I wonder why some women who would give anything to be a mother don't get to be, and some have children who don't have it in them to parent."

"That, my dear, is one of life's eternal mysteries. Mary's not a bad person. She's just not a *warm* person. She doesn't know how to be. I've watched you with my grandchildren and you've given them more attention in a short period of time than she has since they were born. I finally figured out she probably can't learn how: she is who she is."

She kissed him on the cheek. "Thank you for talking about her. I feel like I talk about Matt all the time and you rarely say anything about Mary."

"My daughter is the best thing about my marriage to Mary, so there's not much to say about her beyond that. I suspect you'll meet her someday, and you can make your own judgment. She will charm you, I'm sure. She does have *that* skill."

"I sometimes wonder when Matt will just slip away. I used to talk to him every night. I don't do that as much anymore. I think time would make that inevitable, but loving you makes it possible."

"Bella, my Bella. Matt will never be gone. He is in your heart and soul. And that's okay. There's room for both of us. Don't you think?"

She started to hum. "Somewhere in my youth—"

Chad's secure phone rang. He knew it by the ring. He jumped up to get it from the kitchen counter.

Bella pulled the throw she had on her legs up to her neck and stared at the fire. She continued to hum as she watched Wizard's paws twitch as he slept on his bed.

"Oliver."

"Sorry, sir, I know—"

"What's happening?"

"Sir, I can't reach Sergeant Whitehorse and Sergeant Douglas said to get you on the phone. Putting you through, sir."

"Douglas here."

"What's up, Eddie?"

"Sheriff, sorry—"

"Get on with it."

"Just got word that the police chief in Round City was shot and the suspect has fled. There's concern he might head this way. I can't reach Whitehorse."

"Put patrols on alert. Put the station in lockdown. I'll call you back."

Chad hung up and dialed Sylvia's personal phone. "Whitehorse here."

"Chad." He told her what was going on.

"No one has called me, sir." She realized he was on her personal phone. *Where's my secure phone?* "Sorry, sir. I'm afraid I left my secure phone at the station. Inexcusable."

"Happens. Just glad I don't have to worry about you. Know where Williams is?"

"Home. He was off today."

"Okay. I'll call him."

"I'll head back to the station. I can stay there tonight. Mike's working."

"You sure? I can go in. I'll call Williams. You stay home."

"No, sir, you are not to go in. We'll handle this. I can call Billy—"

"I've got it. Thanks, Sylvia. I owe you big time."

"Honor to serve, sir. Mean it."

"I know you do." He hung up and dialed Billy's secure phone. As it rang, he wondered why he automatically called Sylvia's personal number.

"Williams."

"Oliver here." He told Billy what was going on.

"You stay home, sir. I'm putting on my boots. I can stay at the station tonight. We've got it."

"Thanks, Billy. Appreciate it." Chad hung up.

He put the phone down on the kitchen counter, leaned on his elbows, and ran his fingers through his salt-and-pepper hair. He felt Bella wrap her arms around him from behind, and he pulled her tightly to him. She rested her head against the back of his. He fought back the tears he felt welling. *Mary would have never done that. Never. Maybe somewhere in my youth I, too, did something good.* He turned and hugged her. He saw on the clock behind her that it was almost nine o'clock. "Did we really leave Florida this morning?"

"Funny, I was thinking the same thing. I think we did, but whether we did or not, I'm tired. I'll let Wizard out . . ."

"Tell you what. You go take a hot shower; you'll feel better. I'll take Wizard out then I'll be there in a few minutes."

"Thanks. Sounds like a plan. I love you."

"I love you too. Now, scoot."

He walked into the living room to grab a jacket and Wizard's lead off the coat tree.

"Let's go, boy." Wizard sat up, stretched, and then scampered towards the front door. "Don't know who'll be happier about your new run at Drellag Caban, you or us." Wizard's tail hit against Chad's leg. "Okay, *you*. I get it."

Bella turned on the shower and stood under the hot water for several minutes. Even though she had showered before they left Florida, it felt good to let the water hit her back and neck. She had not realized how tense she was. Her mind turned to Jocelyn. *How can one person have so much hatred? Could I have handled things differently? I honestly thought I handled it as I would with any student. Did she think I rejected her because she was a woman?*

The hot water started to work its magic and, as her muscles relaxed, her thoughts drifted to walking on the beach this morning with Chad. *That's the memory to hold on to.* She turned off the shower, put on her nightgown, and crawled into bed. She was asleep as soon as her head hit the pillow.

Chad returned to the house with Wizard. He stopped in the bedroom doorway and saw the gentle rise and fall of the covers. He was glad she could sleep. He leaned down and whispered to Wizard, "Go lay by our Bella. I'll be in shortly." He had to sort out his reaction to David Nelson being shot.

At the Station

Billy's phone rang as he drove to the station. "Williams."

"Billy, it's Quinn."

"Where are you?"

"At the office. Did you get a call about Chief Nelson?"

"Yes, I'm headed to our station."

"Were you called?"

"Yes, looks like it was related to that caravan of immigrants I mentioned."

"Where's Chief Nelson?"

"At the hospital. I don't expect to get updates. If you do, will you call me?"

"Sure. What are *you* going to do?" Billy hoped his concern for her was evident.

"I'm at the office and talking with my counterpart in Knoxville. He just had another call come in so I expect him to call back any minute."

"Okay. I'll be at the station. Call me if you learn anything. We're on the lookout over here."

"10-4. Gotta go."

He pulled up to the gate to the back of the station and called the gate guard.

"Opening now, Detective. Didn't expect to see you here tonight."

"Duty calls. Thanks for opening up." The gate moved to the side and he drove through. He parked and sprinted for the back door, scanned his badge, and headed for Sylvia's office. She was already there.

"Any word?" he asked.

"Not yet. I had Eddie send two more cars down to the gap. Unless whoever did this is from here, she or he isn't going to know they hit a bottleneck that we'll have covered."

"Always been one of my favorite things about our little valley. Our own built-in protection."

"I suspect our ancestors on both sides figured that out long ago." She smiled at him.

"I'll be in the lab if you need me."

"10-4."

CHAPTER 21

One can make a day of any size and regulate the rising and setting of his own sun and the brightness of its shining.

John Muir

Early Morning Shift

Doc Fred could usually do rounds at the hospital on the weekends, if needed, later in the morning, but the physician who usually handled weekends had called in sick. He and Nora were in the kitchen enjoying the quiet time they had together before the children woke up. "Glad to hear your dad and Bella are back. Did they enjoy the beach?"

"It sounded like they did. Felt like there was a lot on his mind, but then when isn't there?" Nora shrugged.

"Goes with the job. Sort of like mine: you can take time off, but the job never turns off."

"I know. Wish I could make it different for you." She kissed her husband.

"If I'd wanted it to be different, I'd have taken up plumbing, not medicine. Doubt they worry about pipes and drainage at the end of the day."

"Oh, I don't know. Maybe they do. I'll ask ours the next time he comes."

"Shhh . . . Let's hope that's no time soon."

"True. I really appreciate your understanding about my impulse to buy Daddy and Bella's tickets and house rental. I should have asked you."

"Nora, you know better than that. I appreciate being informed; I don't need to give permission. I'm glad it's something we could do for them. I just hope this is all behind them soon."

"Me too. By the way, Nancy isn't going to the jamboree tonight, so she said she'd keep the kids."

"That's nice of her. Are you upset it was changed to Saturday night?"

"Not really. It's been a hectic week. Now I can enjoy it."

"I'll swing by the jamboree and see you before I go get the kids. How's that?"

"Sounds nice. I'll look forward to it. At first, I was disappointed about not taking the children since it's the first night we'll do some Christmas singing, but then I realized Nancy was right."

"About what?"

"About not getting them excited about Christmas too soon." She laughed.

"Something to be said for that. Little Lilly will have a super Christmas this year, won't she? Two and half is the perfect Christmas age."

"I agree. And just think, we'll have Bella with us too." She looked at him. "I hope."

"What do you mean? You don't think she'll stay in the mountains?"

"I do. Well, I assume so, especially now that she doesn't have another home. I don't know—she seems to love being with the kids. I just don't want her to think that we only have immediate family."

"Well, maybe your dad's going to ask her to become immediate family." He raised his eyebrows and wiggled them.

"I'm trying. Maybe *you* need to have a man-to-man talk with him." She wiggled her eyebrows at him.

"Whoa! I'm not about to interfere in my father-in-law's love life. I love your dad as if he were my own father...but... no way." He put his hands up. "They are two mature people; they'll work it out."

"Yes, my wise husband. You're right. We just need to make sure Bella knows she's welcome."

"I think she knows. Now, patients await. I hope you have a lovely day. Seems I don't get to hear you play the piano much anymore." He kissed Nora.

Nora clapped her hands. "Then let's have our own Christmas sing. We can invite Daddy and Bella and a few friends over. What do you think? Tomorrow night, okay?"

Fred couldn't miss the excitement in her voice. "Make it an early evening and you're on. I'll even flip the burgers."

"Deal. Have a good day. Go forth and heal the sick. I love you."

"I love you, Nora Oliver-Smith, for ever and ever."

"Amen!"

Fred put on his top coat and sprinted across the courtyard to the garage. She watched him through the glass panel in the door.

Up With the Sun

Bella woke at six a.m. and Chad was sound asleep. She had slept through the night. *I didn't hear Chad come to bed.* Wizard stirred and looked up at her. "Shhh ..." She ruffled his ears as she slipped out of bed and grabbed her robe. She was almost out the bedroom door, with Wizard at her heels, when she heard Chad speak.

"I'll make coffee. Be there in a minute."

"No hurry. It's actually Saturday morning." She said softly and kept walking.

She hoped he'd fall back asleep; she was very quiet as she moved around the kitchen. She pulled the kettle off the stove just before it whistled, but Chad walked in as she was pouring the steaming water into a mug.

He went to the kitchen sink and looked out the window. "One of the things I don't like about winter, besides the cold, is closing the drapes at night on the sliders to the porch blocking the view of the mountains. So, I walk in here and raise the shade to get a read on the day."

She smiled. "I like that phrase: a read on the day. What is your read on this day?"

"Grateful it's one I get to share with you." He turned around and looked at her sitting at the counter with her tea. "The sky is crystal clear, which goes with this cold weather, there's a hint of first light across the mountains, and a beautiful, intelligent woman graces my home."

"Poetry first thing in the morning. I love it."

"How are you? Did you rest?"

"I slept. Obviously. Yes, I think I rested. I was so exhausted I must have fallen asleep as soon as I put my head on the pillow."

"Part of my plan. A hot shower is a great antidote for all that ails you."

"So I see." She sipped her tea. "Do you think they arrested Jocelyn?"

"I'm sure they'll let us know. Now, you had a pretty skimpy supper last night. How about some ham and eggs and toast?"

"I can help."

"I know you *can*. That means you're able, as Mac would remind us." They both laughed. "No need. I can handle it."

"Thanks. I love work; I could sit and watch it all day."

"Speaking of all day. Something you'd like to do today?"

"Just the jamboree this evening. I have a book I can read if you need to go to work."

"Running me off? Too much time together?"

"Never. Just don't want you to feel you *have* to be with me all the time."

"Bella, if I am with you twenty-four seven for the next fifty years, it won't be enough. You will likely tire of me, so I'll spare you. The good news about my job is that I'm elected. My term is up next year. We can talk about whether I run again or not."

She stared at him. "You aren't serious?"

"I'm certainly thinking about it. I want you to think about it." His gray eyes conveyed his desire for her opinion. "Then I want us to discuss it. I have to qualify by February. Of course, if I'm *not* going to run, I should make it known as soon as possible."

"Chad, I'm speechless. It never occurred to me you'd consider retiring."

"Me either, if you had asked three months ago. Shoot, maybe even two months ago. Now it's something I'm thinking about a lot of the time—when I'm not thinking about you. *And* when I *am* thinking about you."

"I would never want to be the reason you left a job you love and obviously do well."

"There are many ways to serve this community. Some of the things I've wanted to do as sheriff, I've not been able to do. You talked about helping with recycling—that appeals to me too. Anyway, let's have this discussion on a full stomach at least. You think about it, and we can talk about it later. You okay with that?"

"Sure. I'm just not sure I should weigh in on it."

"Okay, last thing for right now. I get the intellectual Dr. Anderson taking that position. I want, and need, the woman I love to weigh in on it." He kissed her, pulled back, and looked into her dark brown eyes with his soft gray ones. "I love you, Bella Anderson, with all my heart."

"Okay, okay. I surrender. I'll think about your decision. Right now, though, I *can* make toast."

Chad's personal phone rang. He saw it was Nora and picked it up. "Hey, favorite daughter of mine."

"Am I calling too early?"

"Call anytime you like."

"Thanks, Daddy. I know it's only seven, but my day is about to get hectic. I'm calling to see if you and Bella can come tomorrow night for burgers and a Christmas sing-along."

"Let me ask her."

He asked Bella. She nodded and smiled.

"We'd love it. What time and what can we bring?"

"Oh, I hadn't even gotten that far. Just yourselves."

"We'll bring beer and wine. How many folks?"

"Gray and Nancy, Joshua and Carla, and Harold and Julie. I think that'll be it."

"Good, glad Joshua's coming. I'd hate being the oldest one there." He saw Bella wagging her finger at him. "There's a lady here wagging her finger at me."

"Why?"

"Because . . ."

Bella took the phone from him. "Hey, Nora. Because . . . he knows I'm nine days older than he is and he's afraid to say it."

"Hey, Bella. That's funny. Put me on speaker phone, please."

"Daddy, I'm glad you have an older woman in your life. Be easier for her to keep you in line. She can always say, 'Mind your elders.'"

"Argh . . . daughter of mine. It's too early in the morning for that."

"Nora," Bella hesitated. "Thank you for your quick action and the wonderful gift of our trip to Florida. It was just the balm I needed, and I don't think it did your dad any harm either."

"That's all I needed to hear. Fred and I were happy to do it. Now, I'll let you two get on with your day—see you at the jamboree tonight and tomorrow at six. Love you both. Bye now." She hung up.

Bella looked at the phone and then handed it to Chad.

"See. I told you my family is your family now."

"That was sweet."

Suspect

Detective Burton decided to call FBI Agent Michaels first. He picked up the phone and was about to dial when the forensic artist walked in his door.

"You wanted to see me?"

"Thanks for coming by. Are you normally here at this hour and on a Saturday?" He looked at his watch and saw it was seven fifteen.

"Depends. Late night usually means late morning the next day. No late night, I come in around seven and leave by three thirty, which means I can pick my kids up from school once in a while. But, yes, it's Saturday and I had to do a drawing in the middle of the night. So, late night, early morning. Headed home shortly."

"This job doesn't lend itself to normal family life, does it?"

"I don't know what normal is. My husband teaches at the technical college and he can have an eight a.m. class and one at seven p.m. We just make our own normal. Fortunately, it's easier to juggle now the kids are in high school. Anyway, how may I be of service?"

"Heard you were in the building and wanted to show you the picture of the person you drew."

"You got her?"

"Middle of the night, too." He showed her the photo.

"Oh." She studied the picture carefully.

"Notice anything?"

"No tattoo."

"Right. We found a sticker sheet of them in a drawer in her apartment. Seems it was all part of her messaging."

"How's that?" She continued to study the photograph.

"Seems the homeowner has a thing for dragonflies." He opened the portfolio and put the drawing the artist had done next to the photo. "Fine work. Mighty fine work."

"Thanks." She pulled up the chair next to his desk. "May I?"

"Of course. Sorry, I should have offered."

She shook her head. "When I'm doing a sketch based on someone's description, or from a video like this case, I'm aware the person is likely a criminal. It intensifies my focus and determination to get as accurate a depiction as the information I have will allow."

He knew to let her talk.

"It's something else when you see them vulnerable. Detective, do you think there's at least a little bit of good in everyone?"

"I have to think that. Couldn't do this job if I didn't. People have mental health issues, get a bum deal in the parent department, or just started hanging out with some bad folks. What I try to remember is there are a lot more good folks who count on us to protect them from the bad things others do, no matter the motivation. It's up to the courts what happens to the criminal. So, don't carry that burden. Your drawing led to her arrest."

"Thanks, Detective. Thanks a lot. That helps. If you don't need me further ..."

"Thanks for coming down and for the great work you do. I've told our Chief."

"Nice of you to do so. Might get me a ten cents an hour raise." She chuckled, shook her head, and walked out.

Detective Burton sat back in his chair and looked at the drawing and mug shot of Jocelyn Walters. He picked up the phone and decided Michaels could wait a few more minutes. He dialed the Valley Sheriff's office.

"Whitehorse."

"Sergeant, there's a Detective Burton from Statesboro, North—"

"Please put him through." She didn't usually cut off the dispatcher. She heard the click. "Whitehorse here."

"Sergeant, Burton in Statesboro here. I'm calling to update you on the suspect in the fire at the Anderson property."

Conference Room

Detective Burton told Sylvia he would contact Agent Michaels.

As soon as she hung up, Sylvia called Chad.

Chad answered. "Any word on Chief Nelson?"

"No, sir. I'll let you know when we hear anything."

"Got it. What's up?"

"Just got off the phone with Detective Burton. He had news on Jocelyn Walters."

"I don't want to hear it. We were headed out for a hike, but we'll come by the station first." He looked at his watch. "We'll be there by 10:30."

"10-4." It was 10:15 a.m. Sylvia called Billy.

"Billy, I'm not sure why I'm finding it hard. I think we'll just give the sheriff and Bella the facts. Wouldn't you want it that way?"

"Sure, Sylvia, but hypotheticals are always easier than the real thing."

"What do you think about the document Burton sent? Should we share it with Bella?"

"I don't like people playing games with me, and I don't like them thinking I can't handle bad news. We've seen Dr. Anderson handle the things that have happened since she's been up here, and I'm sure she'll handle this. And, besides that, now she has the boss to help her through it. Win-win. Right?"

"Billy, you have always been able to cut to the chase."

"Thanks. That's why I'm a detective. And you, Sergeant, are a whiz at problem solving and managing people. I'm hopeless at the latter. Just look at Alexander."

"Speaking of Alexander, is she back from Knoxville?"

"Thought I told you she'll be back today. I think I told you they catalogued all the arms and ammunition that Harris had in his truck?"

"Oh, yeah. You did. Sorry—not like me to be distracted."

"Alexander's still intrigued with the wildlife poisoning."

"I thought we'd wrapped that up and passed it on."

"We did. It's in the hands of Wildlife Resources, so technically no longer our case. Elizabeth thinks she's found a new substance. She's trying to determine if it exists in nature or if it's a manufactured chemical. She'll pass it on if she does."

"Sure hope she doesn't find playing with the big city folks more appealing." Sylvia raised an eyebrow.

"She sounded pretty happy to be coming home."

"Yeah. This *being* her home helps, don't you think?"

"Always did for me; I'm guessing for you too?"

"Always."

"Okay, let's get some coffee and make sure the conference room got cleaned last night after our meeting."

"Billy, you never cease to amaze me. Not to sound sexist, but I doubt if ten percent of our male staff would think about whether the conference room was clean."

"Mr. Perfect, that's who I am." *Sure hope Quinn figures that out.*

Sylvia laughed then turned serious. "Any word on Chief Nelson?"

"Not yet. He was in surgery a long time. No evidence of anyone trying to come our way."

"I suppose we'll hear something today." She stretched. "I forgot how rough those bunks are."

"You're telling me!" They walked towards the conference room.

"Going somewhere, folks?" They both turned and saw Chad and Bella coming from his office.

Sylvia looked at her watch. "Sorry, sir. It's a little earlier than I was expecting you. We're headed to get coffee. Get you some? Dr. Anderson?"

"None for me, thanks," Bella said.

"I'm good." Chad held up his mug. "Just mentioned to Bella we don't accommodate hot tea drinkers here."

"Well, sir, in a way we do."

"Really? How?" It was a question, not a criticism.

"A couple of our folks just buy the bottled tea in the drink machine and heat it in the microwave." She shrugged. "Guess we could do better."

Bella laughed. "Well, that's a new one on me. Why didn't I ever think of that?"

Billy wondered if she'd still be laughing after they met.

"I'm good, though." She pointed to the iced tea drinks in the machine.

Bella shook her head. "Thanks, though."

"We're ready when you are. Meet you in the conference room."

Billy entered the conference room last and closed the door.

"Dr. Anderson, Sheriff, I received a call this morning from Detective Burton of the Statesboro Police to inform us that they picked up Jocelyn Walters."

Sylvia looked at Billy.

He nodded slightly. "Ms. Walters was arrested."

"How? Did she resist arrest?" The words poured out of Bella.

"No, ma'am. She didn't resist arrest." Sylvia looked at Chad. Then she realized she didn't have to give the same level of detail she would give the sheriff if he were by himself. That's what she'd been struggling with.

"Oh my." Bella sat quietly. "Do they know now if she actually burned my house."

"She actually handed them a letter when they arrested her." Sylvia looked at Chad and he nodded. She slid a photograph of the note towards Bella.

"To whom this may concern . . ." The letter rambled. Jocelyn wrote that she had been rejected by the woman she loved most in the world, whose work she admired, and who she wanted to be like. Bella looked up from the letter. Then she continued to read: "I believed her that she didn't have relationships with students, but she does." The letter went on about finding out Victoria lived in Bella's home. She called Victoria a third-rate hack and some other things. Bella pushed the letter back towards Sylvia.

"Thank you, Sergeant. Uh, Sylvia. May I call you Sylvia here?"

"Absolutely. Please do."

"Thank you for telling me and showing me the letter. I am deeply sorry to have contributed to her anguish. If you need anything more from me, you know how to reach me."

She stood. "Chad, I'll wait for you outside." She walked to the door.

He stood up and walked out with her. They left the building.

Sylvia and Billy sat without saying a word.

"Come on, Sylvia, let's get out of here. Is Mike home?"

"Yes."

"Then I'll drive you home and you can have someone come get you for your next shift."

"Okay. I'll let you."

Round City

Billy was driving back to the station when his personal phone rang. "Williams."

"Isaacs."

"Hey, what's up?"

"Where are you?"

"Just took Sylvia Whitehorse home."

"Why? She isn't hurt, is she?"

"Only in the place that aches when we can't fix or make something right." He told her about the woman who had burned down Bella's house.

"Well, that just caps an already really lousy morning."

"Why?"

"You're working, right?"

"Quinn, if you need to talk, I can come to Round City. We're allowed to take leave by the hour, and I can take the day. We're finally getting back to our slow-paced ways in the valley and surrounding hills. Where shall I meet you?"

"My house. See you when you get there."

"Thirty minutes or less." He called dispatch and told them to sign him out. He expected to be back by three and was reachable by phone.

Quinn's SUV was sitting in the driveway when he pulled up. She was at the open front door when he climbed the steps two at a time. She pointed towards the fireplace in the living room. "Have a seat."

Billy saw coffee and a pitcher of water on the coffee table. *Guess that's why they call them coffee tables. Never thought about it before.*

"It's not been announced yet, but Chief Nelson died about an hour ago."

Billy let out a long, low whistle.

"Well, that's one way of putting it."

"Did you know him well?"

"We worked on quite a few cases together over the ten years I've been here, and he was one of the best cops I know. I can't say the same for his lead detective."

"Am I to assume that means he'll be the next chief?"

"Hard to tell. It could be the administrative captain, at least temporarily, although I've heard he's going to retire in July. It's up to the city council who they appoint. There'll be a process—it just makes an already difficult job for me even more so."

"Why?"

"They arrested the guy who shot him and he's an illegal immigrant. I've interviewed him. He claims he was told to do it or the runners who brought his family into the US would kill his wife and children and make him watch."

"Son of a . . . Sorry."

"I know those words. Don't like them, but sometimes they are the only ones that work."

"What does it mean for you?"

"I don't know. It could mean nothing. It's only my job to translate, assess, and give my opinion of the veracity of the man's statements. They will, of course, have other native Spanish speakers interrogate him. The issue for me is that I already have an uncomfortable situation at my own agency. Now, the local law enforcement I work with the most will have a new leader."

"Quinn, my mother was a very smart woman. In situations like this, I always think of something she taught me. 'Will a decision on this, unmade by you today, result in life or death?'"

"Are you asking me that question?"

"Yes." He gave her a smile of encouragement.

She sat for several seconds. "Not that I know of."

"Then you have time to sort it out. Even on the job, we don't have to take ownership of the circumstances presented to us by others." He watched her face. He could see in her eyes that she was thinking. *What* she was thinking he didn't know yet, but she *was* thinking.

"Thanks, Billy. I think I'm struggling with the nagging feeling I have about the young agent and now the loss of a man I respected greatly."

"Yeah, that was his reputation. Do you have work you *have* to do today?"

"I have work I *should* do today. But the caravan, the one we knew was headed this way, left the shooter—that's how he got caught. They crossed into another IEA jurisdiction during the night, so now another team picks it up."

"The word we got was he escaped. Don't know if it was said or was just assumed he was in a vehicle. We went into virtual lockdown." Billy continued to watch her.

"Billy, the suspect was not in a car. He was in sandals, shorts, and a short sleeve shirt. Yeah, the guys who transport these people across the border and drop them off along the way are real sweethearts."

"Any idea why they targeted Chief Nelson?"

"I can only assume it was because he worked with us at Immigration to catch the mules moving people through here. The challenge of the mountains is that their routes are limited, so they couldn't bypass us."

"Where are they headed?"

"Mostly to the northeast. Folks can disappear in cities, and there are plenty of folks willing to hire them and not talk about it."

"I think I like my little corner of the world."

"You should." She stood up and turned her back to the fire. "The least I could do is buy you lunch."

"Let me make another proposal. Take the rest of the day off. Pack a bag and come to the valley. You can stay in my guest room, or you can stay at Joe's house like you planned. We'll go have lunch at a place I know off the highway, then you can put your feet up until time for the jamboree. If paperwork is overwhelming you, go in tomorrow or Sunday afternoon."

"Maybe the jamboree is just what I need. Will they have it if word travels about Chief Nelson?"

"I'm sure. At our jamborees, we celebrate the lives of folks who've left us. I'm sure the sheriff will see that it happens if the news is public by then. What do you say?"

"I'd already told Joshua I was coming over tonight. Will you drive and bring me back home anyway?"

"I will. Now, go pack."

She walked away towards what he assumed was her bedroom.

He walked out on the porch and called Sylvia. He wanted to call Chad but decided he had enough on his plate. Sylvia could decide when to let Chad know about the chief of police.

CHAPTER 22

Come to the woods, for here is rest.
There is no repose like that of the green deep woods.
John Muir

Drellag Caban

"I'd like to go to Drellag Caban. Do you have time?"

"For you, I have nothing but time. We could go for a hike up there."
He put the SUV in gear and drove out of the parking lot.

Bella looked at the CDs on the visor in front of her and read the labels of songs Nora had recorded on each of them. She pulled the one with "Where Rainbows Never Die" by The SteelDrivers and put it in the CD player. She leaned her head against the headrest and closed her eyes.

Chad drove up the county road towards Bella's cabin. He glanced at her when she joined in with Nora, his heart ached for her. When the song ended, Bella turned off the CD. "How do you reconcile your role in the life, or death, of another person?"

Chad knew it was a rhetorical question, and one he asked himself every single time he pulled the trigger and it resulted in the loss of life. *More than that ... I have to ask myself if I am justified in being judge, jury, and executioner even to save my own life or someone else's.*

He was on the last sharp switchback, lost in the question she had asked.

"Chad! Look out!" A deer darted across in front of them.

He slammed on the brakes. *How do I reconcile the distractions of love, life, and death?*

"Bella, I am sorry. I should have had a closer eye on the road."

She reached over and touched his arm. "No, I'm the one who should apologize. In my own little pity party, I failed to consider my rhetorical question might be far more than that for a man whose life involves fighting crime. I *am* truly sorry."

"Let's get to the cabin and then we can regroup. Good with that?"

She nodded, and he continued driving, crossing over into Bella's land. He realized that he had no idea the actual dimensions of the eighty acres she owned. The space for the cabin—now cabins, plural—was likely less than one of those acres. He pulled up and parked. They sat in silence, watching as the workers finished up the final touches on all the projects: cabin, garage, dog run.

"*Home*. I've always thought of this cabin as my family's ancestral home. The home of my great-grandparents and a place my Grandmother Hazel loved. She fed me the stories and showed me the beauty of every element of these magnificent mountains." Bella stared out the windshield across the tableau that had now changed for the first time in more than fifty years.

Chad took her hand in his. "Why did you choose the song you just played?"

"I don't know. I guess because for me it's about the awareness you reach at a point in life, a point where you know too much and not enough."

"Meaning? I know what the words *say*, I want to know what it means to you."

"We haven't done a great job in our culture of teaching children the value of aging. We've allowed a scripted, Madison Avenue version of ourselves, focused on being 'forever young.'"

"Being young is overrated."

She chuckled. "Of course you'd say that. Just wait until you've lived as long as I have."

He relaxed. She was finding her way back, shedding the shock. He squeezed her hand. "When I first started in law enforcement, the sheriff was a good friend of my dad and a man for whom I had the greatest respect. He used to tell me that young people waste the carefree days of their youth trying to replace the old folks, only to learn they get the real work when they get old themselves."

She smiled. "Maybe the moral of the story is we don't know how to enjoy the time we're given at any point in our lives."

"Maybe we could learn and show others." He leaned over and kissed her cheek.

Arthur came out of the shed and waved.

Bella opened the door and hopped out of the Jeep. Chad followed.

"Morning, folks. Lovely day, isn't it?"

"It is, Arthur. How are things going?"

"Floors dried up well in Solasta Caban. Want to go in?"

"If you're sure. Otherwise, we can look in the windows."

"I'm sure. Wouldn't say so if it weren't the case." He headed to the front porch.

Bella and Chad followed him, walking hand in hand. They stopped as she looked up at the sign: Solasta Caban.

"Do you like the sign?" She turned to look at Chad.

"I think it's a perfect complement to Drellag Caban. Good choice, Bella." Chad put his hand behind her back as she stepped up on the front porch.

Arthur unlocked the door and stood back.

Bella stepped into the doorframe and stopped. "Oh my! It's beautiful."

"A few more finishing touches, but it came together pretty quickly." Arthur didn't tell her it was the only work his full crew had over the past month. "I'll leave you to it. Let me know if you have questions." He went down the steps.

Chad and Bella stepped in and slipped out of their boots. Each looked out the windows which gave a sprawling vista of the mountains.

"Oh Bella, it's amazing. What a stunning view." He pulled her to him. "I'm glad you added your own touches to the original cabin design." He smiled at her. "I love it. Do you?"

"I do." She took his hand and walked across the open living and dining room. The sun was sending light across the matte finish of the floors and warming the space. They stopped in front of the corner that was framed on both sides by glass. She turned to look at him.

"I want us to live here." She stopped. "When you can be away from the valley." Her eyes were pleading. "It's big enough to be comfortable and guests can stay at Drellag Caban. What do you think?"

"I think you had me at 'us.'" He embraced her and kissed her deeply. Then they stood, an arm behind each other, and looked out to the mountains.

"Chad, I have a ton of thinking to do to sort out what has happened and why. I hope you can handle the randomness with which I am likely to ask to talk about it."

"Talking has not always been my strong suit, but I'm a good listener. I'll give you my opinion when I have one, but I want to make sure you know that I don't ever mean it to be the *only* answer that is right for you."

"Back at 'cha."

Chad loved it when her often formal language slipped into mountain colloquialism.

She took his hand and headed for the door. "I want Arthur to show me how to handle the heated dog run …" She stopped. "Why didn't I think of it? I should have had him do one here, too."

"Still can."

"Ah, yes. The thinking man. Please remind me to tell him."

"Done."

"I don't suppose it will need to be as elaborate, will it? This one can be just Wizard's."

"Seems fair."

She laughed as they walked towards the garage.

Lunch Encounter

There was a small, narrow road that pulled off the highway underpass off Route 54 between the valley and Round City. Billy drove about five hundred feet and turned into a secluded parking lot.

"What's this?" Quinn looked around and saw a cabin located toward the back.

"One of the best kept secrets for the last fifty years—give or take. It's a local restaurant you have to know about or stumble upon."

Quinn looked at him. "I've been to some of those places in these hills, and I don't think I'm welcome."

"Yes, there are some private clubs that don't let women in without 'their' man, and truthfully, they prefer men only. I don't go to those places. The owners here are actually distant cousins of mine and they have welcomed anyone who found them."

"Little hard to find with no signs."

"Keeps it interesting. If you're uncomfortable when we get in, we don't have to stay."

"Okay." She opened her door and got out.

They walked up to the front, and she looked in the plate glass window. "Is this someone's home?"

"It was, decades ago. The highway noise ran them off. They live in Round City now." He opened the door.

Quinn looked around as she walked in. It was early for lunch so there weren't many people. But there were two highway patrolmen, both Hispanic, two women in professional business dress, a four-top table with two Anglos and two local tribal members. *Why did I expect something different? Maybe I'm the one with the closed mind.*

"Want to try it?"

"Works for me."

"Hey, Billy." A man in uniform stood up in the back corner. Billy saw him and waved, then noticed the black band on his badge. He was a Round City policeman. He and Billy had gone to high school together.

"I need to speak to him," he said to Quinn.

She saw the band. "Of course. Please introduce me."

"Sergeant Steve Clark, IEA Agent Quinn Isaacs. Quinn, this is Steve Clark. Sorry for your loss."

"Pleased to meet you," Quinn said. "Sorry about the chief. I had the utmost respect and admiration for him."

"Your reputation is well known, Agent. Pleasure to meet you. I just stopped in for a coffee and cinnamon roll—best in the area. Comfort food on a day like today. Care to join me?"

Billy looked at Quinn. She nodded. "If you don't mind the company, we'd be honored."

They sat down, and a server got their drinks while they read the chalkboard menu.

"If it's lunch you're having, nothing better than their egg salad sandwich. They make the bread too." Steve pointed towards the special on the board.

"Do they just serve breakfast and lunch?" Quinn said.

Billy and Steve spoke in unison: "Yes."

Quinn nodded.

Once their food was ordered, the three law enforcement officers talked quietly about the chief of police and the loss to the community. After their meals arrived, the conversation was sparse as they focused on the food in front of them. Sergeant Clark finished his cinnamon roll and took out his wallet.

"Put it away, Steve. I've got it. Good to see you again. Sorry it's been so long. See you next week," Billy said. They both knew he meant the funeral of the police chief. He stood and shook hands with Steve.

"Nice meeting you, Quinn. Be an honor to work with you if the situation arises."

"Likewise—see you next week." All three knew every law enforcement officer in the area would be at the funeral, whether they knew the chief or not. It's what they did.

Billy looked at Quinn as Steve walked away. "You okay?"

"I'll be fine. Guess this might have been the most gentle way to make the news real."

"How's that?"

"I'm very sad at the loss of Chief Nelson, but this man just lost his boss and likely a friend."

"True. It's a reality we all know and never want to face in our line of work."

"True. Finished?"

Billy swooped his hand above his plate like a game show model showing a prize. "Empty plate." He took out his wallet and nodded. "Let's go. We pay as we leave." He put a tip on the table and headed towards the front.

Back in his SUV, Billy reached across Quinn to his glove compartment. "Excuse me."

"Sure. What's up?"

He pulled a small box out of the glove compartment. He took his badge out of his pocket and took a black band out of the small box and placed it across his badge.

Quinn stared out the window when she realized what he was doing. Her black band was in her desk at work.

"Not sure about your tradition in the IEA, but we wear the band from date of death until after the funeral if the officer is in another department."

"And your own?"

"Thirty days."

"Billy?"

"Yes?" He had been about to start the vehicle, but he took his hand off the key and waited for her to continue.

"Do you believe our lives have a plan?"

"You mean, has God already decided our fate?"

"I guess that's what I mean."

"Quinn, I'm not the most philosophical guy in the world. I think God expects us to use the brains He gave us, or else why bother giving us one in the first place? What do you think?"

"I think the day I am most religious, and the day I am least religious, is when a fellow law enforcement officer is killed in the line of the duty."

Billy didn't comment. He started the SUV and drove out of the lot towards Route 54 and the valley. They were nearing the pull-out to overlook the valley and Billy turned onto the approach to the rise. "Have you been up here?"

"No. What is it?"

"You'll see." He drove up close to one of the benches along the overlook, hopped out, and went around to open her door.

She sat staring out the windshield and was startled when the door opened.

"Billy, it's like a movie set. The Corral, the Valley Store, the sheriff's station, the hospital. I can see the tribal grounds off in the distance. What is that small building?" She pointed to a small structure.

"That's the library and just beyond it is the post office and the elementary school."

"Oh, then that's the high school?" She pointed to a red-brick two-story building.

"You win the prize. It's actually the joint middle and high school now, but when I attended it was kindergarten through twelfth grade." It was the fanciest building in the valley. "We don't have enough kids to warrant a separate building."

She sat down on a bench, put her hands beside her and pushed her shoulders forward against them. "I love how the community is protected by the mountains. When you look at the ocean, it goes on forever. When you look at the mountains, like from here, they go on forever too. But somehow it seems you can navigate them. You can imagine the possibilities of what lies over the next hill. I've always loved the blue-green of these mountains; have you seen the Rockies?"

"Not yet."

"Bare cliff faces, sometimes for as far as you can see. There are places that remind me of these mountains, but it's not the same. They are beautiful in their own way. But, for me, there's nothing like the Smoky Mountains."

"Me too."

Peace and Quiet

Chad and Bella talked with Arthur as he showed her the switch in the shed and Drellag Caban to turn on the heat for the run. "I put them on a timer so you don't have to heat it all the time, but you can."

"Arthur, how much trouble would it be to put in a run, not as fancy as this perhaps, on Solasta Caban?"

"Would you want it off the back?"

"I think so." She looked at Chad. "What do you think?"

"Makes the most sense. I don't think you want to change the view at the crest."

"Good point. So, yes, the back."

"I can figure something out and get you a drawing."

"Surprise me."

Both men looked at her.

"Ma'am? Are you sure?"

"Arthur, there is nothing you've done that I've felt the need to change, and you have improved upon the structures that are here. I'll be pleased with whatever you do. Is it a deal?"

"Yes, ma'am. If you're sure."

"I'm sure." She extended her hand, and he shook it. "Okay, we'll get out of your way now. Remember, I'm looking forward to meeting your family tonight at the jamboree."

"Sure thing. Catch you later, Sheriff."

"Have a good rest of the day."

Chad took Bella's hand and turned towards Drellag Caban. "Need to go in?"

"No. I just needed a reality check."

"Want to go for a hike?"

"Not today. Thanks for coming up with me."

"My pleasure. Now, here's my suggestion for the rest of the day. Let's go back to the valley, figure out something for lunch and relax for a few hours, then be some of the first to the jamboree. It gets crowded when we move inside, and we'll want a table."

"For sure. I remember the last time it was inside. It got pretty loud."

"It will be for sure tonight. It's the first night of Christmas songs."

"That will be nice."

They were at the bottom of the switchbacks when Chad's secure phone rang. He pulled over and stopped. He wasn't going to be distracted again; the deer would be running and he needed to remind Bella of that in case she came up here on her own—it was hunting season.

"Oliver."

Cecelia said, "Sir, sorry to bother you. We just got word that Chief Nelson passed away early this morning from his injuries."

"Arrangements?"

"Unknown at the moment, but probably Monday."

"Okay. I'm headed home. I'll send a notification to the department."

"Yes, sir. I think that would be best. Sergeant Whitehorse said they can follow up in roll call."

"Fine. Thanks, Cecelia, call me if you need me." He looked at Bella, who was watching him. "Police chief in Round City passed away this morning."

"Oh, Chad. I met him."

"You did? When?"

"When we were trying to find Billy. He's the brother of the State Bureau Assistant Director, Elliott, right?"

"Good memory. I had forgotten you'd met." He was relieved she didn't ask him what happened.

"When's the funeral?"

"Unknown at this time." He caught himself. He sounded like he was reporting to his deputies. "Cecelia thought it might be Monday."

"If it's appropriate, I would like to go."

"Always appropriate when we honor the departed, don't you think?"

"I do."

They drove on in silence.

Chad backed into his garage. He was so accustomed to a quick exit that he was around his Jeep before Bella could open her door. He opened it for her and she stepped out. They walked into the kitchen together. Wizard was sitting by the kitchen island, his tail drumming against it in a steady beat.

"Hey, Wizard. You missed us, didn't you?" Bella squatted down and nuzzled his head. "Want to go for a walk while I still have my coat on?" She stood and turned towards Chad. "You go take care of your people. We'll be fine. We'll go for a walk, then I'll settle in and read. I think you should go to the station."

He shook his head.

"Yes. Don't argue with me. I can only imagine the thoughts running through the head of every law enforcement officer in the area right now. Go. Please."

He wondered if she had heard the conversation with Sylvia last night. He replayed the phone call in his head. He knew he had not mentioned the chief being shot. Then he remembered telling Sylvia to go into lockdown. *Bella must have heard me say that and put the two together. One smart lady.* He kissed her then went to his dresser to get the black band for his sheriff's star. He heard the jangle of Wizard's leash followed by the creak of the front door closing. He headed to his SUV. As he drove out of the garage, he could see Bella and Wizard walking across the front lawn to the hedges on the far side.

Chad rolled down the passenger window. "I'll be back as soon as I can. I love you."

"Take your time. Love you too." She threw him a kiss and waved.

Sheriff's Station

Chad pulled in the back and parked his Ford Interceptor—his official vehicle. Three deputies were walking towards the station and saw him. They stopped, came to attention, and saluted. This carryover from the military to law enforcement was not something they normally practiced, but he knew the deputies must have already heard about David Nelson. They were honoring *their* boss *and* Chief Nelson. He saluted back and waited for them as they approached him.

"Afternoon."

"Afternoon, sir."

"Sir." The female deputy gave a deferential nod of her head.

"Good afternoon, Sheriff."

He stepped to the side and let them pass him. Each swiped their ID cards as they entered. He followed and swiped his ID.

"Thanks for your commitment," Chad said. "Stay the course."

They nodded and kept walking.

Chad wondered if there were ever words you could say when a fellow officer was killed in the line of duty. He'd only had one other experience, and it was one of their own whose vehicle had been forced off a mountain road by a drunk teenager. He was a detective then. The sheriff had gone into full leadership mode. Bella was right—Chad knew that was what he would do too. He stopped at Sergeant Whitehorse's office.

Sylvia was on the phone but looked up and saw him. She held up one finger. He pointed towards his office, and she nodded. Chad headed down the hall and had just sat down at his desk when she appeared in the doorway.

"Sorry, sir, it was Deputy Thomas. She said the word was spreading among the deputies. I emphasized she should just say what we know: Chief Nelson passed away this morning from a gunshot wound in the line of duty." Her eyes roamed around his office. "Do you think that was too much?"

"Sounds perfect. It's what we know. The circumstances will only matter if they can inform us in ways to improve our practice in the future. Come in! Come in!" He motioned to the round table.

They had just pulled out chairs when there was a knock on the door frame. Billy and Quinn were standing there.

"Come in, please." Chad remained standing. He extended his hand to shake theirs.

"Glad you're here. Quinn, good to see you." He saw the weary look in her eyes.

"Good to see you, sir. I'm the interloper here. I can wait outside."

"No need. You can contribute to the brainstorming I'm about to ask of these two."

All three looked at him.

"Give me just a minute." He walked to the door connecting his office to Cecelia's and asked her to join them. He wanted to remember to include her in any leadership meetings.

"Quinn, have you met Cecelia?" Both nodded.

"It's important that I get official word out to the troops right away so they don't wonder if the loss of one of our neighbor's leaders has debilitated our own leadership. Thoughts on what I should include?"

There was silence for a few minutes.

"Respect," Sylvia said. "Something about respect we have for each other and for the work we all do in keeping our community safe."

"Support," Billy added. "I like knowing others are here to support me all the time, but especially in times like this."

"Commitment," Cecelia said. "Everyone in this department is committed to the work we do. Those of us in this building know we're supporting the people on the front line."

Chad looked at Quinn, who was scanning from one face to the next.

"Team. You are a team in this department. I'm not sure if you take it for granted, but it is obvious to an outsider that there is a strong team here. That has to matter in difficult times."

Chad nodded his head. He made a few notes.

"Anything else?"

They each shook their heads.

"Then I'll get a note out to everyone." He turned to Sylvia, "I'll be at roll call this afternoon. Anything else?"

Sylvia stood. "Thank you, sir."

"Shall I draft something for you, sir?" Cecelia said.

Chad sat for a moment. He wasn't accustomed to having a full-time assistant. "Thanks. That would be great. Wait, Cecelia. It's Saturday. You aren't scheduled on weekends."

"No problem, sir. Sergeant Whitehorse asked me to come in. I'm here to assist."

"Thanks, Cecelia. I'll be over in a minute."

Sylvia closed his door on her way out.

"How are you, Quinn? I think you worked with David on several cases, didn't you?"

"I did. I actually asked Billy to see if we could talk with you. Well, if I could talk with you."

Billy started to stand.

She looked at him. "You can stay. I just meant it's my struggle, not yours." Quinn took a breath. "The loss of Chief Nelson came on the back of a situation at work that I don't know how to handle." She told him about the young agent, the director, and the receptionist. "I don't really care what the relationship is between any two people. The challenge is that it's interfering in the work. The young agent distracts me by his comments and phone calls, although it hasn't kept me from doing my job—*yet.*"

Chad was pleased to have this opportunity to talk with her because he had seen her leadership potential the first time he met her. He also thought it could be a growth opportunity for Billy. What he knew he *wouldn't* reveal was the personal connection the three people she mentioned might have.

"It sounds like you've handled it well with them, so far. That doesn't always mean the circumstances don't stir our inner thoughts. In my opinion, the first thing you have to do is speak to the young agent. It's always best to try and smooth out rough edges at the source. Let him know you welcome him to the agency and your regional office. Take ownership of your preferred style and tell him you would find it helpful if he saves phone calls to emergencies. He can let you know anything else by pink note or whatever electronic system you use."

Quinn nodded as she listened.

Billy watched both of them. *The direct approach. That's good.*

"Then, if it doesn't smooth out the relationship, you have no choice but to go to the director. It sounds like the comment from the receptionist wasn't really a problem, just an anomaly, right?"

"Right. I've found myself thinking it was more adoration. Like she needed me to know she was taken with the young agent."

"No harm. Might make Rachel more approachable."

Quinn's eyes narrowed. "Do you know her?"

Chad nodded. "Small community in these mountains. Let me know if I can help you further. I think you'll be fine."

Billy knew Chad's way of dismissing folks. He stood.

Quinn took her cue from Billy and extended her hand. "May I call you if I have questions?"

"Any time."

"And, Chad," Quinn's voice turned personal, "I hope Bella's going to be all right."

He nodded. "Me too. Thanks."

Chad walked to the door with them and then stepped into Cecelia's office.

"It's going to take some time for me get used to having your help. Thanks for this." He waved the paper she handed him with a printed draft for him to check and send out.

"My privilege, sir. I sent it to you electronically as well."

He nodded and turned back to his office as he read what she had written. He pulled up the electronic copy, made one small change, and sent it to the entire department. He leaned back in chair, locked his hands behind his head, and thought about loss and the possibilities life offered—no matter how old you were.

The ringing of his personal mobile jarred him from his reverie.

"Hello, beautiful daughter of mine."

"Hey, Daddy. Busy?"

"At the station."

"What? I thought you were still on leave. Aren't you coming to the jamboree?"

"I am. We are. Bella's at my place. What's up?"

"I just wanted to make sure you were coming tonight and to tell you the kids won't be there, but you'll see them tomorrow evening. Daddy, are you okay?"

"Sweet Nora, I'm fine. It's others on my mind right now. Speaking of which, we just learned that David Nelson passed away this morning."

"Oh, Daddy! I know some of the Nelsons."

"Yes, he and his brother were born here; both went into law enforcement." He paused. "We'll want to honor him tonight."

"Done. I'll handle it. Thanks for telling me. I'm sorry for your loss, Daddy."

"Seems the order of the day."

"What is? Sorrow?"

"Nora, I never wanted to burden you with the seamier side of this work, but maybe I've sheltered you too much. We learned that the woman who burned down Bella's home in North Carolina was one of her former students."

Nora gasped. "Oh no! Should I go to Bella?"

"No. She needs some space right now. I know you'll show her your welcoming self tonight and tomorrow. That'll go a long way."

"Of course, Daddy. Of course. I love you."

"I love you too. Hug Mac and Lilly for me. See you soon."

Families: love and loss. And sometimes love regained—sounds like maybe Rachel may have met the child she gave for adoption.

CHAPTER 23

Headed to the Jamboree

After roll call, Chad headed home. He wasn't on duty tonight, but the jamboree was an event he always attended as sheriff, not just a local citizen.

"Hey, lovely lady." Bella was facing the stove, and he quietly put his service weapon in the small gun safe by the door. He walked up behind her and kissed her on the neck. "Something smells delicious."

She turned her head and kissed him. "Chicken and dumplings. I assumed you didn't eat any lunch and decided we could eat here before we go to The Corral. Is that okay with you?"

"Perfect. We have about an hour and a half before we need to leave. Will it keep?"

"Absolutely. I just need to add the dumplings about fifteen minutes before we eat. I'll set a timer for thirty minutes, which will give us forty-five minutes to eat and be out the door."

"Thanks." He waited for her to set the timer and poured himself a glass of iced tea. "Need a fill-up?"

"I'm good. Shall we sit by the fire?" She picked up her glass.

Chad nodded toward the living room. "Following you."

They set their glasses on the coffee table and sat on the sofa together. Chad put his arm around her and laid his head on top of hers. "I missed you."

"I missed you too. How'd it go?"

"Hard to tell. Not only is the loss of a fine man a somber moment, but the cause is sobering for all of us." He lifted his head and faced her. "I don't know if you figured it out, but the chief was shot on the job. I didn't tell you earlier because I honestly didn't know how to navigate it for myself, or for you, on the back of everything that's happened this week."

"I was going to ask when you got home. I think I told you some time ago that if I wanted to know more, I'd ask. It seemed to me that was the most probable situation given the call you got last night."

"Nora called me this afternoon. I've come to understand that I've spent my life trying to shield her from the ugly side of what I do. I'm learning I don't have to give all the details, but I can't expect her to be realistic about the changes in the world if I don't make her aware of what happens here. I now know I should do that for you, too." He waited a beat. "And, more importantly, I've let go of the voice of Mary in my head that always popped up when I spoke about work. Sometimes I *need* to talk about it; I need perspective."

"Anytime. I'm a big girl. I don't like the ugly in our world, but I know it exists. Doesn't seem fair that we ask law enforcement officers to bear the burden of protecting us from harm *and* from knowing what it is." Chad smiled and kissed the tip of her nose; they sat in companionable silence for several minutes until Bella spoke up again.

"I called Victoria."

"Good. How is she?"

"She already knew it was Jocelyn. It was the front page of the paper today. She told me not to worry about her personal things in my home. She even laughed a little and said she had the most important things with her: her thesis and her computer. She's sleeping on a friend's sofa." Bella sat up straight, turned sideways, and tucked her legs under her. "I called a friend of mine, Mark Franklin, who leases executive apartments, and I'm going to pay for Victoria to stay there through next semester. Mark said he'd take care of it, and I called Victoria back and told her."

"That's nice of you, Bella. Victoria okay with it?"

"She cried. I cried. I told her I hoped the fire didn't sidetrack her on finishing her thesis."

"Will it?"

"I don't think so. She told me she had gone to the counseling center at the university because she felt guilty. She feels she was responsible for my home, and if she hadn't gone to the conference, it might not have happened."

"Probably not true."

"That's what I told her. I've been thinking about Jocelyn, and I can see some signs from her as a student that she had mental health issues. I just wish I had picked up on them then. I might have been able to get her to counseling."

"Hindsight is too often 20/20. It's easy to second-guess ourselves. Don't." He lifted her hand and kissed it.

"I'll try. Not my strong suit. I'm pretty good at beating myself up for what I think I should have been able to see, or figure out, or know. Hopefully you can help me with that."

He didn't speak.

"I'm not ready to know what you've dealt with when it comes to deaths directly related to your job, but I will ask you someday. My intellectual self knows that I did not cause Jocelyn's choices, but my emotional self will need time to come to grips with it." She squeezed his hand. "I don't know if I'm ready for the answer, but will I have to testify?"

Chad thought for a moment. "It's doubtful. She confessed. She wrote a confession even before being interrogated. An attorney may try to get her a light sentence since no one was physically harmed. In that case, I think you would be able to speak if you wanted..."

She held up her hand. "That's enough for now. We'll talk with Gray if it comes to that. Thanks for the perspective. Not something I know much about."

"There are days when my life is so routine it's hard to remember that people's lives can depend on what we do. Then there are days like today."

"Did something else happen?" She knitted her brows and her dark brown eyes showed concern.

"Aside from David Nelson and your news, nothing major, but Quinn Isaacs came to see me. She wanted some advice about handling a situation at work."

"Oh, Chad, I'm glad she confided in you. I'm sure you gave her good counsel."

"I hope so. What I wouldn't tell her is what I *do* know and what I suspect about the situation."

"Is it important for her to know?"

"That's what I don't know." He told her the issue revolved around the receptionist, the IEA director, and a new, young agent.

"Sounds like you gave her the advice I would give someone on handling a workplace interaction."

"Yeah." His gray eyes sparkled in the light of the fire. "Rachel worked at the sheriff's office here for a while, about twenty-five years ago."

"Stop. Does this involve you?"

"No." He chuckled. "No, not me. But I knew she was dating a guy in Round City. I'm about ten years older than she is, and I was already a detective. She came to me one day and asked me if I could find out if an IEA agent was married. I asked her if there was a crime involved. I haven't seen her in years but, in those days, she could be quite blunt. She said, 'Only if you call falling in love, getting a girl pregnant, and then saying you can't marry her a crime.'"

Bella took his hand.

"I told her the woman should talk to a lawyer as there could be paternity responsibilities and rights that needed to be considered. She never said she was the woman or who he was. But about two months later she moved to Knoxville. Seven months or so after that, she went to Round City. About ten years ago I heard she was the receptionist at the Immigration Enforcement Agency regional office. I remember thinking she was lucky to have a good job and didn't think any more about it."

"So, how does this affect Quinn?"

"I don't know that it does, and I'm not one for speculating. But given what Quinn told me happened with her supervisor coming out of a storeroom, what Rachel said to her as she was leaving the office, and the young agent's interactions with both of them ..." He got very quiet. "It would not be beyond the realm of possibility that the young man has found his birth parents."

Bella blinked and shook her head. "Why, that would be wonderful, wouldn't it?"

"In an ideal world, I'd say yes. Not sure if the workplace is always an ideal world for the day-to-day lives of folks."

Bella nodded. "I see what you mean. I admire you for not telling Quinn what you know and what you suspect. It's not relevant to her unless the workplace becomes untenable. If it does, she has a whole system in place to file her grievances."

"I agree. What actually concerns me is that I think she may feel she can't do the work she needs to do in the current environment and transfer to another region."

"I hope not. From what little I know, it seems she's been an asset here. I think she'll come back to you for advice before she does that."

"Could be. It also comes our way because I think she and Billy have more than a work interest in each other."

Bella started laughing. "The long and winding road of life. I think I should write about that."

"I do too."

The timer went off. She kissed him on the cheek then went to put the dumplings in the chicken stew. "I'm dressed for the jamboree, so if you're changing, now's the time."

"Got it." Chad stood and went to put on his jeans and a plaid shirt. "We can go in matching outfits."

The Jamboree

Chad and Bella walked into The Corral through the side door and crossed towards the community room beyond the bar. James waved at them.

"Hey, James," Bella said and kissed him on the cheek.

"I think I'm not supposed to know, Bella, but I do and I'm sorry for your loss." He shrugged. "Carla's always told me everything."

"It's okay. Won't mean anything to most folks up here, but it helps when your friends look out for you."

Chad and James shook hands.

James pointed towards the room. "There's a table marked reserved. I have strict orders you are to sit there."

"Honored," Chad said. "Didn't know you reserved tables."

"Didn't until my baby sister wasn't on the scene here every day." He leaned in and spoke in a low voice. "Besides, I have to protect her right now." His eyes lit up.

Chad slapped him on the back. "You have always protected her, and you're going to make a fine uncle."

James grinned from ear to ear. "Poor kid doesn't have a chance. Parents old enough to be his or her grandparents and a widowed uncle with nothing better to do than spoil a kid."

"Sounds like a great family to join," Bella said.

"See you inside," Chad said as he and Bella walked into the room.

Nora was warming up. She stopped and jumped off the small stage.

Chad pointed. "There's a step, young lady."

She shrugged and pulled her dad and Bella into a hug. "So glad to see both of you."

"Nice to see you too, Nora. Thanks again for your kindness." Bella kissed her on the cheek.

"Had a change of plans. The kids were going to stay with Nancy, but Fred and I talked about it and decided who cares if they go ape over Christmas this early? So, they're coming."

"Good for you, Nora. If memory serves me as a father, although it doesn't always, by the time they're fourteen or fifteen they'll be shrugging and saying, 'Mom, do I *have* to go to the jamboree?'"

"Daddy, I *never* said anything like that for anything you wanted to do." She rolled her eyes. "Okay, I can get in trouble for lying to a police officer." She laughed and hugged her dad.

"Apparently, we're at a reserved table," Chad said.

Nora pointed. "Looks like it will be a full house. You're over there." A table for ten was along the window wall and a smaller table for kids with four chairs was between it and the music stage. "James even set a place for the kids. Wasn't that sweet?"

"Looks like he's ..." Chad stopped himself, "... thinking about his future customers."

Bella smiled. *Takes a lot for a man to know some happy news and not share it with his daughter.*

Harold and Julie were already at the table when Nora walked Chad and Bella over. Nora had her arm around Bella. "I think you folks all know each other. I'll leave you to each other's fine company." She kissed Bella and then her dad and headed back to the stage.

They were just about to sit when they heard Mac. "Miss Bella! Miss Bella!"

She turned and squatted down. He fast walked over to her and threw his arms around her neck.

Chad took Lilly from Fred and put her on his shoulders. *Thank you, Nora. You knew we needed this.*

Cheri came and took their drink orders. "I'll just put pitchers of tea and water on the table with the buckets of beer. Just let me know if you need more. Miss Carla should be here shortly."

The Greg Brothers started warming up and people began to trickle in, tapping their feet in time with the music.

Arthur Gillett walked over to Bella and Chad and introduced his wife and oldest son.

"So happy to meet you! Your husband does such fine work. It's a privilege to have him taking care of things for me." Bella shook their hands.

"He speaks highly of you, ma'am. Nice to meet you."

They turned as they saw Nora pick up the microphone.

"Catch you later, Miss Bella." Arthur waved as they moved off.

It was 7:00 p.m. on the dot.

Nora tapped the microphone. "Good evening."

Folks started clapping. "The Greg Brothers ..." She had to hold her hands up to get them to stop clapping and calling out. "We're glad you came out on this crisp Saturday night in our fine hills. It's not the coldest it's going to get, but let's see if we can warm this place up."

The band started playing "Rocky Top" and everyone jumped to their feet. Mac stood in front of Bella, stomping his feet in time to the music. Lilly sat in her daddy's lap, trying to get her two hands to connect more often than they didn't. Chad leaned back against the wall and smiled as he took in the scene of his family and his community.

After the last verse was repeated multiple times, the band ended the song. It was only one of Tennessee's ten state songs but clearly the favorite here. "And if timing counts for anything," Nora said, "those fine folks who keep us all in milk and bread are coming through the door. Let's welcome Mr. and Mrs. Johnson. Hello, Carla and Joshua." Everyone started clapping. They expected Joshua and Carla to go to the dance floor, but they didn't. They made a beeline for the table with their friends.

Nora picked up on it and said, "Folks have been saying there's some competition for the title of the best cloggers in these parts. Let's get the high school cloggers out on the floor and let them show us the future of clogging in these mountains." The band started playing "Devil Went Down to Georgia" and four teenagers went to the dance floor. People turned to watch them and forgot about Carla and Joshua.

Fred leaned in to speak to Carla. "Glad you didn't go on that dance floor. Probably okay, but no sense pushing it."

"True, Doc. Joshua and I talked about it, and we're going to tell the other folks at our table tomorrow night at your house. Still think it's okay?"

He smiled at her. "Up to you." He prayed he didn't live to regret it. Carla's pregnancy was developing quite normally despite her age, and she was certainly in far better health than many of his younger patients. He knew if things turned out differently, at least they would have had the joy of conceiving a child. *Why shouldn't they celebrate that?*

After several dances, the teenagers received a huge round of applause. Nora noticed some of the Nelson family come in. David and Elliott's parents had been gone for some years, but their cousins and their families still lived in the area. Nora said, "Folks, if I can have your attention for a moment." The chatter died down and all turned to her.

"I'm going to ask our sheriff—my daddy as y'all know—and Pastor Fisk to come to the stage."

Chad clipped his sheriff's badge on his shirt. Three deputies in the room took theirs out and clipped them on. Pastor Fisk followed Chad up to the front of the stage.

"Ladies and gentlemen, it is my sad duty and personal regret to share the loss of one of our own." There were gasps in the audience. Not everyone would have heard the news already, and he realized the way he said it would make some would think it was a valley deputy. Everyone took to their feet without a sound. "Chief David Nelson of the Round City Police was one of our own. He was born and raised here. This morning, he passed from an injury sustained in the line of duty. He was well respected, and we will miss his presence among us."

Chad stepped to the side and handed the microphone to the pastor. "Heavenly father . . ." Everyone bowed their heads. The pastor finished the prayer, "Amen."

"Amen" echoed through the hall.

As the pastor handed the microphone to Nora, Chad's eyes turned towards the far wall where the Nelson family were standing. He walked over to them and offered his condolences. "If you need anything at all, just let me know. We will be represented at the service." He shook hands with each of them.

Bella watched Chad. She had never thought about him being in office on the votes of his community. *I doubt he has to do much work to get elected. He knows everyone.*

Nora had been humming when Chad turned back towards her and nodded. He saw that Sylvia was up there with her, and Nora walked to the edge of the stage and motioned for Bella to join them. She set Mac next to Nancy and Gray's three-year-old son and climbed the stairs to the platform. Nora started quietly singing, "Amazing Grace." Everyone let her sing the first verse before joining in.

Chad leaned in to speak to David's first cousin. "Anyone in the family want to speak?"

The man looked around. "Reckon I could say a few words for the family."

Chad said, "Come with me." They walked along the wall towards the front of the stage but stood off to the side until the last verse was sung. Sylvia and Bella had moved to step off the stage during the last verse, leaving Nora to finish by herself. The fiddle player quietly continued the hymn and Nora handed Chad the microphone. The fiddle player stopped.

"Most of you folks know David's cousin. He'd like to say a few words."

"Yes, sir, Sheriff. It'll be a *few* words, all right. Not much for public speaking."

"He don't speak much at all," someone called from the audience.

Folks gave soft chuckles around the room.

"Those that knowed David will always say he was one fine man. Our family was always right proud of him and Elliott. They was always law-abiding men and expected it of the rest of us."

"Hear, hear," came from the crowd.

"Amen," someone else called out.

"He was also a God-fearing man. We know he's met his Maker."

"Amen," was repeated around the room.

Bella wondered what it was that made people lose this simple community connection when they moved into the cities and took on more formal ways of interacting.

"One thing for sure about David, he loved some clogging. He'd be real happy if he could know these young folks was going to get up and dance for him and his late wife, who he's joined in heaven today."

The four teens looked at each other and shrugged as they walked to the dance floor. The Greg Brothers started playing "Sold." While folks turned toward the dance floor, Ken Bennett, Billy, Quinn, and Sylvia slipped out the door into the restaurant.

Chad looked over at Bella and she nodded. He followed his folks into the restaurant and found them gathered in the corner. The badges had returned to pockets since they weren't on duty, and it was a protocol they all knew. Chad took his off as he approached them.

"Heading home, Sheriff," Bennett said. "Let us know where to be."

"Fine words there, Sheriff," Billy said.

Bennett headed out the side door. Chad noticed Sylvia and Billy had moved towards the door to shake hands with Bennett. In that moment, he knew that whatever decision he made about running again, everything would be all right.

"We've got the weekend covered, Sheriff. See you for the leadership meeting on Monday morning." Billy and Quinn shook Chad's hand and headed out.

"Well, Sylvia, we're pretty fortunate, you know."

"I do, Chad." She knew there was no one around and, in this moment, he was her friend, not just her boss. "I hope Bella can start to heal over this weekend. Guess we'll sort out the leadership meeting once we know about the arrangements for Chief Nelson."

"Sounds good. Bella's doing better than might be expected. I'll tell her you asked about her. Now, you do better than I've done. Let Eddie pick up some of the slack."

"He is. Good man, Eddie is, good man."

"That he is. He always knew he didn't want to be the sheriff." Chad looked at her. "How about you?"

"Sir?"

"How about you? Am I going to lose you to Round City?"

She shook her head. "No way. I'm not leaving this valley even when my life is done. I'll be buried right here with my ancestors."

"Two friends standing here on a tough day. Okay to give you a hug?" Chad waited.

"Yes, friend. Anytime." She reached out first. They exchanged a brief hug.

"Now go home and rest. We'll talk over the weekend."

Glad she might consider being sheriff. After all, she didn't say she didn't want the top job, she just wasn't leaving the valley. Fine with me. He stood in the quiet of the restaurant and found he was humming the various Christmas songs he'd heard Nora leading: *Santa Claus is coming to town, Joy to the World, I'll be home for Christmas...* He knew they'd go on for a while. He entered the community room to see Fred walking towards him with Mac at his side and Lilly asleep on his shoulder. He picked up his grandson.

"Grandpa, I want to hear this song."

"I'll sing it to you on the way to the car." He started humming *Jingle Bell Rock*. He whispered to Mac, "A man named Bobby Helms first sang this a long time ago." *Thanks for teaching me, Dad. Memories now passed to your great-grandson.*

Back seated with Bella and their friends, he saw the nod from Nora to the Greg brothers that this was the last song. The fiddle player started a soulful opening to the song all expected at the end of this night's event. The crowd stood, joined arms with family and friends as Nora started singing, "Silent Night, Holy Night." Chad decided he actually liked that this was a song to send them out in somber, yet hopeful, fashion on a day when a fellow police officer lost his life in the line of duty.

Sunday Evening

"Bella. Hey, sleepy head," Chad had covered her up when she fell asleep reading on the couch. "We're due at Nora's in an hour."

She stretched and looked at him. "What? How long have I been asleep?"

"Does it matter?"

She raised her hands over head. "Guess not if we're not late to Nora and Fred's."

"We'll be fine. Nora called and said the dress is festive casual."

"What does that look like?"

"Like this." He ran his hand down the front of his vest. He was wearing dark blue chinos, a white turtleneck, and a blue and red plaid vest. "It's my attempt at Christmas red." He grinned.

"Got it. I think I have something to wear. Give me a few minutes to sort through my clothes in your guest room closet."

"I'll be ready and waiting. No rush."

Chad was sitting in front of the fire in one of the brown leather armchairs, and he looked up when he heard her shoes on the wood floor. He straightened up and whistled. "If that's festive casual, I'm underdressed." He saw her eyes widen. "Hold on. Not a criticism. You look fabulous and it's not overdone. I'm out of practice at compliments."

She turned around and her flared black skirt twirled over her black stockinged legs. Her long dark brown hair fell over her shoulders as she curtsied. "You sure it's not too much?"

"I think you look lovely, and you will be the belle of the … well, the sing-along." They both laughed.

"I took Wizard out while you changed, so we can head over anytime you like."

"I'm ready. Since we're just going from the car to the house, I'm not wearing a coat."

"I'm with you. Let's go. Glad we delivered the beer and wine this afternoon. Hate to get stopped by one of my deputies with that much alcohol in my SUV."

"Good point."

As they pulled up to the Oliver-Smith house, Chad noticed Nora had been busy decorating since they had dropped off the drinks. A fresh Christmas wreath was on the door and candles flickered merrily in the window. *This is the year I should decorate for Christmas. Been far too long.*

When they stepped inside, the great room was a swirl of activity. Bella looked around the room, capturing vignettes in her head of friends chatting and laughing together and enjoying a casual supper of hamburgers and hotdogs. Words were starting to play in her head. She wanted to write. *Soon.*

"Miss Bella, do you like hotdogs?"

"I do, Mac. Shall we both have one?"

"Okay. I like them too. Mommy told me not to eat too much so I can sing."

"Good point. It affects your diaphragm."

"What's that?"

She took his hand and put it on his abdomen. "Take a deep breath. Feel the air filling up right here?"

"Yes, ma'am. Is that my dia … what?"

"Diaphragm. I bet you've seen the Scottish bag pipers, haven't you?"

Mac moved his fingers to his ears. "Miss Bella, I like music but they're loud."

She laughed. "They can be, but the big bag that they use fills up just like your diaphragm. You have air to push out when you sing. But if your stomach is too full, you don't have room to hold as much air."

"Oh, I get it. Thanks." He took her hand and they walked to the table. "Mommy said I could ask you to help me get my plate."

"Happy to do it."

Bella and Mac had just finished their hot dogs when Fred tapped a knife against his bottle of beer. Everyone got quiet. "Thanks for coming, good friends and family." He lifted his beer bottle. "Nothing better than a spur of the moment gathering of good company. *Yeh-chid da!*" The Welsh rolled off his tongue, and the adults in the room raised their bottles or glasses in return.

"To your health."

"Cheers."

"Salud," Bella said.

"Daddy," Mac said.

Fred leaned down. "Yes, Mac."

"May I say grace?"

"You certainly may."

Everyone got quiet.

"Thank you, God. Amen." Mac lifted his head and beamed.

"Amen," they said in unison.

Chad whispered to Bella. "That's my grandson: a boy of a few words and to the point."

Bella kissed him on the cheek. "He's a bit more talkative than Grandpa, I think."

Nora moved to the piano. Before she sat, she turned to their guests. "Joshua and Carla have asked to speak to us before we sing. Mr. and Mrs. Johnson."

"Well, ya'll know if we wait on Joshua to speak we'll be here all night. We aren't telling the world yet, but want you as our closest friends to know..." Carla took a breath.

Joshua blurted out, "We're going to be parents."

Breaths drew in, claps started and everyone lifted glasses and made toasts—all at the same time.

Joshua hugged Carla and looked at Nora with a fervent plea to play.

She turned on the TV which was camouflaged as a painting on their mantle; winter scenes began to scroll across the screen; and she started to play. "Let's sing!"

Folks joined in the songs as they moved to wish Carla and Joshua all the best. Friends supporting friends. A hush came over the group as Nora started the last song, "Winter Wonderland."

CHAPTER 24

No matter what, I always make it home for Christmas. I love to go to my Tennessee Mountain Home and invite all of my nieces and nephews and their spouses and kids and do what we all like to do—eat, laugh, trade presents and just enjoy each other ... and sometimes I even dress up like Santa Claus!

Dolly Parton

Christmas Eve Afternoon

Wednesday, Christmas Eve, came quickly. Billy had been shown to the guest room at Quinn's parents' home in Knoxville by a uniformed maid. Quinn had assured him that she was a part-time worker at her parents' home and normally did not wear a uniform. He was glad he knew not to tip her when she asked if he needed anything after showing him the bathroom and the small fridge hidden in the wall of cabinets in the sitting area. He wondered if he should have brushed up on his manners, though. *Sure glad my mama taught me how to behave in polite company even though she didn't expect it of others. Some of the best advice she gave me is still with me: 'Billy, when you don't know what to do, watch your hosts. Even if they are not in keeping with others—they are the host.'"* There was a soft knock on the door. He opened it to see Quinn standing there looking sheepish.

"Okay if I come in?"

"Is it allowed?"

"Far as I'm concerned. My very proper mother also knows how to turn a blind eye as long as I don't misbehave in front of company." She shut the door behind her and walked over to the sitting area. She poured herself a glass of wine. "Something for you?"

"Just water, thanks." He sat down in the wingback chair upholstered to perfectly match the décor of the room. "Don't want to risk embarrassing you tonight." He looked out the window at the formal garden, which he had already decided must require two or three full-time gardeners.

"No worries on that score. You'll be the most authentic person here."

"Next to you."

"Ha. I still play the game. I love my parents, and they're good people. They both came from very affluent families—generations of wealth. They have no experience with anything different. I don't want to live like this. I admit I like that money allows me to live comfortably in a lovely home, but I could live in a one-bedroom apartment and be perfectly content. My mother would never understand that."

"Doesn't cost much to humor our parents. We wouldn't be here without them, and I think respecting them is pretty high up on my expectations of myself."

"And of me?"

"No judgment. Looks to me like you do a pretty good job in showing respect."

"Thanks, kind sir. Thanks also for coming. I promise I will whisk you back to the safe haven of the mountains right after Christmas breakfast."

"Won't your parents expect you to stay for Christmas day?"

"They are so happy to have me here for Christmas Eve dinner, their most formal charity event of the season, *and* with a man, that they would let me leave at three in the morning and never say a word."

Billy laughed. "Well, let's just hope they don't kick us out at three in the morning. Tackling the road we would have to drive back on in the dark isn't high on my list anymore." Billy's recent experience of getting forced off the road and trapped in his car hadn't affected his sense of humor, but Quinn realized it had made him a little more cautious.

"Okay, no three a.m. escapes." A smile spread across her face. "Well, I'll let you settle in and see you in the drawing room for cocktails at six."

"You're going to feed me to the lions alone? I'd much prefer to enter with you."

"Then wait for me at the bottom of the stairs at 5:56."

He lifted his arm. "Let's synchronize our watches."

Quinn tapped his wrist, kissed him on the cheek, and said, "Don't be late."

"Not one second."

After the door shut behind Quinn, Billy turned to survey his luggage. He took the rented tuxedo out of the hanging bag—grateful Quinn had told him it was black tie. He decided to make sure his shoes were sufficiently shined and then shower. *Held up pretty good from the shine I gave them for Chief Nelson's funeral on Monday. Shouldn't take much to buff them.* He pulled them out of a bag and took a cloth to them. Satisfied he could see himself in them, he set the shoes aside. He stepped out of the hot shower at 5:35 p.m. and dressed. He adjusted the cuffs on his shirt, double checked his tie and cummerbund, and walked out of his room at 5:54 p.m. He did not want to stand in the foyer too long by himself.

He was halfway down the stairs when he heard a door close. He assumed it was Quinn's, but he did not turn back. At the bottom of the stairs, a young man in a white jacket offered him a drink. He took a whisky and turned to look up at the top of the stairs.

Quinn was standing there in an emerald green, off-the-shoulder dress with a pin in a shape he couldn't distinguish. He couldn't miss the sparkles though. Her shoulder-length hair was as shiny as the pin. He had to bite his tongue to avoid letting out a whistle.

He felt a hand on his elbow and had to stop himself—the cop—from reacting and reaching for the service weapon he wasn't wearing.

"Welcome to our home, Mr. Williams."

Billy turned and saw a handsome man in his late fifties with sharp Spanish features.

"Buenas noches, señor." He extended his right hand to shake with Quinn's father.

Quinn slowed her walk down the stairs.

"¿Habla español?" Dr. Isaacs smiled, flashing perfect teeth.

"No, sir. I'm afraid you've heard the extent."

Quinn continued down. "And, Daddy, he practiced all the way here." She stepped off the bottom stair and kissed her father on each cheek.

Billy saw that it was really just a kissing noise when their cheeks touched. He was surprised when she turned to him and did the same.

She whispered in his ear. "Sorry, should have prepared you for this." She turned and took his elbow with one hand and a glass of wine off the tray the waiter put in front of her. "Lead the way, please, Daddy." Her father turned toward an open double door opposite the staircase.

Billy whispered, "You look stunning."

"Been known to clean up pretty well. Don't get used to it. Not my cup of tea."

He chuckled. He was relieved they were the first to enter the drawing room, and he began to wonder if he'd make it through the evening without committing a faux pas. *Or a 'fox paw' as I called it in my younger days. Might know how to pronounce it now, but I'm not sure I'll be able to avoid one.*

Quinn chose a high table by the windows looking out onto the garden, which was lit with tiny white lights sparkling from every tree. Soon they were chatting with people who stepped over to them after greeting her father.

"Billy, in less than five minutes my mother will make her appearance. Just watch the doors."

Billy had been charmed by Quinn's mother and her elegant, gracious manners when he and Quinn had arrived in the afternoon. Although she was as formal as Quinn had said, she was warm and seemed pleased to have him in her home. He had even managed to get her ti-tles correct. Quinn had explained that because both of her parents had doctorates and taught in the Spanish department at the university, students called them Dr. Mr. and Dr. Mrs. Isaacs, which was the Spanish form of address. He tried to imagine his mama in this house as he continued to hope he didn't embarrass himself—or Quinn.

Quinn saw her father walk to the doors of the drawing room, and the string trio in the foyer started playing "White Christmas." The lights dimmed in the drawing room and were turned up slightly on the stair-case. He watched Dr. Mrs. Isaacs walk down the stairs, her right hand lightly on the rail, in a cream-colored gown with an emerald brooch at the waist. Billy thought the dress she had on probably cost more than his house. Her husband met her at the bottom of the stairs, and, as they entered the drawing room, the twenty-odd guests clapped politely. The couple moved among their guests, greeting each one.

Billy followed Quinn's lead and air-kissed her mother on each cheek.

"We're so happy you could be with us tonight, Billy." She turned to her daughter, "You look lovely, dear. Thank you for coming home."

Billy wondered if there was more to that statement than he knew. *This will definitely be a Christmas Eve to remember. Keep watching over me, Mama, it's going to be a long night.*

Supper is Served

Sylvia and Mike had been at Chief Whitehorse's home all afternoon. Mike was an excellent cook, and he took over on Christmas Eve. Sylvia and her father were sitting beside the fireplace waiting on her sister, Jackie, to arrive from Atlanta—apparently, she was bringing a friend. "Daddy, how are you feeling this evening?"

"Fine, daughter. Just fine. Thanks for asking. How are you these days? Things settling down at work?"

"I'm fine, thanks. Yes, things seem to be running smoothly. The sheriff has included his leadership team more in the decision making, and we're trying a new shift rotation."

"What do you think of it?"

"Well," she dragged out the word as she turned to look at her father. She knew he was sicker than he let on. She had tried to get her mother to convince him to go to Knoxville to the hospital at the university, but he wouldn't budge from the valley. "I'm the one who proposed the rotation. Some agencies in the state are doing twelve-hour shifts, but they're just too long for people on these mountain roads, especially in the winter at night."

"So, what did you propose?"

"Eleven hours a day over four days, with two forty-five-minute meal breaks and two fifteen-minute walkarounds in their patrol area. It means their start time shifts each of the days, and we have some overlap, but then they have three days off."

"How's it working?"

"Too soon to tell, but if the talk is any indication, folks seem to like it. May just be the novelty of it. On the traditional system of forty hours over five days, they only get a thirty-minute meal break. This way they get two breaks, work one day less in the week, and ... well, I guess we'll see."

"Sounds like a good way to solve a problem that's plagued us for years."

"What's that, Daddy?"

"Manufacturing needed a work force routine, which forced every job and industry into the same model of eight-hour days. Worse yet, in my opinion, it forced our schools into it."

They both turned as Sylvia's mother entered the room. "Mighty heady talk for Christmas Eve. Please, our youngest daughter and her guest are here. Let's enjoy some non-work talk for the rest of the evening."

"Daddy!" Jackie ran past Sylvia to their father's chair. She gently sat down on his lap and threw her arms around him.

Sylvia smiled and walked over to her sister's guest. "Hey, I'm Sylvia. Welcome to our hills."

The young woman smiled and extended her hand. "Hey, I'm Jen."

"We're happy to welcome you. Did you meet my husband?"

"I did. Gotta love a man who can cook."

"Indeed. May I get you something to drink?"

"Just tea for me, thanks."

"Iced or hot?"

"Iced tea if you don't mind."

"Coming right up." Sylvia smiled at her mother, who was watching her youngest daughter chatter away to her dad as if no one else were there. The petite poverty lawyer had reverted to childhood and Christmases past. Sylvia disappeared into the kitchen to speak with Mike and pour the tea.

When she returned, she handed the glass to Jen before passing on Mike's announcement: "Christmas Eve dinner in five minutes. Wash up."

Sylvia saw the effort it took their father to stand. *I hope this visit will bring you home a little more often, Jackie. He needs your special medicine. You have a lightness I never had.*

Christmas Eve at the Johnsons

"Honey, are you almost ready?"

"Just finished lighting the candles on the mantle. The Christmas tree is plugged in and lights up the front window in a way it hasn't been for far too many years." Joshua turned when Carla tapped his shoulder.

She pulled him into an embrace, and they stood bathed in the light of the tree. Carla didn't have a lot of experience with soothing ragged emotions. Her bantering in the restaurant had always been a way of pulling people out of their troubles, if only for the time they were there to eat. This was different. She knew Joshua had to be thinking of the loss of Jan, his wife of more than thirty years. *It's been barely four months since Jan passed after a long illness and then he lost his dad.*

As happy as Joshua seemed to be with their own decision to marry so soon after losing both Jan and his dad, Carla was a smart woman. *Christmas often brings out the heights and depths of emotions in folks. I want to say the right thing.*

She looked up at her husband's face. "Christmas is a holiday of joy and sadness for me."

"Me too. It just seems more than normal this year."

Carla gave him a squeeze and stepped back. She took his hand and guided him toward the sofa in front of the fire. They sat and Joshua put his arm around her shoulders. Carla reached in her pocket.

"Joshua, James and I have been alone on Christmas for years now … since his wife passed away. So, I'm used to it just being the two of us. I propose a new tradition, starting now."

Joshua seemed to perk up and squeezed her shoulders. "Do tell." He tried to imagine what she had in mind. He had accepted an early present of new corduroy slacks and a complementary turtleneck, but now he couldn't figure out what she might have planned. He moved back to look at her but never let go of her.

Carla pulled her hand out of her pocket. She had a stack of small velvet bags and set them in her lap. "I like keeping the memories of life's events. Sometimes it's hard to navigate the loss of people we love, especially at holidays, but I've learned to remember all the good and focus on celebrating the person's life."

Joshua nodded his head. He smiled at her and leaned in to kiss her cheek.

She handed him the first bag. "Each year I'd like us to add an ornament to our tree that brings all of us together in some way. It might be about a person, or it might be an event. Open it."

Inside the bag was a flat silver angel and Joshua saw something had been engraved on it. Tears started down his face as he read the text: Jan Johnson—daughter, wife, friend, beloved teacher. Joshua closed his hand gently around the ornament. Carla leaned her head on his shoulder and gave him space to have his own memories. After a few minutes, Joshua leaned forward and set the delicate angel on the coffee table.

Joshua wasn't sure he could get through what he expected the next ones would have on them. He took a deep breath and whispered, "Thank you. I love you, Carla."

"I love you too. Let's open these together." She took the little bags by the strings and held them between two fingers.

"Choose one."

He pointed. She was surprised he didn't pick the lone red velvet bag, but they took turns opening the black bags one at a time. There were three more with angels which shared something about her parents, his parents, and her brother James's late wife. For her brother, she had chosen a silver bell which read: James Long—son, brother, husband, uncle, friend.

"I wanted you to see the one for James, but I'm going to slip it back in the bag so we can share it with him at supper. Okay?"

"Perfect." Joshua had become more talkative since he married Carla, but he reverted to being a man of few words when emotion was involved.

The red bag was still in her hand. She smiled at him.

"Let's open this one together."

They could barely get his finger and hers in the tiny opening but each gently tugged. Carla pulled her finger out, leaving Joshua holding the small bag. He pulled out the gold heart and looked at her, then he read it aloud: "Carla and Joshua: New beginnings." It also had the date of their marriage.

Joshua smiled broadly. "I'm going to like this new tradition. Thanks for thinking of it."

Carla had one tiny bag left in her pocket, which she had separated by wrapping it in a tissue so she wouldn't pull it out with the others. She pulled the white velvet bag out from the tissue and handed it to Joshua.

His hand shook as he opened it and pulled out the thin gold ornament in the shape of a baby. On it were engraved the words: *Carla and Joshua's son.*

"What? How do you know it's a boy? I thought the ultrasound was inconclusive." Joshua stumbled over the words as they flew from his mouth. He leaned across the coffee table and put it on the basket Bella had bought for them at the powwow last month—the one with three hearts on it.

"Modern times, even in these hills. There's a blood test Doc Fred did, and he said it's 95% accurate. So, promise me you won't be disappointed if we have a daughter."

"If she beats those odds, she'll be on the path to being a strong woman like her mommy." He pulled Carla up to her feet and rubbed her abdomen. "No matter who you are little one, we will love you with all our hearts."

Carla couldn't speak. She was with the man she had loved since she was a small girl. They were going to have a baby. It was Christmas Eve and Carla's brother would be here any minute. She was overcome with joy.

The doorbell rang and James walked in. She smiled; James considered their home his.

Christmas Eve at the Oliver-Smiths

Chad straightened his turtleneck and slipped on his sports coat. "So, Doc Jim liked the finished dog run? Nice of you to take him up there."

"I had promised to do it last week and didn't. He doesn't seem to get out much. I want to try and make sure I take him out from time to time."

She put on her silver earrings and tried not to focus on the fact that most of her jewelry was gone forever.

"That dress is lovely on you. I think royal blue might be your color." He stopped and studied her face. "Am I allowed to say that?"

Bella laughed nervously. "I try to give compliments and I enjoy getting them. Thank you for the compliment. Complimenting the color of my dress, however, is not why I'm uncomfortable."

Chad walked towards her and held out his arms. "What then?"

Bella walked into them. "I just don't want to interfere . . ."

He put his finger on her lips. "Shhh . . . don't even *think* that. They all love you. Nora has been so worried you might not *want* to be with us tonight."

Bella stepped back. "What? Why would she think that?"

"My daughter is pretty smart and a keen observer of people. She respects that you have some reserve about you when it comes to social situations."

"Ha! Some? You have no idea how many years I've worked to take the best of my mother's very formal ways and my Grandmother Hazel's live-life-to-its-fullest ways and make them mine."

"Maybe you don't need to work so hard. You're pretty awesome just the way you are. Now, come on, there will be no better family get together in these hills tonight than the one at the Oliver-Smith household." He took her hand and walked over in front of the Christmas tree.

"Thanks for helping decorate this old house. It's long overdue."

"New beginnings." Bella kissed him lightly.

"New beginnings. Shall we go?"

"Can we wait a minute." She reached for a small box under the tree. "Please open it now."

He studied her face, but didn't object. "I love presents." He unwrapped the box. "Oh, Bella. The watch. . . the one with the altimeter." He kissed her. "Thanks for remembering I asked Santa."

"Yes, Santa whispered in my ear. Now, lead the way. The Oliver-Smiths await."

"Another minute." He picked up a package from under the tree. "I was going to wait until morning, but I want you know how important you are to all of us."

Bella gently tore the paper off the package.

"Nora was able to track down the artist who did the original drawing of the Anderson property."

Bella sat—unable to bear her own weight. "How? When?" She stared at the almost identical drawing—but it showed the changes to her property which she had done.

"I'll give you the whole story tomorrow. Seems Ken Czarnomski was a very young man when he did this for your parents in the 1960s and was happy to update it for you. He had to rely on Nora's explanations of the cabin and walk/dog run to the shed."

A single tear dropped on a piece of the wrapping paper. Bella quickly wiped away the others in her eyes. She stood up and pulled Chad into an embrace and kissed him.

"Thank you. This means more than you can ever know."

"Then mission accomplished. Let's go join the family."

He turned his wrist several times looking at his new watch, then got her coat out of the closet by the front door and held it for her. "Just so you know, Wizard has been out, and he'll be fine. I'll come up the front stairs to get you."

Once the front door closed behind her, Chad took his service weapon out of the safe and slipped it in the holster under his jacket.

After pulling onto the driveway, Chad hopped out of the SUV to collect Bella from the front porch, grateful he had remembered to salt the steps and walkway this afternoon. The early snow had long since melted but he knew his grandchildren hoped for some tonight. As Bella settled into the heated seat of the SUV, she was delighted to hear Nora singing "Deck the Halls" through the audio system. She started humming.

They were at Nora's door in less than ten minutes. The unusual warmth of the day had brought moisture into the air and the roads were starting to get slippery. Chad hated that the salt trucks would have to work through the night when folks wanted to be with their families. *So do my deputies. Be nice if everyone could be safe and behave one night of the year.*

Fred opened the door, kissed Bella on the cheek, and took her coat. "Lovely dress. Great color on you."

"Thank you."

"Miss Bella, Miss Bella!"

"Wonder if my grandson thinks that's your name."

"I think he's a mountain boy practicing his echoes." She squatted down to hug Mac when he reached her.

"That's a pretty dress, Miss Bella. I like it very much."

"Thank you, kind sir." She kissed him on the cheek.

"Miss Bella, I'm not a sir."

"You are a very polite and thoughtful boy, though."

"Thank you, Miss Bella. Here comes Lilly. Doesn't she look beautiful?"

Bella looked down the hall and saw two-year-old Lilly in a green velvet dress with white tights and black patent leather shoes. She had silver bows in her hair. "Oh, Mac. She is absolutely beautiful." She let go of Mac's hand and held out her arms for Lilly. Chad picked up his grandson and hugged him close.

"B'la, B'la." The toddler made her way to Bella's arms. She picked her up and hugged her.

"Hey, sweet girl. You look so pretty."

"Gra'pa, Gra'pa." Lilly reached out her arms for Chad.

"I was beginning to wonder." He winked at Bella as he took Lilly. Bella took Mac's hand. They walked into the living room where a CD of Christmas music was playing softly in the background.

Nora took off her apron and came over to them. "Sorry I couldn't meet you at the door. I needed to get the roast out of the oven to rest."

"Miss Bella, did you know that meat has to rest before you can cut it?"

"I have only recently learned that, Mac. It's a good lesson to learn early in life."

"Okay ..." His quizzical look amused Bella. He looked up at his mother. "My mommy looks beautiful too."

Fred handed Nora and Bella a glass of wine; he and Chad stuck with water. Both men knew Christmas Eve was an unpredictable night in law enforcement and medicine.

"Here's to my beautiful wife, my smart and delightful children, my special father, and a lovely lady we hope will always feel a part of our family. Cheers!"

Mac pulled on his father's pants leg. "Daddy, I want to say something."

"Sure, son." Fred turned to Bella and Chad. "Please, have a seat." Fred picked up Mac and put him on the sofa next to Bella. He then went and sat on the arm of the chair where Nora was holding Lilly. "Okay, son. What do you want to say?"

They were all expecting him to make a toast as he had heard his father do.

"Grandpa, is Miss Bella your wife yet?"

Nora almost spit out her mouthful of wine.

Bella set her glass of wine on the coffee table. She hugged Mac.

Chad looked at his grandson and tousled his hair. He turned to the other three members of his family.

"Well, Mac, I asked Miss Bella to be my wife."

"You did?" Nora moved to the edge of the chair. Fred's hand squeezed her shoulder.

Mac looked at Bella. "Did you say okay?"

She smiled and her eyes danced as she looked at him. "I told your grandpa I thought you and your mommy and daddy should tell me whether you think it's okay for me to become part of your family."

"Yes." Mac said it with the finality of a four-and-a-half-year-old. "But I have one question."

Bella glanced at Chad then Mac. "Sure, Mac, what is it?"

"Do I get to call you Grandmother Bella instead of Miss Bella?" Bella knew he called Nora's mother Grandmother Mary.

"How about Grandma Bella?" She smiled at him.

Mac jumped in her lap and hugged her. Nora jumped out her chair and ran to her father and Bella. "This is the fourth best Christmas in my adult life!"

Bella looked at her. "Fred, Mac, Lilly?" She nodded her head towards each of them.

Nora grinned.

"I'm happy to be the fourth best."

Fred stood. "This calls for another toast."

Chad stood. "Hold on a second, please." He reached in his pocket then took Bella's hand and helped her to her feet. "I want us to pick out rings together. I know you didn't have a say in this choice . . ." He opened a small jewelry box. "I want this to be a symbol of our family for you from this moment forward." Inside the box was a gold necklace with four heads in profile: an adult male and female, and a male and female child. Each of the Oliver-Smiths' initials were on the back.

"Oh, Daddy, it's perfect. I hope you like it, Mom Bella." She hugged Bella even before Chad could put the necklace on her.

Bella held her new daughter tightly. She whispered in her ear. "Thank you, sweet Nora. Thank you."

"My turn." Chad said. He kissed Bella and fastened the necklace on her before turning to his family. "We'll let you know where and when to show up for the wedding."

They all laughed.

"Let's eat," Nora said. "Fred can make the toast at the table."

"Come on kids, let's wash your hands." Fred took his children to the sink, then they all sat down at the dining table. It was draped in a festive red tablecloth embossed with leaves, and the centerpiece was made of white twigs decorated with sequined silver balls. Candles in pinecone-shaped holders completed the setting.

Bella helped Nora put the food on the table while Chad carved the prime rib. Once they were all seated, they held hands.

"Let us pray," Fred said. "Dear Lord, wherever people are tonight and however they may worship, may they know your message of love and redemption. Thank you for bringing Bella to our family. Bless this food to our use and us to Thy service. Amen."

"Amen" was echoed around the table—little Lilly said "'men."

Halfway through eating, Mac said, "Mommy, I'm sleepy. Is Santa going to come tonight?"

"He is, sweet boy. Daddy and I will put you both to bed in a couple of minutes. You've eaten a good dinner. Let's put out Santa's cookies before you go to bed."

"Grandma Bella, did you know that we don't put out milk for Santa 'cause he told Mommy the cookies were enough?"

"Nice of him to tell her, right?"

"Yes, ma'am." He tried not to yawn.

Fred pushed his chair back to take his children to put on pajamas. His phone rang.

"Dr. Smith." He listened. "On my way."

Chad's secure phone rang.

"Oliver."

Nora took the children from the table. Fred was already out the door and gone.

Bella watched Chad's face turn pale and his shoulders sag.

"I'll be at the hospital when they arrive." He hung up and gave a sad smile to Bella. "Chief Whitehorse has apparently had a heart attack. I need to go meet Sylvia."

"Of course you do. I'll stay with Nora and the children. If Sylvia needs me, just call."

"This is my life, Grandma Bella. I'm grateful you've accepted the vagaries of it. This, however, will be a special Christmas Eve the rest of my life." Chad kissed her and headed for the front door.

She smiled that he called her Mac's special name. "I love you, Chad Oliver. Go now and take care of Chief Whitehorse's family—*ours* will be right here when you return."

Bella started putting away the food and cleaning up the dishes. She was sure Nora would come and get her to say goodnight to the children.

"I would have done that," Nora smiled with a sadness Bella could feel.

"Happy to be useful. Are the children ready for bed?"

Nora nodded. She reached out her hand. "Come on, my new mom. Let's go sing to the children. Do you know 'Circle of Love?'"

"By Dolly Parton?"

Nora nodded.

"I do. It's lovely."

They stood in the doorway between the rooms of the two children. "Lilly's already asleep," Nora whispered to Bella. "You can go and tell Mac goodnight."

Bella stepped into Mac's room and sat down on his bed.

He plopped his hand on her lap. "Grandma Bella, I'm sleepy."

She leaned over and kissed him on the forehead. "Then may you sleep soundly and dream of Santa. I love you, Mac."

"I love you, Grandma Bella."

Nora was fighting tears. She grieved for these special moments her mother would never know—she just wasn't capable. She started to hum and thought of the new circle of love her family now had with Bella.

Bella stepped away from Mac's bed. She was pretty sure he was already asleep. The two women stood in the doorway and sang. At the end, Nora hugged Bella. "We're going to make so many wonderful memories. Welcome to the family."

Nora kissed her son goodnight and then went to Lilly's room. Bella was standing beside Lilly's bed. Nora heard her soft voice say, "Sweet dreams to you too, precious Lilly. We have lots of adventures to come at Drellag and Solasta Cabans." She kissed the sleeping child.

"Good night, my angel. May your guardian angel watch over you. Tomorrow will be a great Christmas morning."

The women returned to the kitchen and finished putting away the food and stacking the dishes in the dishwasher.

"I didn't realize you had two dishwashers."

"Smartest thing I ever did. Big crowd? No problem. No time to empty the dishwasher? No problem."

Bella laughed. "Now that's planning!"

The kitchen cleaned Nora took out the bottle of wine and poured some for each of them. "Do you remember when you were so impressed with my dad because he had Kim Crawford Sauvignon Blanc?"

Bella laughed. "I do. I don't know if I ever told you that he went up a notch when he told me he could not take credit for it—that it was your wine of choice."

"I know you've been through things I don't even really know about since you came back to the mountains in September. I'm sorry for the pain. But I'm also glad that some of that distress brought my daddy to your doorstep."

"Me too, sweet Nora. Me too. I want to thank you for the very special gift of the drawing of Drellag Caban and Solasta Caban. As much as I play with words, mine are inadequate to let you know what important it is to me."

"I found Ken soon after Solasta Caban went up, so he was able to get it completed." She hesitated. "Of course, I had no idea it would turn out to be so important."

They sat in companionable silence for several minutes. Then Bella told Nora their men had gone for Chief Whitehorse. They chatted while listening to a recording of Christmas music played on a piano. Occasionally, they hummed or sang a song.

"Nora, it just dawned on me . . . is that you playing?"

Nora nodded. She saw the lights come on in the portico. She knew Fred was home. It was almost midnight. He'd only been gone three hours or so—that was not a good sign.

The front doorbell rang. "It's Daddy. I'll get it."

Bella wondered how she knew it was Chad. Fred opened the kitchen door. He nodded at Bella and walked towards the back of the house to kiss his children.

Nora was talking softly with her dad in the foyer. She heard Nora say, "I'm sorry he didn't make it, Daddy. I know he was a special friend to you."

Tears began to run down Bella's cheek. She had spent many hours over the past month with Chief Whitehorse. He seemed determined to give her the stories he wanted her to write. She was honored she had learned about the history, tribal life, and customs from a venerated chief in such a short time. She felt Chad's hand on her shoulder and heard footsteps coming down the hall and into the great room.

Chad sat beside her on the sofa, and Nora and Fred sat across from them in the wingback chairs. Nora reached out to hold her husband's hand.

"The chief had given explicit instructions to his wife that when he passed, I was to be present along with his tribal council. He wanted me there when she gave the senior elder a letter he had written. Thanks for understanding." Chad stared at the fire.

Bella smiled at him through her tears. "Can you tell us what the letter said?"

Chad looked at each of them. "I don't think I'll ever forget it. 'The Great Spirit has come for me. I leave you my first-born daughter to be the first female chief of our tribe. She has wisdom and skill, and she has served us all well. She will lead you until such time as the Great Spirit calls her. I know you will welcome her counsel.'"

Bella now knew she had the closing for the series of stories Chief Whitehorse had asked her to write. The sound of a bell striking midnight caused her to look up. The TV showed St. Patrick's Cathedral in New York City, and their choir started singing, "Silent Night."

Bella's voice was soft when she spoke. "May Tom Whitehorse rest in peace, and may the spirit of Christmas fill us all with joy, love, and peace, whoever we are and wherever we walk."

Merry Christmas! Feliz Navidad! Ulihelisdi Unadetiyisgv'i!
Nittak Hullo Chito Na Yukpa! Happy Hanukkah! Joyous Kwanzaa!

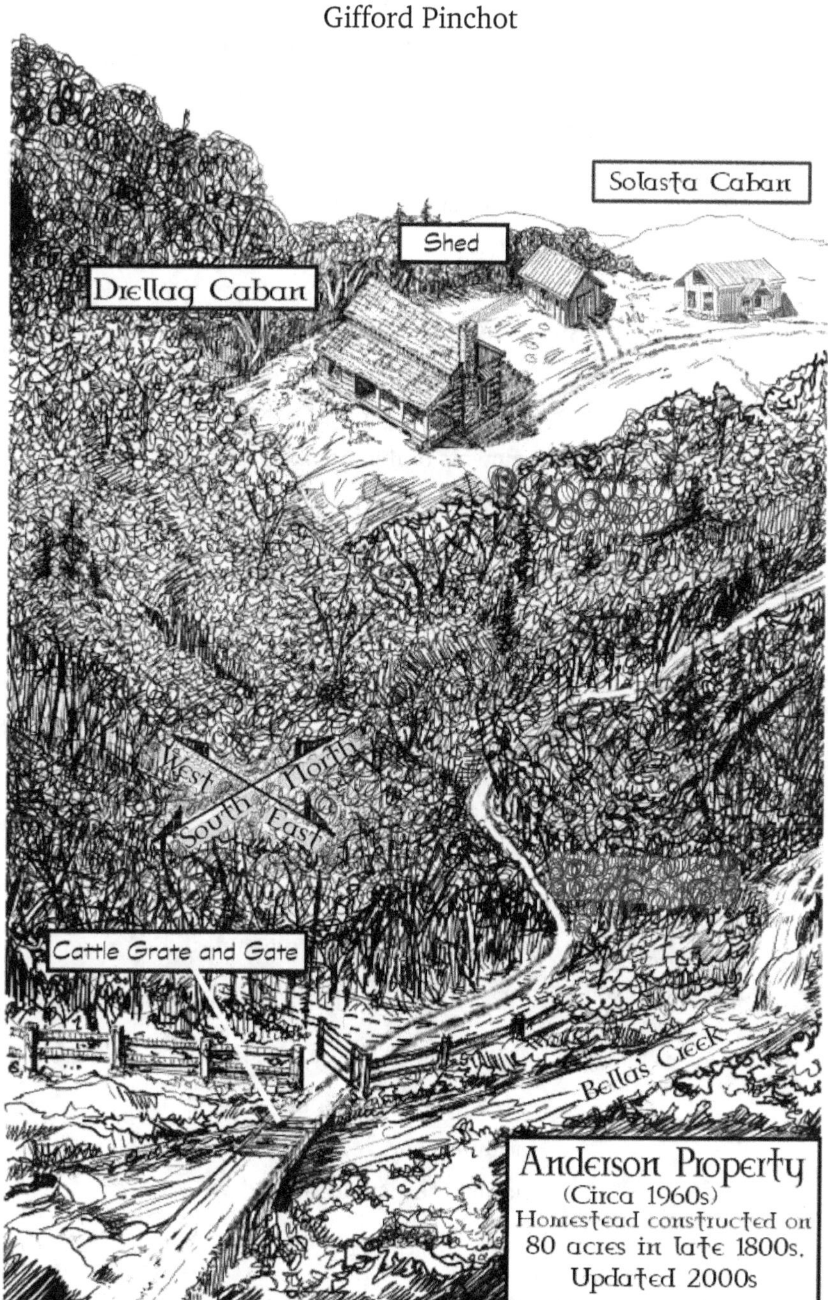

Drawing by Ken Czarnomski

Christmas on the Valley Floor
(Chris Erdman, December 25, 2017. Based on work by John Muir, 1838 – 1914)

Christmas brings a cordial, gentle, soothing snowstorm—
a thing of plain, palpable, innocent beauty
that the frailest child would love.

The myriad diamonds of the sky
come gracefully in great congregational flakes,
not falling or floating,
but just coming to their appointed places
upon rock or leaf
in a loving, living way of their own—
snow-gems, flowers of the mountain clouds
in whose folds and fields all rivers take their rise.

The floral stars of the fields above
are planted upon the fields below.
The pines, the naked oaks, the bushes,
the mosses too
and crumpled ferns
are all in equal bloom,
and belong to the same one great icy order.

Now the last sky blossom has fallen,
the clouds depart in separate companies,
leaving the valley open to other influences and communions.

Every tree seems to be possessed
with a new kind of life—
in sounds and gestures
they are new creatures,
born again.

The whole valley, sparkling in the late sunlight,
looks like a trim, polished, perfect existence.

The dome Tissiack, *
looks down the valley like the most living being
of all the rocks and mountains;
one would fancy that there were brains in that lofty brow.

How grandly comes the gloaming over this pearly beauty!
What praise songs pour from the white chambers of the falls!
Surely the Lord loves this new creation,
and His angels are now looking down
at this new thing that His hands have wrought.

Muir's journal, December 25, 1869, John of the Mountains: Unpublished Journals, p. 39-40. *Tissiack is the name given to the image of a young woman that can be seen on the face of Half Dome. Indigenous legends tell of an Indian maiden turned to stone by the wrath of the gods; some say her tears are still visible on the north face of the monolith.

About the Author

Jacqueline Evans Jacobs, PhD, lives in Vero Beach, Florida, but considers herself a citizen of the universe. She has had the good fortune to live on five continents and visited Antarctica in 2012. In those travels and living abroad, she has experienced Christmas and Hannukah in many states in the U.S. and thirteen countries on four continents.

Jacque was born in a small community in middle Georgia of parents whose home of birth and heart home was always the Smoky Mountains. As a voracious reader, she dreamed of seeing the places and knowing the people around the world she only read about as a child.

Regardless of any individual's personal religious or spiritual beliefs, millions of people around the world recognize the symbol of peace and hope represented by Christmas. Jacque works to promote peace among all she meets and celebrates the gifts of her family by birth and marriage, in all of who they are individually and collectively. She encourages each of us to promote a world which embraces the individual person and whatever identities they claim or have adopted. She believes love of our fellow travelers on this earth is what matters most in making us human.

AUTHOR'S NOTE

My journey in writing this series of six novels has been one of creative joy and intellectual challenge. I understand the importance of research in presenting information that can be verified by readers and have tried to do my due diligence in being accurate in those details. I am grateful to the experts who contributed to that information, particularly related to criminal actions and consequences.

At the time of my retirement from Western Carolina University, I was one of less than twenty women there who had earned the rank of full professor. Women, as represented by Bella, have continued to achieve in ways my mother's generation thought would never happen. I think many women have also learned not to be compelled to achieve in the ways defined by others.

Self-publishing in the context of higher education is generally unacceptable and, in most universities, will not help you get tenured or promoted. I had academic publishers for my academic writing, and am thankful to *EDIE*, *Eye on Education*, *Rowman & Littlefield*, and *Routledge* for the publication of my work. Even though I am retired, I did a lot of soul-searching before I could allow myself to self-publish. I would encourage any young person to accept the challenge of becoming commercially published. Like it or not, publishers still control what most people have access to read, and certainly control the book industry. Times are changing though, and I learned a great deal as I figured out how to publish my work and how to find a high quality editor, format person, and book cover creator. It can be done.

In the final analysis, what matters to me is best expressed in the words of Samuel Johnson (1709-1784): "A writer only begins a book; a reader finishes it." Thank you for coming along with me on the journey of Bella Anderson and for "finishing" this work.

Peace,
Jacque